The Tale of
~~King Arthur~~
MORGAN LE FAY

Copyright © 2024 Sarah C.E. Parker

All rights reserved.

Sarah C.E. Parker

Other Works by Sarah C.E. Parker:

Flames of the Ether

The Realm of Night Saga:

Book 1: Shadow of Destiny

Book 2: Building Darkness

Book 3: Land of Shadows

Book 4: Hand of Night

Book 5: Heart of Darkness

All works available at https://parkerpublications.com

Prologue:
Shall We Start at the End?

It was hardly the worst thing that Morgan had done, burning a woman to death right in front of her fourteen year old daughter, but the ironic thing was that this was supposed to be her path to redemption. Putting end to ancient evils and recovering holy relics, that was a noble quest, now wasn't it?

So why was it all turning out so terribly again? She was fighting alongside noble knights, including the man she loved. She was not at the head of a foreign invasion anymore, killing thousands with lightning strikes, horrible sickness and deadly tricks. She had atoned for all that villainy.

Or at least... She was trying to atone, alright? The work of redemption was much bloody harder than ruthless, rampaging villainy, as it turned out. She offered merciful solutions, and her companions outright laughed at her, thinking it all some jest or lie covering up some horrid scheme.

But Morgan had long since given up on scheming. It was not even in her nature to be brutal. Merlin and Arthur and her horrible family and marriage had been the ones to make her brutal. Those men were to blame for all her monstrous acts, or so she insisted.

From the day she was born, she had been ostracized and hated. Even when her magic was used for nothing more than harmless pranks, it still caused outrage and near riots. And when her magic was used for self-defense, like at this very moment, she did not appear as some avenging angel, she was perceived as an abominable demon acting without restraint.

She found herself wishing now that she could mimic her mother and put on the air of a gentle princess to comfort this weeping child, huddled on the floor over her mother's disintegrating skeleton.

No words came to her though, because Morgan had never been a true princess. She failed at even the mantle of esteemed wizardess that she had tried so hard to project. This entire country termed her a witch, a disaster and terror.

Even among her own family, that's all anyone had ever seen. It's no wonder she still felt resentment and the need to lash out, because she was getting really, homicidally sick of that perception.

Time to haul this shaking child to her feet and kill another of her family members.

The Tale of ~~King Arthur~~Morgan Le Fay

I. Sixteen Years Prior

Morgan Pendragon never had the right to live in a castle and call herself the daughter of kings. She had heard the whispers all her life, from the servants, and visiting nobles, and even her own nursemaid. She was a changeling, an imposter who had snuck into the cradle the night Uther's heir was birthed and taken her place. With her shock of black hair and sour disposition, there was no way she could be the true daughter of the golden-maned Uther, the great unifier of Britain driving out the Saxon threat. There was no way this plain-faced girl with her frightfully dark eyes and sallow skin could be the daughter of Igraine, the blue-eyed muse whose every smile weakened the knees of even the most stalwart knight and made even the youngest of maidens weep with envy. This surly child was naught but a malevolent fay, some mischievous pretender seeking to take over the kingdom.

Such grand plans of conquest were a little beyond a child of eight however. Sitting up in her bedroom, Morgan's only wish at the moment was that she could undo the damage to the sad, straw doll lying charred on her floor.

She had not meant to start the fire. She never did, but her maid, Beatrice, had gotten mad at her again, after finding her lurking near the war room where the lords of Logres had gathered to lay battle plans.

Morgan was not like most children. Her perception and intelligence grew quickly and ceaselessly, considered by the palace staff as unnervingly keen for anyone, let alone a girl of her age. She understood enough of tactics to take interest in the matters the lords discussed around that massive oaken table in the war room, and idling in the hall with her father's familiar baritone booming in her ears was a far better way to pass the day than locked in her rooms having one of the maids fearfully try to show her the 'grand art' of needlepoint that all ladies dithered away the days with.

Her father did not wish for the other lords to see his charmless daughter however, and so Beatrice always hauled her back to the tower before she could be spotted, berating her with stern words about the importance of obedience and a sensible bedtime. She fled today the moment the doll caught fire, backing away with eyes shining with fear.

Reports of the spontaneous combustion would only add fresh fuel to the maids' gossip about her, Morgan knew. A child should not have to worry about such things. A child should not be so keenly aware of the bitter eyes always watching her from around corners whenever she descended her stifling rooms and dared roam free about the castle.

"But I am far smarter than those air-headed other ladies, so it is my burden to be cursed with insight." Morgan smiled, repeating something Merlin had told her just this past week when she had tearfully asked him why the other lords' children avoided her so.

"Power makes people afraid. And you are not only the daughter of kings, you've magic in you, and a keen enough mind to make use of it. It would be a tragedy for you to wind up a regular lady of court, a useless wallflower, stranded on the sidelines stitching needlepoint with nothing of worth to say and no power to effect true change."

"A tragedy to wind up like mother, you mean," Morgan had responded, and the wizard gave a vehement shake of his head.

"Your mother is no ordinary woman either, Morgan. She helps your father more than you know. A single word can build a man's strength or lay him low, and your mother always chooses the best ones."

Merlin's eyes had that same dreamy look to them that all men had whenever he talked about Igraine. It made Morgan lose respect for him somewhat, seeing him act so average, a blushing fool whenever he and her mother were in a room alone together. He never lost face that way when her father was around at least. To the eyes of any other he was stately and wise, a juggernaut of confidence and power. It was only Igraine who seemed able to crack that composure, and only Morgan's shrewd surveillance that revealed to her that fact.

Morgan would not resent him this one flaw of fancying her mother though. At least he was sincere. He never lied to her the way the other adults did. He was a powerful wizard with a million important duties of his own to see carried out, and he made time for her anyway, not just because he was her tutor she decided, but because she was special. The magic made her special.

"And I shall become a wizard too," Morgan nodded to herself, waving the smoke from her ruined doll toward the window with a pillow. "if only he would bloody teach me already."

A disapproving cluck echoed from the doorway. "How would your dear mother feel hearing you use such language?" Merlin teased, and Morgan rolled her eyes.

"I imagine she would be bloody embarrassed and blushing a bright bloody red, as she murmured many an apology to every noble within earshot."

The Tale of ~~King Arthur~~Morgan Le Fay

Merlin stifled his smile and cleared his throat imperiously, adopting a stern expression. "No lord will take you seriously if you start talking like a village boy."

"It is the lords themselves who use such language I will have you know. The bloody Saxons this and damn King Octa that cursed, blackguard, bastard."

"Well, you are to be better educated than those foul-mouthed lordlings, so there is no need for you to be bandying about such language."

Morgan crossed the room in a swirl of skirts and dipped into a dramatic curtsy. "Alas! I am ever so sorry to have offended you, sir. In the future I shall ensure that my curses are only the practical kind of long Latin phrases with crippling, transformative effects."

"Speak all the Latin you like, child. That's not how magic works."

Morgan frowned, running over in her mind the gossip she had heard in the city of witches and blood rites. "Sure it is," she insisted. "Why, they arrested a woman just this week, saying she talked in the tongue of Satan, casting curses, and I heard it quite distinctly. It was Latin."

"That woman was likely not a proper witch. She was probably just a foreigner."

Morgan's frown grew even deeper. "Why would they arrest her then?"

"The masses are ignorant. It is why you must be careful," he chided, brushing up the ashy residue of her doll into his handkerchief and dumping it out into the open air of the night. "You must learn control and not threaten maids with sudden conflagrations to send them screaming from your rooms."

"It was only a little fire, and I didn't mean to do it. Beatrice was the aggressive one, shoving the thing into my arms and forcing me down upon the bed with her never ending lecture of how I should already be asleep, as if a person can simply force themselves unconscious just because some adult declares it time for rest."

"Well, you must admit it is far past your bedtime, Morgan," the traitor declared, taking the side of her obnoxious lady in waiting and all the other adults. "The mind needs sleep. Go too long without it, you shall fall prey to delirium."

"De-leer-ee-um, hmm?" It was a word she had not heard of yet. She would have to look it up later.

Morgan glided over to the bed, sprawling out across the covers. "Teach me a sleep spell then, and I shall retire immediately."

Merlin raised a finger to his chin, taking clear note of the excitement in her eyes and hemming and hawing loudly before giving a firm, "No."

Morgan glared. "Why not? I need to learn something, don't I? Otherwise you'll have burning dolls and ceilings, and their whispers about me will be proven right; I will bring nothing but wanton destruction to all!"

"Being a little overdramatic again, now aren't we?" Merlin chided, settling down beside her.

She buried her head in his lap, trying to fight back her sniffles. "It is not drama. I mean every word. You should have seen Beatrice's face. She hates me, just like all the others. Even mother's face when I froze that stable boy last week..."

"I told you what to practice, Morgan."

She huffed, fists knotting in his robes. "Breathe in, breathe out. Clear your mind. Control your temper. None of that is magic."

"They are stepping stones, a foundation you must establish before learning any true spell. I will tell you truly, I have run across many a wild sorcerer blowing themselves up with torrents of fire and winds they do not control."

"Lucy has already paid the price of my torrents of fire," Morgan stated dryly, referring to her cremated toy. "Beatrice may be next."

"Why not tell Beatrice that?" Merlin teased. "Then she is certain to flee the castle, sparing us all the bother of her constant nattering."

Morgan smiled. "Mother would have said not to joke about such things, that a sweet little girl such as I could never harm a soul."

Though Igraine would have said it with smile cracking, eyes glittering with worry she tried hard to conceal. Igraine would have lied. Morgan's smile turned bitter at the thought.

"A sweet little girl? What a thin lie that would be." Merlin tore apart her musings. "We both know Princess Morgan is a stubborn little nightmare who may very well hurt someone, should she fail to practice what I have been teaching."

Morgan raised her head, fist jabbing out into his arm. "What an awful thing to say!"

"You want to prove me wrong? Practice your breathing, control your temper. Think calculated thoughts."

"Not happy thoughts?"

"Happy lies serve no one," the wizard dismissed. "Think instead of *why* you would do something. *Why* destroy your own cherished toy? Who does that benefit? Even your maid, only ill would come of harm befalling her. The

The Tale of ~~King Arthur~~Morgan Le Fay

castle would be a hungry, filthy place without all these maids, a cheerless place should they all be terrified of burning to death on whim of a young wizard, and you would be all the lonelier. So, stop seething on resentments and the accidents will stop." He patted her on the head. "Now go to sleep."

She grabbed his arm. "I want a story first."

He settled back in his seat. "And what tale would the young princess like to hear this evening?"

"A tale of the great Merlin praising his own exploits of course."

The wizard smiled. "Oh yes, of course."

"But tell it like the bards do!" she demanded, sitting up eagerly.

"You mean the fearful fireside recitations they chant when I'm away? The whispered tales of the mysterious and terrifying wizard." Morgan nodded, and Merlin cleared his throat. "Let us start at the beginning then, as far back as any of us commoners have heard rumor of this most dangerous sorcerer."

He leaned in toward her, eyes grave and dark, and tone conspiratorial. "They say a man walks the roads in the dark woods of England, known to all but trusted by none. For no one would dare to truly confide in an adviser with such strange and unnatural powers as Merlin of Carmarthen.

"He came first to England as an orphaned youth, a hermit already with no sign of his parents. The long shadow of Castle Caerfryddin lay over the boy from the moment he set foot within village borders, and some say it was with an ulterior motive that he entered town that red dawn. A quiet grief hung heavy over these dung-spattered streets where no child remained free and at play following the dreadful declaration of King Vortigern."

"Usurper of the throne and pagan-blooded butcher!" Morgan interjected with a flourish.

"Oh yes, quite so." Merlin grinned. "Foul, foul Vortigern whose adviser had bid him sacrifice a dozen young that very day and forge in their blood his victory over the Angles gnawing always at the border of his domain, seeking to unseat him.

"Hearing of this, Merlin set off immediately to the castle gates, and the words he spake to the guards who sought to bar him entry, no man has dared recount. But whatever foul prophecy or spell it was that fell upon the men's ears that day, they dropped their weapons and abandoned their posts before the eyes of the whole village, never to return."

"What did you say to them?"

"Nothing a hotheaded child like our princess could replicate." She frowned. "Anyhow, young Merlin did stride unopposed into the hall of false king Vortigern, facing down in enrapturing silence all the bared blades and blustering words of the king and his shield-bearers gathered there. And with a frail and bony finger, the boy did lay pointed accusation on the druid stood cowering alongside his lieges' throne, denouncing him a traitor and deceiver. 'No sacrifice this day shall win you the coming battle!' the young prophet relayed his first warning."

"For the serpent at your side hath struck an alliance with your enemies, sabotaging the mechanism of your gates to swing open for the lords of Logres the moment their army arrives upon your doorstep!" Morgan recalled, and Merlin nodded.

"Being led outside to the town wall, the king's men saw this to be true, but the druid Malifol did hiss that it was Merlin himself who wrought the sabotage through some foul trick of witchcraft. 'Falsehood drips from thy forked tongue, charlatan,' came Merlin's sage response."

"Quite an eloquent ten year old, wasn't he?"

"A strange criticism coming from our oh so eloquent princess."

"Yes, but I am much better educated than you were."

"Did you want a grand retelling or not?"

"I did, I did. Please continue, my courtly bard."

"'This simpleton's deal with the enemy is but the most recent treachery he hath wrought upon his lord,' young Merlin so very eloquently concluded. He led them then to the east corner of the wall in the castle courtyard and tapethed firmly a stretch of dirt. 'Here lies Vortimir, thy son and heir, neither dead of illness nor laid in his proper resting place in thy family tomb as yonder serpent hath proclaimed to you. Poison stole his life so that you would be robbed of legacy, your lands passed on to your magician's pawns. His royal bones lie buried here to cement the curse upon your reign.'

"Silver-tongued Malifol did plead with Votigern to ignore Merlin's words and have the impetuous youth sacrificed along with the others, but suspicion did, as always with Vortigern, heavily outweigh his trust, and so the grounds were exhumed and the bones discovered.

"The only blood shed that day was old Malifol's, as Merlin had warned the king that were the village children to be sacrificed as planned, Malifol's dying curse would take its root and the king would not live out the year. So it was the children returned to their homes in shadow of Castle Caerfryddin and grew to see maturity and families of their own. Merlin left the village that very next dawn with the prophecy that Vortigern would see the end of his reign in ten years time, dying without heir on the first moon of spring under a banner of gleaming scales from the east.

The Tale of ~~King Arthur~~ Morgan Le Fay

"The death came to pass exactly as Merlin had foretold, and Carmarthen soon fell under the rule of Uther Pendragon, king of many a scattered piece of Britain's lands. People whispered of Merlin's deeds and his hand in such battles. The whispers stretch on to this day in arguments that shall never be settled on whether the man was prophet or jinx, fay and foul trickster or true-born druid."

"Or crotchety wizard far too well paid for his work sitting around Uther's halls and refusing to teach spells to his pupil, the brilliant Morgan Le Fay."

Merlin arched an eyebrow. "Morgan Le Fay?"

The princess shrugged. "Why not? They all whisper it about me anyway, just like they did you. So, if I am to become a great and powerful sorceress, I might as well have a great and powerful name."

"The name of Pendragon is a far better title, princess. Do not toss it aside so callously." He stroked her hair, pulling the covers up under her chin. "Now go to sleep."

"Wait. What about the battle of Essex? It's practically the next chapter in your tale, so the story is not finished."

"Sleep."

Her head thudded back onto the pillow, and her eyes began to grow heavy. "You dirty, bloody... cheater..." she mumbled.

The man didn't even have to use spells. It seemed all the tales she'd heard of how magic worked were outright lies.

I'll be just as powerful as you someday. She swore to herself, a smile gracing her lips, as she drifted happily off to sleep with dreams of battle and sorcerers dancing on back of her eyelids.

II. A Fitting Heir

The castle was a far noisier and unwelcoming place after Arthur was born. The kingdom had been anticipating his coming for nine long months, and so Morgan should have been well prepared for the little black hole that drank up all attention. She had expected the fuss to die down after the baby was delivered, but even after the heralds' horns echoing over town had fallen silent and the many celebration banquets had wound to a close, Arthur continued to incite endless visits and commotion.

The golden haired boy with the bright blue eyes was fawned over and adored by every lady in court. He was adored by her father, who would show him off proudly to all visitors, even praising him for the loudness of his crying. "Has the lungs of a warrior!" He laughed.

She had never seen her father laugh like that with her. He never even smiled at her like he did for his guests. With her, he was always stern.

"Sit up straight," Beatrice chided.

Morgan shot her a glare, and the maid paled, averting her gaze and giving no further corrections to her ward. Morgan had recently learned the effectiveness of her glares. If the entire castle insisted on being afraid of her, then there was no point wasting effort feigning charm and kindness. It was much more fun to lay them low with the weight of her eyes and watch them squirm, terrified of all the horrible fates she could inflict upon them. *I could turn you into a toad.* She thought, still glaring down at Beatrice. *An ugly, warty toad.*

Though granted, she had never attempted a human transmutation before. It was likely much more complicated than floating rocks or conjuring flashes of flame. She had heard stories though, of how Merlin changed his shape, and so she knew it must be possible.

I could make everyone a toad. She thought, scanning the room of chittering waifs around her, done up in their fine dresses and ridiculous hats, cooing over the blond haired baby at the head of the table. *It's not like any of these idiots contribute to father's war efforts. They just hang around, drinking and gossiping, with their fake smiles and compliments. They'd be far more fun hopping around the floor, a grand and shocking entertainment.* She smiled.

Her smile died as she noticed Merlin, stood by Uther at the head of the grand table with all the other lords. This feast was ostensibly to celebrate the king's recent victory quelling an uprising in Cornwall, but once again Arthur had become the center of attention, twirled around by the high-spirited

The Tale of ~~King Arthur~~ Morgan Le Fay

conqueror and bragged about loudly as the heir to this newly forged nation. The boy was not even a year old. He had no place in a feast hall. He aught to be crying, covering his ears and tantruming like the spoiled brat he was. Instead, he giggled and cooed, far too used to the noise and crowded motion that had been surrounding him every day of his charmed little life.

The worst traitor was Merlin, stood so imperiously by the side of his liege. He smiled at the baby the same way the others did, oblivious to the glares of his surly student sat shoved in her shadowed corner of the feast. Before Arthur, the wizard would have noticed Morgan's ill tempered smile. He would have known immediately the twisted fantasies that had been darting through her mind as she wickedly considered the transformation of the feast hall before them into a gathering of amphibians, but the princess was nothing but a forgotten shadow to him now, with endless meetings and war campaigns keeping him constantly away from the castle. Now, even when he and Uther did return, Arthur was all that mattered. Why waste their time exchanging words with a charmless girl when a true heir lie before them? The son her father had always wanted.

"I think that's enough of that for now." Igraine laughed, taking Arthur gently back from his father's rough-handed grip. "The young prince must be headed off to bed, my lords."

Uther protested, a slurred and berating rant, but Igraine's gentle words and soft touches instantly had him turned around on the subject, and he turned his attention back to the sickly smelling beer his servants continually tipped into his drinking mug. He was drunk already, Morgan could see, even though they were a mere hour into the night's festivities. Why was it only ladies who had to sit upright and prim, sipping their wines and holding their tongues while the men went about boasting and draining horn after horn of vintage?

The musicians seated at the side of the hall struck up another soulless tune and many a lord and young lady took their place upon the open floor set up in the center of the great tables lining the walls of the room.

"The young princess should be participating in the dance, don't you think?" Igraine gently prodded. Morgan did not know why she bothered to pay visit to this gloomy little corner her daughter had quite purposefully worked to clear of company.

"Shouldn't you be fussing over my dear little brother?" Morgan prompted dryly. "Reading him bedtime stories. Then holding his hand throughout the long night, so he doesn't ever have to feel alone, until morning light doth pierce the windows and the crowd of sycophants flocks to his bedside to rouse him from his slumber."

"What an evocative picture that paints." Igraine smiled. "You could write such lovely sonnets, if only each line were not dripping with sarcasm and insults. I hardly like you referring to our hard working staff as 'sycophants'--"

"The word I learned this morning is *pariah*," Morgan cut her off bitterly, eyes cold and distant. "Now that describes only one member of this castle, don't you think? Perhaps I shall write a sonnet about that. *The hideous little spitfire, less princess than pariah...*"

"You are not an outcast. You are the king's daughter and..." She had not the right words to reassure her, to make her laugh and lighten her mood. The one with the right words had already vanished from the hall, slipping away from the bawdy festivities the instant the opportunity had presented itself in a move Morgan dearly wished she could replicate. "Why not go speak with the other children? Young Lord Bastion over there is about your age," her mother nattered on.

"Yes, and his father Lord Ruthien is oh so eager to have him betrothed to pay off their house's debts and secure them a place at the king's side. Though I think at nine years old I'm still a little too young for you to be plotting my sale. From the best bred mares to common whores after all, they at least wait until they've reached sexual maturity before pairing them off."

"Morgan!"

"Yes, mother, I know *you* were only nine when your father sold you, but you're a far prettier piece of furniture. A nice little lamp that lights up rooms rather than dousing them in gloom--"

Igraine seized her wrist. There was real anger in her eyes, anger and hurt, but she had nothing to say, no counter or comfort. For all Merlin's talk of her amazing skill, always picking the best words, she seemed completely inept when it came to her daughter. She looked anxiously to the lords seated at the head of the table, but none there had noticed their spat.

No one had noticed, except the servants lurking in the shadows of the room, already shaking their heads in judging disapproval. *"What an awful girl!"* they would be whispering. *"And our poor, precious queen, cursed with such an ugly, evil child. At least she has Arthur..."*

Morgan shrugged free of her mother's grip and shoved back her seat. She headed straight out the doors, easily cutting down with her eyes the few servants like Beatrice who dared step in to stop her.

She felt rather pathetic. She was not some bloody flower. She had never needed showering praise to keep her from wilting. She needed no attention

The Tale of ~~King Arthur~~ Morgan Le Fay

whatsoever, not from these pretenders. She hated absolutely everyone in this court, servants and noblemen alike. Arthur should be a welcome distraction. Better to be forgotten by her father after all, than still under the weight of his stern-eyed anger. The more the visitors flocked to her brother, the more chance she had to study, alone in the blessed solitude of the emptied out library and towers. No one had even noticed the last of her outbursts, supernaturally shattering the vases in the upper hall, as no one had been present, not even Beatrice.

She yanked the flowers from her hair and set spiteful fire to them, before deciding that wasn't nearly dramatic enough and torching the gaudy tapestry of the great King Uther and his queen hung on the wall beside her.

"I myself have always hated that tapestry," Merlin noted coolly. "The clumsy weaver made your mother look far too blank, empty eyes and distorted features. We should hang an image of the princess in its place. I'm sure they could make a grand and impressive portrait, if only she would allow the artisans to capture her."

"I'm caged enough. I've no need to be flattened and bound on a wall, a leering ghoul, haunting the halls."

"A ghoul you are not, my lady. Yet leering and scowling is all I have seen from you today."

"You would rather I smile?" She spread her teeth, a wild eyed and chilling expression. "You would rather I lie in endless, exhaustive play, like mother and all the other ladies of court? Only, the men wouldn't swoon before me. They would faint in fear!"

"A dramatic claim from a nine year old. Would you care to test it? I would quite like to see Lord Cadry collapse like a maiden. It would humble him considerably."

Morgan did not feel like laughing. She would not allow her smile to turn genuine, because Merlin had abandoned her. He had given up on her lessons to go serve mysterious purpose in pointless skirmishes against the Saxons. He had been gone for six months and not written her once. Returning today with a host of knights, he had not even acknowledged her! He had abandoned her and...

She was crying, fat, ugly tears far from suited to a great and powerful wizardess, even one in training. She clamped her sleeve over her eyes to hide the childish breakdown, and Merlin knelt solemnly across from her. "I... I should have stopped by earlier for a greeting I suppose?"

Her fist jabbed out into his shoulder, but her eloquence had deserted her, and she had no words to reprimand him. All she could do was sob, stuck firmly in the grips of her pathetic meltdown, as if she really were some ordinary child succumbed to her tantrum.

Merlin's arms closed about her, awkwardly patting her on the back. "Uh, there, there. I should... I should fetch your mother."

She hit him again, much harder than before, and angrily lowered her sleeve, puffy eyes losing none of their glare. "You didn't even write. And you were gone so long..."

"I... Yes. But I had little time. You understand this, yes? The king keeps me very occupied these days, quelling fires and keeping down the increasing chaos of this ever spreading conquest of his."

"Yet you return not in w-want of intelligent conversation, but instead spend your whole day f-fussing over d-dusty maps and w-wailing infants!" she accused, trying to quell her shaking shoulders and adopt an air of controlled uncaring, the cold facade she was able to maintain before everyone else in court. It eluded her sorely.

"Ah, so this *is* about Arthur." She raised her chin, lips pursed and eyes flashing. "Jealousy is the natural reaction of older siblings. Actually getting to know your brother might quiet quite a lot of that resentment, rather than spending all your time squirreled away in your rooms, mired in dark tales."

"I am honing my mind!" she snapped, eloquence returning. "An admirable quest far wiser than the causes taken up by witless idiots hammering away at each other on the battlefields. And what would you know of jealousy or siblings?"

"As everyone knows, I know everything." Morgan glared, not amused. "Though I myself was an only child. I can only imagine how distressing it would be to have had a little brother or sister," he continued in dry hyperbole. "Or to have parents, actually present, living and breathing there to raise me. How awful that would have been. And God forbid there be a brother by my side, someone for me to protect and teach and share the burden of our unique family, someone who understood the stresses of court and--"

"He's six months old! I am quite sure he would not understand were I to waltz up to his crib and start ranting complaints about the pressures of court. He will probably never understand, because he will spend his charmed little life as crown prince having the entire court swoon over his every unimpressive act!"

"And you could be a friend, an adviser of unselfish intent. You could ground him, help him."

The Tale of ~~King Arthur~~ Morgan Le Fay

"He doesn't need any help. He is Arthur Pendragon! I will not be some unremarkable relation hanging around in his court, known for his legacy and the shadow of our father, where my only role is to be married off to some grimy old lord..." Her eyes filled with tears.

Merlin reached out, taking her hands. "You are far too young to be worrying about such things."

She ripped free of his hold, sniffling in the embarrassing line of snot now sliding down her face. "I am old enough to understand my inevitable place in this horrid castle. And you still have not apologized!" Her voice broke.

"I am sorry I did not write. But I will not waste words consoling your bleak imaginings about the future, nor hear you defame those you should care for most. Family is a gift. Cherish it. Do not waste your energies setting fire to those ties. Your mother loves you. You must know that."

Morgan rolled her eyes. "The Lady Igraine loves every broken bird, even an ugly crow. There's not a soul on this earth she would not pity and care for, no matter how despicable their character."

"Well... I... have a fondness for you as well," Merlin declared, drawing back his hand and stiffening primly. "And I disdain most everyone. That makes you most special."

"Disdain everyone except mother, and Arthur, and--"

"Good God, you jealous child. The boy is a delightful, laughing baby. Of course I smiled. Do you wish for me to start kicking puppies, turning candy into coal and scowling at sunsets?"

"I think a great and powerful sorcerer would be far more suited to a scowl." Her eyes narrowed, cocking her head. "And a beard. A long, white beard. As it stands, your hair is far too dark, and your robes are far too gray. They aught to be blue. Or purple. Covered with the glitter of the caged stars themselves."

"You have been reading too many epics. Come along, young sorceress, to bed with thee. When you become a great and powerful wizard, you can wear whatever you like."

A smile did finally find its way onto her countenance then, and she allowed herself to be led off to her rooms.

Merlin set off the very next day, gone for months on some mysterious mission. He never wrote once.

Just like all the others, he was a liar.

III. The Rose's Thorn

More whispers filled the castle in those long and dreary months while Merlin was away, more malicious, fearful gossip, though for once the rumors had nothing to do with Morgan.

The whispers spoke of Uther and the unseemly pallor that had taken over his face, the rasping wheeze that tinged each cough and clearing of the throat, and the blood that spotted the linens that the maids were tasked to scrub clean each morn, despite all of them knowing he bore no wounds from battle. The injuries eating away at him seemed purely internal, a deadly illness slowly stealing his life, but the king refused to hide from his people. He kept his head held high and threw feast after feast, desperate events of raucous crowds where he blustered and drank even more than usual.

Morgan stayed well away from those events, and no one seemed to miss her presence. Even Igraine and Arthur made no appearances at those gatherings, though the servants gossiped of the king's complaints. The shouted beratings of his wife shook the corridors in the late hours of the evening, as he criticized the queen for her lack of support, lending fuel to his enemy's defamation of his manhood by refusing to attend him.

Morgan did her best to block out all the noise and keep her mind on her studies, until one afternoon she was pulled most rudely from the library and brought before her father, sunken on his throne in the great hall with features sallow and brow stained with sweat.

Uther eyed her up and down in weary disapproval. "You will attend the feast tonight and try to look presentable," he muttered. "Our kingdom is in dire need of more troops to drive back the incursion into York, and I have not heard from that cursed druid of mine in months."

Morgan raised her head, eyes flooding with worry. "You haven't?"

"Your king is speaking," Uther thundered. "Have your tutors taught you nothing of etiquette?" Morgan bit her tongue. "Anyhow, I've no need of that wizard's meddling. A union of our house with that of King Lot of Orkney shall win me all the backing I require. He lost his wife in childbirth this past winter, though the babe appears hail and fit."

"A match for Arthur then?" she warily pressed, crossing her fingers and desperately ignoring the clear implication in Uther's words and his purpose in summoning her here.

The Tale of ~~King Arthur~~ Morgan Le Fay

"A match for you," the king gruffly deflated all such hopes. At least being betrothed to an infant she had over a decade to wiggle her way out of the arrangement and-- "The wedding will take place as soon as you come of age in... when is that exactly? Next spring?"

"Almost three years," she corrected him scathingly. "I'm ten years old."

Uther grunted, eyes narrowing. "Thought you were twelve. I suppose this is why your mother kept insisting you were too young for this. The wedding will take place in three years then, giving you ample time to temper your tongue."

"Three years? This boy is but an infant..." She trailed off, realization dawning in slowly settling dread. "I'm to marry King Lot? You would sell off your daughter to one of your contemporaries?!" she demanded, eyeing the rotting forty year old before her with pointed disdain. "To tend to him while he dithers away in his sickbed--"

Uther leapt to his feet, eyes burning with rage. "You *will* temper your tongue! I have made you a fitting match to a powerful house of the heir to the entire country of Norway, wherever that is. A *distant* noble house who has not yet heard ugly rumor of the cursed changeling child of Britain's king!" Morgan flinched. "You have caused me nothing but grief since the day you were born, but you will serve me now as a daughter must. You will attend the feast tonight, and you will smile and be *silent* in presence of your betrothed. Is that understood?"

Morgan said nothing for a moment, powerless before the fury of a father who had never loved her, a father who saw her only value to be traded away as livestock in exchange for added soldiers to his conquest.

Uther settled back in his throne, contented with her silence and with the fear in her eyes. "Good. You are dismissed. Have your mother pick out something suitable for you to wear. The maids have terrible taste."

"No."

Uther grunted. "Fine. Pick a dress yourself then, but it had better be something--"

"No," she repeated, chin raising and eyes shining with shaking resolve. "No to all of it. I will not be promised to some pervert who takes not even the time to grieve his own wife before agreeing to wed a child. I will not be used as a bargaining chip in your war."

"You disrespectful brat!" He stalked down from his pedestal, seizing her arm. Morgan could not think of fire or spells as that fist drew back. Her mind had gone blank with panic, and all she could do was stand there and stare.

"My lord?" A gentle voice echoed through the audience hall, and a pale and delicate hand settled atop Uther's own, still clamped about the frail arm of their daughter. Igraine interposed herself between the pair of them as if it were the most natural thing in the world, eyes holding those of her husband. "You promised I would be the one to tell our daughter of this match, should it come to pass," she reminded him quietly. "You swore last night that I would have that privilege, did you not? Did I misunderstand your words?"

"You... you did not," Uther grumbled, cheeks flushing. "But the courier arrived this morning while you were away at mass. And I had heard from her nurse that this heretical girl was just sitting out the service again, nose buried in books of stars and other meaningless drivel. She needed a scolding, not from you women who let her get away with all her glares and caustic outbursts. King Lot will be attending the feast tonight. I needed her to know of this, to treat him properly. To hold her tongue and not sabotage my... my..." He broke off hacking.

Igraine pulled out her kerchief and dabbed at the blood that poured free of his lips, speckling the fair hair of his beard. "I understand, my lord. And I commend your enthusiasm. I feel that same wistful pride when envisioning our daughter's wedding, still such a *distant* day." Morgan caught clearly the subtle emphasis on the word, though Uther, still hacking with kerchief clutched to his mouth, nodded along blearily. "Your alliance with such a powerful house as that of King Lot is a masterful stroke of politics, truly. Morgan should indeed know of this, now that Orkney has assented to the arrangement. I am simply saddened you did not think to share it with me first."

"I apologize, Igraine."

Morgan blinked. He'd apologized. The bear had actually *apologized*.

"I hold nothing against you, my king. But perhaps I should speak with our daughter now, prepare her for tonight's festivities."

"She insulted..." he murmured.

Igraine stroked his back, whispering in his ear, "She is a child, wracked by nerves at the high pressure of her position being daughter to such a great man, responsible even in small part for the future of his line. You put a critical political treaty quite bluntly on the shoulders of a ten year old, dear, and she is but a frail maiden. Of course she had not the confidence to assent to it."

"I do not need her consent. She is my daughter. She will do as I say."

"Of course. Of course." Igraine guided him back to his throne, sitting him down. "But the Lords of Logres will be here shortly with news from St.

The Tale of ~~King Arthur~~Morgan Le Fay

Albany. You should remain here to greet them. I will have a word with our daughter."

Morgan stood fuming alone on the cold stone floor of the chamber, watching the whole ordeal with tongue frozen from shock rather than conscious effort. She wanted to set fire to her mother's efforts in stepping in to shield her. She wanted to scream at this beast of a man, not lull him to sleep with gentle strokings of the ego. Her mother's words were treachery. Morgan was not a fragile maiden. Her defiance had not been weakness. Even that simple word of protest had taken immense strength. She was not a quivering child, fainting under the pressure of her duty...

That last part was a lie though, because she was shaking under this strain. She was nothing more than a little girl in the face of her father's fury, eyes filling with tears, as she stared down the bleak future racing now to seize her.

She allowed Igraine to take her hand and lead her to her room, back up the many steps to the blessed silence of her remote tower. No servants dared to follow them. Igraine bolted shut the door and knelt gently across from her daughter. "I know that must have been--"

"You traitor!" Morgan shoved away from the woman, the torches in the room flickering under the sudden winds of her mercifully returned rage. "You agreed to have me wed to some lecherous old mummy!"

"The man is thirty two," Igraine stated wearily. "Hardly a shriveled corpse, but regardless, I did not assent to it, and you will *not* be marrying King Lot." Morgan blinked, the winds vanishing.

Igraine stroked her hair, eyes gentle but tone fierce. "I would never allow that, not for you, my beautiful baby girl." She kissed her forehead. Morgan grimaced. "You are far too young to be getting engaged. Your father is simply not himself these days. His illness and even worse, the rumors of that weakness, have made him desperate. He acts rashly now to seize more land and solidify our borders. The alliance with Orkney is a necessity, a shrewd maneuver to cement his power. But if you are to marry anyone from that house it will be young Gawain, over a decade from now."

"Gawain?"

"Lot's firstborn son."

"But... what you said before father in the throne room..."

"A gentle side-stepping of the issue," her mother assured her, "laying it to rest until after tonight's feast. I read the missive from King Lot's courier. He said he would *consider* an alliance with our house, after an appropriate period of mourning for his dear departed second wife. He needs your father's troops as much as Uther needs him. So you must indeed hold your tongue at this feast tonight." Morgan flushed. "Present yourself with short-spoken decorum and stay seated with the other children at the side of the hall. I will see Lot's attention is otherwise occupied."

"What do you mean?"

"Your cousin, Anna De'gaur, turned fifteen this past cycle. She already has a flood of yet to be accepted marriage proposals from the men here at court due to her rapidly developing... attributes. King Lot will be taken with her instantly, be assured, and she will be happy to indulge him."

"If he swears himself to your niece, that will no doubt upset father."

"Your father will be dead inside of a year," Igraine bluntly countered, all gentleness gone from her eyes which sat flat and cold now like chips of ice. "The sickness will take him, but he has Arthur as his heir, and I will be dowager queen, in charge of day to day matters until your brother comes of age. You will have a casual betrothal to Gawain of Orkney to keep their house loyal to us and our borders strong, but that marriage will be years and years from now, and you will have all the time in the world to decide whether or not you want to honor it. Alright?"

"You planned all of this?" Morgan murmured, caught completely off guard by the sudden fierce cunning from a woman she had always assumed to be nothing but a compliant doe. "You have a plan for his death."

"Of course. A good and solid plan. We will survive Uther's end, my darling girl. We may even be better for it." She gave one final stroke of her hair and headed for the door. "I shall have Beatrice come get you ready for the feast. Wear the blue dress, the one with the lace right up to the collar. And no more setting things on fire this time. Please? That lace takes days of care to craft and only seconds to destroy."

Morgan numbly watched the door click shut, her mind racing in careful analysis of looks and whispers she had never bothered to pay attention to before. Her father was dying, and her mother did not seem to care about it at all. True, he was an awful person, mulish and cold, but the fact that he had fallen ill so suddenly, a scarce six months after Arthur was born, an heir to hold the throne afterward...

Morgan cleared such malicious doubts from her mind, as Beatrice stepped into her chambers. She gave no resistance this time, sitting by silently and allowing the maid to dress her and pin up her unruly curls in a painfully tight crown of braids.

King Lot was not nearly so disgusting as she'd imagined. He had a strong sort of face, bearded and lined only with a faint scattering of smile lines

The Tale of ~~King Arthur~~ Morgan Le Fay

around his eyes. He was built like a warrior, tall and broad-shouldered, just like his new liege lord, her father, though without the swelling girth that marked most older kings. He had brought none of his sons with him on his long journey south. An unsurprising choice, since even the eldest of the four was not yet trusted to ride any great distance on horseback, being only six years old.

Lot gave Morgan a cordial and dismissive greeting, as she did as her mother had bid her and acted like a shy and stupid child, what she imagined an ordinary girl of her age to be like.

"How old are you?" he hesitantly pressed at the end of the fumbled exchange.

"Ten."

He grit his teeth. "Indeed. I'm not certain that was mentioned in your husband's missive," he muttered to Igraine. She laughed off the misunderstanding with wide-eyed innocence and clear implications that the union between their houses had indeed been concocted as a far future wedding between two promising *young* nobles, neither of whom had come of age just yet.

Uther did not overhear any of his wife's careful sabotage of his plan, too busy drowning his pains in liquor and exchanging boasts with his brother about the coming campaign to lure out the Saxons from their mountain stronghold in Gywnedd.

They settled down to eat, and Anna De'gaur with her low cut dress and clearly developing "attributes" was seated directly before the eyes of King Lot at the corner of the maidens' table nearest the head of the feast. The foreign king was indeed instantly taken with her, just as Igraine had promised, and Anna was all too eager to indulge him. Morgan supposed her cousin was just like most ladies of the court, eager to pin down a man with title and lands far greater than their own.

Morgan endured all the hours of chatter and dull music, wondering bleakly if there would be anything left of the royal treasury by the time Uther was dead. His constant military campaigns and displays of wealth were quite costly after all, even with the ever increasing taxes on his citizens. She would have liked to discuss it with the royal treasurer, to get an exact run down of the figures, but the snobbish old noble refused to speak with her about such things.

Even Igraine had told her to hold her tongue this evening, to act like nothing more than a stupid child, a vapid young princess contributing nothing to her father's kingdom. Morgan obeyed that dreadful prompting and sat in gloomy silence in her forgotten corner of the table, fading slowly into the background, until the opportunity presented itself and she abandoned her seat, setting off toward her solitary tower. No one would notice her departure. Even the servants only made note of the princess when she was making a scene.

She did stop by Arthur's nursery briefly before retiring back to her books. She had never done that before, never intruded on the babe and his constant string of ogling visitors. There should be no one there this evening however, with King Lot visiting and the festivities in the banquet hall keeping the guests thoroughly occupied.

The door was locked, a strangely paranoid precaution to Morgan's mind. She shrugged aside the inconvenience and brushed her finger over the mechanism. She had no need for something so mundane as a physical key.

"Unlock."

The spell did nothing.

She frowned, certain that such minor telekinesis was well within the realm of her abilities. If only Merlin had bothered to teach her, so she did not have to spend so many hours combing through vague texts with only cryptic references to such powers.

"I command you to **open**!"

The door flew open in fearful obedience of her will, and the nursemaid cooing at Arthur's crib-side started to her feet with a scream.

"Oh, uh, princess Morgan? I-I thought the door was locked."

"It was. I unlocked it."

"Your mother gave you the key?"

Morgan exhaled, drained and exasperated. "Just shut up and sleep."

"Excuse me? Princess, that is not the proper way for a lady to address someone. I may be a lowly nurse maid, but I am still your elder--"

"Sleep." She snapped her fingers this time, holding compellingly the gaze of the woman across from her. That seemed to do the trick. Evey's eyes fluttered shut, and she collapsed to the ground, thumping her head against the flagstone.

Morgan winced. She had never considered head injuries as a consequence of sudden collapse. Fainting was such a regular occurrence here in court, and no one ever died from it.

Though she supposed all those maidens had eager knights there to catch them whenever they swooned and thus were not at risk of cracking their heads on the floor.

The Tale of ~~King Arthur~~ Morgan Le Fay

She tucked a pillow beneath the minor lump forming on back of Evey's head, hoping it would do something to mitigate the pounding headache that would likely torment her the moment she awoke.

Arthur was wailing in his crib, rudely awakened by the screams of his nurse a minute past.

Morgan whirled on him in anger. "Be silent, will you? I stopped by to see you. You ought to be used to that. And grateful, bloody grateful. I have far more rewarding things I could be doing with my time right now." The baby showed no such gratitude, distressed screams only growing in volume. "Shut it! You are going to draw more of them."

She leaned over the edge of the crib. The babe whimpered, bright blue eyes glued to the pale-faced girl staring him down. He seemed scared, like he wanted to know what was wrong, wanted to know what he'd done to earn such a glare. He was frozen the same way she had been in that throne room before their father.

Her eyes instantly softened. "A few more months and you'll be king, do you understand?" The baby said nothing. He did not in fact understand. "Our father will be dead. And our mother maybe planned it. But I'm still being used as a bargaining chip of breeding married off to a foreign child instead of an old man while you get to be boy king of a country. Understand?"

A little hand reached up toward her hesitantly, winding his fingers around a lock of hair that had come free of her braids, dangling right above his face. He yanked on it. Hard.

Morgan bit back her curse, hand locking around those annoyingly strong stubby fingers in an attempt to pry them loose. "Bloody great conversationalist, just like I suspected," she grumbled, jerking back her head. Tiny fingers twined around her own, and the baby stared at her. She stared back solemnly.

The door thudded open. "Who goes there?"

Morgan glared over her shoulder at the packed doorway of guards and cowering maids.

"Princess? What are you--?"

"Sleep!"

Everyone dropped. Arthur giggled. He really was just adorable when he smiled, insufferably adorable.

"You sleep too," she muttered. "And let go of my finger already." The baby's eyes fluttered shut, hands weakly uncurling.

Morgan picked her way over the snoring masses and set off down the hallway.

Her mother's plan tonight had been a shrewd one, pulled off without a hitch, as she manipulated everyone around her toward a happier but still miserable future.

I wish no part in your plan. I will make my own fate. Morgan swore. *I am the daughter of kings, a powerful wizardess. I am no one's chess piece.* So what if she lacked sorely the skills to steer those knights and play the game as a proper queen, the most powerful one on the field? Morgan had no need to win by capturing kings. She'd flip the board and be done with it.

The Tale of ~~King Arthur~~ Morgan Le Fay

IV. The Feast to End all Feasts

A blessed calm had filled the castle this past month, as the ailing King Uther set out to ill-advised battle with his host of knights in tow. That peaceful silence was set to end tonight. The heralds had announced a great victory, a grand triumph over the savage Saxon threat on the field of St. Albany, with the final charge led by the great Uther Pendragon himself. The procession of rowdy lords would ride back to Camelot tonight to host a celebration. Morgan's only hope was that Merlin would be accompanying them. She had seen no sign of the wizard in almost a year, but perhaps now, with the immediate threat ended and the war on pause, the mysterious mage would finally be finished with his travels, able to return home to them once more.

The almost completely self-taught wizardess was getting better and better at scrying, an ancient art that involved viewing a target through a pool of water. She had tried the first few times to locate Merlin and mistakenly believed herself an utter failure, as searches for the druid revealed only haze and clouded waters. She read more scholarly commentary and tried again, day after day. She knew her preparations were correct, and her stubbornness would not allow her to quit at anything before she succeeded in her goal. Still, she could see nothing of the druid.

She passed a group of maids in the hallway on the day of her fifth consecutive failure. They were most noticeably and obnoxiously giggling, but they fell instantly silent at her approach. Paranoid curiosity prompted her to try her scrying again with those twits as her targets, and she found it to be perfectly effective. She could observe each servant as they went about their day to day lives, gossiping and sowing rumors. It worked on anyone she could envision. Anyone but Merlin.

She tried the art next on some of the local children who dithered away their days in the woods just outside the castle, gathering firewood or squiring for knights. Those girls and boys had such boring little lives, stitching endless needlepoint or completing common chores of dishes and wood-cutting. She decided to liven up their days by conjuring up snakes to come crawling up out of their chamber pots. That trick was even more delightful when played upon the adults. The great knights screamed just as loudly as their page boys when the serpents brushed their backsides.

No one really came to Morgan's rooms anymore, not even to investigate her hysterical laughter. She was rather lonely, she discovered, even with her little pranks, and her mother's company made her most uncomfortable these days.

She tried once again to catch even the briefest glimpse of Merlin. Nothing but clouded waters. So, with a heavy sigh she went looking for her father instead, out on his war campaign with the other lords. She saw from her own observation of the battles that all the herald's tales of Uther's undampened battle prowess were complete and utter lies.

The king had been kept soundly at the back of the lines throughout each skirmish and clash, swaying in his saddle and barking confused commands to generals who for the most part ignored his input, forging ahead with their plan to route the Saxons. The sights on that first battlefield churned Morgan's stomach. It was all mud and gore and flailing mounts. There was no glory or decorum, and she found she could not sleep at all the night that followed her first scrying of it. She looked again the next day, regardless of her discomfort, and watched the entire brutal battle on the field of St. Albany, where Britain's ailing king had allowed King Lot to take charge of their armies, playing brief pantomime out on the field before retiring to the warmth of his pavilion, as the killing came to a close and the leader of the Saxons, King Octa, was slain.

Now the sun was sinking, and the feast hall was filling with knights raving endless lies of Uther's valor. Uncle Aurelius took charge of the narrative, insisting his brother had ridden with head held high throughout the long march to their eastern border and won yet another legendary victory, striking down this horde of Saxons almost single-highhandedly. No one challenged that narrative, not even King Lot, who had done most of the work out on that field.

Uther drank in those lies with smiles and blustering embellishments of his own. He was in genuinely high spirits, for the first time in almost a year. His pallor was not as poor tonight, and he had much to celebrate. King Lot's aid in subduing the north had made Uther's dream of a unified Britain quite near a reality. Even those few stubborn pagans and foreigners who clung to chunks of land to the far west and south dreaded the approach of the Pendragon armies, yielding their cities and castles and striking up treaties often at the mere glimpse of the red-scaled flag. The feast tonight seemed a heartfelt farewell on part of these knights, a joyous salute to a dying monarch whose legacy would live on long after his sickness won out.

The Tale of ~~King Arthur~~ Morgan Le Fay

Morgan had not been invited to that feast. No servant had been sent to fetch her, but she eased her way into that crowded hall anyway, eyes scanning the chaos for some sign of her long missing mentor. It was just as she'd feared from her scrying however. The druid was nowhere to be seen.

"That's right, your majesty, you never had the chance before we set out to meet my cousin, the little prince, now did you?" Morgan overheard Anna De'gaur somewhat loudly exclaim from her position fawning over King Lot near the head of the feast table. "Where is he, Aunt Igraine? Won't the little heir be joining us this evening?"

"Yes, where is he?" Uther eagerly agreed. "Haven't seen the boy in ages."

Igraine forced a smile and whispered a quick command to one of the servants. "He will be out here shortly," she assured her husband, and Uther's smile returned. Arthur had been kept from these feasts lately, what with the increasingly vocal guests coupled with Uther's failing health and unpredictably flaring temper. Still, the king seemed in a stable mood tonight.

Stable enough to answer a simple question surely. Morgan prayed, making her way tentatively over to the crowded table where her father loitered amidst his circle of praise. She waited patiently for an opening in the conversation of laughing lords exchanging compliments and lies with their king. She waited an entire five minutes and was left with no choice but to cut one of them off. Lord Cadry would do.

"Father?" she pressed.

Uther ignored her, seeming not to have heard.

"Lord Uther."

Still no response.

Morgan's eyes darkened, finger twitching up in a sharp and purposeful command. The wine on the table before Uther went up in a sudden flash of steam and crimson flame. The lords started back from the sight, and the hall fell silent.

"What the devil?" King Lot whispered.

"No devils, just a flaming rum punch," Morgan assured him dryly, lips spread in a smile. "A common sight here in the hall of the Pendragons. When a dragon is a blowhard, it is only to be expected there will be flames. Anyhow, father," Her eyes shifted back to Uther. "welcome home. I have been needing to speak with you all day."

"Surely it can wait." Uther's brow had lowered, eyes darkening dangerously. He did not scare her this time, not here in a hall of so many witnesses. Anyway, there was no real strength to him now. She had seen it herself, out on that battlefield. He would be dead inside of the year, just as her mother had said.

"It cannot. Seeing a king return without his chief adviser is most concerning after all. Was Merlin not with you on the campaign?" she pressed. "You said before that you had not seen him in months, but I thought surely--"

"That useless wizard has not been seen in the king's lands for almost a year now," Lord Cadry sniffed, turning up his nose. "He has betrayed his post and his duty."

"Indeed," Uther growled. "I sent him out on an errand, and he has yet to return. Now, daughter," The word seemed almost an insult. "we will speak no more of this."

"Your son, my lord."

The announcement cheered him instantly, and Uther stood up in his seat, reaching out his hands for the towheaded babe being carried over by Igraine. "There he is!" Uther clapped in delight, seizing up the boy. "Won't be long till we get a sword in your hands, now will it, my boy? Get you out on that field fighting alongside your old man..." A bought of sudden coughing took him, and Igraine gently eased Arthur free of his grip, passing him on to his nursemaid, Evey.

"Fetch the king something to parch his thirst," she ordered one of the servants. "The dryness of the room has caused quite a tickle in his throat. Isn't that right, my lord?"

"Yes, indeed." Uther forced a smile, hiding the red at the corners of his mouth with a quick swipe of his sleeve.

"Here you are, my king." Anna De'gaur gave a low curtsy, presenting him with a chalice.

"Thank you, Anna." He raised the cup in salute. "A toast. To the defeat of the pagan King Octa and the future of our lands. To Britain!"

"To Britain!" the knights howled in response.

The men all drained their horns, as Igraine and all the other ladies took delicate sips from their own chalices in graceful support. Morgan drifted to the back of the crowd and drank not one sip, eyes still burning into her father and his crowd of posturing liars. *Better if you were all of you dead.* She thought to herself.

Uther's hacking worsened with abrupt suddenness, and Igraine looked over in alarm, hand settling on his back. "My lord? Perhaps you should retire for the..." The queen's breaths became suddenly erratic.

The Tale of ~~King Arthur~~ Morgan Le Fay

Igraine looked to her niece in alarm, but Anna made no move to help her, as the queen swayed, pitching forward across the table.

"My lady?" Lords and knights rose to attend her, only to falter themselves, knees buckling. They crashed to the ground in a clamor of metal and shattering glass.

Uther's hacking had ceased, as his own labored breathing grew jaggedly still, glassy eyes staring unseeingly up at the ceiling, as he slumped back in his chair. Uncle Aurelius was dead at his side, skin pale and slack, just like Lord Cadry and a dozen others throughout the hall. It all happened so fast. Morgan didn't have time to react or do anything to stop it. She just stared in shock at her father – dead. And her mother... Igraine was dead. Her mother was...

It wasn't me, was it? Morgan questioned herself in sudden panic. *It was just a thought. I didn't actually kill them, did I? I couldn't have. I wouldn't!*

"What treachery is this?!" King Lot cried, bounding to his feet with sword in hand and eyes sweeping the crowd in angry accusation.

"No treachery. Witchcraft!" Anna De'gaur gasped, clutching a hand to her breast and whirling to face the pariah stood frozen in the corner. "That cruel fay hath slain her own father, our king. You all saw what she did to our liege's cup!"

"I didn't... I didn't mean to," Morgan stuttered, and the surviving knights before her paled with instant rage. The vast majority of them were King Lot's retainers, with only a few of her own countrymen that she recognized: Lord Maleagant and Duke Kador, and a handful of others. All of them usurped heirs of formerly independent duchies like Cornwall that had sworn begrudging allegiance to Uther, but she had no time to give thought to how composed they were about the sudden death of their liege. She had no time to think at all, mind frozen with fear and self-doubt, as the ring of armored men closed in around her.

"Witch," some of them muttered, hands drifting to their swords.

"She is a witch!" Anna wailed. "A known changeling, now a murderer! Strike her down, my lords. Quickly! Before the same sadistic fate that befell our liege is cast over us all!"

A dreadful figure clad in layers of black steel stalked grimly through the crowd and reached to seize her. Sir Turquine, a butcher of most frightening prowess from what she had glimpsed of him on the battlefield. His blade was already bared at his side, raising now to strike. She needed to fight back, flee, but the fear kept her frozen, powerless, and all she felt was small, tiny and despised, unable to do anything as that blade came hurtling toward her head and passed right through--

Empty air.

Her arm had shrunken and slipped from Turquine's grasp, leaving behind just an empty pile of fabric, as the sword whistled through the area where her head had been and clanged against the wall. The nobles gasped.

"So it was a specter," King Lot stated, strong voice quavering. Even Anna De'gaur, who had been witness herself to many of Morgan's strange outbursts and powers just stared on in shock, completely caught off guard by the strange vanishing of the cousin she had condemned.

None of them noticed the tiny black furred mouse that slid out from under the hem of the deserted dress and shot off down the hall, keeping to the shadows with little heart thundering away within her transmuted chest. Her mother was dead, and her father's own knights, all those who had survived, blamed her for everything. *But it was only a thought. I didn't mean it!* She swore. Her eyes were growing damp, blurring her vision with tears. It appeared even mice could cry, and the fear and panic felt so natural in this state, scurrying across the floor in desperate search of cover. Those angry shouts were still booming through the halls. The servants were wailing. Awful things would happen here tonight. She needed to escape, flee, run!

A long hanging tapestry rose up before her, a perfect bit of cover from the booming footsteps she could feel shaking the floor behind her, closing in on her back. The mouse scooted beneath the fabric and crouched there, shaking, as the footsteps thundered past. A baby's cries were echoing through the hall, and chasing after the sound were the awful clanking footsteps of a brute. It was that horrible knight, Sir Turquine, the man who had attacked her in the hall, fully set on murdering his princess, a ten year old child. She was too frightened to feel angry about that. She was a murderer after all. She had killed her own mother, even if it had only been an accident...

But why was he chasing Arthur?

That thought froze all her guilt, and her beady eyes tracked the brute making his way after the frail, fleeing figure of Evey, scurrying off down the hall with the wailing heir to Britain's throne clutched desperately to her chest.

All thoughts of flight and her own safety were instantly smothered by worry. What was that brute of a knight doing, reaching out so menacingly to rip the young prince from the arms of his caretaker? Why had he been so calm about the death of his liege and so eager in wake of his passing to

The Tale of ~~King Arthur~~ Morgan Le Fay

dispose of his heirs, both she and her brother? Morgan's guilt and doubt turned instantly to rage. She had no need to hide from this traitor. She was not some cowering rodent. She was Morgan Pendragon, a great and powerful sorceress!

That thought was a mistake. In an instant, the mouse was gone and so was her cover, as she found herself returned to her regular shape, naked behind the tapestry and silently berating herself for her lack of control, or any sort of plan here.

She peered around the edge of the heavy hanging fabric. Turquine had not noticed the rippling surface of the tapestry that concealed her. His attention was fixed on Evey, screaming now in protest, as he seized her by the shoulder and reached for the babe in her hands.

"What treachery do you plan here, peasant, smuggling away the king's heir?" Turquine demanded in sneering accusation, one hand clamped around frail Evey's shoulder and the other still fixed about his sword, hanging bared at his side. "Do you not realize the dangers this night in wake of his father's passing?"

"Get back, villain! I see through your lies. The danger is you!"

"Be silent." Turquine seized the nurse by the throat, but Morgan knew well how to deal with a rampaging beast. You lulled it into lazy slumber, just as her mother had so deftly done with her own powers of influence.

Though Morgan's own influence was much more direct. "Sleep!"

The black knight dropped, pitching forward and thudding face first into the stone. Morgan felt no regret whatsoever for the injuries that time.

Evey clasped a hand to her mouth and turned her eyes to the princess peering out from the corner of her tapestry. "Princess?" Those eyes flooded with fear, and she tightened her hold on Arthur. "No. I saw what you did, even to your own dear mother. You will not have our prince. Do you hear me, demon?!"

More footsteps sounded at the head of the hall, clamoring towards them. Evey took off, Arthur in her arms.

"I saved him, you thankless crone," Morgan muttered, knowing she needed to flee herself, and quickly, but running naked through the halls was clearly not an option.

Her eyes settled on the narrow window just across from her. She was a changeling, she reminded herself grimly, a powerful magician fully able to transform herself completely, as she had already proven once this night. All she needed was something with feathers, to carry her away on the winds, out into the freedom of the open world. That craving for flight, escaping this cage, brought forth the change instantly. Glossy black feathers sprouted all along her arms and back, and the ground raced up to meet her, as she shrunk down with stomach churning suddenness, her toes curling into sharpened talons.

The armored troop of traitors charging up from the head of the hall staggered to a halt, as the raven spread its wings. She hopped off toward the window in a somewhat less than impressive fashion, struggling to flap her way free of the tapestry and into full on flight.

"Shoot it down, you dullards!" Anna shouted with a decided lack of decorum, and the knights all looked at her aghast. "I mean... Ahem, that demon is clearly on its way to devour my dear cousin, our king's precious son. We must hasten to find him and shoot down that-- Oh curse your sluggishness! She's already gone."

Morgan could hear quite clearly the angry stamping of Anna's foot, as the young sorceress plummeted out the window in a streak of black, calling up her instincts and spreading her newly formed wings to slow her momentum and glide off into the night. It seemed her tantruming cousin was not nearly as grown up as she pretended. Though she had indeed displayed some shockingly developed attributes that Morgan was just now catching sight of, as she fought down her own doubts and panic and reflected back on all her cousin's cruel words and dramatically staged reactions this night.

The princess's resentment of her father had not poisoned anyone at that feast. There had been no accidental spell or magic involved in their deaths. Her cousin had been the one to give Uther his chalice, and it was the servants of King Lot who had poured the rest of the libations for the now dead Lords of Logres and their queen. Morgan had underestimated her cousin sorely, just as she had her own mother in the past. The wicked girl was a traitor and a murderer of most ruthless efficiency. She had emptied the throne for her new suitor, King Lot, and framed the known sorceress, Morgan, for all of it, painting her a devil and an enemy.

Morgan wanted to scream with frustration, though all that emerged was an echoing caw. She had no idea where her brother was now, or even if he had escaped that castle. Evey had spurned her aid. She despised her just as all the others did. Morgan had lost her family and a home that had never truly been hers to begin with. She had graduated from outcast to exile in truth, alone in the world, with her powers perceived as always as nothing but a condemning curse. She needed to be planning her revenge, plotting her return to the halls of her murdered kin to inflict gruesome punishment upon Anna De'gaur and each and every treasonous knight and honorless noble that had aided in her scheme. That righteous fury would not stay with her at the moment though, cracked with grief and self-pity, until the rage became nothing but little knots in her chest, useless wads of despair that drained away her energy.

She found an abandoned barn and turned back into a frightened little girl, sobbing in the corner in stinking borrowed sackcloth. She had not the control to take vengeance upon her cousin. All her study and effort were worthless out here, exposed and alone with few reliable tricks to call upon to aid her. She needed more power, the control and poise to wipe out all that threatened. Her sniffling petered out, teary eyes hardening with resolve. She needed to find Merlin.

v. The Lady Of the Lake

The soon to be great and powerful sorceress awoke within the moldering hay, as dreams of fiery vengeance gave way to bleak reality, and she found herself back within a collapsing barn abandoned far outside the gates of the great city of Camelot. The rains of the evening prior had left the princess decidedly chilled, huddled there in the damp all night. She had attempted repeatedly with masterfully contrived anger to start a proper campfire during the night to keep her warm. Each and every time the magical flames came in contact with her selected soggy fuel source however, they did nothing but sputter and smoke. Be it hay or wood beams, every single item within this barn was far too drenched to serve as proper tinder. The summoned flames only further exhausted the young sorceress, until her traitorous eyes gave in to the invisible weight pulling them shut and she drifted off into a light and uncomfortable doze. Now her shoulders were shaking with shivers, her stomach was rumbling, and her nose was crinkled up in anger at the stench of her makeshift burlap dress.

This was not a den befitting of either princess or wizardess, and she decided immediately to forsake the sad amount of shelter it provided. She shoved open the door and slogged barefoot through the mud toward the firmer ground of the forest ahead. She needed to find a standing pool of water, first to quench her thirst, and then to use for scrying to find out where Merlin had wandered off to this past year. It did not matter that she had never once successfully conjured even the briefest glimpse of the wizard. Whatever obstacles or enchantments existed clouding her sight, she was determined to break through them and track down her mentor.

Unless he too is--

She did not allow herself to finish the thought. Merlin was not dead. He was a druid of unparalleled power and wisdom. Only the devil himself could strike him down, and she did not believe in the devil, so alive the druid must be. He had simply wandered off somewhere, neglecting his responsibilities. He needed only to be located and informed of the dreadful usurpation that had taken place within the castle he had so carelessly abandoned.

Morgan closed her eyes and tried to turn herself back into a crow, to take to the skies and scout out a lake or a pool with far more efficiency than the scrawny legs of the cold and weak body in which she was currently trapped. She felt far too soggy and sad to focus on feelings of flight this morning however. She felt more like a bear, a miserable, lumbering beast rudely ousted from its den and now wandering the wilds with half a mind to maul any that approached.

The hair had just begun to sprout and her shoulders to swell, when a tinkling laugh firmly scattered her concentration. Her eyes darted angrily to the dew-drenched bushes at her side. Eyes of luminescent green boldly met the glare of the shivering princess, and a figure emerged from the tangle of budded branches. It was a fairy, thrown into the shape of a little girl with green skin and hair of stringy moss curling around tiny horns: the mark of Satan, as the bishop back in town surely would have decried. Morgan was not at all intimidated by this frail magical creature however. She was enraged, as she stood there shivering with arms crossed across her chest and the little terror continued to stare and laugh at her.

"Oh come on, why'd you stop?" the little fay demanded, lips pursing in a pout. "I wanted to see what animal that was, be it beaver or bear. You shift so slowly after all. It is quite strange but oh so fun to watch. Left me just brimming with anticipation!" The fay cocked her head, smile twisting with puzzlement. Flesh became mist, and she zipped right up to Morgan, a dog sniffing at her backside, changing shapes with liquid ease, as she shifted from mutt to boy then back to girl, leaned right up in Morgan's face with nose pressed against her own. "How come you can change, anyway?" she demanded, poking a rude finger into her chest.

Morgan shoved her away, and the fay tumbled to the ground in a flurry of snaking vines, making odd patterned faces at her. "You little pink people are supposed to stay solid, one shape that just stretches and swells and crinkles over years and years." The vines wove themselves into a little boy, lying on his stomach, staring up at her and kicking his feet. "You're just like that other one, aren't you?"

"What other one?" Morgan demanded.

"The *other* one," the green boy emphasized, as if it were the most obvious thing in the world. His face became suddenly middle-aged and bearded, taking on an instantly familiar cast of brown eyes twinkling with smugness, though his skin was still green. "Someone like me," the fay huffed in an exaggeratedly gruff version of Merlin's regular timber.

"Merlin was here?" Morgan smiled, eyes lighting with hopeful excitement. "When?"

The druid melted back into a moss-haired child, her fingers twisting mist, as she waved her hand airily from her missing stump of a wrist. "Hmm, months... years... Who keeps track?"

The mist flowed right between Morgan's legs again, and the fake Merlin was back, towering over her sternly. "Do you want to play a game?" he pressed, stroking at his beard.

"What sort of game?" the princess pressed.

Fake Merlin put a hand on her shoulder. She batted it away, only for the arm to puff to mist and reform back into a little girl with head settled on Morgan's shoulder and arms clutched tight about her waist in an uninvited embrace. "You can remember time by losing it."

"Get off me!" Morgan swore, twisting free of the strangely slimy grip.

The fay kept a hold of her makeshift dress, picking with webbed fingers at the back of the sleeveless burlap in clear judgment. "That's not a dress for a princess."

"How did you know I was a--?"

"You need some better clothes. Why don't you make some?"

"I can't," she snapped. "Now tell me when Merlin--"

"Why not? The other one could do it."

"He could?"

"Mmmhmm. Like this." The fay's body became flowing fabric, wrapping around Morgan's shoulders and unrolling right to the grass in the form of a horribly heavy dress with sleeves trailing along the ground and tight-laced bodice squeezing at her rib cage. Morgan could hardly breathe it was so tight, with the vines laced straight through the corset still pulling themselves steadily tighter.

She clawed cursing at fabric that dripped right through her fingers wherever she sought to tear it free.

"Look, you're changing again!" a disembodied voice echoed in a sing-song taunt. "Such a pretty color, blue. Blue lips, blue skin, blue--"

"Get off me!" Morgan screamed, and the edges of the unnatural garment went up in flames.

The fay screamed and solidified back into a little girl, rolling in the dirt and patting frantically at the green flames still sputtering along her legs. "Ouch," she sniffled, still trailing smoke that did not for once seem to be of her creation. "You're not a princess at all. You're a devil."

She turned into a snake, slithering back into the bushes and eyeing Morgan with wary anticipation. "Only devils play with fire."

"I am not a devil," Morgan could not help but protest, voice hoarse and breathing ragged. "You are!"

"Am I?" The snake became a smiling imp with curving horns and goat's feet. "Mmm. I like this game."

The Tale of ~~King Arthur~~ Morgan Le Fay

"I am not playing," Morgan grated. "Now where is Merlin?!"

"He was no fun," the imp asserted, "but the lady said he was. Keeps him locked away like her other toys."

"Where?"

The imp vanished in a surge of wind, ruffling her hair with a tangle of leaves and dirt, as the boy reappeared with hands around her waist. "What will you give me if I tell you?" The lips seized hers, stealing a kiss, and the fire burst back against the fay's chest, hurling him away from her.

The fay howled and retreated back into a tree, smoking skin melting into the surface and leaving behind only the pouting face of a little girl with moss for hair. "You're no fun." The teary eyes melted back into the tree trunk, though the wood retained a bit of charring, right by the spot where Morgan had burned her.

Morgan was quite seriously in need of a lake now, to wash out her mouth. She wiped at her lips in angry disgust and slogged on through the woods. At least the kiss had not been slimy or stolen her breath like that deadly trap of a dress. She decided in that moment that she firmly hated fairies. Maybe Merlin had been right about the value of the name Pendragon, for Morgan Le Fay now seemed the title of an irritating troublemaker, just like that changeling who had accosted her.

Morgan was grateful for the sheltered shadow of the trees as the day wore on and the heat rose, evaporating the mists and dew of the early morning, though strange faces continued to leer at her from among the vines and brambles. She supposed there was a mystical quality to these woods so seldom traversed by travelers. Why had Merlin come here then? Why suffer through the tauntings of fairies, even if you had the power to repel them? *That changeling had to be lying.* She told herself. *There's no way he could be trapped. He's a druid. He is far more powerful than these simple woods spirits.*

Morgan stumbled more and more throughout the hours, as a terrible dizziness overcame her. This was no fairy curse. It was simple dehydration, eating away at her equilibrium and blurring her vision. She spotted water finally, just as the sun began to set. This was the lake she had been looking for, much deeper into the wood than it had appeared on the maps she had studied. Those had clearly not been drawn with proper scaling. She collapsed onto hands and knees and gulped down greedily handful after handful of the pristine crystal liquid. She heard more little voices murmuring and laughing at her from the fringes of the lake, but she made a point of ignoring them, slurping in more and more of the precious liquid and regretting sorely that she had nothing else to fill her stomach.

A pale white arm darted up from the surface of the lake, and she jerked back in alarm, scrambling back along the shoreline. The perfectly manicured hand was holding up an apple, its glistening red flesh calling to her in tantalizing allure, as the fingers splayed open in clear invitation for her to take hold of the fruit so appetizingly displayed upon this stranger's palm.

Morgan was not near foolish enough to consume such a suspicious offering however. She knew all too well what happened to princesses who went around impulsively biting into apples without a second thought. A mortal could not consume the food of the fay without being made a permanent prisoner to their whims, and whoever the master was of this disembodied arm, they most certainly had an ulterior motive for offering her this far too desirable fare.

It was getting exceedingly more difficult to resist the demands of her growling stomach however, with that fat juicy fruit sitting right there in front of her, so Morgan snatched the apple from the open palm and hurled it out into the lake. The fingers curled into a bitter fist, and the hand sunk slowly back beneath the darkened waters.

Morgan felt a sudden angry twist within her gut and promptly vomited up all the water she had taken in so eagerly just a few minutes past. Perhaps it had been a mistake to drink of these waters in the first place.

"It appears the water, like the apple, was not to your liking, child," a lovely voice of echoing strength taunted her coolly. The speaker was a woman, rising up from the darkened waters of the lake with her silver hair and trailing white dress giving off a steady effervescence that far outshone the frail light of the newly risen moon. She was the most beautiful creature that Morgan had ever seen. Her perfect curves and angelic features made Igraine and all the muses of legend look plain and dull by comparison, and Morgan instantly, instinctively disliked her. "A wayward doe, ragged with mange, comes lost into my wood, and so generously do we provide thee charity, only for you to spurn the offering."

"I need not your charity, Lady of the Lake," Morgan insisted, shoving herself swaying to her feet. "I have come here for Merlin."

The lady glided across the waters toward the mortal on her shores, her pale bare feet causing not so much as the slightest ripple on the mirror-like surface as she walked. "I think not, little one," she challenged, stalking right up to Morgan and holding her captive with the alluring force of those beautiful green eyes. "You came here simply to sate your thirst."

The Tale of ~~King Arthur~~ Morgan Le Fay

She drew a silver chalice from her sleeve, holding it out to the parched and starving child stubbornly attempting to maintain her decorum. "Go on, drink. I would not let so precious a bud wither and die before she has yet had a chance to bloom."

The purple wine within the chalice was giving off a most fragrant aroma of berries and honey. Morgan was already salivating, much to her irritation. She wiped angrily at her lips and stubbornly pulled back her head, staring the lady down sternly. "Where is Merlin?" she repeated.

The lady frowned and drew back her hand, dropping the cup. It puffed into mist the second it left her hand, and the lady eyed her up and down in glaring judgment. "A favor demands a favor in turn. This is why you are so reluctant to accept my gifts, even those you are in sore and urgent need of. If you want to see your druid, then look for him yourself." She waved her arm over the waters behind, and a sudden glow appeared from beneath. Morgan squinted, leaning forward, and her eyes widened in wonder. It appeared an entire city lay out there, far beneath the surface of the lake.

The lady arched an eyebrow in clear challenge, and Morgan waded out into the waters without further hesitance. If Merlin was down there then she had no choice but to go rescue him. *And if you wind up trapped yourself?* She pushed away the thought. She would cross that bridge when she came to it.

The water remained shallow, only coming up to her shoulders, no matter how far out she strode. The city seemed to draw further and further away from her with each and every step. The lady glided up beside her, cold eyes weighing into the child now level with her feet. "No visitor may come into my kingdom so poorly outfitted for the feast. Stretch out thy hand."

Morgan glared at her, wading forward another few feet before diving beneath the surface. It was useless. The city vanished and her face hit the soil at the bottom of the lake, arms becoming tangled with weeds. She thrashed her way back to the surface, spluttering angrily.

"Stretch out thy hand," the lady repeated irritably, holding out her own pale unblemished palm.

"Fine," Morgan snapped, slapping her own tiny hand right into the infuriatingly superior fay's. "I agree to attend your feast, and I will wear whatever you wish, so long as you swear not to strangle me with it."

The lady arched an eyebrow, letting loose a wonderful, melodious laugh that Morgan judged as decidedly shallow and synthetic. "I swear no harm shall befall you, little doe. Come now." She pulled her up out of the waters and into an embrace.

"You fairies have zero respect for personal space," Morgan muttered, though the rest of her criticisms cut off, as she was suddenly plunged back beneath the surface, hurtling through darkness and raging currents, until her senses gave out.

The Tale of ~~King Arthur~~Morgan Le Fay

VI. The Room of No Exit

When Morgan's eyes fluttered open, she found herself perfectly dry, seated at a seemingly endless table in a golden banquet hall of luminescent walls and sparkling crystals that lined the walls and ceilings in place of ordinary smoky torches or candles. It was indeed a feast. Set right before her was an already filled plate of figs and warm bread and glazed, juicy meat. The smell of it sent her reaching instantly forward, even as her other hand angrily forced down her wrist, reminding herself sharply that this was all some elaborate trick to trap her here forever. That sweet smelling berry wine was sitting in a chalice right before her though, and her throat was burning with thirst that could only be sated by seizing that cup, draining every last drop of the no doubt delectable...

She shoved back her chair and bounded to her feet, tripping over the hem of the long emerald dress that clothed her, a perfectly fitted finery that clung to her waist in layers of heavy embroidered velvet that somehow felt light as air, billowing about her as she walked.

A hundred pairs of lovely luminescent eyes tracked her stumbling movements, as she stalked away from her seat. She scanned the crowd of dangerously fair humanoid creatures seated or dancing around her, searching for the normal skin tones of Merlin or any other human.

It was hard to focus though, with those mouth-watering scents of roast beef and wine still flooding her nostrils and the colorful swirls of fancifully clad fay twirling all around her in graceful dance. Their trilling voices filled the air with laughter and music so much richer and more compelling than the dully plucked dulcimers that had petered in the background of her father's own feasts.

She wanted desperately to join in that dance. The rhythm was infectious, and as a young boy seized her hand, pulling her toward the center of the floor, she could not help but go along with him. He had lovely eyes, brilliant green, just like the Lady of the Lake. Where had the lady gone anyway? Morgan had seen no trace of her here. And where was--? *Merlin! I came here to find Merlin.*

She broke free of the boy's waltz and tried to fight her way to the edge of the crowd, only to be swept up by an even more lovely partner with ghostly eyes like shining glass and strong slim fingers twined tight in her own, as he guided her hand to his lips. "A single dance, my lady?"

She gave no answer or affirming nod but could offer no resistance either. He pulled her in, and she glided across the floor in thrilling, spinning synchronous with the silver clad fay. He was smiling at her so invitingly, and she could not help but smile in return, laughing along with the musical chorus of tinkling voices around her. They were all of them smiling, eyeing her with hunger, as she spun from partner to partner, with that wonderful, terrible music overriding her senses. She could not stop laughing, giggling and losing her breath. Her stomach hurt, but the action would not cease, and her throat was so dry...

Another dance, another song, its beat manic and enrapturing. The room was spinning now, and she felt so faint... The smooth hands fixed tighter about her waist as she swooned, twirling her about and lowering her into a chair. Those lovely fingers held a chalice to her lips, a mercifully refreshing wine of berries and honey...

She spluttered, shoving away the cup and spewing her mouthful of vintage out into the face of the green-eyed knight who had so manipulatively dosed her.

The fay wiped irritably at the dripping red stains running down his cheek and staining the pristine white of his tunic with an all too fitting crimson taint. "A princess aught to have more manners," he chided. "A princess aught to be more gracious."

"And a knight aught to have more honor than to drug an exhausted damsel," Morgan panted. "Now stop trying to feed me your magic and just answer my bloody question of where Merlin is, so I can leave this place already!"

"Leave? Why would you want to leave?" a beautiful fairy girl demanded, spinning past her and into the arms of another of the green-skinned knights. "It's so wonderful here. You'll be happy forever."

"You can be whoever you want," a little pixie whispered in her ear, settling on her shoulder and turning her chin toward the mirrored wall at the side of the room. The little fairy blew her dust over Morgan's perfectly coiffed curls, changing them from black to shining gold and her eyes to a brilliant blue, the color she'd always envied. "You're a changeling, one of us. You belong here. That's why the lady brought you."

"You belong here," the boy who had first pulled her out onto the dance floor repeated, pulling her back to her feet.

"Have a drink," a beautiful woman with eyes of solid black added sweetly, folding a cup into her hands.

The Tale of ~~King Arthur~~Morgan Le Fay

"Eat," another whispered, pushing her back into her seat at the head of the banquet table.

"Drink."

"Eat."

"You belong here."

"Drink with us." That horrid knight was holding the chalice right to her lips again.

Morgan struck him, elbow driving sharply into his stomach, as she angrily shoved back her chair and drove back the crush of devils hovering over her with a burst of blistering fire.

Ladies and lords alike began shrieking, batting at the flames eating away at their fine tunics.

"I am not some play thing for you to twirl about and force feed!" Morgan thundered. The entire banquet hall had gone silent, all the hundreds of guests glaring at her in anxious silence. "I am Morgan Pendragon! Heir to my own kingdom and sorceress of unrivaled potential! I do **not** belong here, and I will **not** suffer any more of your games!" The fine crystal lights shattered, the ground quaking with the strength of her fury. "Now where is Merlin?"

"A dragon she is not," one lady spat in cryptic criticism.

"Yet a dragon she is," another added sullenly, clutching in teary eyed pain at the smoldering remains of what had once been a tail.

"Not dragon, devil."

"Devil," they all agreed, an echo of unified judgment.

"Be gone from this place."

"Be gone from this place!" Each and every infuriating trickster took up the angry jeer, and clawed hands reached to seize her, only to jerk back just as quickly at but a lick of Morgan's flames.

"I shall take my leave," Morgan retorted haughtily, raising her chin. "As soon as I get what I came for. Now stand aside."

The crowd parted, leaving open the path to the doorway, a looming portal of pitch black menace stood at the very end of the impossibly long feast table. Morgan stalked toward that opening with no hint of fear in her proud, brisk stride, bearing easily the glares of those around her. She was well used to such expressions. She had already endured a lifetime of blistering regards and scrutinizing stares, and these creatures were not kin. They had not been friends, no matter all their smiles and possessive embraces. They had simply been trying to kidnap her and keep her trapped down here as some sort of pet or amusement. They had zero right to change her hair or invade her personal space or set her to drooling with their evil magic brews. She felt zero remorse for burning them, and she would feel zero regret for shunning their offer and breaking free of this horrid place, or so she harshly insisted.

Still, her throat was achingly parched, and she might very well still be headed into a trap, as she crossed through the ominously dark doorway, the only visible exit to this cage of a banquet hall. She stepped boldly into that blackness and found herself in a gloomy, stone room. This was the base of her tower, her home in Camelot. The winding stairs leading up into the turret that housed her rooms were unmistakably familiar, though the tapestry of Igraine that had been hung on the wall right at the base of the stairway was mysteriously absent, as were the windows and arrow slits that had previously let in the light of day outside. Perhaps this was not her tower after all.

She crept up the stairs of the eerily silent turret, lifting the hem of her long velvet dress that had grown irritatingly heavy the instant she left the feast hall. "Bloody fairies," she cursed, tripping over the insanely long sleeves of the gown that had given her no trouble throughout her hours of dancing yet now seemed determined to send her tumbling down the stairwell.

It was a horribly long hike. This winding staircase seemed much longer than the one in her home, and she feared she was indeed caught in another fairy trap to keep her here indefinitely, fighting her way up an endless stairway until she collapsed from exhaustion. "Merlin!" she puffed, the desperate shout taking up far more air than her burning lungs were want to part with. "Bloody show yourself, you damn, lazy druid!"

She collapsed, as she reached a landing, staring hopelessly at the line of fresh steps curling up and away from her. Her frustration boiled over, but she would not cry. She was Morgan Pendragon, brilliant sorceress in command of powers that could damage and frighten even these immortal tricksters with their infinite hallways and changing shapes. She would fly free of this cage as she had all the others.

The feathers sprouted, and she went streaking up the stairwell in a blur of black, flapping wildly and picking up speed with every smoothly banked corner and landing passed. She soared on, faster and faster, as the steps blurred by until--

Thwak. She hit the door with bone cracking force and collapsed to the ground, her right wing a crooked mess, and her mind a haze of pain. She curled up into a ball on the floor and became herself again, back in that

The Tale of ~~King Arthur~~ Morgan Le Fay

horrid velvet dress that even her transformations would not free her of, with the tears finally flowing and her arm clutched tight to her chest, even though she could feel that it was no longer broken. Changing her shape had healed her it seemed, grown new bones to replace the damaged crow's wing. It didn't matter. She was still miserable. This damn door had just risen up out of nowhere, with no one coming to answer it or check on her, even after she had so loudly thudded into its surface.

She wiped away her tears and staggered to her feet, gripping the handle with the calm assurance that she had finally reached her destination.

The door was locked. It would not budge. Her eyes grew black with rage. "OPEN!"

The door near blew off its hinges, and a useless old wizard, sat placidly on the window sill of the room ahead, dropped his book in shock, jerking up to face her. "Morgan? What are you doing here?"

"What am I doing here?" she snapped, stalking forward into the bed chamber but leaving the door carefully open behind her as she did. "What are *you* doing here? Why did you come here?! Why didn't you leave? Or come back? Or--"

"Wait! Do not leave the..." The door thudded shut behind her, locking soundly. Merlin exhaled. "The door. It locks on its own, and no one within can open it. No one but the Lady Viviane."

"Viviane?"

"The Lady of the Lake." Merlin sighed. "Surely you met her. She brought you down here I presume?" He crossed over to her wearily, putting a hand on her head. Morgan expected him to hug her, to say he'd missed her, to apologize, or thank her, or explain. Instead, he was simply measuring her, drawing a line toward his chest and frowning decidedly. "You are much taller than before," he murmured.

She threw off his hand. "Of course I'm taller! You were gone for over a year!"

"Only a year? Are you sure? Because you are *much* taller. I mean it. You've grown nearly a foot. How old are you? Twelve?"

"No. I'm only ten..."

The denial trailed off, as she caught sight of herself in the mirror at the side of the room. She peered closely at the lines of her face and found she was indeed noticeably older than when last she'd looked. She did look about twelve or thirteen. How long had she been trapped down here?

"Time passes down here as Viviane wishes," Merlin illuminated. "A single day can feel a second or a year for a mortal, depending on her preference. Just where were you before this?" he murmured, hand to his chin, eyeing her unhappily.

"What does that matter?"

"You didn't do any feasting, did you?" he worried. "Or drinking? Because you are far too young for the beverages here, being that their side effects are permanent slavery."

"I am not a fool," Morgan croaked. "I have not eaten or drunk anything. Apparently for years now, so I am clearly far more disciplined and wise than you are getting yourself trapped here!"

"Not eaten for years, hmm?" Merlin parroted back, sinking down at a simple wood table and tearing into a bread roll. "Well that certainly explains your temper. Your stomach always did make you irritable. You may not be able to starve to death down here, but it certainly feels that way, doesn't it? Come on then." He poured a glass of water, holding it out to her insistently.

Morgan balked. "So what? The lady told you the door would not open, so you just went ahead, believed her, and permanently trapped yourself by eating the food of the fay?!"

"This is not the food of the fay. I conjured it myself. It is perfectly safe, so sit down and eat your dinner."

Morgan sunk down sullenly in the seat across from him, guzzling down the water in a single messy gulp and draining five more full glasses in shocking succession, before the burn in her throat finally began to abate and her pounding head to calm. Her stomach was still rumbling though, and so she greedily devoured the roast chicken Merlin summoned to the center of the table, washing it down with more precious, sweet water, and wishing in bitter envy that she had known how to do this herself.

"Your mother must be worried sick," Merlin muttered, and Morgan froze, gut twisting with grief. The wizard did not seem to notice, eyes on the window beside him, blocked off by a wall of water. "You should not have come here," he continued callously, and Morgan flushed. "Sneaking out from the palace and hiking alone into lake country, you ought to know better. Now you may never see your family again, do you realize that?" Morgan pursed her lips, her eyes veiled and dark. "We are both of us trapped here, forever."

Morgan was instantly irritated by the resigned assuredness with which her mentor made that declaration. No cage could hold her, as she had already proven in each and every trap these fay had thrown at her. The door had opened for her once, and it would open again, the second she willed it.

The Tale of ~~King Arthur~~ Morgan Le Fay

She shoved back her chair and stalked defiantly back up to the portal. "Open!" she commanded. The door didn't budge. "I said **open**!" A blast of flame appeared, charring the portal black. The door let loose a nervous creaking, yet still refused to budge.

Merlin exhaled. "I have already told you, Morgan, it is impossible to leave."

She whirled on him, fists curling in anger. "How hard did you try? That door will give under another blast, I know it."

"Then you will wander endless corridors and staircases before winding up right back here in this same very room," the druid dryly illuminated. "No one but Viviane may open this tower, princess. It is a trap of quite unbreakable cleverness. I should know."

"What do you mean you should know?" Morgan prompted, eyes narrowing in suspicion.

"What I mean is... beside the point. The only point you need know is that I will get you out of here. I swear it. We just have to wait for Viviane to come back."

"*If* she comes back," Morgan snapped. "How long has it been since she trapped you in here?"

"Well, I've no idea. It has felt as mere weeks, but she always comes back," Merlin smugly asserted. "It does happen rather out of the blue, but she has visited dozens of times in... however many years it's been. I do not imagine she shall ever tire of me. She called me most extraordinary, and I must admit that she in turn is quite..."

The man had the same starry eyed look to his eyes now that he'd had around her mother, and Morgan felt an angry flush of judgment, understanding instantly the nature of he and Viviane's relationship.

She chucked a bread roll at his head. Merlin flinched, jolted out of his daydream. "Baked projectiles, now is it? That is a shameful waste of food. My conjurations have limits, and this bread was not created. It was simply pulled from someone else's table, a necessary pilferage."

"You got trapped in here on purpose, didn't you?" Morgan accused. "You fell for some silver haired fairy lady and let her trap you in a spell of your own construction you conjured up simply to impress her! Does that sound about right?"

"I came here for a most practical reason, I will have you know," Merlin retorted primly. "King Uther required a sword, a legendary blade prophesied to be wielded by the only rightful king, the man who would unite all of Britain and bring about a time of unprecedented peace. Even the old bishop in Canterbury buys into that prophecy, which is why a mischievous fay did steal that most holy sword a century past, handing it over to his mistress to be locked away with all the rest of her treasures. Our country has seen nothing but war and ill fortune ever since that day, which is why the sword must be returned to the possession of our king, along with all the other sacred hallows."

"Sacred hallows?" Morgan pressed.

"The Holy Grail and the tainted spear that pierced the Lord's side on the cross, along with the sword of the true king, Excalibur, to defend the sacred objects and keep them from use."

"Who cares about a cup and a lance no one can use? This sounds like some bishop's nonsense, sending followers out on pilgrimage for relics that will do nothing but sit in his church collecting dust and drawing in fresh paying crowds to come gawk at them."

"The curse these hallows bear is very real, Morgan, I assure you. Though Uther certainly does not have the right temperament to protect them... Still, your brother shall do much better as their keeper. This I know."

Morgan pursed her lips, thinking herself that Arthur may already be dead, what with multiple years having passed and no one to protect him from that dreadful black knight and their treasonous cousin, Anna, who had wanted him dead, no one but ignorant Evey.

"Not that I have yet figured out where these hallows are exactly..." Merlin rambled on, completely oblivious to the grim reflections of his pupil. "and not that I ever shall I suppose, being trapped in this tower for all eternity."

"What kind of druid are you?" Morgan snapped. "Giving up so easily and abandoning the world?" She started to her feet again, taking up an angry pace from one side of the room to the other. "No spell is unbreakable," she insisted, studying shrewdly the lines of the room around them. "Simply tell me how it was cast, what the rules are, and what you have tried to undo it. Then we shall find a way to unravel it, and we shall *both* of us break free of this place."

Merlin's answer was long and littered with strange concepts and theory. He had to go over it with slow patience, repeating it twice, before Morgan finally began to understand the workings of the spell that had created this inescapable tower. "So... it's like an infinity," Morgan cemented, tracing out the shape on the wall. "You think you're headed in a straight line out, but all the halls just curve right back to here." She gestured to the room

The Tale of ~~King Arthur~~Morgan Le Fay

around them. "The crossroads, the center, but this is the exit as much as it is a cell. We are right above that doorway where I entered, are we not?"

"That door both exists and does not exist," Merlin countered. "It is here and not here. Invisible and intangible, until the Lady Viviane--"

"That stuck up fay is not the all powerful warden of this place," Morgan asserted. "She cannot violate the rules. She can trap no mortal here who does not willingly eat of her fare, and she holds no power outside of the rules of the spell you crafted to create this tower, a spell made with clear openings for one to come and go, to visit whenever she pleases."

"The caster can never undo this cage," Merlin repeated, "nor can I add to it an exit that will accept me. The maze is finished and locked, secured in infinity. I am trapped here for eternity. Though I am sure I can convince Viviane to let you out. She likely does not want you in this room anyway. It would cause far too much of a disruption to our time together."

"I am not staying here and waiting docilely for a slim chance to argue with that manipulative kidnapper! I am not the caster of this spell, so I am not rendered powerless to unravel it as you are. I can find a way out of this loop. I just have to find the right..." Her eyes settled on the open window beside them, looking straight up through the shallow waters of the lake shimmering in the distant sunlight. "That's not a part of your original design for this trap, now is it?"

"No. That is Viviane's own embellishment, one I most appreciate. There are such interesting fish out there."

"Then that is our exit," Morgan cemented, jabbing her hand through the opening. The rippling waters sought to repel her, but she clenched her fist and forced her way through the invisible barrier and into the chill wet of the waters beyond.

"That will not work," Merlin protested. "Even if you go through there, you'll just wind up--"

Morgan ignored him, seizing his wrist and pulling him with her, as she took a deep breath and plunged head first out into the waters. She thrashed her way past the tangling weeds that curled around her limbs, seeking to drag her back toward the window. She tensed her legs and launched herself upward, up from the soil and straight toward the shimmering sunlight, so close within reach. Her speed increased with alarming suddenness and up became down, until she and Merlin both dropped back through the window and into the stone walled bedroom, hitting first the far wall and then the floor, as gravity returned to normal and the ground became down once again.

Morgan's cheek smacked into the flagstone with a wet slap. Sopping wet and spluttering, she pushed back her dripping hair and glared angrily at the window of rippling water. She knew it was an exit. She could feel it.

"As I warned you," Merlin chided, ringing out his beard. "I have tried that before. It is part of the loop. There can be no escape, unless Viviane…"

Morgan blocked out his words, closing her eyes and sinking back on her knees with hands held out in front of her. She could *feel* the exit, beside her, below her, and all around her. The crossroads where the loops all began and ended, here and not here all at once, three halves of a doorway. She just had to bring them together to open the doors.

She flexed her fingers and seized hold of the window and that darkened doorway far below at the base of the infinite staircase that had brought her to this room. She brought her hands together, and window and room and the door she had entered through all became one and the same. The walls shuddered, and the floor crumbled beneath them, opening into a massive void of watery darkness surging up to swallow them.

Druid and sorceress both instantly dropped, plunging back into the waters of the lake outside. Morgan could not open her hands to swim, knowing they were not yet free of this trap and keeping her fingers knitted tight together to keep in place their exit, as the current picked them up and sought to drag them back into the weeds. Merlin seized her about the waist and kicked his way free of the grasping tendrils seeking to tie them down.

Her head popped above the water's surface, and Morgan finally released her hold, fingers unclenching, only for a massive whirlpool to form, instantly seeking to suck them back down into the depths.

Merlin raised his hand and the waters around them retreated and froze, forming an icy barrier around a narrow corridor of exposed lake bed. Fish flopped in panic on the weed-covered sand, as the two wizards stumbled their way to shore. The ice melted, and the waters rushed back into place the instant they set foot on the grass.

Morgan felt drained and dizzy, and she collapsed onto the springy turf with breathing ragged, sopping wet and freezing once again, with her fine velvet dress returned to ugly foraged sackcloth.

A bush sprouted up around her suddenly, and Morgan opened her eyes in alarm, only for Merlin to hold a finger to his lips, crouched close beside her within the cover of the conjured leaves with eyes on the other side of the lakeshore.

The Tale of ~~King Arthur~~ Morgan Le Fay

Morgan followed his stare and spotted instantly the glowing figure of Viviane making her way through the woods and back toward her lake with the richly dressed figure of a dark-haired toddler giggling in her arms. "Who is the most adorable princeling, the most handsome little lord? It is thee! Indeed it is. My little... Lancelot. Yes, a fitting name. You are going to make such a dashing servant in my kingdom, yes you are."

Morgan shook her head, glaring out at the angel faced demon and her freshly snared captive. It seemed the fay's fondness for abducting people was not limited to wizards and fellow changelings. She raised her fist, pointing an angry finger at the fair-haired devil before her with the firm intent to set her on fire and free the little boy she was but seconds away from carrying beneath the water and imprisoning forever.

Merlin seized her wrist, forcing down the hand and instantly breaking her focus. "You mustn't attack her," he ordered, his voice a harsh whisper. "The Lady Viviane is an ancient and important being, a protector of these waters and the surrounding woods."

"Protector?" Morgan scoffed. "She's a psychopath! A selfish, vainglorious, child kidnapping, sword stealing maniac who aught to be burnt to a crisp in penance for her many crimes! Honestly, what about that boy's parents? Do not you think they would wish for us to rescue him and put a stop to that terror?"

"That boy will be fine," Merlin shrugged off callously. "He will grow up well fed and coddled in a land of magic and music."

"Never allowed to leave!"

"Yes, but that is not so horrid a fate as you make it out to be. His parents might be dead for all we know. The last child Viviane took in was abandoned in the woods to die because his mother could not feed him. Now he is a healthy young bard in her court. She is not the monster you make her out to be."

"Well she is certainly not the saint you somehow see her as!" Morgan railed. "She *imprisoned* you."

"Yes, but it was quite the clever trick, using my own hubris against me by presenting me a puzzle and then trapping me with it." He smiled, eyes dreamy and distant. "She is an extraordinary woman, and we still need her to give us that sword. We shall never reclaim it from those hidden depths without her consent."

"Just as you would never be free of that tower without her consent?" Morgan criticized. "You are a wizard, you old fool! You do not need anyone's consent, not for anything, and neither do I! And my father does not need for you to succeed at this stupid errand and bring him that sword anyway, because..." Her voice cut out, as the tears returned, choking her. She still had not avenged the wrongs of that awful night, a tragic betrayal that Merlin still knew nothing of, because he did not even care to ask. He was too swept up in daydreams of the fairy who had held him captive, and it seemed he no longer cared for her mother. Why should he? She was another man's wife, so why spare a thought for her? Why would he care that she was dead?

Merlin put a hand on her shoulder, eyes heavy with sympathy. "If your father has fallen to his illness... That is what is best for the kingdom, Morgan. You know that as well as I," he insisted, completely misreading her grief. She was not crying for that bear of a man. She was crying for herself and for--

"Let's just get back to your mother, alright?" Merlin ignorantly prompted. "It has been a hard night, or... two years, as it were. We need to get you home and lay to rest the no doubt devastating heartbreak of our dear queen, thinking her only daughter gone. Though perhaps do not mention my recent, ah, diversions with the Lady Viviane? Not that there is anything to forgive, of course. I mean, I was kidnapped and the lady was so very forward with her advances. Any man in my position would have acted the same. But do not say that to Igraine. I would just... I would prefer it if you left it at 'imprisoned by a manipulative fay'. No need to even mention she was a woman, or tell of her beauty, or--"

"The queen is dead." It felt better to say it that way, cold and detached, with the tears run dry and the calm insistence that it was a tragedy long past. "As is King Uther and the lords Ruthien and Brenin and..." She told the whole tale of that dreadful night in flat and somber monotone, with Merlin's features growing paler and darker with every second that passed.

"What about your brother?" the wizard demanded, as her story wound to a close with her escape out the window of the palace. "Where is Arthur, Morgan?"

Her brow furrowed, eyes flooding with resentment, as she remembered the encounter with horrid Evey, saving her brother from the black knight, Turquine, only to be cursed at in return as devil and danger. "How should I know where he is now?" she grated, teeth grinding. "I was imprisoned in a fairy trap for two entire years while trying to rescue my fool of a tutor who has yet to even thank me or apologize!"

"I understand this has been hard on you," Merlin offered hollowly, his callous calm only deepening her fury. "But we haven't time for this now.

The Tale of ~~King Arthur~~ Morgan Le Fay

We are both of us fine and safe, but your brother may not be."

"Then look and see if he's dead already, why don't you?" she snapped, gesturing to the placid surface of the lake beside them.

"Not in this place," Merlin insisted, taking her hand and leading her off into the woods. "Viviane will discover our absence in mere moments if she has not already. We must hasten to be gone from here. There is another pool out near the edge of the woods. We can use that for scrying since conjured water will not hold the image." Merlin looked back at her with eyebrow raised in clear expectation. "You said you knew already the trick of transformation?"

That was it. No praise for all her progress, just the silent expectation that she follow along with his orders now and do as he demanded to save dear little Arthur, the one who really mattered.

Morgan ripped free her hand, crossing her arms, with eyes glued to the grass beneath her bare feet. "Yes, I know the trick. Though how do you make clothing afterward?"

"I will tell you once we land. We've no time to waste," the wizard insisted, spreading his arms and snapping instantly into the shape of a falcon, soaring off above the trees.

Morgan stared after him sadly and moved not one step. He was not waiting for her to follow. She did not think he would turn around to look for her either. All that work and suffering, venturing bravely into this wood and the realm of faerie, refusing all temptation and breaking her tutor free of an inescapable cage, and yet the man had shown not even a moment of gratitude, or pride. He had abandoned her in an instant. He had left her behind to go chasing after Arthur, a hapless babe who might already be dead. *I hope you are dead.* She thought without charity, as the distant speck of the falcon vanished from sight.

Just like she'd suspected, he never turned around to check on her.

VII. The False Queen of Camelot

Morgan slogged off into the woods in the precise opposite direction that Merlin had gone, numbing her resentment and taking to the skies in a blur of black feathers. She soared through the heavens, free of tethers, free of ties. She flew far away from Camelot and far away from England to an abandoned castle known as Cader Idris, a said to be haunted hall sitting in shadow of the looming peaks of the Welsh mountains. No mortal dared approach that place, but she was not afraid of ghosts. She found a single, lonely banshee and promptly chased it from the castle, savoring the silent solitude that came in wake of its departure. These cobweb covered spires were a place of solemn majesty, a den befitting of a sorceress.

She was the bane of fairies and ghosts alike, and she did not need a tutor to instruct her. She would master all these powers on her own, the way she always had. She was Morgan Le Fay, a changeling of great power who could become anything and everything she wished. She would punish Anna De'gaur and take back her home, and she would do all of it alone.

She did perform a quick scrying that same night she landed however, and discovered that Arthur was indeed alive and well, living in abject poverty in a tiny hovel in the filthy streets of a village in Essex. Evey was still watching after him, laboring away the days stitching up clothes and begging for coins, as four year old Arthur toddled along at her heels, helping out however he was able. Morgan kept watching the pair and saw Merlin come to retrieve the boy that very same eve. Evey instantly recognized the druid and followed him without objection out to the estate of Sir Ector, one of the few lords of Logres who had not been present at that bloody banquet where King Uther had met his end. The old knight's manor was a far more fitting place for a young prince than the filthy streets of Saxon slums. Now he could grow up with all the pampering and training and splendor that everyone believed he inherently deserved.

Morgan dashed apart the image and continued with her studies. Basic tricks like conjuring clothes and food were easy enough to perform now that she had observed Merlin doing it. The rest of her powers grew through months of careful cultivation and toil. She could indeed become anything she chose, be it bird or spider or shadow itself. She could move any

The Tale of ~~King Arthur~~ Morgan Le Fay

object and paint the walls with frost, and her torrents of fire became all the more fearsome and precise.

She was more than powerful enough to take whatever horrid revenge she wished on her filthy cousin. Anna was now the wife of the king who had usurped her father's throne. King Lot called himself a peace-maker, keeping the kingdom together while scarcely leaving the walls of his stolen palace, as the other lords all warred and squabbled over who was truly the heir now that they believed Uther's son, Arthur, to be dead.

The exiled princess made her return to Camelot without glory or fanfare, gliding in over the gates, then taking the shape of an old beggar woman, as she worked her way closer to the castle ahead.

Anna De'gaur spent her days in the most disgraceful of behaviors, drinking and abusing the servants while carrying on an obvious affair with one of the young knights in her court, vocal and frequent afternoon meetings that her husband seemed completely oblivious to. Morgan had seen all this in her scrying these past few months. She knew well her cousin's fondness for the bottle and her propensity for boredom.

It would be a simple and fitting revenge to simply poison her drink this night, leave her choking on blood in a dramatic and painful end before the whole court at dinner. Such just deserts would instantly be labeled as treason or the work of some devil however, making the conniving traitor's death a tragic and deeply grieved affair. Morgan needed first to destroy her reputation, reveal her for the horrid rat she was, for revenge (as she had learned from the many epics she had read) was an effect best achieved over years of careful torment. The end had to close in slowly, the agonizing approach of a dreaded inevitability.

Morgan started simply and slipped inside the castle kitchens wearing the face of one of Anna's ladies in waiting. She served her at the feast that night celebrating King Lot's temporary alliance with Lord Maleagant, and watched with amusement as the false queen vomited all over both her dress and Lord Dolor, seated at her side.

Anna turned quite a satisfying shade of crimson, but Morgan's enjoyment of the moment was instantly spoiled, as the knights all carried their "poor queen" off to her rooms and she made a great show of moaning and ladylike faintness, until the entire castle staff was fussing over her with pity. It was not the shameful criticized embarrassment that Morgan had been aiming for, but she refused to be disheartened by the failure.

She set right back to work, covering her cousin's sheets with an alchemical powder that left her itching without rest, until she awoke the next morning covered in hives. Anna kept bundled up in shame the entire day, claiming to still be "ill", as she spent a million hours bathing trying to rid herself of the unnatural irritation driving her mad with discomfort and marring her flawless complexion. She even canceled her evening engagement with Sir Lucan, but King Lot had called off his weekly hunt out of concern for his wife and spent a good portion of the day fussing over her, spoiling her with sweets and offering to send for doctors to treat what Anna claimed was a simple unease of the stomach.

Morgan found it absurd that the king believed that lie given how greedily Anna sucked down those pastries. She found it especially absurd, as Anna claimed coyly that she believed what had happened last night to be no illness or poisoning but simply the morning sickness of a woman with child – King Lot's next son. The king was brimming with joy at the news, announcing instantly another feast to celebrate.

In the form of a hanging spider, Morgan gaped at her cousin in angry disgust. The traitorous queen was in no way pregnant. She had gone through her cycle of bleeding a single week past. The woman just seemed to lie without restraint, speaking falsehood with a casualness and constancy that was not only despicable but reckless. Each and every time she was caught in a lie however, Anna would simply attack the accuser and lay even more lies down on top of it, with her quivering breast and tearing eyes for some reason instantly turning each and every man she spoke to into a dim witted sop.

Morgan kept watch as a shadow in the corner of the room that night, looming over her cousin menacingly as she tossed and itched between her torturous sheets. She waited most impatiently for Anna to open her eyes and catch a glimpse of the monster leering down at her. It happened finally, around three in the morning, and Anna shrieked.

"You know what you did," Morgan rumbled in a whispery rasp of barely formed vocal chords, "murderer of kin."

Anna's screams intensified, and she scrambled from the bed. Her servants came rushing in with lit candles, but Morgan's shadow became easily a natural part of the floor, invisible and untouchable.

"My lady, what is it?" Anna's head maid pressed, but the queen waved her away with a look of annoyance, blue eyes narrowing shrewdly as they scanned the room around her.

"Burn those sheets," she ordered her maids, scratching angrily at her shoulder. "And draw me another bath."

The Tale of ~~King Arthur~~ Morgan Le Fay

The maids looked at her in clear concern and confusion, but did as ordered for fear of the wrath of their queen, which had shown in the past as wicked bruises and nail marks on the wrists of those women who defied her.

Anna changed to an entirely new mattress and coverings for the rest of that night, so Morgan sent her screaming awake by summoning a flood of spiders that came streaming out the sides of her new bed. Anna's screams once again brought the maids rushing into the room, though they all instantly fled the plague of insects, with Anna retreating to the bedchamber she shared with King Lot. It was a room she often came up with excuses to avoid, such as her recent illness that demanded she stay in seclusion as she recovered, even though the "morning sickness" she claimed was not at all contagious.

Lot asked his wife instantly what the commotion had been and why the maids were now whispering of Satan's influence. Anna declared it laughingly to be nothing more than a single spider that the ladies had in their womanly weakness overreacted to most sorely. She had indeed been terribly frightened though, and King Lot spent the next few hours until dawn holding her tight and comforting her dutifully, but Morgan was not about to allow them such peace.

She scanned through the alleys of the streets below until she found what she was looking for. Camelot was far more filthy than she remembered it, with the children bony and malnourished, and trash and numerous dead birds and rodents littering the cobblestone. That gave her plenty of amo to choose from. She scooped up a pair of rats she found rotting in the east district and flew back through the open window of King Lot's bedchamber, depositing the carcasses right ontop of the sleeping monarchs, and changing quickly to a shadow hidden in the corner as they both awoke shrieking in disgust.

The king did indeed become paranoid about curses and ill omens then, and Morgan fed into that fear with grim delight over the next couple of days, filling bread with weevils and shattering glasses to splatter Anna and her husband both with fitting red stains.

The king went to church every morning that week, giving hollow confessions of the wrongs he had done. This most recent confession was for failing to avenge his former ally, Uther Pendragon, taking his throne and allowing his heir to be smuggled off and slain. A brief note of sincerity did enter his voice finally, as he spoke of how he feared now for his wife and sons. Perhaps the devil did want to end his line. Both his previous wives had died in child birth after all, and his youngest child, Morin, had fallen to illness just two springs past, never living to see his second birthday.

The bishop prayed a blessing over him, with the hollow assertion that Christ had chosen him to rule over these people and protect this city. The Lord would not allow any harm to befall him or his other heirs.

Morgan rolled all eight arachnid eyes at the assertion. The priest said that exact same thing to every king. He had said it to her father, and he would no doubt say it to Arthur the second the boy reclaimed his throne. *"Happy lies serve no one."* She remembered Merlin's words, but thought of the druid instantly filled her with nothing but grief and bitterness. She blocked the wizard firmly from her mind, focusing on the scene below, as King Lot took his leave of the confessional and her cousin entered the church, veiled and demure.

She told her husband that she would be spending many hours in prayer and would meet him back at the castle for dinner. He kissed her hand and assented, taking his leave. Anna then followed the priest, not into the confessional booth, but into the locked rooms in back of the cathedral.

The old bishop hesitated to give into his desires, pressing Anna about these supposed signs from Satan. Perhaps he was worried that the queen's clear unfaithfulness to her husband really was cursing their kingdom. Anna responded tearfully that there was indeed a devil after her. "But with your holy guidance, I know I can be saved," she whispered, pressing up against him. "With you I feel the love of Christ. The Lord would not fill me with these feelings were they not true love. Just hold me for a while. I feel so frightened…"

The supposed holy man gave into his cravings quite thoroughly then, and Morgan knew this was not the first time. Anna asked the man with manipulative insistence afterward for each and every word her husband had said during his lengthy confessions. The bishop told her everything, and hearing King Lot's arrogant defense of his actions seemed to bleed the tension from her frame. She bid the priest farewell and headed back toward the castle.

Morgan stood in the guise of a beggar boy and glaringly watched the ironically chaste dressed queen exit the cathedral, angrily kicking aside a cat who lay sleeping on the step. The woman was a complete and utter swine.

The thought was far too potent. With alarming suddenness, Anna pitched forward to hands and knees, her perfectly manicured nails turning instantly to calloused hooves and her face a bulging snout. Now she *really* was a swine, and Morgan could not help but laugh.

The Tale of ~~King Arthur~~ Morgan Le Fay

She knew in the back of her mind she should have saved this trick for during the feast, a display before all of court. There was hardly anyone outside to see it now, on this rainy day within the inner city.

Still, Anna the pig was shrieking in panic, swelling sides ripping right through the seams of her dress, and Morgan simply could not stop laughing, so much so that she did not even notice when the illusion of the beggar boy fell away and she was back to her regular shape. She fell back against the wall of the cathedral, cackling and pointing. "Oh... Oh my. That is such a *fitting* shape for you, cousin."

The pig glared at her in outrage, trying to snap out a response that emerged as nothing but breathless snorts.

"Perhaps I shall leave you this way forever!" The pig grew deathly still, eyes widening in panic. "It would certainly be a sound revenge, don't you think? Just look at you, so plump and tender. Maybe they'll serve you up at the next feast. Now wouldn't that be wonderfully horrid? Though most of that court has already had a taste of you, now haven't they?"

Shrill and strident oinking rose in response to the comment, but Morgan had no idea what the beast was saying. She did not care to hear any of her cousin's cruel words anyway. Better for the entire kingdom if they never had to hear the manipulative lies of this harlot again.

Morgan sauntered off down the street, back toward the filth of the lower city. The pig scrambled free of its torn dress and plodded along after her, still shrieking in protest. Morgan rounded a corner and vanished into the wind, leaving the floundering swine alone in the churchyard, stampeding about in disoriented panic.

The guards seized it an hour later, utterly inundated with reports of the commotion the mysterious pig was causing, charging up to any and all passerby with insistent snorts of panicked, oinky nonsense. Anna the swine wailed all the louder, as she was hauled off in a cage to the palace kitchens, assumed to be the escaped main course of next week's feast, despite the chef's insistence that she had never before seen the beast and had ordered no hogs be brought in for slaughter. The woman was not about to turn away good meat however, and she took the shrieking sow into her custody, penning it up in the cellar where the heavy door blunted its ceaseless cries that were already driving the palace staff mad with irritation. The pig slumped down within its cage then and set to quietly weeping.

Morgan refused to feel pity for the wretch. This was exactly the fate this lying traitor, the murderer of her mother, deserved. Despite that grim insistence, her amusement was rapidly waning, replaced with a sick sort of nausea, as she thought of King Lot's sons. The young boys would wind up eating their own step-mother without even realizing it, if events continued on their current trajectory. A proper witch would not have minded that, but at thirteen years old with pranks and lies her only evils, Morgan found she hadn't quite the stomach for it.

She flew away from the kitchens, too stubborn still to free Anna of her cage. She soared out over the churchyard and found an entire patrol of knights, up in arms with a furious and grief-stricken King Lot at their head. They had found the torn remains of the queen's Sunday dress and assumed she had been brutally abducted. The knights were already sweeping the whole of Camelot, interrogating the citizens with brutish shoves and threats. And with no witnesses or news of Anna, King Lot was preparing to send out his riders, to charge to the gates of every fortress of every enemy nearby to find who had kidnapped his queen and demand she be returned. It was a chaos far beyond what Morgan had envisioned. The people were suffering, not just the virtueless nobles, and she decided it was time she ended this game.

She slid as a shadow beneath the cellar door and retook her own shape, sauntering up to Anna with dark eyes weighing into the sow in cruel condescension. "It won't be long now," she asserted, savoring the trembling gaze of the arrogant villain who had thought herself queen. "The court has assumed you most brutally murdered," she lied. "They have found your remains and are now hard at work planning your funeral. For the wake of course, a spread of pork." Anna whimpered. "Though I think a few moments back in your own skin is required," Morgan mused, putting a finger to her lips. "A chance for you to give confession and spare your soul the fires of damnation."

Morgan envisioned her cousin back with her regular face, and the hog lengthened out into Anna, naked and shivering within her cage. "You killed your own aunt, a true queen who was nothing but kind."

"I'm sorry," Anna wept. "I didn't mean to--"

"Liar!" The cage roof above Anna became lined with flame, and she screamed, covering her head.

Even after all her practice, Morgan was still not in control of her temper, but she pretended the flames were intentional, a dramatic punctuation to her words. "You are a power-hungry sociopath who feels clearly no remorse, not for any of her evils!"

"I am sorry," Anna insisted, eyes raising to lock with her own. "But not for poisoning Igraine. She was superior and vain. She made me feel an

The Tale of ~~King Arthur~~ Morgan Le Fay

ugly cow, the way everyone fawned over her, always comparing me, comparing us..." Morgan's jaw clenched. She did indeed remember that feeling, how ugly she was standing in Igraine's shadow. "I wanted to love her," Anna insisted, voice breaking. "I wanted her to love me. I worked so hard, so she'd be happy. We all could have been happy without that awful bear in charge!"

She was speaking of Uther. She had poisoned Uther. Of course he had not died of some regular sickness, and of course her mother had not been the one to deliver him that cruel and drawn out end.

Anna drank in the dawning realization in her eyes and simply cocked her head, a cruel smile teasing out the corners of her lips. "Oh come now, Morgan, do not tell me you never realized..." She laughed, eyes softening. "Are you just a little girl after all?" Morgan's hands clenched. "Just as ignorant as all the rest of them, believing it to be natural illness? Granted, that was my design, slipping him such slow acting and carefully spaced out doses that no amount of bleeding or purging supplements could cure. But I thought you of all people would have deduced its source, especially after that bloody feast. You always act to be so much smarter than all the rest of us, and yet you never even saw--"

"I never saw what a monster you were," Morgan cut her off with a snap. "No, I suppose I did not. I did not think you worthy of any regard, and so I never saw your treachery--"

"It was not treachery," Anna grated. "It was loyalty. At least... it began as such. I got rid of him *for her*."

"You poisoned your king, so you could steal our throne," Morgan insisted, eyes hardening with anger. "So do not dare try and claim you killed my father for the sake of my mother--"

"She was my mother too!" Morgan blinked, staring at her in tense suspicion, but Anna stared right in her eyes, and she knew it to be truth. "She would not claim me as her daughter, offering hollow lies of how it was to protect me, claiming I was the daughter of her long dead brother and not the seed of Gorlois, her first husband and Uther's hated rival. I knew the truth however. She disowned me for the sake of our king, that possessive savage. And yes, I hated him for that. I hated being some shameful secret, but I never once acted selfishly," she declared, eyes holding Morgan's with compelling insistence. "I waited until she had Arthur as heir and our family was secure. She could have held the kingdom together once Uther was dead, and I never would have taken or even coveted that throne. I just wanted her thanks, for one time in my life. I just wanted her acknowledgment." Her eyes flooded with tears. "I had given her salvation, an absolutely perfect plan, and yet she terms *me* the monster!" She straightened, eyes burning into Morgan in unchecked resentment. "She betrays me completely and demands a cure, else she will report all I've done and have me executed!

"I lied and said there was one, said it would take weeks of regular doses to work. And then, and *then,* she asks me to indulge the advances of King Lot to keep little Morgan, her only true precious daughter, safe from marrying him." She shook her head, tone bitter and eyes dead. "And King Lot of course is just like all men, just like my father, and that priest who put his hand under my skirt when I was thirteen and came to the church far too late in the night to give confession, not knowing he was drunk..."

She wiped at her eyes, smiling in deranged glee. "But everything taken can be turned into power, all that guilt and lust. You just have to feel nothing and pretend, and any man can be made a slave. I did it to that priest, and then the bishop, then even to King Lot, though he was much more forward than even I expected. He took me that very first night we met." Morgan crossed her arms, gut twisting with sickened sympathy in spite of herself.

"I rather think he would have been done with me after that had I not faked enjoying it so, and kept visiting his bedchambers, and listened so raptly and eagerly to all his vented frustrations about Uther in the days that followed. After the victory in Saint Albany, he knew he could take all of Camelot with ease. He had the superior troops, and Uther's allies, Kador and Maleagant and a dozen others, were already eager to betray the ailing dragon. I gave him a simpler method, to keep him a hero and spare our city from siege and bloodshed. I brought death to only those who would never swear him allegiance. And our mother..." She exhaled. "Well, if I hadn't killed her, Lot might have married her instead, so I simply had to paint her as a threat and poison her. But still," She held Morgan's gaze, blue eyes fervent and compelling. "I was not lying about my regret of that day. For one thing and one thing only, I am deeply sorry. It was out of jealousy alone that I blamed you, painting you a devil, and that was a grievous error. I should have embraced you instead, my sister, and we could have weathered this horrid family of ours together."

She closed her eyes. "Just do me this one kindness, Morgan, and kill me now. I cannot bear just waiting here in terror, waiting to be slaughtered and fed to..." She shivered. "You are as powerful as Merlin himself, and you have taught me my lesson. Take no vengeance on Lot though, please? His boys need him. Horrid as their father is, they are not old enough to defend

The Tale of ~~King Arthur~~Morgan Le Fay

themselves from his rivals if left alone in the world. I rather enjoyed being their mother for a time." She smiled. "I would have liked to have a child of my own someday..." Her smile died, and she cleared her throat, wiping away her tears. "But you've no interest in that. I am but a monster, and monsters can evoke no sympathy. So end me, end it all. Go ahead."

A long minute passed with Anna's eyes staying firmly shut. Then the cage door creaked, and Anna's eyes flew open, staring in shock at the young sorceress holding the portal open for her to pass. "I'm not giving you any clothes," Morgan muttered. "You can creep naked through the halls, because you deserve to be humiliated, you... villain. And you better indeed have learned your lesson."

Anna's eyes flooded with tears. She bounded to her feet and held Morgan tight, kissing her cheek. "I have. I will! I will be so much better, my wonderful, merciful sister! And there will be a home for you here always. This I swear."

Those words should have irritated Morgan. This *was* her home. She needed no invitation to these halls. Anna and her husband had no right to sit on that throne. It belonged to the Pendragons. *But to Arthur, not me.* The thought left her hollow, but she knew it to be so. Her abandoned castle in Wales was far more comfort than these stifling halls always flooded with posturing strangers. Still, she felt a swell of peculiar warmth toward Anna anyway. She had suffered so much, even more than Morgan had, yet here she was, being so gracious, welcoming her home, even after all the torments Morgan had inflicted.

She expressed nothing of such irrational familial affection however. She kept intact her icy facade and melted into shadow, abandoning the castle.

VIII. The Right to Rule

The somewhat spineless feeling sorceress flew far away from Camelot, back to her remote and wonderfully ominous crumbling fortress in Wales. She scried images of Anna most frequently however, to ensure she really had learned her lesson. She was still a rather incompetent mother to Lot's sons, but she always had been attentive to them at least, taking happily their constant, competing gifts, acknowledging their acts to impress her and garner praise, and helping the maids break up their constant, roughhousing squabbles. As for her behavior toward every other resident of the castle, she had indeed reformed herself in the most basic of ways. She stopped drinking so much, and she treated the maids with relative decency now instead of violent impatience and hurtful criticisms. She also ended her affair with Sir Lucan and dedicated all her excessively amorous energies toward her husband alone.

She was still a bald-faced liar though, who explained away her abduction as the work of an ancient and powerful fairy creature who had spotted her leaving the chapel and instantly become enamored with her beauty, sweeping her off to his kingdom. She had staunchly refused all the beautiful creature's advances however, holding chastely to her vows of matrimony. She told this abductor she was pregnant with child already and begged he return her to her lord, until the fay finally assented and deposited her back within the mortal realm.

It was a ridiculous tale, but the northern king and his knights all knew enough to believe in fairies and their propensity for kidnapping people, and so they believed every word of it. Anna kept the king almost solely tethered to the bedchamber that entire month following her return, until her lie of being with child finally became truth. The child was born a full ten months following her disappearance, a beautiful baby boy with the bright blue eyes of his mother, given the name Gareth and baptized in the cathedral.

Anna truly did seem happy now, though she would often watch the windows and scan carefully the corners of her chambers. She knew Morgan was still watching her, though she had no idea how far away the sorceress loomed. Perhaps that was the reason for her incredibly long streak of good behavior this past year. Though she clearly loved her son, taking charge of

The Tale of ~~King Arthur~~ Morgan Le Fay

him willingly, instead of letting his nursemaid see to the work, and showing him off proudly to each and every visitor and noble.

Lot's older boys grew noticeably sullen as a result. Morgan found it somewhat sad how desperately ten year old Gawain acted in response. He trained hard his swordsmanship and riding skills in often dangerous stunts to show off for his father, taking out his frustrations on the hay stuffed dummies for hours afterward when such maneuvers were given only the briefest moment of regard, before the king went back to cooing over his newest son. The little wonders the babe could perform, such as raising his head and rolling over, were far more impressive to Lot than the uncoordinated attempts of a young boy still learning the rudiments of jousting, and the aspiring knight was noticeably disheartened by the reaction.

Morgan knew it was foolish to waste her time watching worriedly over Anna's neglected stepchildren. She aught to be spending those hours on her studies, perfecting her elemental powers, learning more of potions, and collecting more texts from around the globe. She labored away at her spells until her brow was covered with sweat and read until her eyes were swimming with exhaustion on many a long and sleepless day that year. Yet she continued to waste many an hour scrying, each and every day, feeling keenly the isolation of her remote, empty castle. She had not spoken to a single soul in sixteen long months. That is, unless you counted the ghosts, but those wailing dimwits were terrible company, so she inevitably wound up consuming them with hellfire whenever they moved into her halls.

In wake of their passing though, she was left in complete and eerie silence, utterly alone. And that should not have bothered her. She should not be talking to the spiders and playing out imaginary discussions with Merlin or Anna or even poor little Gawain. It seemed even those with an aversion for crowds became somewhat unhinged when left in isolation, and Morgan knew it was time she left this self-imposed exile. Hadn't she been set on taking back her city? She had studied enough, and she was surely as powerful as Merlin already, just as Anna had praised. She wondered if her sister would still honor her invitation and welcome Morgan home were she to stride openly into the halls before the usurper's entire court. She wondered what King Lot's reaction would be were she finally to confront the man who had taken her father's throne in a face to face denouncement of his character.

She found herself rehearsing speeches and acting out that scenario an absurd number of times, before finally cementing her resolve and flying off back to England. She lost her nerve, when she reached the city and looked down at all the people milling about the streets. There were so many of them, commoners, and guards, and knights. None of them friends. She turned right around and found herself for some reason at the manor of Sir Ector far out in the woods.

Arthur was even taller than the last time she had scried him. Six years old, sprinting around the muddy courtyard laughing, as Sir Ector's son, Kay, chased after him. Morgan roosted in a tree and watched her little brother without daring to approach for the longest time. She fluttered down to the corner of the stables and took her own shape but stepped not one inch closer, hovering back in the shadows and wondering if the boys would catch sight of her.

Finally, it began to rain, and Evey stomped out into the muck, ushering the boys inside before they caught a chill. Morgan's eyes narrowed savagely at the sight of the old nursemaid, and she considered most seriously becoming a crow again, launching herself at Evey and tearing at her all too neatly braided hair with her talons. The horrid hag had denounced her a devil and a danger. She would not allow Morgan to take meal inside these halls alongside her brother. The second she spotted the princess's true face, she would raise a shaking finger, shouting out accusations and wild, frightening claims. Morgan could already hear the words, echoing cruelly in her head. The woman was a--

"I know that look, princess, and I would have you refrain before turning dear Evey into livestock," a gruff voice chided, and Morgan jumped, whirling to face Merlin who had somehow snuck up behind her and now stood right at her shoulder.

Morgan's lip quivered and her fist clenched at the mere sight of him. She wanted to sob into his shoulder, bang her fist into his chest. He had never come to look for her. He had probably never even scried her, or bothered to question where she was. Why would he? He had Arthur to watch over, and just like everybody else he cared more for the blond-haired brat than he did his former pupil, a student who had far outgrown his useless instruction anyway, amassing great knowledge and power all on her own. She wanted to confront him with all of this, but she could not find the right words, so instead she just stood there, arms crossed and chin raised, waiting coldly for the druid to speak.

"You should come inside," Merlin prompted, raindrops rolling down his beard, as he squinted up at the gloomy sky. "Evey's made a stew. Perfect fare on a day such as this."

The Tale of ~~King Arthur~~Morgan Le Fay

"Dear Evey can choke on her stew," Morgan responded jaggedly, turning her back to the warmly lit manor and striding off toward the woods. "I must be off now anyway. I have a usurper to confront and a castle to reclaim."

Merlin seized her hand, staring her down gravely. "It is not time for that yet."

"And why is that?" she demanded, voice deathly quiet.

"Your brother must be the one to take back that city, to walk through those gates with Excalibur in hand and ascend that throne as he is destined. It is the only way the other lords will cease this warring dispute. All slaying King Lot would accomplish is throw the city into even more chaos."

"You are erroneous and ignorant," she muttered, eyes lowered and tone bitter. Of course he assumed she was just going to sneak into the castle and assassinate the king, like she was no better, no braver or more clever than those traitors who had poisoned her father. "I can take back that throne without killing anyone, and unlike that six year old, I do not need some fancy sword buried at the bottom of a lake to accomplish it."

She started to pull away, but Merlin's hand tightened about her own, a firm and controlling grip. "You cannot take that castle," he repeated. "Whatever tricks you try and whatever face you wear, you are not the rightful ruler. The other lords--"

"Why not?!" she screamed, ripping free of his grip and whirling on him with eyes burning. "I am Morgan *Pendragon*! I have just as good a right to the throne as my useless *baby* brother."

Merlin sighed, putting a hand to his forehead. "Just... just come inside. We can talk this over as long as you like--"

"What would be the point of that? You *never* listen!" she snapped. "I am going to Camelot, and I am confronting King Lot, who I *could* kill in an instant, but I am not going to, I will have you know, and I am not going to wear any face but my own, and they will abandon that stolen seat at the mere emergence of my presence! Just you watch!"

She turned to leave, but Merlin's hands clamped down upon her shoulders, pinning her in place. "You are being rash and selfish."

She struck him, a quick burst of flame that exploded against his chest, hurling him into the mud. She then shifted into a crow and went to take off, only to slam face first into solid stone, dropping to the ground in a tangle of feathers.

She snapped back into her own shape and sat up with a groan. Her eyes widened with alarm then, scanning in panic the plain stone walls of the chamber around her. She was back in the tower, that horrible, endlessly looping tower the Lady of the Lake had used to imprison Merlin. Only this time there was no door, no window, no escape.

"No," she murmured, hands searching frantically over the seamless wall in search of some hole or crack. "No, no, no!" Fire erupted into the walls, but it did no damage.

Morgan fell to her knees, hands knotted in her hair and breaths quickening into shaking hyperventilation. Two years in that horrid place, stolen before she even realized it. Endless hours climbing those stairs... Now she was trapped once again. She was trapped, and *Merlin* had done it to her. How could he? Just because she had become an inconvenience, a wrench in his plans? What if he never let her out? What if she never got out?

She was never getting out.

There was no air at all, just her thundering pulse, hammering away, driving her mad.

Arms closed around her, rubbing her back. "Calm down. Just breathe. To my chagrin, I... ah, I... did not anticipate this reaction."

Morgan struck the callous traitor trying to soothe away the trauma he had caused. He went flying across the flagstone, thudding into the far wall and rubbing ruefully at his head.

"Let. Me. Out. Now." Morgan grated, rising to her feet in shaking, fragile control of herself once more.

"Not until you calm down," Merlin insisted, tone low and patronizing. "You are a danger to yourself and others, so long as you allow your temper to control you--"

"Let me out, let me out, let me out!" she screamed, fireball engulfing the wizard before her.

It did no damage. He simply vanished. He was gone, and Morgan was alone again. Alone in this room. Forever.

She attacked the walls with chaotic, savage strikes, until her faulty breathing left her unable to stand, room spinning and chest shaking. She curled her knees into her chest and rocked back and forth.

Then Merlin was there, seated beside her, holding her tight. "Alright, alright. This appears a poor strategy for giving you time to reflect. I apologize. Truly. I'm right here, Morgan. I'm not going anywhere."

"L-liar," she gasped. "You-you always leave."

The Tale of ~~King Arthur~~Morgan Le Fay

"Because I have responsibilities. It is a great and terrible power the both of us possess. It must be wielded with maturity and foresight--"

"Leave!" she screamed, jerking away from him, and curling up with cheek pressed to the floor, as she futilely tried to calm her anxious breathing.

The floor beneath her vanished, becoming coarse wool blankets. She blinked away her tears, breaths becoming more stable, as she looked shakily toward the open window beside her, letting in the cool air of the night without.

"D-different r-room. It's still a... a trap," she whispered raggedly, feeling keenly the presence of the druid at her bedside.

"This is no trap, Morgan." Merlin sighed. "This is an inn in Essex."

Essex... Leagues away from Camelot and Arthur. Of course he did not trust her there. He did not want her there, and this was indeed another trap, an imposed exile teleporting her far away from her throne.

"You can fly right out that window or walk right out that door," Merlin hollowly assured her. "But we must talk about this first."

"I will hear not your words," Morgan grated, climbing shakily back into a sitting position. "You wish me to remain in exile, locked away forever, unable to interfere in the grand story of your king. I can see that clearly now."

"That is not--"

Morgan raised a deadly finger, and the druid's words fell silent, swallowed up by an invisible shield she had crafted to block out all sound. He put a hand to his forehead, abandoning his previous course of manipulative denials and clearly pleading with her to dispel the wall she'd placed between them.

She stared him down with eyes burning, remaining stubbornly deaf to his pleas. "I will give you a legend," she whispered. "I will claim your precious sword and bury it in stone, sealed away forever right before the eyes of all of these pretenders, *none* of whom carry the right to be king. Neither treacherous Lot nor rancorous Maleagant nor juvenile Arthur! No man will be able to free the blade until *I* bestow it upon him, because *I* am far more powerful and clever than even the legendary Merlin himself!"

She turned her back to the wizard and became a cruel-eyed hawk with feathers of midnight black and a grand and impressive wing span she showed off in proud pose before streaking out the window and off into the night.

The druid was too much a coward to challenge his former lover, the Lady of the Lake, and lay claim to Excalibur, so Morgan would do it in his stead. Then *she* would walk proudly up to Camelot's castle, denounce King Lot, and dare him to prove that he or any of the lords were more powerful than she, able to prove themselves the rightful king.

IX. Excalibur

Lady Viviane, the beautiful yet dreadful, proved impossible to steal from. With proud confidence had Morgan flown back to the lake shore and reclaimed her own shape, standing with chin raised in the light of the full moon, clad in fine cloak and robes of deepest purple. With great and dramatic demand had she raised her hand to the heavens and easily parted those waters to expose the mystic city below...

There was nothing but lake bed. Just mud and weeds and sadly flopping fish. Her arm dropped back to her side, and the waters flooded back into place. The city emerged again, the instant she did so, shimmering lights and towering turrets revealed clearly on the circled disk of the full moon reflected in the center of the waters.

Morgan's fist clenched, and she walked across the waters and right onto that reflection, plunging her arm beneath the surface with fingers flexed, feeling out the location of the sword she envisioned in her mind. She had no idea what Excalibur looked like of course... but it did not matter! She would find it anyway. She did not need permission to enter this kingdom and reclaim a sword that was *her* birthright as the eldest of the Pendragons. She would force her way back into that horrid trap of a banquet hall if she had to, and she would not leave this time until the relic was in her hands.

The very thought of going back there caused her breath to quicken with unsettling suddenness however. Her outstretched hand began to shake, and she lost her ability to remain levitating on the surface of the lake. She dropped into the water with an ugly splash, and the image of the city vanished once again. She would summon it back...

She couldn't. Her breathing continued to spiral out of control, and she felt keenly all the many luminescent eyes watching her from the bushes and from right beneath her feet. They would drag her down and cage her.

She thrashed noisily back to shore, feeling herself about to keel over and cursing angrily this strange breathless weakness that continued to afflict her. She was not a little girl anymore, and she was not afraid of the fay! No being could entrap her, as she had proven a hundred times over now. She was not afraid.

"...great and powerful wizardess," she murmured to herself, and her breaths finally began to slow. She closed her eyes and focused, breathing in and out in slow and careful control.

The shaking stopped, and she opened her eyes to find a bright red rose shoved right up into her face. She flinched back, flames sparking at her fingertips, only for the fires to vanish, as she saw the little pink hand clutched delicately around the stem. It was a little boy, seated beside her on the mud-bank, offering her a flower.

"You shouldn't be afraid," the boy soothed, cocking his head and proffering up the rose with renewed insistence. "All ladies like flowers. They make them smile. So go on. I brought it for you."

"For what purpose?" she demanded, rising to her feet and looming over the child, though he showed no trace of fear within his frank and open gaze.

"Well, you were crying."

"I was not!" she snapped, rubbing angrily at the tears still misting out the corners of her eyes. "Anyhow, I need no fairy tricks. The scent of that rose is likely cursed with some sleep spell or other deadly nonsense."

"Is not!" the boy protested, flushing with anger. "And why would I send you to sleep? Bedtimes are horrible." He started picking off the petals. "I just thought you'd like it. You're supposed to say 'thank you'."

The boy really did seem like an ordinary human child. Perhaps he wasn't a changeling. His skin was a healthy, pale pink after all, with deep brown eyes and curling chestnut locks, and none of the green tinge or glowing eyes of the fairies Morgan had encountered in the past. He was certainly just as fair as any fay child though, and Morgan's eyes narrowed in weary suspicion, realizing slowly that she had seen this boy before. He had only been a toddler then, dragged below the waters by the Lady of the Lake. "Lancelot?" she pressed, and the boy smiled, jumping to his feet.

"You know my name. But wait, how come? I don't know you, do I?"

"I saw you here, three years ago," Morgan muttered. "The day that damn psychopath, Viviane, abducted you, though you probably don't remember."

The boy flushed, drawing a dagger from his waist. "Do not insult my lady!"

"She gave you a knife?" she asked incredulously, eyeing flatly the sharpened implement in the hands of the brash six year old before her.

"Every knight must have a blade, to defend our mistress from those who wish her ill!" the hardly grown squire asserted. "Though mostly it is to trim the roast. I fill our lady's plate and stay seated at her side *all* evening. It is a most honorble persistion."

"Then why are you up here?"

The Tale of ~~King Arthur~~ Morgan Le Fay

"Well... she sent me to bed, but I was not tired. And I get so bored when she goes away. She won't allow me at the feast or the hunts without her. I'm not s'posed to leave my room. But Belle lets me sneak out to the woods if I ask nicely. She says it is a joy to see me in sunlight. And I played all day long, and I am still not even tired, so bedtimes are clearly a bad rule, something I shall tell our lady."

"Lancelot!" a panicked voice called, and the tiny light of a pixie came darting into view. "I told you not to wander off while I..."

The pixie froze in panic, as her pitch black eyes fixed on Morgan, stood haughtily on the lakeshore beside the abducted young prince. She blurred toward the pair of them in a streak of steadily growing light, intending no doubt to lay hands on the child and send him instantly back to the kingdom hidden beneath the lake. Morgan caught the tiny winged creature in her fist, and raised it up to eye level.

The pixie's sharp teeth bit down hard into Morgan's thumb, but she kept her hold, raising Lancelot's rose right up toward her lips and blowing its scent straight into the face of the struggling pixie with the firm command of "Sleep."

Proper tools only strengthened the trick that Morgan had mastered years ago, and her enchanted slumber seized easy hold of even one of the magically resistant fay. The pixie's eyes fluttered shut, and she slumped in Morgan's hand.

Lancelot jumped, holding a hand to his mouth. "It *was* a sleep flower? I didn't know it was. I'm sorry. I didn't mean to be bad." He caught little Belle, right as she dropped from Morgan's disdainfully opened fist. "She's... she's alright though? She'll wake up soon?"

"She will wake eventually," Morgan corrected, kneeling down to be at eye level with the tender hearted boy. "Now, do you want the chance to be a real knight and not a kidnapped slave?"

The boy cocked his head. "Slave? What's a slave?"

"Someone turned into property and worked against their will."

"But... I like my job. It makes our lady happy."

"The name that horrid lady gave you literally means servant," Morgan harshly illuminated. "That is your entire identity to her. You have a real name and real parents out in England somewhere, parents she stole you from."

"W-why are you saying such horrible things?"

"Because I can free you of her," she whispered, hand settling on his shoulder. "I just need a quick favor from you first."

"Free?" He shook his head, throwing off her hand. "I... I don't need you. I love my lady, and she loves me! What did you do to Belle anyway? That wasn't the flower, was it? It was you. You're a witch! A bad, bad--"

"Fine, I am bad!" Morgan snapped. "I am an evil, ugly witch, and I hate all the fay, so I am going to kill this little devil." She snatched the unconscious fairy right back from the hand of the unsuspecting six year old, easily holding him at arms length, as she dangled the pixie out over the waters beside them. "I will encase her in ice, and she will *never* wake, not unless you head back into Viviane's palace and bring me out Excalibur!" The frost was already forming over little Belle's wings, a clear and serious threat.

"Not if I slay thee first, witch!" Lancelot snarled, sounding much more brave and grown up than he had any right to be, as he drew his dagger and swung for her.

The knife puffed into mist the second it brushed her arm, and young Lancelot blinked in shock, staring down at his empty palm.

"Little boys cannot strike down great and mighty sorceresses," Morgan informed him coldly. "Now do as I say, or this frost shall become flames." She raised her free hand and summoned a spiraling ball of fire, looking suggestively toward the unconscious, shivering fairy in her other hand.

"Stop! I yield!" Lancelot cried, raising his hands. "But... who is Excalibur?"

"It is not a person. It's a sword. A great and holy sword belonging to the true ruler of Britain, which is my family. Me. The Pendragons. So go bring it to me, and I will return your little pixie, awake and completely unharmed."

"You're horrible!" Lancelot denounced. "A thief and a witch. You don't deserve a flower."

"You insulted me first, you little brat!" Morgan snapped, irrationally wounded by the disdain of this child. "I just wanted to help you."

"Merlin's lost little bud has bloomed into quite the carnivorous flower, it seems," an all too familiar melodious voice condemned, and Morgan turned her eyes to Viviane, stood on the surface of the lake behind them with lovely eyes glowering. "You dare threaten my subjects? Try to pilfer what is mine?" The winds rose, and the waters churned with anger.

Morgan refused to be intimidated. "Not everything you lay hands on becomes your possession, *my lady*. I will release your captive subject and your kidnapped little cup-bearer, but I will not leave without that sword."

The Tale of ~~King Arthur~~Morgan Le Fay

"You have no right to this blade," Viviane denounced, drawing Excalibur from the folds of her robes. "It is mine to bestow upon whomever I choose, and you, rancid flower, are not even a knight. You are far from a worthy wielder."

Morgan studied the gold-inlay of the cerulean sheath around the shining silver blade gripped so arrogantly in the fay's slim fingers. Telekinesis was such an easy trick. The blade should have been ripped from the lady's grasp the second Morgan laid eyes on it, sent hurtling toward it's **rightful** wielder, stood with hand outstretched, waiting for it to obey.

The sword resisted her call, and Viviane smiled, an ugly smirk, with eyebrow arched in clear, gloating challenge. The flames emerged at one glimpse of that expression, but the waters swirling around the lady extinguished Morgan's fires before they could blister and char the supple white skin of her enemy.

Morgan screamed in frustration, and the fire became lightning, crackling toward her target, only to fizzle out with an ugly hiss, the same as her flames. Something struck her from behind, a tree branch, slamming across her shoulders and sending her face first into the waters of the lake. She came spluttering upright and lashed blindly out at the source of the attack.

Little Lancelot was flung from his feet, landing hard with tree limb shattering in his hands. His head cracked against the ground, and he gasped, holding his bleeding, splinter riddled hands cradled tight to his chest and trembling with pain.

Morgan felt an instant swell of shame, and she rushed to aid the poor child who should have run far away from this fight. He should have never attacked someone who was clearly so much more powerful than he.

"That is true virtue," Vivian asserted, appearing right in front of her and blocking her path. The fairy knelt down by Lancelot's head, holding his gaze and tenderly brushing aside his tears. "Risking thyself and defending so valiantly thy lady." She kissed the boy's forehead. "You are a true knight, and you will be worthy of this sword and all the other hallows once you've grown enough to wield them, now won't you?"

He nodded, biting his lip to fight back the sobs that would surely escape were he to try and voice a stronger reply.

"You however, will never be worthy," Viviane condemned, eyes weighing into the intruder still frozen on the shores of her lake. "Not of Excalibur, not of a throne, and not even of Merlin's love." Morgan flinched. "Those are, all of them, mine. Though England's throne is meaningless. You mortals can squabble over that worthless seat in Camelot as long as you wish. I am ruler of these lands." She gestured to the woods around them. "And that is all that matters."

She lifted Lancelot into her arms and carried him back beneath the waters, whispering soft words to him the entire time of his greatness and a destiny she would no doubt ensure and control.

Morgan let them leave, powerless to do anything, even attack. She looked down at the abandoned little pixie still snoring on the shore and pitched her angrily back into the lake, snapping her fingers at the last second to wake her from her slumber and ensure she did not drown.

The cowering eyes of the common fairies were watching her warily from the bushes and trees, but she ignored them, stalking back into the woods. She did not need Viviane to give up her sword. That 'legendary relic' was nothing but a hunk of metal, assigned significance and reverence only by the belief of those fool priests and prophets who guided the lords of this land.

She held her hand out to the side and summoned her own sword, crafting the blade with pain-staking care, an exact replica of the holy blade she had been denied. She held the sword up to the light and smiled at the fine detail of its construction. Even Merlin himself would never be able to tell the difference. Let Viviane hoard her own Excalibur for all of time, safe within the vaults of her kingdom. Morgan's sword would serve just as well in humiliating her enemies and crowning a true king for these lands.

The Tale of ~~King Arthur~~Morgan Le Fay

x. The Sword in the Stone

It was a sunny morn of twittering birds and clear blue skies, and such weather was not nearly dramatic enough for Morgan's tastes. She raised her eyes up to the cheery blue depths, and her potent, tumultuous mood became easily rapidly darkening wisps of cloud that swelled and blackened until they covered the whole of the heavens. The thunder rolled in right as Morgan drew up to Camelot's gates. She wore no false face this time. She carried the conjured Excalibur proudly at her side and walked right up to the helmeted guards with the hood of her fine cloak lowered and her face bared for all the world to see.

"My lady?" the captain at the gate prompted hesitantly, not seeming to recognize her. "It is unseemly for a young damsel to be wandering those woods without protection. Did some evil befall thy escort?" he pried, eyes settling on the sword in her hand and assuming it no doubt to be the weapon of some fallen knight that had accompanied her. His eyes widened then, as he saw the name graven on the sheath: the sword of legend that had long been lost. "Where did you come by that blade?"

"I reclaimed it from the hands of treacherous fay," she declared, just as she'd rehearsed. "It is mine by right, as all of you should recognize. Just as you should know well my face. I am Morgan Pendragon," The men paled, hands tightening about their polearms. "great wizardess and royal heir. Now run to your bishop and your false king and inform them I come to confront them."

She started forward through the gates at a stately walk, and the weapons lowered foolishly to block her advance. "You are the witch who slew King Uther--"

She cut off the captain's words with a turn of her head, staring him down coldly. "I will hear no such lying slander. The poison that stole the life of my father and mother was the work of weak cowards who then blamed a child for their actions. The pretend nobles infesting this country, the men who told such lies and the fools who believed them, they have no right to Camelot's throne, and they have no right to wield this weapon." She hefted Excalibur, keeping her voice loud and authoritative, so it carried past the guards to the nervous villagers inside the gates watching her arrival. "Your false king, Lot, will come to realize that truth this very morn, and you will all of you bear witness."

She strode through an arch of spears that parted involuntarily at her approach. The captain's voice returned to him in a fit of violent coughing, and he eyed her with obvious fear. He barked an order to the younger man beside him, and the soldier went sprinting off toward the keep.

Morgan kept up her slow and commanding advance, striding calmly through the filth-stained streets of the lower city with the eyes of the skeletal peasantry tracking her advance. She would return to feed them later, she swore, but she could not afford to waste her energies on food conjurations just now. Such charity would only ruin her ominous air anyhow. She never earned love, not even from those she aided, but fear and respect, those she could command with ease, so long as she kept her composure.

An entire procession of knights waited for her at the castle gates, and stood right at their head was the usurper and his queen, wearing somewhat nervously their stolen crowns. Anna was whispering a ceaseless stream of urgent advice to her husband, no doubt warnings to stay rash action and leave the threat of the approaching sorceress to his queen.

"Cousin!" Anna greeted with a smile, as Morgan finally reached the head of the rise. "I am so happy you have returned, and with such a kingly gift!" she noted, eyeing hungrily the mimicked Excalibur and looking to her husband in clear prompt that he echo her welcome.

"Er, yes." Lot sighed, hand clutched tight about his own sword hilt, sheathed at his side. "We would of course be happy to receive you, my Lady Pendragon, and discuss the… misunderstanding of that bloody feast all those many years past. And this kingdom is of course grateful of your gift, if that is indeed Excalibur…"

"It is! Oh praise the Lord, it is!" The bishop scurried right to the front of the crowd, studying the sword in Morgan's hand with dreamy eyed delight. "It matches exactly the illuminator's drawings. You can see its title and inscription, laid right there upon the scabbard. That is the holy sword of England's king, returned finally to its rightful home!"

The robed priest reached to seize the weapon, and Morgan coolly pulled back her hand. She held the model Excalibur point up toward the sky. "You will not lay hands on this holy sword, bishop," she denounced, "for you are not a holy man."

She looked pointedly between the bishop and the queen. The man flushed in nervous rage, not daring to look over at the liege he had cuckolded, though oblivious King Lot clued into none of these implications.

The Tale of ~~King Arthur~~ Morgan Le Fay

"Of course the priest is holy!" he snapped. "Why bring the sword if you do not intend to return it to your king?"

"You are not my king. You are no Englishman's king, pretender." Lot flushed. "You are a foreigner and a usurper, and you aught to be grovelling before me, because *I* am the rightful queen of this city." The lightning flashed to emphasize her point, and King Lot looked nervously to the heavens, grip rigid around his sword hilt.

Anna seemed to share none of his unease though. Smile still in place, she sidled up to Morgan and took her arm, whispering in calm advisement, "Oh, Morgan. You cannot be queen without a husband. This you must know. As regal as your blood, you would need a fitting suitor to ever be a ruler. My husband may indeed not be the rightful holder of this seat, but this throne must have some kind of steward, a powerful warrior, to keep back those greedy other lords who think they have a claim to it."

"You are as foul as any of those lords," Morgan denounced, voice ringing out over the crowd. "I have watched you closely, usurper king. You feast in splendor while the people starve. You train your sons in warcraft and continue the bloodshed that tramples the farmlands and worsens this famine. The people in Camelot are living in squalor--"

"No different than it was under your father, King Uther," Lot retorted. "I inherited a bankrupt treasury and have kept taxes high because of this, to keep our armies fed, because they are needed to defend this city. The spoils of battle these brave knights and I bring back to this city has kept our populace from death, and we take first part and feast on those spoils before they rot, as is our right. The curses of plague and malcontent that have ravaged these citizens..." He faltered, then his eyes became steely once more, chin raising. "Perhaps that is because you stole that most holy relic now clutched within your tainted hands, witch. This curse upon our kingdom came about because a changeling demon slew a king!" Morgan's eyes darkened dangerously, and Anna put her hand on Lot's arm in clear warning, but the man shrugged free of her grip, continuing on stubbornly. "I am the chosen king! God willed Uther dead so that I could take his place and better rule these lands!"

"You dare paint yourself a righteous man?" Morgan mocked. "You know as well as I, it was a mundane hand that poisoned Uther and his lords. There was no witchcraft." Her eyes settled on Anna then, and she considered quite seriously proclaiming her treason before the entire square.

And Anna, bizarrely, nodded in gentle encouragement. "Indeed," she boldly announced. "My dear cousin, Morgan, was the victim of that tragic feast. It was--"

"What madness do you speak?" Lot snapped, hand squeezing Anna's shoulder, until his queen fell meekly silent. Lot turned his eyes back to Morgan then, thundering, "Every man here knows whatever accusation you lay is but falsehood, witch, to allay thy own guilt!"

Morgan's eyes darkened, deciding firmly that Lot was an evil manipulator, far worse than young Anna, whom he had taken and pressured into poisoning Uther and Igraine. He lied to his people, and he had lied even to his bishop, spinning a false image of nobility and ignorance simply for the sake of stirring sympathy.

"The names of the guilty are easy to uncover for any *righteous* man seeking to avenge his king," Morgan countered coldly. "From Sir Turquine the butcher, to the usurpers before us, traitors to their liege and false rulers of this kingdom. You would be worthy of this sword..." She drew Excalibur from its sheath, leveling it at King Lot. "...only in death. I dare you to lay hands on this holy relic, and witness for yourself God's judgment of your greed."

"I fear not your empty threats. Seize her and take it!" Lot snapped, and his knights surged forward.

Morgan gave a disproving cluck. All twenty men froze instantly in place, feet glued to the ground and muscles gone rigid. She tried not to show how difficult it was to speak while holding so many targets transfixed, but her slow dictation only added to her imperial air. "Like any uncultured brute, you resort straight to violence and force, but no bloodshed can win you this blessed sword." The men all regained control of their muscles with abrupt suddenness then, but Morgan pretended it was intentional. She was tiring rapidly now, but she had not yet reached the end of her performance. She needed her energies for three more essential stunts.

"Just because it is guarded by a witch?" Sir Lucan snapped, drawing his own blade. "We do not fear you, woman! The power of Christ shall protect us as we strike you down!"

He looked in clear expectation toward the bishop, and the man gave a hesitant nod. "Indeed, a true knight of virtue cannot fall to Satan's spells."

"I use no powers of Satan," Morgan asserted coolly, stalking over to the old anvil sat off to one side of the gates. "I am *not* a witch. I am like any other druid, a prophet and councilor, teaching God's lessons to you, the corrupt and naive."

The Tale of ~~King Arthur~~ Morgan Le Fay

She drove the blade right down into the stone, putting in place a complex and unalterable spell to make anvil and sword one and the same object. The two of them could never be separated, not until she willed it. She kept her hand fixed about the hilt and tried to mask the fact that she was leaning on the weapon, as a flood of energy left her. Then she turned back toward the host of knights with a ladylike grin of subtle triumph. "Whoever pulls this sword from this stone and anvil is the rightful king of all Logres!" Morgan proclaimed before the crowd, finally lifting her hand from the hilt. "The power of God will indeed support the true ruler of these lands, and no spell or trickery could defy him."

Dead silence hung over the assembly for a full minute then, as the knights all shuffled their feet and stared nervously at Morgan, and then the sword, and then the sorceress once again.

"I shall free the sword of England's king and deliver it unto its rightful master!" Sir Lucan proclaimed, stalking arrogantly up to the stone-embedded blade.

Morgan waved him forward with dry amusement. He was clearly not after the weapon for Lot's sake, and Morgan suspected he would wear all too eagerly the title of "rightful king".

His eyes drifted to Anna with a show-boating smile, right as his hand settled on the pommel of the legendary weapon. Perhaps he also assumed if he were named rightful king, then Anna would desert her current husband and resume sleeping with him again. He heaved back upon the hilt, but the blade refused to budge. He glared over at Morgan, fingering the blade at his side.

"Strike me down if you wish." The sorceress shrugged. "It will avail thee not. That sword will stick fast to its new sheath long after I am dead. Only God's blessing can wrench it free."

King Lot did not seem to buy into that assertion. He grabbed a crossbow from his guard and launched a bolt straight at Morgan's back, despite Anna's shriek of protest.

The bolt passed only through empty air, as the wizardess dropped into shadow. The crowd gasped in wonder, and King Lot spat, angrily handing off the bow. "Dispel whatever evil hex she has laid upon that blade," the king growled to his priest.

Morgan stayed watching as a shadow on the wall, as the bishop strode forward with arms raised in sanctimonious theater. He prayed loudly over the anvil and sword in long verses of archaic Latin for a full twenty minutes, then declared that God would indeed now allow the *rightful* king to pull it free.

He gave clear emphasis to that word before the mob of citizens gathered watching this event, endeavoring to enforce that King Lot was indeed God's chosen ruler. No doubt this was an effort to finally silence the years of rioting against the foreign king, as Camelot's people still spoke of him disparagingly as an invader undeserving of his seat.

King Lot stalked arrogantly forward and fixed his hand about the pommel. A bolt of lightning arced down from the sky and smote the lying usurper, flinging him to the ground in a ruin of smoking robes.

Morgan rematerialized, leaned back against the wall, eyes drooping with exhaustion, though she portrayed it all as arrogant lounging. "God has judged thee, false king," she denounced, as Anna fell weeping to the side of her dead husband, tearing at her hair in impressively vocal grief. "It is a blasphemy for a serpent such as thee to lay hands on a holy relic."

Morgan stalked inside the castle then, and no man dared step up to stop her. She sent the servants fleeing from the halls with a thundering announcement and sunk down upon the throne she had finally emptied. She could not smile for some reason. Perhaps she was simply too tired for such strenuous expressions. She sealed the doors with a quick charm and fell instantly into exhausted slumber. The proudly returned exile, snoring away within her rightful seat.

The Tale of ~~King Arthur~~ Morgan Le Fay

XI. The Curse of a Witch

The new queen of Camelot awoke alone in her hall and knew by the gummed up discharge of her eyes and the dryness of her mouth that it had been many hours, if not a full day. She shoved herself wearily to her feet and conjured a grand dress of royal purple and a fur trimmed cape, completing it with the simple crown her mother had always worn. She then settled back in her seat with a cup of tea and studied her reflection in the massive polished mirror settled directly across from the throne. She had a strong suspicion it had been Anna who had put that thing in place, so she could admire her reflection while seated here.

Even in her grand outfit, Morgan's image was not nearly as resplendent as her sister's. She looked bony and small, and the mirror made it uncomfortably obvious that the seat beside Morgan's lay stark and empty, as did this eerily quiet hall, devoid of all the chatter and music that had filled it in the past. None of this should bother the new queen. A king did not need a queen at his side to rule, and she did not need a husband. She was powerful in her own right. Wasn't that what all great rulers aspired to? Morgan slurped down the last of her conjured tea that tasted far too strongly of licorice and tossed aside the teacup, letting it shatter with a satisfying explosion on the flagstone and leaving in place the mess of its remains as she stalked with echoing footsteps over to the door of her throne room. It was time she greeted her subjects.

She ran over the speech, murmuring the eloquently phrased rhetoric over and over again beneath her breath, as she made her way through the empty halls and toward the open air of the courtyard and the castle gates. She stepped out through the grand main doors of the fortress, and-- was instantly soaked. It was pouring rain, a prickling deluge of unpleasant force that turned her grand dress and cape into dragging weights, tangling her feet and pulling at her neck.

"Cease!" she commanded, but that simply summoned more lightning, a dazzling bolt of force that touched down right in front of her, shattering the cobblestone and near bursting her eardrums. "Damn it! I said cease!" The thunder shook the walls, and the rains only intensified. She found herself unable to see and barely able to breathe, as the water dripped down her brow and over her sputtering lips. It seemed it was far easier to summon a storm than it was to dispel it.

She stalked back inside and firmly shut the door, wiping the water from her face. "It appears more study is in order," she muttered, summoning forth the book on weather patterns that she had left back within her castle in Wales. She had learned that trick of teleportation from Merlin himself, even with so brief and shaky an observance as the day he had transported her off to Essex. Now she could fold space and pull other objects toward her position or cast them away, and she would master the trick of her own transference soon enough, just as she would figure out how to dispel this damn lightning storm blocking her exit.

She read and experimented for many hours, and learned much to her irritation that tampering with the wind currents and clouds caused chain reactions of weather that were much harder to control. Her only chance of dispelling these rains was to remain completely calm and pull apart the clouds, dispersing their moisture back into the higher altitudes. She attempted this trick, only to lose her temper once again and find it began hailing.

She slumped down beside the fire in her old bedroom, healing her weather-inflicted bruises and sullenly gave up for the day, hunkering down beneath her blankets and going stubbornly back to sleep.

It was sleeting the next morn, and she angrily re-shuttered her window, stomping down the stairs and pouring some water into a wide brass dish, so she could scry what was happening outside these walls. She saw a figure making her way nervously up to the sealed portcullis of the castle with hood raised against the chill damp. The woman was flanked by a host of knights, seated on horseback with lances raised in preparation to attack. The hooded woman knocked upon the gates. "Morgan? We only wish to talk! It is a fine and impressive storm you have conjured here, but it is growing rather tiresome, is it not?"

A crash of thunder sounded in seeming response, and Anna flinched away, turning her back in dejection. Morgan put a hand to her forehead and wearily summoned a portal, jerking her sister from the freezing rains outside and into the throne room where she was seated.

Anna staggered, looking about in bemusement, as she pushed back her hood and wrung out her hair. A smile graced her lips then, and she strode up to Morgan, seated coldly on the throne ahead. "Your majesty." She gave a little bow. "I most appreciate this audience. Though after two days of standing out there yelling in the rain, I may soon fall ill to pneumonia, so if you have any potions of warming tonics..."

The Tale of ~~King Arthur~~ Morgan Le Fay

Morgan twitched a finger, and a swell of hot air ripped through Anna's hair and clothing, instantly drying her.

Anna smoothed down her tangled locks. "Why thank you. Though when you announced you had come to retake the throne, I did not imagine you would find it appropriate to keep walled away in a cursed castle surrounded by a permanent storm."

"That is not intentional." Morgan sighed. "These rains are not my conjuration. They are a... unforeseen side effect. Now why are you here?"

"To visit my family of course." Anna beamed, settling down in the chair at Morgan's side. "To congratulate our magical queen on her impressive, dramatic conquest, and bring her news of the city outside. Though it seems I am the only one brave enough to enter these halls." She laughed. "What with my husband a smoking corpse and every knight who approaches this place falling quivering to the ground at even the most distant crash of thunder."

Morgan eyed her sister narrowly, noting that her ready smile seemed not at all forced this day, despite the frightening storms and the aforementioned murder of her husband. "You are so very composed for someone I just widowed. You were stricken enough, out in the square the other day."

"And why would Lot's death grieve me? I never loved him. His every invasive touch repulsed me," Anna denounced. "That performance of grief was solely for the sake of the crowd, just as all your speeches were. I've nothing but respect and even gratitude for your most masterful revenge against the usurper who poisoned our family."

Morgan arched an eyebrow. "*Our* family? You were the one that killed her! What makes you think you can act so casually friendly toward the victim you framed?"

"Victim?" Anna laughed, pushing her playfully. "Oh, please, Morgan. You will never be a victim. You are a great and powerful sorceress. And I thought this bad blood had already been settled. I thought you understood, that you'd forgiven me." Her smile faded, eyes flickering with fear. "Was Lot's death not enough of a revenge? If you will not take my life then... Oh please, Morgan, do not even threaten such things."

"Threaten what exactly...?"

"I need to know my son is safe."

"Of course he's safe! I would never hurt Gareth. He is an infant," Morgan asserted in outrage. "I am *not* some child-eating witch. I am a *wizardess*, teaching valuable life lessons to all."

"With strikes of lightning and horrible curses," Anna retorted, shrinking away at Morgan's responding glare. "I mean no offense, of course. You are as wonderful and merciful as ever, and it was a grand and impressive play you put on the other day, but now you've a deserted, rain soaked castle the entire court is too terrified to approach. What is the use in that?"

"I do not need a horde of courtiers scuttling about and annoying me!" Morgan defended, unable to admit that she herself was somewhat trapped here until she discovered a way to dispel these rains.

"Every queen needs courtiers," Anna countered. "And maids and subjects, otherwise you are not a queen. You are a squatter." Morgan's glare deepened, but Anna continued her meek wheedling. "Why did you not take back your throne in the normal, logical manner? You could have married King Ban or Meliodas or any of a dozen others and set him up to slay my husband in respected battle, instead of this ominous show of cursed storms and imprisoned holy swords."

"I will not be the brood mare of some old man to be ridden and churn out children! I am the rightful ruler. I have taken Camelot already, and if I do decide at some point in the future to accept the adoration of some suitor and have him pull Excalibur from that bloody rock, cementing my claim, then I will do so. It is a sound plan." She pouted. "Regardless of a few... weather related setbacks. This is not some rash siege."

"It is a sound plan, I suppose. But you should have found your king first. I could be an invaluable advisor in that respect," she insisted, all smiles and trusting confidence once again. "With the proper approach, it would be an enjoyable and easy game, awing some dashing young noble to defend and legitimize you."

"I do not need to be legitimized! I am the rightful--"

"But Morgan, it is so very nice to be fawned over, to be held. And you are the most blessed of women. You can shape yourself however you wish," she whispered enticingly, drawing Morgan's gaze to the mirror on the wall across from them. "You could be the most beautiful woman in the kingdom, the most beautiful woman on earth. Why settle for plain brown eyes and unseemly freckles when you could have flawless skin, and full lips, and shining eyes to match the stars?"

Morgan threw off her hands. "I ought to reshape you again! I do not care how ugly I am. I will have admiration anyway for my extraordinary cleverness and power!"

"Well, you will have fear and envy for those things." Anna sighed. "And I never said you were ugly, Morgan. You are far from ugly. But why

The Tale of ~~King Arthur~~Morgan Le Fay

settle for..." She eyed her up and down. "that, when you could effortlessly become breathtaking and snare any suitor you wish without the need to coerce and frighten?"

"Get out of my castle," Morgan muttered, calling up a windowed portal back to the rainy streets outside. "I care not for your company."

"Then why invite me in?" Anna challenged, seizing her hands. "We are all in want of company, dear sister, and I want no distance between us. You have forgiven me my mistakes?"

"I mean..." Morgan faltered, all eloquence deserting her, as she searched her feelings for an answer to that. "No. No matter what you do, she'll still be dead and..." Her eyes flooded with involuntary tears, and Anna's eyes softened.

She pulled her close, a tender embrace. Morgan instinctively remained rigid, and Anna sighed. "Well, if I cannot atone, at least let me grieve with you, my sister. I trust you, Morgan. I do. I trust you will do what is right."

"Well... Thank you," Morgan awkwardly muttered.

"That said, you really must leave this castle," Anna whispered in her ear, "and dispel this horrid storm. Because we are mere days away from rioting and calls for witch burning, with even our cowardly knights soon to be storming these gates."

Morgan pulled back from her with eyes burning, but Anna gave only an innocent smile, raising her hands in meek surrender. "Tis but a heartfelt warning, Morgan."

She rose smoothly to her feet, raising her hood and starting toward the portal shimmering in the air ahead. "You should come by the manor where the boys and I have taken up rooms," she called back over her shoulder. "I should like to introduce you to my Gareth. I know you've already seen him, seen his perfect little face and his adorable wittle hands, but I should like for you to meet him anyway. I would like for him to know his aunt."

"I'll... consider it," Morgan muttered, and Anna smiled once again, stepping trustingly off through the portal and vanishing from sight.

Morgan knew her sister was simply trying to manipulate her. The woman was callous and conniving and all too wisely wary of the sorceress that had taken her throne. She wanted to work her way back to a seat of power by influencing her, but Morgan did not really mind all that much, not at the moment. She was still terribly lonely, she discovered. She was not the master of magic and channeler of storms that she had thought herself. Even once she did dispel these rains and attain even greater powers... She would still be left sitting here, alone in this hall. It might be nice to go ahead with Anna's plan, to find some handsome but unavoidably dimwitted young lord who was actually kind, who adored her, who called her beautiful...

It disturbed her how easy of a trick it was, enhancing her features and her other assets, transforming from a bony, plain-faced girl to a long-lashed muse whose beauty far surpassed even that of her mother. She found her features had unconsciously taken on a cast far too close to the shrew Lady of the Lake however, and she quickly scoured away the porcelain face and bright blue eyes, retaking her normal appearance before she forgot what that looked like.

She sketched a quick copy of her normal features in paranoid fear immediately after the experiment. The image of her true face looked even more plain and disappointing now however, and she set fire to it without a second thought, deciding instantly that it did not matter what she looked like. She would simply cease to own a mirror.

She shattered every single reflective surface in every room of the castle then stayed lounging alone in her reclaimed throne, reading through her weather texts, until she finally managed to rein in the storm, reducing it to a tiny radius of darkly swirling clouds that stayed around the spires of her keep instead of sheeting over the entire city.

She could walk out into the courtyard now into perfectly dry and airid conditions. Still, she hesitated to venture out into the city. She never made her grand speech to the people, and she did not take Anna up on her offer to visit. She did scry her repeatedly though, both she and the boys. Little Gareth really was adorable, but Gawain and his brothers, Gaheris and Agravain, were quiet and bitter in wake of their father's passing.

The aspiring young knights kept visiting the sword cast into its anvil right outside the castle gates. The legendary weapon received constant visitors, from townspeople to noblemen, always hovering about it, whispering. Some few brave men even tried to pull it free, though the first was shouted at as a rash fool, with his companions fearing he would be roasted with lightning, just as had befallen King Lot.

Morgan launched no crackling attacks against these blustering fools however. She just sat back and watched in amusement, as they pulled, and strained, and struggled, though many of them muttered that the sword would never come free so long as 'the witch' remained in their castle, cursing their lands. She hated those whispers, but she could not help but keep listening to them.

The Tale of ~~King Arthur~~ Morgan Le Fay

Gawain himself was never brave enough to lay a hand upon the sword. He hung back always at the edge of the square, just staring at it, as did Agravain, whom the whole family had always called "Agi" in the past, but who now insisted he be called by his full regal name, because at nine years old he was clearly not a little boy anymore.

Both blustering young nobles remained far too traumatized to dare touch the "cursed" object that had killed their father, despite Gawain loudly proclaiming to his step mother each morning that he would free the blade and reclaim their throne. Anna told him irritably the seventh time he said it that he was wasting his time. He was clearly too afraid to even touch the sword, which meant he was in no way strong or noble enough to be the rightful king. It was a cruel thing to say to an eleven year old, and Morgan could not help but feel pity for him.

She felt more pity for herself however, wandering the deserted halls of the former home she had reclaimed while the people she had liberated all rioted in the streets below. She had disguised herself as a common woman the first week and gone down to the slums with baskets of bread and fruit. They had tried to beat her for the fare, but she had melted into shadow before the fists connected. Following that, the peasants had all been too terrified to eat the cursed food, murmuring of "poison". The entire wagon load had just rotted in the street, with even the children who tried to sneak up and lay hands on the fare being hauled away by their elders before a single bite could cross their lips.

Morgan had sealed herself back up in the throne room, seething in frustration, as a few more failed efforts at charity on her part only resulted in more riots at the castle gates, as well as the people becoming exceedingly paranoid that their neighbors were not their neighbors but a witch in disguise.

She stayed stubbornly in her captured castle for an entire six weeks with the depression eating away at her. These deserted halls were even worse than her ghost infested fortress in Wales. The people blamed her for the bad weather and the dying crops, and not a single one of them believed her proclaimed innocence that she had not in fact poisoned her parents all those years ago. Why should they believe her? She had killed their king. Though a few of the common folk did mercifully whisper that it had been God himself who punished King Lot. All those storm clouds were surely God's displeasure, judging the witch that had invaded their city and sealed away His holy sword. Excalibur could not be cursed. It was a divine instrument. It simply needed the right man to free it of its prison.

It was the first day of the seventh week that Morgan discovered she was incapable of scrying Arthur. She had wanted to see something happy, even when she knew it would only churn her guts with envy, but when she envisioned her brother's laughing face, all she saw was clouded waters. No matter how hard or long she looked, all she saw was shadowed gloom, and her anger deepened tenfold. Merlin had probably smuggled the boy away, hiding him from her sight. He believed her a curse and a danger, just like everybody else.

She found herself crying then. Weeping and shaking, and acting not at all queenly. She could hear the mob of commoners and knights battering at her gates, as she chugged down wine and thought what a miserable fool she was. She was a usurper even less competent than Lot, and nothing she said, no act of charity or greatness, would change these people's opinions.

She transformed into a crow and flew away from her captured castle, taking with her the swirling storm clouds that had hovered over the place since the instant she sat upon the throne. Maybe that was God's glaring judgment, or maybe it had been caused by all the bottled up pain she had been brooding on and worsening this entire disastrous visit.

She could not hold her throne after all. She did need a husband, a rightful king to sit at her side and act as a warrior of esteem to keep the people from shunning her. She did not want to admit that defeat however. She did not want to become someone's wife, hanging off their arm with a fake face and a million lies on her lips like Anna, endlessly stroking the ego of her puppet so he stayed beneath her thumb. She flew with no real destination, then watched through all-seeing waters when she stopped at a lake, as far back in Camelot the knights reclaimed the deserted castle with cries of triumph, emptying out the larders for the peasants and sounding the celebratory trumpets.

The appointed temporary steward of the throne, Sir Lucan, summoned the arch daises of Canterbury himself that very month and had him cleanse both the castle and the sword in the stone of evil influence. Even after all the rituals and lead up however, Lucan could still not pull the false Excalibur free of the anvil.

None of the knights could. Not even Gawain, who finally worked up the nerve to try, alone in the courtyard one night after a full two months of fearful procrastination. Morgan was highly tempted to let the boy pull it free. Instead, she did nothing, watching his shoulders slump in weary defeat, eyes flooded with frustrated tears, as he finally released his cramped and shaking hands after hours spent yanking and kicking in an attempt to wrench free the blade he no doubt saw as his destiny, stalking away with hands bloody and brow covered in sweat.

Morgan could not allow his family to once again steal her throne, however bad she felt for him. She would not allow Arthur to steal it from her either. She needed time, and a plan. And she needed to find out where Merlin had hidden the boy, because not knowing was driving her mad.

XII. In a Country Churchyard

Morgan, the shunned and despised, flew back to the estate of Sir Ector in a somewhat hopeless attempt to pick up Arthur's trail. She expected him to be long gone from these halls, smuggled away by Merlin to some even grander hideaway safe from the evil influence of his dangerous sister. Sure enough, the courtyard where her brother and Kay would host mock sword battles and chase each other in endless tag lay stark and empty this rainy day. The room where the boy had been quartered was likewise deserted, though a little wooden sword and a few other odd toys still lay scattered around the bed, as if the room was still in use.

Morgan became a racing shadow and searched the whole of those halls but passed only the faces of unfamiliar servants, along with Sir Ector and his eight year old son, Kay, picking away at their dinner in uncharacteristic silence. There was no trace of Merlin, and there was no trace of Arthur. Still, Arthur's former room with the rumpled sheets and many present toys had made her suspicious, so she flew off to the nearest town, just to be sure he was not off on some errand or little adventure with the wizard tutoring him. Even the thought of that scenario filled her with instant, bitter envy, but she kept in line her temper and kept constant her feathered shape, as she soared off to the nearby hamlet of Hewelsfield and its little country chapel.

The streets were rather empty of people this dreary, drizzling eve, yet out in back of the old churchyard lingered an all too familiar pair of figures. Arthur was knelt before a freshly filled in grave, pants soaked with mud, and tears mixing with the rain rolling down his cheeks. Behind him stood Merlin, arms crossed and cowl raised.

His eyes locked instantly on the crow, as she fluttered down to roost on the roof of the cathedral beside them. Morgan prickled, feathers ruffling in irritation that she had been so easily unmasked. The druid should not be able to see through so flawless a disguise. There were crows all over this churchyard. What made her look any different?

"You should head back to the manor, Arthur," the druid advised his young ward, eyes still locked on Morgan, glaring down at him in angry challenge that he dare attack or seek to trap her again. "We've lingered here far too long already. You are late for dinner."

The Tale of ~~King Arthur~~ Morgan Le Fay

"Why couldn't you save her?" Arthur whispered, and Morgan's fierce gaze darted past Merlin and over to the gravestone. *Evelyn Copperlane.* So dear old Evey had finally met her end. *Serves her right.* Morgan brooded.

"When she got sick..." Arthur continued, voice breaking. "Why didn't you save her?" He turned on Merlin, but there was no anger or accusation in his eyes, only hurt incomprehension.

"No spell or potion can fend off the ravages of time," Merlin responded sagely.

"Rav-a-jes?"

Morgan rolled her eyes. She had known that word at his age. She was so much better than him, so much smarter and... harder hearted. She looked again to Evey's gravestone and felt nothing but spite.

"The natural order," Merlin carried on. "Steady deterioration is the way of all mortal creatures." Arthur's blank look of confusion did not abate. "Everyone dies eventually," the druid clarified.

"Oh," Arthur mumbled, voice quieting. "You weren't here at all though. I've seen you help those people, like in the village last year when everyone got sick. Maybe if you'd given Evey one of those drinks, she would have gotten better."

"I am sorry I was absent," Merlin offered hollowly. "I failed to return in time, so I can offer you no specific diagnosis."

"Di-egg...?"

"Identifying labeling of the specific illness that brought about her end," Merlin rephrased, and Arthur blinked, trying to process the dump of words and clearly not at all succeeding.

Dullard. She seethed. It did not matter that he was only six years old, he was clearly as average as they came. Why was Merlin even bothering to teach him?

Arthur turned back to his solemn contemplation of the gravestone, and Merlin's hand settled on his shoulder, such a protective and fatherly concern. "You yourself are going to catch a serious cold should you stay out here any longer, son."

"Son." Morgan wanted to attack him. She already felt the shape of her crow melting away into that of a tiny black widow, deadly and venomous, yet so easily overlooked.

"I don't want to leave her," Arthur whispered, head dropping against the tombstone. "I don't want her to go away."

"Yes... but... She's already gone, and away you must go." Merlin fumbled for the words. He was dreadful at comforting those in pain. He always had been. "Just... look at old Bailey over there." He gestured to the sway backed mare that Arthur had no doubt ridden into town. "She looks absolutely miserable shivering in this rain, now doesn't she?"

Arthur's lip quivered in shame. "She does. I'm sorry. Can you send her back to the stables?"

"No, because you must lead her back there. With all haste. Go on now." He pulled the boy to his feet, steering him toward the horse. "And wash your trousers. You've gotten them dreadfully muddy. Whatever would Evey say?"

It was an idiotic comment to make at a time like this. Arthur instantly started sobbing, collapsing back to his knees like the broken babe he was.

"Oh dear," Merlin fretted, hands hovering over the boy uncertainly. "I should... I should fetch Sir Ector. Yes. That's it. Though..." He looked nervously toward the chapel eaves where Morgan had last been sighted.

She had already flitted down to the grass however, snapping into the form of a kindly looking baker's wife, as her arms closed around the sobbing child before her without a second thought. Arthur sobbed into her shoulder without question, even as Merlin stiffened in alarm.

"There, there, little boy," she cooed, glaring up at the wizard, though her next words were not the threat or curse he had clearly been expecting. "Those who love us are never truly gone," she whispered. "They are with you always. You had a mother who loved you and a crotchety nursemaid who loved you just as dearly. The entire kingdom loves and needs you, so stop sitting out in the rain," she ordered sternly. "It only makes it feel worse, now doesn't it?"

"Y-yes," Arthur sniffled. "I s-suppose it does. T-thank you, Mary."

"Yep. That's me. Mary. Mary the kindly baker's wife. Now get up, go home, and eat your dinner," she commanded, lifting him up onto old Bailey's back and sending him off up the road to Sir Ector's estate.

Merlin breathed a sigh of relief. "It is wonderful to see you so... supportive."

Morgan's eyes darkened, bleeding back into her own face, with softhearted Mary running off into the muck at her feet.

"After your last visit, and with all your glowering up there in the eaves, I had quite worried you would--"

"Kill him? Well I could, you know. It would be so very effortless to strike down that sobbing brat in any of a dozen ways, but unless it were a creative enough end, it would simply be boring, now wouldn't it?"

The Tale of ~~King Arthur~~Morgan Le Fay

Merlin's brow lowered. "I beseech you not to threaten such things, not even in jest--"

"In jest? Who said I was jesting?" she snapped, keeping her back firmly to him and her gaze fixed off down the road. "I am nobody's jester or puppet. What I do have is a wicked wit of my own paired with the dazzling talent to incinerate and terrify, and I absolutely aught to make use of those talents, inflicting horrible ends on every idiot in this country, as absolutely everyone just automatically assumes I will!"

"I never meant to..." He reached for her shoulder, and she vanished into mist, twisting away on the winds of the steadily worsening storm.

"Blind me all you want," she snarled, an echoing voice howling past his ears. "A lioness always finds her prey."

"I blocked your scrying, so you would be forced to visit," Merlin asserted. "I wanted you here--"

"So you could trap me again? Give it your best shot, old man. Bottle the winds themselves." The currents rose, driving rain into his face, as she drifted farther and farther away from him.

"This is not a game!" Merlin shouted, finally losing his temper. "Now get back down here and listen, for once, as I explain and put an end to all these paranoid delusions you've been--"

The shriek of the wind rose to drown out his words, and Morgan drifted away.

He just wanted to explain. That's what he claimed. Explain why he'd felt the need to blind her, isolate her, trap her? Explain why he never sought to help her with any of her own goals, or check in, or visit, or even *scry* her? She had no patience to hear such excuses, so she floated away on the winds. Her heart was too heavy in the end, and she thudded back to the earth, floundering through the muck of Sir Ector's courtyard and shrinking down into a rat, clever yet despised, and thus unable to help but frighten even those who aught to pity her.

XIII. The Tale of the Lady of Cornwall

Morgan the conniving rat scuttled into the chambers of the precious boy king curled up beneath his blankets. He seemed in a better mood now, after a warm dinner eaten in company with his wonderful adoptive family and all their many smiling servants. Each and every one of those adults had put aside their own grief at a single look at Arthur, returning from the graveyard all filthy and somber. They showered the boy with concern and blankets and sweets to accompany his dinner, pouring absolutely all of their effort into desperately trying to cheer their precious little prince. He had smiled at many of their antics, but he had not laughed as he normally would have. Still, his expression remained calm and his eyes less distant, as his young maid, Cara, bundled him off to bed, tucking him beneath the covers and carting away his muddied clothes without a complaint.

Morgan hunkered down in the rafters just above the boy's bed, her beady yellow eyes glowing sinisterly in the darkness. He caught sight of the rat finally and gave nothing more than a faint grimace, before closing his eyes anyway and settling down to sleep. She aught to drop down and bite him, start him crying again. It would only be fair, after all the misery he'd caused her.

The door thudded open, and Arthur sat up with a start, staring quizzically at Merlin, standing flustered in the doorway. "What's wrong?" the boy murmured.

"Er, nothing," the wizard asserted haughtily, instantly composing himself, though his eyes still flickered to the rat crouched prickling in the rafters. "I just... came to check on you."

"I'm not crying anymore." Arthur shrugged. "And Cara said she would wash the mud from my trousers."

"You should wash them yourself," Merlin clucked. "It is a mess you made. You must be the one to clean it."

"I suppose." Arthur sighed, pushing back his covers and trudging toward the door.

Merlin caught his shoulder. "You don't have to go now, Arthur. That was more of a metaphor than an actionable order for the present."

"Huh?"

The Tale of ~~King Arthur~~ Morgan Le Fay

"It was advice for later in your life, a symbolic lesson from a literal scenario," he enforced, looking pointedly back at the rat glaring down at them. "Rash action, driven by emotion, causes unintended consequences. And then you must clean up your mess."

"Um... Alright," Arthur murmured. "So... I *do* have to wash them myself?"

"Yes, but I will let Cara know that, so go back to bed. You can see to it in the morning."

Arthur obeyed without comment, climbing back beneath the covers.

"You shall have safe and happy dreams," Merlin announced, nervously meeting Morgan's gaze, as he proceeded with his patronizing speech. "for I *know* you are in no danger tonight and that nothing within this room would harm you. I trust that nothing shall happen. So, I shall be off." He started backing toward the door. "Off to the courtyard, where I will be waiting expectantly for an old pupil who truly must allow me to explain recently perceived slights of scrying and neglect."

Arthur eyed him in clear confusion. "I don't know much of what you mean. But it is awful late for visitors coming to our courtyard, is it not?"

"This visitor is already around." Merlin sighed. "She does not follow normal rules of etiquette."

Morgan changed into a fly and flitted out a crack in the window. She'd had enough of the wizard's pointed comments and far too easy tracking of her disguises.

Merlin put a hand to his forehead, rushing back through the door.

"Mary said I had a mother." Arthur's comment put a halt to both the hasty exits of the sorcerers, bringing all eyes back upon him, as his fists knotted up the covers in clenched little bunches. "I suppose everyone has a mother, even if they've gone away, like Kay's, and Evey..."

Merlin eased shut the bedroom door, sinking down onto the bed. "You had a mother, yes, and she loved you dearly, just as Mary said. Her name was Igraine."

"Igraine," Arthur repeated, brow scrunching. "Evey wouldn't talk about her. Not even when I asked. Why is that?"

"Well, no one's told you this yet, but your mother was the queen of all of Logres and your father was King Uther Pendragon, which makes you heir to all of Britain."

Arthur's eyes widened, and Morgan fluttered her wings in annoyance. Merlin always did pick the *best* times to dump out overwhelming information.

"Anyhow, your mother was a wonderful lady, compassionate and clever." He paused, eyes drifting to the spec of a fruit fly on the window sill. "I don't suppose a boy your age has any appetite for epic tales of misleading truths recited in the style of the bards?"

"What's a bard?" Arthur demanded.

"A sometimes musical and somewhat obnoxious storyteller."

"Ob-nocks-is? Doesn't sound like a good thing."

"It seldom is, but a good bard is a rare delight. Anyhow, I've all the stories in the world about me, whispered over campfires, recited in the taverns, so did your father. But for someone so remarkable as the Lady Igraine, mother of kings and sorceresses... For her they sing no tales. I suppose it was the nature of her husbands, both so similar in the end, determined to hide away her beauty, to keep it for their own."

"What do you mean?"

Merlin's eyes shifted again to the window, but Morgan did not run from him this time. She wanted to hear this story, perhaps just as badly as he wanted her to hear it.

"The life of the Lady Igraine could easily be a tragic tale. She was sold off in marriage at the age of nine to settle the debts of her family, and her breathtaking countenance as it blossomed was hidden jealously away by her ever-cautious husband, the aged duke of Cornwall, Gorlois, lest she be stolen from him. No fortress or heighted tower could defy the all-seeing eyes of the druid Merlin though. A druid's eyes can see in dreams a limitless distance, into even the most closely guarded chamber. And so it was that Merlin, while keeping vigilant watch over the enemies of his liege, did spy the lonely eyes of Igraine staring out the window of her tower in unspoken pining. She sat there often with little to do between the brutal nightly visits of her husband, visits that bore the heavy-hearted Igraine nothing but misery and mourning. Three times you see, she had born the duke a child, only for the babe to be ripped from her arms and locked away, most of them dead in a matter of months from illness and neglect. The duke never shed a tear, for they were all of them female, and thus seen as useless to the aging Gorlois, who sought only a son to carry on his name."

Well this is a great story to be telling a six year old. Morgan thought dryly, but listened raptly herself, in spite of her cynicism.

She had indeed never heard this tale.

"Igraine sat there in her sliver of a window, staring out at the misty trees that surrounded her castle and thought to herself that she could bear it no more. The window was too small for her to hurl herself free of her

The Tale of ~~King Arthur~~ Morgan Le Fay

confinement, but a dinner knife would serve just as well this morning to slice open a vein and free her of her misery."

Arthur burrowed anxiously deeper into his blankets, but Merlin carried on with his grim tale, oblivious to his distress, with eyes still fixed on the changeling in the window.

"The sparrow came in a panic just in time to stay her hand, and the druid Merlin did reveal himself to her, providing her a promise that he would free her from her prison, if she would only abide another fortnight. Igraine did tearfully consent, and Merlin immediately set into motion a most clever plan to free the dear lady.

"King Uther had long disliked the Duke of Cornwall, though their armies moved in unison to battle against the Saxons ever seeking to seize their lands. It took only the briefest urging from one such as Merlin to goad Uther into unseating the brutish codger and having him replaced. Merlin made no mention of Igraine in his persuasions, speaking only of the abuse of Gorlois's subjects as a way to stir the king's heart to anger in proclaiming war against his former ally.

"Igraine's image was kept a carefully guarded secret for the druid alone to look upon in his mirror each dragging day he spent apart from her. Igraine too yearned for his company, and so it was the druid would change his shape and visit her each and every day in the long month of preparations leading up to Uther's attack on her lord husband's castle. Simple tricks and headaches would keep her husband occupied throughout the night in the lower levels of the palace, until he became too weary to make the long trek up the winding stairs to the locked door of Igraine's tower, and the druid and his lady would be left to their own company."

Morgan blinked, following finally the implication of Merlin's story. *He couldn't mean...*

"The few who dare share this story proclaim quite cruelly that Igraine was fooled into sin, that Merlin did adopt the shape of old Gorlois to seduce her. The truth however, is that the lonely lady did fall for her strange visitor upon seeing his true face that first and fateful day he came to her.

"The happy weeks wore on in hopeful anticipation for Igraine, as the moon did wax and wane. Finally, the last sliver of glowing white vanished from the sky, and the night of new beginnings arrived. Uther's troops stormed Castle Cornwall, trailed by a triumphant mob of Cornwall's peasants along with all the lords of Logres sworn to follow the Pendragon banner. Uther slew Gorlois with a single blow, as the prideful codger tried and failed to win the younger man's retreat from his lands with a duel. The peasants cheered, and the guards surrendered, bringing forth the duke's nephew, Kador, and the Lady Igraine to pledge new allegiance to the Pendragon banner.

"Alas," Merlin's tone turned bitter. "Uther's heart did seize at one look upon the fair duchess's face, and so he immediately claimed her as his wife, giving no chance for objection from any man around him, least of all his faithful adviser, Merlin, who would have most sensibly forbade such a rash and unwanted proposal.

"Indebted to Uther for freeing her from Gorlois's oppressive ownership, Igraine did serve him faithfully as his wife and bore in his halls another girl, Morgan, a scarce eight months after their meeting." His stare weighed into the girl. "The people did whisper that the child was not a true Pendragon, and most cruelly did they treat her. Despite all Merlin's efforts to provide to her comfort and instruction... Perhaps he should have told her this tale long ago."

"I have a sister?" Arthur haltingly put together, and Merlin blinked, seeming to just now remember the child was there beside him.

"Yes. Morgan Pendragon, a stubborn but powerful sorceress who I wish most deeply had taken after her mother."

"What happened to her?"

"That is a story for another day." Merlin sighed.

Arthur nodded solemnly. "I'll have to learn more words before then. I didn't really understand this story. Not at all."

Merlin looked away sheepishly, laying a hand upon his head. "You're doing just fine, Arthur. It is my failing for having so badly alienated my audience. Now go to sleep."

"I... I will try."

The boy closed his eyes complicity, laying back upon his pillows and sparing Merlin the need for a spell. *What a model of bloody obedience.* Morgan seethed, turning away from the window and finding to her chagrin that her disguise had already melted off, returning her to the shape of a shivering fifteen year old, stalking off across the courtyard with nails biting into her palms, as her shock gave way to steadily mounting rage.

"Now do you understand?" Merlin pleaded, appearing right at her back with uninvited hands settled on her shoulders. "Of course you are dear to me, my girl, and of course it was difficult with this deadly secret--"

"Difficult?" She whirled on him, throwing off his hands. "You know *nothing* of difficulty, of hardship! You never wanted a child, did you? It was just an accidental seed of your affair seducing the legendary beauty right

The Tale of ~~King Arthur~~ Morgan Le Fay

above the head of her husband! How thrilling that must have been. How thrilling to keep having your fun with your paramour under the nose of her new lord, until a different beauty caught your eye and you vanished off into a lake!"

"I loved your mother truly," Merlin insisted, "yet she was faithful to Uther, showing only a single night of weakness across a decade. And that single night near crushed her with guilt, because her husband had been loyal to her, yet she had betrayed him. So I had to respect her wishes and pretend indifference and... Those years were a horrible trial for me--"

"I do not care to hear about *your* suffering! I'm sure it was so very hard for *you*. And I must have made your tragic life just that much more unbearable. Poor you, having to watch your nightmare of a daughter floundering her way through court and the powers you had afflicted her with, never once stepping up to defend her from any of the cruel comments or rumors, but why would you? You were probably elated to have that burden of a child shoved off as some other man's responsibility, his cursed spawn, with all her evils blamed on her alone and whatever hell she sprang from!" Her voice was cracking from the strength of her screams, and the winds were rising, whipping about the courtyard in chaotic, targetless turmoil.

Merlin pulled her in, hands clamping around her back and head. "Calm down!" he ordered, the words a commanding hiss. Every time he hugged her it was simply to manipulate, to restrain, control. "I am putting an end to the secrets, the misunderstandings. You have a home *here*, with me, not off in Camelot causing hurricanes and riots with impulsive and half-learned magics."

She stiffened. "You saw that?"

"Of course I saw it. I was there."

"Then why didn't you dispel it?" she grated, raising her head. "Why didn't you do anything to assure the people, to help me?"

"It was your mess, Morgan," the condescending traitor pronounced. "You had to learn yourself how to subdue it. I could not have intervened, dispelled the rains and dragged you from that castle. You had to come to your own realization and see for yourself that simply seizing a chair does not make you a queen."

She shoved away from him. "I am already a queen! And I *will* have my throne, regardless of your sabotage! You think you were teaching me a lesson? You have never taught me anything worthwhile! I had to learn it all myself, and I did admirably! I am brilliant! And that is why you hate me, isn't it? You don't want any child stepping in on your immortal legend. The great druid, Merlin, the best and wisest there ever was! Of course you love Arthur! Of course you want him as your son. He is such a docile little pet, so obedient and good and *average*. You want me home? You want me here? You are a LIAR!" she screamed, driving him back with a wall of fire. "You simply wish to trap me here in exile, because you cannot control me out there." She gestured to the distant castle. "Because out there, I am impressive. Out there, I outshine even you, and I will prove it!"

She took off in a blur of feathers, only for a massive pair of talons to clamp around her back, bearing her to the ground. She became a scorpion and jabbed her stinger into the cage of claws surrounding her, causing the eagle to flutter back with an angry caw.

"You cannot cage me!" she shouted, back to her own shape once again, as was Merlin, clutching at the swelling mark on back of his hand.

"I am not trying to cage you!" Merlin thundered in response, and she flinched, shrinking back in spite of herself. "I have never tried to trap you, and I never abandoned you! You flew off on your own that night, before I even realized it, and of course I could not follow! I have a responsibility. I needed to protect your brother. There is an entire class of powerful people looking to kill him, and he has not your powers, Morgan. He is a little boy, and he is the hope of an entire people, the future of our country, and the only one who can stop this endless war."

"Yes, Arthur is so very special. The entire world revolves around him, the chosen one savior who will unite all of Britain with nothing more than his goodness and the power of his adorable smile! I grew up hearing it, *father*. And it is all bloody unjust bullshit!"

"Morgan--"

"I should be ruling England! Me! I am the eldest. *I* have the power. I--"

"Am not of Uther's bloodline."

"Who the hell cares? Who cares what they whisper? My true father is too cowardly to ever tell anyone about me, so in the world's eyes I have every right to rule!"

"To be married off and used as a pawn by some honorless noble seeking to be king," Merlin whispered. "That is no future, Morgan."

"I will never be a pawn. The play king will be my pawn, and you will all of you regret having been so bloody awful to your queen!" She was crying now. She did not know why. She wasn't a child anymore. She was a full grown woman, awesome and intimidating, yet she was sobbing like an infant.

The Tale of ~~King Arthur~~ Morgan Le Fay

Merlin reached for her, and she struck him, a blinding flash of fire and fury. The flames around him died in an instant, leaving him unscathed.

"I hate you!" She hurled another bolt, just as easily deflected. "You are a scheming, cowardly liar! Worse than any of them! You are nothing to me. You hear me? You are nothing!"

The fire grew more intense, and Merlin staggered, batting at his smoking beard to quell the damage before it spread to his skin. Morgan made a point of ignoring her own seared hands, nails digging into her blistering palms with anger only growing. "I indulge your scheme, wizard. Groom your prop, set up your play king. I will tear him down and bring this kingdom into line beneath my heel. I will find a champion far greater than that golden haired brat, and I will have my throne."

Merlin stared sadly at her shaking, damaged hands, but for once spewed forth no false wisdom or self-serving order of manipulation. He let her words hang in the air, as she threw up her cloak and transformed, turning her back on the lying tutor who had sired her and the coddled child he had long since replaced her with.

XIV. By Any Means Necessary

Morgan the false Pendragon went to seek the venomous council of Anna De'Gaur, only to find her sister was otherwise occupied. Morgan flitted away from her window in blushing disgust, as she heard the noises from within. It was not Sir Lucan this time, but someone much older, likely some ploy to regain the widowed queen status, though she was not sure why she bothered with that now. Anna was back on the throne, wasn't she? With Sir Lucan at her side and young Gawain declared to be the heir to the title of king of Orkney and Logres alike in wake of his father's passing. Though granted, she had not scried them for many weeks now.

Morgan fluttered down to the abandoned north courtyard and roosted on a rain-filled water trough, taking a long drink before a sharp pain struck her in the back and the tale of the great and mighty sorceress near ended in an instant. Her vision flashed black, and she snapped instinctively back into her own shape. A grievous error. The arrow was still in her heart, jutting out between her shoulder blades. She would be dead in minutes.

"I knew it was thee, witch," the high-pitched voice of an idiotic child denounced. "Now I shall cleave thy head from thy body in penance for--"

She became shadow, arrow clattering to the ground, as she passed right between the legs of the boy who had dared to draw so close and press his blade against her neck. This shadow left blood spatters along the ground as it moved however, with her sight still steadily dimming, and so she coalesced back into a solid, envisioning her organs as whole and mended. The wound in her back vanished, but the pain did not, leaving her shivering on the filthy flagstone with the chill of death still hanging over her.

She kicked out in angry reprisal at the back of the knee of the would-be knight just now turning to face her. He dropped to the ground, and her heel slammed into his face, knocking him on his arse.

"Have you spent all these months just shooting down every poor little crow that happens to cross your path, all in the futile hope one would turn into a witch as it died?" she croaked, glaring at bloody-nosed Gawain, already bounding back to his feet with short sword in one hand and bow in the other.

The courtyard around her was littered with dead birds and rats. She should have noticed it before. "You are nothing but a butcher," she denounced, "and you can do no harm to one such as I."

The Tale of ~~King Arthur~~Morgan Le Fay

His eyes sparked with defiance, and he swung at her. She became mist, savoring the thrill of that blade, as it whistled only through the empty air where her neck had been. "No mortal can kill me," she asserted, rematerializing right before him with hand locked tight about his jaw. "I am Morgan Le Fay, soon to be queen. I am a great sorceress! The greatest there ever was! An untouchable and bloody terrifying witch…" Her voice was quavering, her eyes tearing involuntarily. "Go on, little boy! Scream, run away!"

"You're… you're just a girl," Gawain muttered, sword hanging loose at his side. "You seemed… different before." He frowned, looking down at his blade. "Can you… turn into a dragon or something? It feels wrong, hitting a girl."

"I am not a little girl!"

"I never said little."

"I am the awful power that struck down your father the lying usurper. You should be quivering in terror!"

"A knight does not tremble in face of danger," he asserted, defiant brown eyes rising to meet her own, though he just as quickly lost his resolve, fist turning into an awkwardly hovering hand, agonizing over her fingers, still clamped tight about his jaw with her face only inches from his own. "Could you… stop touching me though?"

She blushed, quickly releasing her hold and primly straightening her dress. "What? Are you worried I was bewitching you or something?"

"No. I mean, were you? You were, weren't you? Get back from me!" He raised his sword, waving it between them menacingly. "I… I will avenge my father. Whatever false, dewy eyed tears you shed. I… I feel nothing for Satan's temptress."

"Satan's temptress?" She stared at the boy in cynical disbelief. She hadn't even put on her bewitchingly beautiful face. She had changed nothing of her features, yet this child the paranoid crow killer was leering at her with face bright red and palms sweating. He really wasn't afraid of her. He was… "You're just a child, so stop looking at me like that. And stop shooting crows, or I'll turn you into a newt."

With that she vanished into mist, billowing past the boy and into the halls of the castle.

What was Gawain even doing in the deserted north courtyard? The gate there had been broken and bricked up for near as long as she could remember, and no one used the overgrown garden and its adjoining crumbling tower for much of anything. It was just a damp ruin riddled with mold. The fact that it was always deserted was precisely why she had chosen it as her resting place, but now Gawain and his looking to be self-made bow had gone and ruined her solitary hideaway.

She drifted through the tower and, sure enough, found not a single servant within those cold and larder-less halls. Though both Gawain's brothers, the twins: Agravain and Gaheris, were slumped sadly in separate chambers, looking far more filthy and miserable than the last time she had glimpsed them, as they picked away at bowls of gruel. These were the king's sons... What on earth was going on in this place?

She came to the door of the north wing and found it not only locked, but barred from the other side. She slipped past it with formless ease and continued her exploration of her former home until she found young Gareth, locked alongside his nursemaid in the remote south tower of the castle, a place that was not nearly so frigid as the cells his brothers had been assigned, but an apparent prison nonetheless.

The banquet hall and other rooms of the castle were stuffed to the brink with barrel chested knights that Morgan did not at all recognize, all of them strangers, except for the dreaded figure of black-armored Turquine, lounging uncaringly in a corner of the mess hall with drinking horn in hand. Morgan drifted over the heads of these mean-eyed warriors like a restless ghost and decided firmly that she really did need to speak with her sister, the one person in this castle still quartered within her regular royal rooms while her sons were all mysteriously locked away in isolation and neglect.

She slipped beneath the door of Anna's chambers and found her late night visitor still laying alongside the deposed queen. The man's balding head and hanging jowls made him a far from desirable companion for the evening, as his hairy arms stayed locked around Anna's chest, holding her trapped against him. "I say it's time we go again," he muttered, kissing her neck.

"I'm afraid you've exhausted me utterly, my lord," Anna moaned in breathy performance.

"Then just lay there and enjoy it," he grunted, easing himself atop her, only for Anna to put a firm and restraining hand upon his chest.

"I'm afraid you must retire for the evening," she insisted. "Before dawn breaks and the rest of the castle sees us like this."

"Should my men walk in on us, dear, they'd simply praise my good fortune. They would never tell Constance of this." He pulled her back toward him.

The Tale of ~~King Arthur~~Morgan Le Fay

"Oh, but my lord, my conscience cannot bear this!" Her voice caught, eyes tearing. "For as pleasurable as this night has been, it is a stain upon my honor to give myself up to thee out of wedlock..."

The old man stared her down gravely, wiping away her tears. "You would become my wife then?"

"Eagerly, my lord, but until that joyous day..." She eased herself away from him, climbing out from beneath the sheets. "I'm afraid this cannot continue."

The codger grabbed her from behind, arms cradling her possessively. "I will take you for my wife, Anna, this very next fortnight. We shall go to the church and announce it. Your husband is dead. You belong to me now."

"Constance is already your wife, Lord Maleagant."

"That shriveling hag has born me not a single heir," the callous cad denounced.

"Yet she remains your wife, so the two of us can never be--"

"She will not get in the way of us," the king insisted, but Anna slipped from his grasp.

"Yet until she is no more... My conscience cannot allow this to continue," she repeated, pulling on her dressing gown. Maleagant chased after her, and Morgan turned her shadow eyes away from that disgusting sight of hairy bare backside.

Maleagant seized his harlot from behind, brushing back her hair and whispering insistently, "Constance will be dead by tomorrow night. An unfortunate accident, choking on her dinner. You know a fitting recipe I can feed her, do you not?"

Morgan could endure no more of this, not without losing her stomach. The emptied goblets on the dresser shattered in sprays of glass, and Maleagant shouted out in alarm.

Anna simply put a hand to her forehead. "Such... poorly tempered glass," she announced, eyes searching the shadows and voice tight with strain. "Pushed by the wind, one glass knocked against the other and they appear to have shattered."

"No, this castle is cursed," Maleagant denounced, seizing his sword from the bedside and drawing it free of its sheath. "That witch is still here, isn't she? She never left--"

"I am a witch," Morgan announced coldly, stepping out from her cover. "And you, my lord? You are a fat and lecherous pig."

"Oh no," Anna muttered, and Maleagant gave a panicked shriek, vocal cords shifting along with his snout, as he dropped down to all fours with his round shriveled flesh looking much more fitting now, as he lay on his back with hooves flailing panickedly in the air.

"Sister," Anna sighed, eyes tearing in frustration, as she unexpectedly knelt at her feet. "Please turn him back. You've no idea what I've suffered through to--"

"To bed an old warlord and get him to play along with the poisoning of his wife?" Morgan cut her off savagely, teleporting the floundering swine out to a farm on the outskirts of the city to be free of the disruption of his shrieking. "I do not care what you've 'suffered'. You are as despicable as always! I cannot believe I came all this way to seek *your* council--"

"Despicable though it may be, you left me with no other choice!" Anna shouted, towering over her now and making her shrink back in spite of herself. "You *killed* my husband!"

"And you thanked me for it!"

"Thanked you for your rash, vindictive actions creating a power vacuum and throwing my entire family into danger? Yes, I was so very gracious at the time, now wasn't I?" Anna snapped, and Morgan deflated. "Then, you ran away, and King Maleagant and his armies seized Camelot a mere month after you left! They would have executed Gawain and all the other boys, including my son, as threats to his reign had I not plead upon his mercy. Now we are prisoners, all of us! Nothing but captives, until I worked my way closer to him, so *I* was the one in power! I could have born him an heir and been queen once again, but you just had to go and..." She sobbed, hugging herself and shaking. She really had suffered this night, as despicable as she was... She had suffered, and Morgan had made it all for nothing. "You think it's easy? Being an ordinary woman? The rest of us do not have your grand powers, Morgan. We are at their mercy unless we are clever, unless we do whatever is necessary..."

"I'm sorry," Morgan whispered, taking her hands. "I didn't..." She put her arms around Anna, pulling her close.

"I haven't even seen my son in weeks," Anna sobbed. "Weeks! He may already be dead."

"He isn't. He's fine," Morgan assured her quickly, pointing her toward the wash basin at the side of the room. "Look."

She conjured the image of little Gareth being tended to by his nursemaid in his securely locked tower.

The Tale of ~~King Arthur~~ Morgan Le Fay

Anna smiled, sobbing in relief. Then she wiped back her tears, meeting Morgan's eyes with compelling sincerity. "C-could you bring that wretch Maleagant back now? Before his men notice?" Morgan tensed. "You can vanish his wife from the castle if you want. Then I won't have to kill her. Give her some happy life in the countryside."

Morgan dropped her hand, turning her back coldly and walking off toward the window. "Please, Morgan!" Anna cried out. "We will all of us be killed. Even if you burn all these invaders, drive them all away... More will come, more of the same. I can help you get back your throne. I can. But for now... I need this."

"I will not summon back that disgusting snake," Morgan hissed. "He well deserves the fate I have imparted." She paused. "What of Sir Lucan?"

Anna rolled her eyes. "Lucan is a pauper knight from a landless family with precious few allies. Why do you think we lost the castle in the first place?"

"But he would do anything for you."

"Yes, of course he would," Anna insisted primly, crossing her arms.

"Then he can protect you and your family," Morgan declared, summoning a text from her library detailing the preparations for a particular mystical potion.

Morgan took one of the disgustingly stained sheets from the bed and disintegrated it down into a key ingredient, as Anna eagerly watched. Morgan then used her contraptions of alchemy and distilling equipment to complete for her sister a vile smelling brew that would deliver her the life she wished. "Only until I come to reclaim this seat," she cemented at the end of it. "And you had better not kill his wife, or I shall punish you. Truly."

Anna gave an eager nod and a flowery, vehement swear, so Morgan summoned Sir Lucan from the sorry tavern in Gloucester where he had been drinking away his sorrows. Anna explained to him in detail the scheme, with Morgan standing by in silent, glaring judgment. Lucan gave an eager nod, easily assenting to it.

The potion would allow him to assume Lord Maleagant's appearance and voice for a period of a few hours at a time. The batch Morgan had brewed contained about two years worth of daily doses, so the cheating lovebirds had best use it wisely. The rest of the time Lucan would retain his own face and figure, as that was clearly the only thing about him that Anna was interested in anyway.

Anna thanked her fervently, and Morgan coldly departed the castle. She no longer wished to hear her advice on securing a husband. Anna would simply urge her to seek out the most powerful man possible, no matter how disgusting his character. Better that Morgan be left to her own devices. She could snare any suitor she wished, she reminded herself, for she was not just a witch punishing the wicked. She was a soon to be legendary paramour, the most beautiful woman on earth. The magic would make her beautiful.

The Tale of ~~King Arthur~~Morgan Le Fay

XV. 𝕿𝖍𝖊 𝕷𝖔𝖛𝖊𝖑𝖞 𝕷𝖎𝖊 𝖔𝖋 𝕺𝖚𝖗 𝕷𝖆𝖉𝖞

𝕸organ the lonely changeling spent a long time holed up in her castle in Wales, plotting her triumphant return to Camelot. And then questioning whatever scheme she came up with, overthinking every possible thing that might go wrong. And then correcting all those flaws, and bragging to the most attentive and appreciative seeming spiders every detail of her now perfected scheme. And then waking up in the middle of the night with the panicked realization that she needed to start completely from scratch and concoct a new scheme, because her perfect plan was surely spoiled now that she had said any detail of it aloud, since Merlin was most assuredly spying on her.

Or maybe he wasn't. He was overconfident and fickle, and he cared nothing about her welfare, so why would he waste his time looking in on her?

All the same... she could feel someone watching her. She **knew** she was being watched. No matter how many times she scoured the halls for ghosts, burning away the essence of any she found lurking in her home, she still felt those eyes upon her, so she dedicated a few months of diligent study to reviewing the ancient writings of magicians and scholars from around the world, until she found a way to block Merlin's scrying, just as he had blinded her. She felt better, as she finished casting that masterful bit of cloaking. Now no one had to see her, no one she did not allow into these halls. No one had to see her real face, not ever again.

She scouted out potential suitors in her looking glass and spent day after day envisioning an encounter with them, as she sculpted for herself a face befitting a queen. She scried a dozen potential husbands from names she had heard muttered throughout court by her enemies, those with esteem who could have threatened even someone like Maleagant or her father. King Urien was the most promising. He was King Lot's younger brother, the ruler of all of Orkney and north England in wake of his brother's passing. He was only a single decade older than her, and he was not yet married. He was far more focused on battle tactics and statecraft than he was on the drinking and womanizing that most other men pissed away the evenings with. Still, despite his reserved manner, he would fall for Morgan instantly, at one look at her new face...

She held up nervously the mirror, making cold and careful study of her countenance for the thousandth time that day. This false face did not have the darkened circles that always ringed her true eyes. It did not have the jagged nails bitten down to the bloody quick. This false face covered up every flaw and weakness. She looked absolutely perfect, she assured herself. She looked just like her mother, but at Morgan's own age of seventeen, with lines scored away and a few other subtle changes. She had made her lips a little fuller and her cheekbones a little more pronounced and painted her skin with such an ivory white that it gave compelling contrast to her shining black locks and thick lashes. It looked enchanting. She was as beautiful as any of the women who had driven knights and dukes to war for her hand. Or... she was pretty sure she was anyway. She needed a little feedback to reassure her of this.

She opened the portal on impulse and yanked her sister right out from the middle of her morning tea, plopping her down in the chair beside her in a poof of dust. Anna coughed, dropping her teacup and staring in alarm at the cobweb filled throne room aglow with eerie green light.

Then her gaze settled on Morgan, and her eyes widened further. "Morgan? Is that you?" Morgan blushed. "Why you look absolutely ravishing!"

She seized Morgan's hand, twirling her about, and Morgan could not help but smile. "I know," she murmured, flipping back her hair. "It is the face that all shall adore and fawn over."

"And grow tight in the trousers for," Anna added wickedly, "yet this hellish gloom is doing nothing but detract from it. Do you not have windows in this place?"

"I do not need windows. I can summon any light I wish," Morgan excused, waving her hand and lighting the rusting chandelier along with a host of other candles to fill the room with a warm and brilliant glow.

"Sunlight, Morgan. It is ten in the morning. You need some sun."

"Ten in the morning, yet you were just now rising?" Morgan prompted, looking pointedly to Anna's dressing gown and spilled cup of undrunk tea.

"I had an itch and decided to keep Lucan in bed this morning for a little while longer before he had to put on that dreadful other face," Anna illuminated, already leading her off down the hall in search of a window or balcony. "Good God, this place is dreadful."

Morgan looked down, shrugging. "It is a regal enough estate, a fortress to repel armies."

The Tale of ~~King Arthur~~ Morgan Le Fay

"Filled with cobwebs and mold and not a single servant in sight to serve us tea or set to polishing the rust from these sconces."

"I do not need servants. I can clean this entire castle with a snap of my fingers. Probably," Morgan retorted, though granted she had never researched if there was a such thing as a cleaning spell, as she had seen no use for one.

"And yet you haven't dusted a single table here, now have you?" Anna noted, looking back at her in judging cynicism. "Have you really just been brooding here alone this entire past year?"

"Of course not!" Morgan snapped, throwing open the doors to the balcony ahead and letting in a surge of fresh air and pale gray light. "I have been plotting my ascension to the throne, a plot that involves a great deal of... thinking and practice and study to achieve!"

"Really? Because it rather sounds like you're overthinking it," Anna gently criticized, and Morgan's blush deepened. "All it takes is a good seduction of a man with an army. So draw us up some chairs and tea, and I can shake off this drowsiness and get a better look at that lovely new face of yours."

They sat outside in the open wind of the chill and misty morning, as Anna sipped tea and grimaced out at the lovely scenery of mountains and distant ocean. "Ugh. So quiet, and gloomy. No birds or bustle of townsfolk..." Anna spotted clearly Morgan's steadily darkening expression, and she pasted on a quick smile. "Though I suppose that's why you need to reclaim Castle Camelot, now isn't it? Much sunnier real estate down there, and we have all of us been missing you terribly. So, let's hear it." She leaned forward, setting down her cup. "Which dashing king has the great Morgan Pendragon selected to pull out her sword and put his sword in her--"

"Anna, honestly, if I have to hear another filthy euphemism--"

"You're going to turn so red that blush will overtake your entire face in permanent fixture, ruining your lovely skin tone. Yes, I apologize." Anna giggled.

"Anyhow, I have noticed that King Urien is quite the statesman."

Anna perked up noticeably, slapping her arm. "That's perfect! He is! Lucan and I have been in talks with Urien this entire past year in fact. We're trying to get him to send a procession to Camelot. When he does, you can be there to greet him and snare his little heart so he will cease causing 'Lord Maleagant' and I such difficulty."

"I am not going to appease him for your sake," Morgan reminded her sharply. "I am simply going to use his impressive armies to retake my lands. Though..." She faltered. "Surely he would have a grudge against the sorceress who slew his brother, even if he has not spoken of it that I have observed. And I am not sure how to allay that hate. Every other candidate I considered to... aid me is either too weak or too old or already married..."

"Which is why Urien is certainly the right choice for you," Anna supported. "And I will have you know he hated Lot. That's why he never visited his nephews, even the world's best behaved and most enchanting boy, my beautiful Gareth."

"Just because he disliked his brother, does not mean honor will not still compel him to..."

Anna seized her hand, and her words trailed off, as the smiling queen stared her down compellingly. "It was God himself who smote down my former husband, Morgan. I know it, and so does all of Camelot. In fact, we have been experiencing a time of great prosperity and bountiful crops this year, and many proclaim, with my support, that it is the presence of our holy sword Excalibur that has caused this sudden change in fortune. Were a true king to emerge and pull it free now with the dazzling new you at his side, I can only imagine the great blessings that would come over our country. I can hear already the people's celebrations, accepting eagerly their one true king."

Morgan smiled, nodding along and feeling the tension ease from her shoulders. "It is a perfect plan. I have laid all the groundwork. Now I will wed Urien and have him play out my legend, and no one will have any claim to challenge us."

"Indeed. It is a flawless plan," Anna supported. "So long as you do not use the name Pendragon."

Morgan blinked. "Excuse me?"

"Well, just look at you. You're not plain, cursed changeling Morgan Pendragon any longer. You have reinvented yourself entirely, and now require a new name to accompany your transformation."

Morgan's eyes flashed. "I did all this so I could reclaim my throne, not spend my days pretending--"

"No one would trust the man wed to Morgan Pendragon," Anna cut her off coldly. "No one would accept as rightful king the companion of the sorceress who sealed up our holy sword in the first place and plunged Camelot into gloom and crop killing hail storms for an entire month."

"I ended that storm after only a few days!"

"Yet it is remembered as much longer," Anna chided, wincing with feigned regret. "And I do not seek to wound you, Morgan, but you must see sense. Our people will never accept the old you as their queen, even with a pretty face pasted on top." Morgan flinched. "They will however, embrace with open arms a poised and beautiful queen married to the great lord chosen by God who freed the sword Excalibur from its mythically impregnable prison. You will approach King Urien as my cousin, Morganna."

"Morg*anna*?" she criticized.

"What? I thought it was cute. A nod to our unbreakable bond of sisterhood, but you're right. It is far too obvious. What about Genevieve?" She eyed her up and down, nodding to herself. "Yes, you look like a Genevieve. Our bodacious Lady Genevieve, the most breathtaking flower of the De'Gaur lineage."

"I am not some unheard of distant relation of *your* family," Morgan spat, jerking back her hands. "I am Morgan Pen--" Her voice cracked before she could get out the words. She was not in fact a true Pendragon. She was an imposter, the bastard seed of Merlin, unwanted and unclaimed.

"Just come with me back to Camelot," Anna whispered compellingly. "We can speak more of this there. You have spent too long trying to do this on your own, Morgan, holed up in this dreadful haunted fortress--"

"Be gone," Morgan muttered, and just like that she was, vanished back to her city to sit on Morgan's throne, the throne she had stolen from Igraine that Morgan was far too foolish and socially inept to rid her of. Anna's absence left a painful hole though. Even as much as she despised her manipulative advice and her whorish nature, it had been nice to talk about her feelings, sipping tea and giggling in company with family...

She found herself thinking of Arthur then, and Merlin's desire to keep him permanently protected from his dangerous witch of a sister. She was giving the druid exactly what he wanted, she realized, by staying cloistered inside this remote fortress, allowing Arthur to grow up in coddled, blissful ignorance...

She had sworn to humiliate him, to humiliate them both. And she would do that by taking Camelot's throne, by...

By becoming some lie of a persona and selling herself off in marriage. That was the essence of her plan, she reflected, and it was coming off as decidedly depressing today. What was the worth in being named queen of Camelot if she could not even use her own name? Neither Merlin nor Arthur would even know her new face, and...

And damn it, she was questioning her entire scheme. Again.

Yet even the thought of this plan's success, after hammering out the details with Anna... It was making her miserable. Maybe she aught not to bother with marrying some foreign king. Maybe she should just head over to Sir Ector's estate and kidnap Arthur, imprison him forever so that neither of them would ever have the throne.

She changed into a raven without a second thought and flew off to England, right up to the estate of Sir Ector. There was no shield in place to ward against her approach like the one she had put in place over her own fortress. How utterly infuriating. Merlin clearly did not see her as a legitimate threat. He thought he could teleport her away or imprison her again the second she revealed herself here. Still, he would not see her coming this time, she swore. She was far more powerful than the last time she had fought him, and he could no longer keep spying tabs on her movements.

She slipped into Arthur's bedroom and roosted in the rafters right above his head. He was a good deal taller than the last time she had seen him. *Nine years old*, she reminded herself. Anna was right; she had spent too long sealed up inside that castle, with not even the ghosts to keep her company. Time was slipping away from her, and the only true living Pendragon, Igraine's only beloved child, would soon be all grown up, abandoning his safe and hidden nest and campaigning to steal *her* throne.

Maybe she really aught to kill him, end the threat in permanence...

Her talons clenched. The rafter creaked, and Arthur blinked up at her sleepily, having the audacity to smile. "Well hullo. How'd you get in here?"

Damn it, why the hell wasn't he terrified? He was clearly far too stupid to be terrified, but Morgan could quickly remedy the error. Her feathers turned to dripping tar, and Arthur stiffened, blinking in alarm. "Merlin's nowhere near," Morgan called out in eerie, sing-song taunt, rising from gooey puddle on the floor into a looming wraith, clad head to toe in menacing black. "He's abandoned you, Arthur. Left you all alone."

Arthur squeezed shut his eyes, giving a shaky exhalation. "I'm dreaming again."

Morgan's hands clenched. "No. You are not. Now..." He had wrapped the blankets tight around his head, blocking her out stubbornly. "Stop that! You will... You will look at me when I speak to you!"

"Can't hear you," Arthur declared in a muffled blur of sound, and Morgan raised her arm, preparing to disintegrate blankets and bed both.

The Tale of ~~King Arthur~~ Morgan Le Fay

It was just then that Arthur's maid, Cara, came storming into the room, rubbing blearily at her eyes. "I thought I heard..." She trailed off, eyes locking on the mass of black robes. "Oh, Merlin. You're back. Sorry to intrude." She headed back out into the hall with an apologetic bow and not a single follow-up question.

"Merlin?" Arthur repeated hopefully, peeking out from beneath his blankets, and Morgan threw up her hands in incredulous frustration.

"Of course not! But what kind of idiots has he entrusted you to?" she demanded, and Arthur flushed, staring her down unhappily. "A strange cloaked figure appears looming at your bedside and yet your primary caretaker walks right off without sounding any sort of alarm or even questioning its presence! I could be a bloody demon, or a specter, and it would be all too bloody easy to kidnap you, so you know what, just forget it!" She disappeared in a dramatic flash of fire.

Arthur squinted at the sudden brightness, then just blearily shook his head. "Sir Ector was right. No more cheese before bed," he murmured, settling back down amongst his cozy nest of feather pillows.

Morgan stormed out into the courtyard in a thunderous burst of wind, and went angrily searching for Merlin, only to find that there really was no trace of him. He was nowhere within leagues of Arthur. He truly had just left him here completely un-warded, as he set off on some quest again, securing some useless relic or falling prey to some fairy lady's charms. Perhaps he abandoned Arthur just as carelessly and frequently as he had his own child.

That thought was in zero way reassuring for some reason, but she had no desire to waste her time lingering here in this household of abrasively cheery fools, simply awaiting his return. She would best Merlin not by fighting him, but by doing as she had resolved and claiming Camelot's throne. It did not matter what name she used or what means she employed to secure her that triumph.

Let Arthur have his happy childhood. Let him stay naive and coddled. The next time she saw him she would be at the head of an army, with a real king at her side and the people all giving fervent praise to their perfect true queen.

XVI. The Permanent Winter of a Paramour

"I will deliver unto thee that sword and that throne, and I will remain by thy side, steadfast, until the end of my days, my queen." The words echoed in Morgan's ears, exactly what she'd always wanted, but feeling not at all how she thought they would as she stepped out from the carriage of a wealthy foreign king who had taken her hand in marriage and had his way with her countless times already.

She gave the words no acknowledgment, and Urien's smile only broadened. He loved it when she played "hard to please" as he called it. The sad truth was that she was not at all playing. When she acted pleased, and breathless, and lustful, as Anna had trained her, that was when she was pretending, though Urien seemed unable to see that.

She had met him over three years past as Lady Genevieve, cousin to Anna De'Gaur: the wife of 'Lord Maleagant' and reigning queen of Camelot. After some rather extensive training from Anna, the newly minted Lady Genevieve had ridden out with a procession of a dozen of Maleagant's greatest knights to the lands of King Urien to press him with talks of peace and stop the advance of his armies crushing in on their north border. Urien had shown no change in expression that summer day he was greeted with her enchanting countenance and host of glowering killers. Three days of scathing wit and verbal sparring on matters of state and this endless war between lords softened him up considerably however. She indulged him in the dances, and the increasingly amorous kisses upon her hand, until one evening at dinner, he whispered in her ear exactly the words her scheming sister had been hoping for. "Peace could be arranged, as a union between our two families. After all, I shall never find another wife as enchanting as thee, my Lady Genevieve."

Morgan allowed him no kiss upon her cheek, though he leaned in rather obviously. She pulled back her head and turned boldly to face him. "If that is a serious proposal, my king, I will see you in church at the end of the month, and you will not sign that insulting piece of paper my cousin bid I present thee with."

He arched an eyebrow, eyes flashing wickedly. "So you do not wish for Maleagant and I to be allies then?"

"Of course not," Morgan asserted. "Camelot's throne is mine."

The Tale of ~~King Arthur~~Morgan Le Fay

"Indeed?" Urien exhaled with barely tampered excitement. Then he nodded resolutely. "Indeed, my lady, it shall be."

They were wed the next month, but as Urien took her to the marriage bed in privacy of their chambers, Morgan stopped him in his tracks. "I meant what I said, about Camelot's throne."

"I know you did, my dear," he gasped, doing his best to quickly rid her of her dress. "And I absolutely adore your ambition, and I will reward every drop of it. I will take back that throne my brother held from his traitorous whore wife, and I will have you at my side as I--"

She caught his wrist, staring him down with eyes bleeding from blue to their regular deep brown. "There is no Lady Genevieve. I am Anna's kin, Morgan Pendragon. That throne was not your brother's, and it certainly is not yours. It is mine and mine alone. If you please me, husband, I will share it with you, but that is the extent of your entitlement."

It was a dangerous and impulsive move, revealing herself like that. Urien's eyes took on a strange and disbelieving cast, but he did not seize her by the throat, nor call for the guards. Instead, he cupped her chin, pressing closer against her with smile steadily broadening. "Morgan Pendragon," he breathed. "So the stories are true. You truly can look any way you wish... I want your true face." She blinked. "The skin in which you were born, every single inch of it. I demand it now, wife."

Morgan pursed her lips, but grimly allowed the rest of her illusion to bleed away, replaced with a flat chested eighteen year old of plain countenance and unseemly freckles. Urien seized her by the back of the head, eyes searching hers with frightening intensity, until he was assured that this was indeed the truth of her appearance.

His smile returned. "You are glorious, my dear." She turned a bright and happy red, allowing him to strip away all her grand clothes and costumes and most amorously consummate their marriage.

They laid their plans to return and seize Camelot in a haze of newly wed bliss, though Urien demanded more of her in the nights that followed. She indulged him, fulfilling any fantasy, and taking any shape he cared to explore. He praised her so passionately, and she felt so loved and nothing but desirable.

Then the months wore on, and she felt nothing but hollow inside and thoroughly done with this game. She showed nothing of that disdain openly of course. She was the wife of a king, and she needed that status and his armies to retake her throne. There were easier ways than fighting endless skirmishes however, and Urien saw that as easily as she did.

They won battle after battle and spent two years solidifying their territory. Then they sent word to Anna and all the Lords of Logres warring throughout the country, calling for a tournament in Camelot to settle their differences and decide in council which warrior of merit was truly deserving of the crown. Urien had the strongest hold over the land, and his forces were already rapidly encroaching on that seat, so that missive was quickly accepted by all the other lords, and they agreed to send champions to fight in joust and prove their prowess.

Morgan did respect Urien's mind and his blunt confidence. She had rapidly tired of being his wife, Lady Genevieve, however, smiling before his court and indulging his evening appetites. He would cut her off mid sentence, whenever they got into a debate about warcraft or politics, showering her with insistent affection and never allowing her to finish her points. She already had to hold her tongue and pretend before his court, so to be silenced in private as well was beyond infuriating, but when she tried to explain that to him, he insisted she was being foolish. Of course he loved her opinions. The cleverness of her tongue simply made her irresistible.

He took whatever he craved, the moment he craved it, and he never seemed to tire of their nights. Even when they ran out of new things to explore, he simply called for whatever he was in the mood for. Even when Morgan had the shaky confidence to remain in her own skin, he did whatever he pleased to her with no less enthusiasm. "We'll have a son in there soon," he would say, kissing her stomach. "You must be careful to keep your own shape then. I want him to have your eyes, those wicked dark eyes."

He loved her real eyes, and he loved whatever mask she put on, because it was her mind behind it. That's what he claimed. He adored her utterly. It was exhausting, and even somewhat frightening. If he had appetites for other women, that was irrelevant, because she could become any one of them, until he had his way and was done with them.

And he treated Genevieve and the real Morgan much better than he did those pretended harlots. He praised her before his men and spoke to her with all respect and reverence before the eyes of all within his kingdom, his paramour and his superior. That worship at first was such a novelty that it of course made Morgan feel warm inside, even when her physical attraction to the man had been worn down to borderline revulsion. Now even the showering praise simply left her irritated. She must have grown into an incredible actress though, because no one could ever detect her ire, not these days.

The Tale of ~~King Arthur~~ Morgan Le Fay

"This is the day, my lady," Urien whispered into her ear, stepping down beside her with arms closing around her back. He kissed her neck, and she stifled a laugh. He knew she was ticklish there, but he kept doing that anyway, and that too angered her. His hands became more active, and she stepped away coldly.

"We are appearing before all of court today, my lord," she reminded him coolly. "We will be in an official setting before their eyes, as your champion, Accolon, puts each and every challenger solidly on their backside, winning us further esteem, before you set out to find a blade for the final sword bout between kings, since your own is so disgracefully spotted with rust."

"Yes, a rusting sword is indeed a problem," he whispered, running his hands up her side. "And you keep mine in such good repair, though another few minutes in the carriage might be beneficial in easing our bodies of tension on this most important day." He had already opened up the door, and she was once again forced to catch his wrist.

"A good queen is never late."

"Yet a king arrives whenever he pleases."

"A lady does not rut down within a carriage parked in a public space."

"No one is looking, and they would never dare defame your honor, my--"

Curse this man, impervious to hints. He had already lifted her back inside the carriage, continuing with his groping until she quite literally shocked him out of it with a flicker of lightning.

He jerked back with a shout, and she angrily straightened her dress. "Do I have to cull you like a dog to heel?"

He seemed far too excited by the idea yet forced his face to remain serious. "Ah, no. I apologize, Morgan. I thought this was the usual game."

"This is an important day," she enforced.

"I know it is, dearest, and you do not need to worry." He pushed back her hair, kissing her demurely on the cheek. "This is a perfect plan, my Lady Genevieve."

He said that so smugly. He said it to reassure her. He had no idea how much she hated him for it, hated having to be this.

He lifted her down from the carriage once again, and she caught clearly the sidelong glances of envy and craving from all the knights around them. She was the Lady Genevieve right now, after all, enhanced mimic of Igraine, as perfect on the outside as she was filthy deep within.

They were greeted at the city gates by the king of pretenders and his conniving queen, riding out amidst a procession of gaudy armored knights with a fanfare of far too many trumpets and shouted announcements of, "Her grace, Queen Anna of Logres, and the great King Maleagant."

Morgan had to commend her sister and Lucan for their organization. They had rationed masterfully the potion she had crafted for them that allowed Sir Lucan to appear as the aged warlord she had sent out to pasture. The liter of brew had only been meant to last two years at most, yet here they were, going on year six and they miraculously still had enough for Lucan to strut about Camelot in the hairy skin of a so-called king. Though of course Anna had the heralds announce her name first, quite boldly revealing that she was the one in power here.

She wondered how many of Malegant's knights Anna was carrying on with in order to keep them in line beneath their weak imposter of a lord. She had scried her sister only a handful of times these past few years, and yet two of those times she had been forced to cut off the viewing almost as soon as it started, after finding Anna engaged in all too typical unfaithfulness right in the middle of the afternoon with someone like Sir Turquine who carried influence within the castle.

Lucan was pretty much as dense as they came however. He had nothing but oblivious praise for his wife's "masterful diplomacy" in reassuring their troops and allies. The woman was back to her wicked old ways, but at least she had not poisoned anyone recently, so Morgan would permit her those vices. She was far too busy with her own scheme to be bothered to correct her.

"Oh, how it fills my heart with joy to welcome family back to our city!" Anna proclaimed, striding right up to Morgan and pulling her into an instant, near-suffocating embrace. "It has been too long, cousin. I never had the chance to congratulate you on your marriage." She pulled back, looking pointedly over at Urien with eyes hardening noticeably. "Though it is of course such a slight that you never came to visit before this, so rudely responding to all of my many letters. I suppose your king encourages such uncordial acts. Yes you, Urien, the lord who chooses to wage war against your brother's widow, the rightful guardian of Lot's throne."

"It was never Lot's throne. And you lost all sympathy from me the day you bedded that cad," Urien retorted bluntly, nodding to the false Maleagant.

The true Maleagant would have killed him for that insult. Lucan simply looked to Anna, who hadn't a mind to instruct him just now, too busy glaring at her former brother in law.

The Tale of ~~King Arthur~~ Morgan Le Fay

"Your stewardship of this throne was never earned and will no longer be permitted to persist," Urien continued coldly, "not after today. The other Lords of Logres will surely agree with my assessment that you are not fit to hold this city. You have done nothing whatsoever to unify this country. You have only driven us to further division."

"Such pretentious words from a foreign king," Anna clucked, eyes shifting back to Morgan. "Yet it matters not. We came here today for some friendly sport. I look forward to seeing the efforts of your champion, as I know our good King Urien will of course leave that game to younger men."

"As will our false king Maleagant," Urien retorted, and Lucan and Anna both stiffened noticeably. "Though it is a shame we won't be seeing our good Sir Lucan this day. I had heard he is quite the artist on horseback, and he is certainly still young enough to hold a lance, unlike the rotting corpse stood before me."

Lucan looked away in frustrated shame rather than drawing his sword, and Anna's smile grew strained. "Be grateful none of our men were near enough to hear all these deadly insults, brother, else we would have to take action to avenge such slights and drown out this innuendo with much louder revelation. After all, it is your wife's own brew that keeps my Lord Maleagant in such good health, as I am sure she has told you. I would just love to share that recipe with my court, and to talk of old times and feast days..."

"Do you think there is anything you could say that would stir up more gossip than what I could inflict upon you with but a twitch of my finger?" Morgan threatened, and Anna bit her tongue. "I thought we were true sisters, Anna. I thought you understood your place, to graciously give way before the rightful queen of Camelot."

"All thrones hinge on a rightful king, dear sister," Anna breathed, "but yes, I have indeed prepared myself to face this day. I simply weep for what was lost, the chance for us to both be happy, working alongside one another as we once did, instead of bracing for attack."

Anna held out her elbow, and her false faced king led her away at a stately walk toward the colorful pavilions of the field of tourney ahead. "I shall see you in the stands! You may have another dramatic play prepared for later, Morgan, but my house will be the one winning all the laurels this day, be assured."

"I could still have her executed," Urien offered, "for poisoning your mother, ruining your good name."

"No, my lord. Perhaps you would not understand, but I've a fondness for that snake." He grunted, half laugh and half derision. "My little pet may never behave, but she does still seek out warmth, and I rather enjoy that manipulative embrace. Little spats like today are nothing of concern. It is simply in her nature to be venomous."

"Yet should she bite and truly wound thee, I will carve her pretty head from her shoulders, mercy and propriety be damned."

Morgan felt a jarring chill at the words, and she seized Urien's hand, eyes weighing into him warningly. "You will do nothing to Anna," she enforced. "She is not a threat."

"Of course not." Urien smiled, pulling on her hand and steering her toward the field of mock battle ahead.

Morgan headed into the stands and found they'd been saved a pair of padded seats right below Anna and 'Maleagant'. They sat there without protest, as Anna bragged loudly about the skills of their champion. It was Gawain, seventeen years old and sat proudly in a resplendent set of silver armor on back of his stallion impatiently pawing the ground. He locked eyes with Morgan, as he felt her studying him, and he rode right up to the stands, tipping his lance with a flourish. "My lady, I don't believe we've met."

"I am your uncle, boy," Urien responded in her place. "King Urien of Orkney and of Norway and Hampshire and Cornwall. And of course you have met your step-mother's cousin, the Lady Genevieve. My wife."

"Anna's cousin?" Morgan allowed her eyes to bleed to brown for the briefest instant; she was not sure why. Gawain's expression instantly hardened in response. "Indeed it is. Pleased to make your acquaintance, uncle. I do indeed already know your wife. Best of luck with that. I'm sure my father is rolling in his grave, but then you never liked him anyway, correct?"

"Watch your tongue, boy," Urien growled. "Insult my queen in any way, and I shall call for a duel."

"That would indeed be tragic, uncle, as you would surely lose, and I've no mind to slay kin. Our family has lost enough as it is."

He rode off without another word, and Urien sank back in his seat with fist clenching. "Start the match already! I need to see that boy flat on his backside," he added under his breath.

That never happened however. Gawain won easily all of the first four bouts, with his opponents landing at most a single glancing blow before his lance shattered into their helms or threw them from their steeds.

The Tale of ~~King Arthur~~Morgan Le Fay

"I will best that child and win this entire tourney for thee, my queen," Sir Accolon announced, as the next bracket of matches began. Morgan graced him with the briefest, fake smile, and he gave a reverent bow, eyes glued longingly to her lips.

Urien's responding glare quickly shattered the knight's starry eyed enthusiasm however, as he tried quickly to squash the confession. "A-and for thee, my king. Of course. F-for our kingdom."

He rushed off to the field and scrambled up onto the back of his horse. "I think I shall go out there and meet our good Accolon in joust," Urien declared, and Morgan arched an eyebrow. "Run a lance through his eye for daring to look at you like that."

"A king does not joust, Urien. Save your energies for the sword."

"Oh, I've energy aplenty. Though I am shocked at how blind I have been to our men leering at you so openly like that." He paused. "How often has he looked at you like that?"

"They all stare, my lord, but they are only seeing a costume," Morgan soothed, "a woman who does not even exist, whose shape was crafted to distract and stir desire. Do not begrudge them such glances. They are not lusting after your wife. They do not even know the face of Morgan, and never shall they look upon it." The words were distant and hollow, as her false perfect eyes scanned over the crowd of knights and lords all eyeing her with such clear desire.

They would never know Morgan, the scrawny young sorceress. All the sonnets would be about the lovely Queen Genevieve, pretty arm ornament of her powerful husband, the conqueror Urien, who pulled free the mythic sword and became England's rightful king.

Urien had said something in response to her assurances, but she had not heard it. She did notice quite clearly his continued scowls however. It seemed she had not distracted him enough this day. Now that his eyes were off of her and noticing the frequent glances of those around them, he was slipping into that frightening state of jealousy he so often displayed whenever they ventured outside of his carefully controlled court.

"Have you prepared for me a tower, my lord?" Morgan found herself murmuring. "To keep away the eyes of other men? Would you dare such a thing?"

"Of course not, my goddess. I would never seek to clip those lovely wings of yours. I will simply maim any that dares lay hand upon them."

The chill inside grew deeper. "You know they haven't though, and you cannot maim a fellow noble simply for a glance or a misspoken phrase."

"I am a king. I can do whatever I wish. Just as you can," he whispered, kissing her hand. "But I would never ruin your careful plans, my dear, nor make us more enemies we do not need."

"Let's just watch the joust then, shall we?"

"It is perfectly acceptable to unhorse that whelp for staring at you like that however," Urien concluded, eyes going to a new knight just now stepping out onto the field in a set of aged and poorly fitted plate. "Accolon I can punish in private, but first let's see him beat down that wretch."

Morgan followed her husband's glare to the knight in question, and she herself could not help but stare. He seemed to grow bolder at the attention, shooting her a smile. She was far from interested in this stubble cheeked sixteen year old however. She simply recognized him, just as she recognized the young squire staggering up behind him. Kay, Sir Ector's son, had come to joust, and right there at his side was young Arthur, bulky lance shoved rudely into his chest, as Kay stalked cockily up to greet her.

"I invited good Sir Ector's son to our tourney of course," Anna smugly announced, as she took note of Morgan's stare. "It seems you overlooked his invitation. And his young squire over there... Why, he looks so familiar, now doesn't he? Though I did not catch his name... But you know it. Now don't you?"

"Some country kin of a retired and crippled knight is hardly worthy of interest," Urien dismissed, his anger a growing storm cloud, for Kay was still advancing on them.

The boy was blind to Urien's glare of warning, pulled in by the wondering blue eyed stare of the siren before him. "My Lady Genevieve, you are the talk of the tourney," he idiotically proclaimed, giving a haughty bow with eyes never leaving her face. "But I shall win this match for thee."

"You're fighting her own champion, you dunce," Urien spat. "And you've not the status to speak to us, so run off before I have you flogged."

Kay paled at the words and hastily returned to his charger, snatching the lance back from Arthur. He could not help but keep looking back at Genevieve however, and she turned quickly to her husband, laying her hand atop his own. "It is comical, is it not? How the boy thinks he stands a chance with such a great man's wife."

The words churned her stomach, but they bolstered her king's ego, as predicted. "It is comical," he agreed, kissing her fiercely.

"My lord, we are in public," she gasped, breaking away.

"Then God give me the patience to wait for privacy, for I swear to him there shall be no sleep for you this night."

The Tale of ~~King Arthur~~ **Morgan Le Fay**

She forced a smile and feigned the same hungry enthusiasm she saw mirrored within his own gaze. He spent the rest of the matches fiddling with her hand, whispering comments into her ear and using that cover to occasionally seize her earlobe between his lips, all while she sat cold and demure, with eyes straight ahead, fixed on the muddy field of flailing mounts and splintering shafts ahead.

He thought it all a game, an impressive show of control from his glorious ice queen who could act in private whatever base driven animal he commanded. The truth remained however, that the Lady Genevieve was nothing but a black hole of lies. All the adoration and compliments from all these coveting eyes felt like nothing but the stinging howl of winter winds, numbing her much abused flesh.

Gawain won all the matches, sending every single opponent limping off in disgrace. The last bout was between him and Accolon. It lasted three rounds. Then the great northern knight fell flat on his back with fully intact lance lying useless beside him. It was the first misstep in the perfect plan of Queen Genevieve, but Morgan could not help but smile.

XVII. Unbreakable Bonding

Of course, that smile turned to glaring rage the second Morgan realized that not only was Arthur here, but Merlin was as well. The drably cloaked druid was idling right outside the castle where Anna was hosting a dinner that was really just a premature discussion amongst the lords of Logres now that the first day of tournament had concluded and only the sword matches remained. The usurper queen would no doubt try to push Urien into accepting his nephew Gawain as "the true king of England", since that would appease both their houses and secure a peaceful future for their country. Urien would never assent to it of course, but Genevieve aught to be there at his side regardless, encouraging him and steering the discourse of the other lords and their ladies.

She found her pulse quickened with alarming suddenness though, the second she set foot in that feast hall. She could barely breathe, and she had no mind for politics. And she certainly had no appetite to eat or drink so much as a single drop within the room where her mother had been poisoned. She quickly excused herself, instructing Urien to remain and do his duty, posturing politics in her stead. She abandoned those halls and all the many leering eyes and correspondingly possessive embraces of her husband, and went for a walk in the night to clear her head and get under control her ragged breathing before anyone took note of it.

She took a single step out those gates and saw that damn scheming druid. The sight of him turned her jagged breaths into a slow hiss of steam, a blaze of temper that consumed all anxiety and weakness. The traitor was staring right at her sword and anvil, hand to his chin and eyes calmly assessing. "That's not Excalibur, is it?"

She stiffened, eyes flaring. "Of course it is!"

"No. It is a masterfully crafted replica, with none of the blessed properties of its model."

"Properties like what?" she pressed, crossing her arms. "Magic resistance? That really only applies to the two of us, so I highly doubt the people of Camelot will notice."

"They could have used the protection and healing of Avalon though, its scabbard."

She pursed her lips, refusing to admit that she had known nothing of that.

The Tale of ~~King Arthur~~Morgan Le Fay

Merlin glanced back at her coolly, and his eyes became noticeably sad. "You look like your mother," he noted, "much more than you used to."

"If only I had been born this way, right?" she stated airily, forcing a detached and callous tone. "Then I would have been married off much sooner, sparing the king so much trouble fishing for suitors. Though I have to say, the one I have now is quite the enviable catch."

"I'm sorry I missed the wedding." He forced a smile, but his eyes were still sad. "Still, it's good to see you, Morgan. We let a few too many years go by, now didn't we?"

"*We* made no such mistakes," she insisted. "*I* became a master of magic and alchemy and queen of an entire country without allowing you to spy on all my progress, and that I am sorry for. I would have liked for you to see it. I would have liked for you to feel that steadily mounting dread, seeing how powerful I was becoming and knowing I was coming for your little boy, the lost little orphan who will never be king."

"He will be king, Morgan. He will be crowned this very spring."

"That scrawny armed child will win no glory in this tournament. And he will never pull free that sword. You have been examining my spell I presume?"

"Yes, a most unbreakable transmutation. The sword you forged has made its identity the anvil, one essence and one solid block, and so never shall the pair of them be parted."

"There's not even a blade beneath that rocky surface anymore. It's all just solid stone with a hilt jutting out," she gloated.

"Yet you think your champion can still pull it free for you and announce himself the rightful king?"

"My king *will* pull it free, and when he does, maybe I will be gracious enough to tell you how it was done, old man."

"I would like that, Morgan. You could tell me inside somewhere, somewhere you don't feel as if you have to keep wearing that ridiculous disguise."

Her eyes flared, nails biting into her palms. "Ridiculous?"

"I didn't mean--"

"I am a beauty beyond compare! The apple in the eye of every knight and lord attending this tournament. Wherever I go people weep with envy and praise my husband as the most fortunate of men, and indeed he is! He is lucky to have me--"

"You? Or this Lady Genevieve."

"Me! He is in love with me. My true face and my mind and my name!" Though the name was still a lie. She had told no one yet that she was not a true Pendragon. Even in her most naked moments of honesty, she was still a cowering liar.

"Well, I am happy for you then."

"I need not your congratulations! Get out of my city! Get out! Before I tear apart all your lies and mysteries before the eyes of these people, have you chased from town and shouted at as warlock and trickster instead of grand adviser--"

"You think that's never happened to me?" he cut her off bluntly, and her words died out. "You think I didn't spend my youth orphaned in the streets getting chased out of each and every village whenever something strange happened?"

"Well how would I know? You never told me about it," she muttered.

"I am telling you now."

"To make me feel a spoiled brat." He had still never apologized for all he had done to her, abandoning her, hiding her away like the shameful mistake she was. He would never apologize. "I must return to the side of my lord. He values my council, especially at such a pivotal time in our conquest."

"Morgan." She turned back just in time to catch the little velvet pouch being lobbed at her head. She undid the laces and stared suspiciously down at the exquisitely crafted crystal sparrow nestled down inside. "A wedding gift. A bit of crystal on the mantel brings light and clarity of vision."

"What curse or spyware have you loaded it with?" she demanded, and Merlin's shoulders slumped, putting a hand to his forehead.

"By God, girl, nothing. There is nothing magical about that. It is just--"

"A piece of glass you conjured up in half a second. Alright then." She dropped it, allowing it to shatter on the stones. "Give it to me in front of everyone next time and maybe I'll keep it. But I've no mind to indulge your guilty secrets."

"Says the woman walking around with a false name, too scared to even show her face."

Her fist clenched, never looking back to see his no doubt cruel and prideful expression. "I am scared of nothing. That is why I am going to walk right back into that feast, the place where my mother died... I am going to walk right back in, before that crowd, and have nothing but adoration. I do not need your gifts to bring me light. And if you wanted me to cherish it..." She shook her head. "You should have made it a crow. Sparrows are weak and dimwitted, but of course you put no thought into it, so it hardly matters that I've shattered it, now does it?"

She marched off before he could say anything further. She marched right back into that hall of drunken lords and became the star of the room, pulling everyone in with her gravity. The hours blurred by and her smile never cracked, until exhausted from all her acting she slogged off to bed. She remained trapped in the skin of Queen Genevieve that entire night however, servicing her husband and given no rest, just as Urien had earlier promised.

Genevieve was not a happy woman. She was just too stubborn to admit it.

XVIII. The One True King

"Fetch me my sword," Urien's tone was cold and commanding, as he held his hand out to the side and his squire brought forth his weapon. The king drew the blade from his sheath, and his brow lowered in perfectly played displeasure. "What is this?"

"My lord?"

Urien pointed coldly to the crusting of rust where the blade of the weapon joined the hilt.

"I-I do not understand," the young noble stuttered. "It was in perfect repair just this--"

"Silence, boy." Urien shoved the sword back into his chest.

"Is this your way of trying to weasel out of our match, your majesty?" Sir Lucan loudly taunted. The man was back in his own skin this morning. 'Lord Malegant' was supposedly watching the matches from the window of the castle, since the chill morning made his joints ache. Morgan wondered if Anna had finally run out of the shape changing potion or if Lucan had simply demanded this glory for himself after all Urien's digs at him the day prior.

"I never back down from a challenge," the king asserted. "I simply need a new sword."

"We've plenty to loan you from the castle armory--" Anna haughtily began.

"I require a sword fit for a king," Urien coldly rejected, striding up the rise toward the hanging bows of the ancient oak by the castle gates where a legendary anvil lay with the false Excalibur sealed forever inside it. The crowd instantly began to murmur in anticipation.

"No way will he pull it free."

"He is Lot's brother."

"Lot wasn't the rightful king. God himself struck down that pretender."

"Someone should fetch the bishop."

"For what reason?"

"Well, what if he does pull it free?"

"Of course he shall," the Lady Genevieve announced, instantly drawing all eyes upon her. "My lord has never lost a battle. God is on his side, and if that sword is his desire, then God will surely grant it to him."

The Tale of ~~King Arthur~~ Morgan Le Fay

Anna frowned at the words, but raced off with all the others in a crowd of steadily mounting hype to see the conquering king pull the sword from the stone. Even commoners rushed out of their houses and flooded the streets. Then a few of them began to gasp, and Morgan looked ahead in confusion. Urien had not yet reached the anvil. He was still a dozen paces away from it when he stopped in his tracks and looked to her and...

The stone was empty. There was no hilt jutting up from it, no tantalizing foot of shining metal. Morgan scrambled right up to the rock with all the decorum of her stately pace abandoned, fingers tracing in shock the narrow slit where her blade had rested just that morning. Now it was just a hole, but... Damn it, her sword was *still* in there. Merlin had simply compressed it down the rest of the way and sealed it completely inside the anvil, invisible and untouchable. He could not separate blade from stone, and so he had simply pushed them into tighter quarters, still firmly bonded, but with no grip anymore to pull it free.

"That cheating--!"

"My lady?" Urien pressed, hand settling on her back.

"Excalibur is gone," the crowd muttered.

"Someone has drawn the blade!"

"Who did it? Did anyone see?"

"No one has drawn it," Morgan snapped. "It has simply..." The crowd stared at her in confusion, and her words trailed off. She could not really explain to them that the sword was still inside and the druid Merlin was just making it look like it had vanished, putting that stupid little hole there as if someone really had drawn it. Now no one would ever have the sword. Unless...

Unless he'd made another replica.

The thought made her pale in anger, and she stalked through the castle gates and over to the stables, shooing away the horses and waving her hand over the filled water trough they had been drinking from.

Urien trailed hesitantly after her, his voice a low pitched whisper. "Dearest, you are acting somewhat erratic."

"Because that bloody druid is ruining my day! And I need to find out who he has given his fake Excalibur, so get your hands off me and stop ruining my bloody focus!"

"As you wish," he grated.

She hardly heard him, concentrating on the waters before her.

She called up the image of the anvil outside the gates, steadily rewinding time to see exactly when and how her sword had vanished. She watched in rage as Lady Genevieve stalked off back to her feast hall the night prior, only for Merlin to immediately push her sword right down into the stone with a single jab of his finger, pulling back his other hand at the same time and crafting his own blade jutting out from her anvil, a perfect bloody replica.

He then walked off and just left it there. She fast forwarded angrily, until she glimpsed a panicking Arthur just ten minutes past, being shouted at by Kay. "I need my sword! Now where did you leave it?"

"With the saddlebags. I swear. It was there just this morning--"

"Stop lying! You've lost it, haven't you? That is my father's sword."

"I'm sorry--"

"My father is counting on me to represent our house! Do you know how shameful this is, having to go around begging to borrow a blade? They already mock me as some country knight. Now I'm going to be late for my duel and--"

"I'll get you another one. A... a grand looking... and you won't have to ask anyone," Arthur swore. "I'll do it for you."

"They are not going to give away a sword to some titleless fourteen year old!"

"Well... What about that one?" Arthur pointed to the sword in the stone, and Kay scoffed.

"Are you a complete idiot? That's the sword in the stone, Excalibur. It's been stuck there for years."

"Then no one will be using it. It's perfect."

Kay shook his head in disgust, running off toward the square where the matches were just beginning. Arthur turned to the sword, wrapped his fingers around the hilt, and pulled it right out.

No one was around to see it however. The courtyard was deserted, the entire city fixated on Urien's grand show happening far down the street, as he shoved aside his own rusted weapon and marched off to seize the mythic sword...

Morgan dashed apart the image with a heavy exhalation. No one had seen Arthur with Excalibur. This situation could still be salvaged. She just needed to find the boy, now, rip that insulting mockery of a model sword from his hands, and--

"Look! That's it there! Excalibur!" Morgan sprinted back out into the square, Urien on her heels. "In the hands of that young knight, Sir Ector's son!"

She staggered to a halt. The entire crowd of nobles and commoners had indeed located the false Excalibur, held up proudly by Sir Kay with a

The Tale of ~~King Arthur~~ Morgan Le Fay

smile across his peach-fuzzed face broad enough to span the seas, especially as he caught sight of flustered Lady Genevieve staring at him. "Indeed. I... I have drawn our holy sword, drawn it free of its rocky prison!"

The peasants roared in jubilant celebration, as Kay's fellows lifted him up onto their shoulders and the older nobles and kings just stared on in shock.

"You bald faced liar!" Morgan shouted, and the celebrations ceased, as every man and woman looked to the normally cool and composed Lady Genevieve in shock. "You drew out the sword, Kay? Really?"

Kay flushed, eyes lowering. "Of course I... It's in my hands, isn't it?"

Arthur stood by with lips pursed and feet awkwardly shuffling, saying nothing to contradict his friend. What a docile little idiot.

"Alright, fine," Morgan snapped. "You drew the sword. So let's see you do it again."

She snatched the weapon from the stunned knight's grasp and stalked up to the anvil, plunging it right back into the mocking little slit Merlin had left for it. "There. Go ahead."

"What have you done?!" Meliodas, Earl of Lyonesse, wailed in dismay. "You re-sealed our holy relic!"

"If he drew it once, he can do it again," Morgan retorted. "Here, before witnesses."

Kay would fail of course. Then Urien would seize the sword and free it in, granted, a somewhat disappointing show far inferior to her original script for today, but still a functional proof that he was the true king of these lands.

Kay swallowed nervously, trudging up to the anvil and reaching out a shaking hand. Morgan kept the blade firmly sealed in place this time of course, and no matter how Kay yanked and strained, the sword would not come free. "You've... you've sealed it back in place forever, woman," he panted in desperate excuse.

Arthur gave a heavy sigh. "That's not a very knightly way to act," he murmured, and Kay flushed.

"Fine. The truth is--"

"The truth is, only a true king can pull free this blade," Urien proclaimed, taking heed of Morgan's firm nudge and stepping up to seize the weapon.

He shot her a glowing smile and... his hand slipped right off the handle. He staggered back in shock, and Morgan cast about in anger, desperately searching the crowd for that damn intruding druid.

"Simply... lost my grip. Palm sweat, from the heat of the day," Urien excused, rubbing his palms on his trousers and grimly repositioning himself.

The blade would not budge, no matter how he strained, and no matter how Morgan bolstered his efforts, even going so far as to crack open the stone--

The bloody stone mended itself, and Urien slumped to the ground, looking to her in dismay.

"Only *our* true king can pull it free!" a village boy shouted. "That foreign blowhard don't got no right to rule Camelot!"

Urien flushed in rage, but that impishly smiling boy melted back into the crowd before the king could call for him to be punished for his mockery. Morgan knew that smile, and those mischievous dark eyes, but she lost track of Merlin as quickly as she had spotted him. Where had he gone, and who was he now? He certainly would not have wandered far.

"Only our true king can free it," the people were all agreeing.

"Then who pulled it free in the first place?"

"Him," Kay sighed, shoving Arthur forward. "My squire. Arthur."

"Some back country peasant freed Excalibur?" King Marcus scoffed.

"That boy is no peasant!" Anna gasped in dramatic performance, rushing up to Arthur and seizing his hands. "Arthur you said your name was? Not Arthur Pendragon, surely. But, oh! You look so much like my dear little cousin, Uther's son, so long believed dead."

"My mother was Igraine of Logres and my father was Uther Pendragon," Arthur confirmed somewhat shyly, and Kay's eyes bulged. It appeared Arthur had never told him his true parentage.

"Then the true king has indeed returned!" Anna proclaimed, showing him off to the crowd with hands settled possessively on his shoulders. "Come to free holy Excalibur and put an end to all these years of pointless warfare and bloodshed--"

"Enough!" Morgan shouted, and the skies began to darken, causing the crowd to mutter nervously and Urien to whisper urgent warning into her ear.

"Morgan..."

She ripped her hand free of his grasp, gesturing to Arthur in derogatory judgment. "Who cares if that is Uther's brat? He is not fit to rule this kingdom! Just look at him! Put him on the throne, he would be dead inside a month. He is not strong enough to even lift Excalibur, much less pull it free of its prison. He has **not** liberated our holy sword. It still sits there before us, sealed in its stone--"

The Tale of ~~King Arthur~~ Morgan Le Fay

"Because you stuck it back in there, you fool!" Meliodas growled, and Urien looked to him with deadly eyes flashing.

"That is my lady *queen* to you, earl," the conqueror hissed. "Temper your tone, or I will see your entire kingdom brought to ruin in penance."

"It seems we've no gentlemen amidst this rabble of lords," Anna clucked in dismay. "My young cousin seems indeed the only noble hearted one among us, seeking no glory or fame with peacocking shows of arms." Lucan flushed, as did Gawain, eyes glued to their boots. "With great humility did he free our holy relic from its prison, and for love of his friend and the good of the country did he remain silent as that boy dishonorably sought to take credit for the act.

"Perhaps you doubt you are strong enough," she whispered to Arthur, lifting his chin to meet her hypocritically tender stare. "just as cruel Lady Genevieve has so callously denounced, but I believe in you, Arthur. The people believe in you."

"Fine then, Anna. Let's see him do it," Morgan snapped, gesturing sharply to the stone. "Go on, Arthur, pull out the sword. We're waiting."

The thunder crashed, and the people murmured to themselves, as Arthur looked first to the ominously roiling clouds then to the glaring woman stood with arms crossed between him and the stone.

"Have no fear, my child!" the old bishop proclaimed, striding out into the square, only... Curse it all, that wasn't the bishop! That was Merlin. Morgan could see it clearly in his smug, twinkling eyes. "God himself is watching over you this day. No ill shall befall you, should your heart be pure. Stride forth, young king, and seize thy birthright!"

Arthur exhaled, closing his eyes to the crowd of onlookers around him and looking nervously back to the sword in the stone. "Alright then."

He wrapped his fingers around the hilt. Morgan would not allow him to free it. She poured every inch of her concentration into keeping it stuck fast, as the boy heaved tentatively back upon the blade. A force like a behemoth rose to counter her telekinesis, pulling sharply in the opposite direction. The blade pulled back a full inch, sliding slowly but surely free of its prison.

Morgan grit her teeth, so did Arthur, wrapping his other hand around the hilt with foot pushing against the rock to give him better leverage.

That dreadful other force kept pushing back upon her. Merlin wasn't even grimacing. He just stood there with hands calmly folded into the sleeves of his robes, staring coolly at the sword in the hands of his chosen king.

Morgan felt a vein in her temple pop, vision starting to blur, but she refused to give up the struggle. That sword would stay stuck in its prison, until she alone granted it a wielder. This was supposed to be *her* moment, *her* champion, *her* prophecy--

The tip of the sword scraped free of its casing, as the Lady Genevieve collapsed to the ground with eyes streaming blood and perfect disguise melting away. Urien dropped to her side, sheltering her from sight of the crowd, with his cape wrapped around her protectively to shadow her features.

He needn't have bothered. Every eye in the square was fixed on Arthur, as he staggered back from the anvil with 'holy' sword held up toward the sky. A golden beam of sunlight pierced the clouds and illuminated the young king, as if the heavens themselves were proclaiming his victory. The lords balked, and the peasants all gasped in wonder, dropping to their knees.

"All hail King Arthur!" Anna clapped, and the square feverishly echoed the chant, a roar of manic celebration that Camelot was finally freed of the witch's curse and given back their perfect prodigal son to rule.

Morgan's bleeding eyes peered past Urien and fixed blearily on bishop Merlin, eyeing her sadly with lips pursed, though of course he made no move to aid her, doing nothing to dare compromise this moment for his precious new king. Other people were looking at her now, though each lord was driven back from rushing to the side of the fainted beauty by the blistering glare of her husband. Urien bundled her tight within concealing folds of fabric and quickly carried her from the square.

"I'll kill him..." Morgan mumbled.

"I will kill him for you, my love," Urien whispered, laying her down inside the privacy of a carriage and pushing back her sweat-damp hair. "I will cut that boy in twain along with every leering knight and lord who dared cause you such distress this day--"

"Not Arthur," she grated. "Merlin. I'm going to kill... that... traitor..."

She spent a few more minutes spitting blood, before drifting off into a deep and dreamless slumber, with the arms of her lord cradling her fearfully and murmuring sweet threats into her ear of all the damage he would wreak should she leave him.

The Tale of ~~King Arthur~~ Morgan Le Fay

XIX. Unjust Deserts

He was lying right beside her when she opened her eyes, kissing her forehead and spewing forth an endless stream of thanks and praise that his queen had finally returned to him. She had been unconscious for three days apparently, but King Arthur had graciously granted the fragile Lady Genevieve lodging within the castle to recover from her sudden collapse.

"And recovered I have," she stated coolly. "So you needn't sound so wild, my lord. No simple contest of wills could bring an end to a great sorceress such as I."

"Yet it nearly did so," Urien hissed, holding her face so tightly between his hands and staring her down with fevered insistence. "Those deadly gifts of yours nearly stole you away from me. You mustn't push yourself like that. Not ever again. Do you understand?"

"It's Merlin's fault," she murmured.

"Of course it is," he breathed. "Tell me how to kill him, and I will do so. I will do it immediately. Not that I have sighted the villain since he took his leave this morn..."

"He was *here*?"

"Well I needed him, my love. He healed you. But say the word, and I will cleave his head from his shoulders regardless, for he is surely to blame for your distress as much as he is to thank for..."

She held a finger to his lips, and he fell uncertainly silent. She then turned her back, rolling over onto her side and staring gloomily out the window. This was her old bedroom, she realized, her isolated tower where she had idled away the days reading through epics and setting dolls accidentally aflame, all safely away from the eyes of the great lords and true ladies always prowling the halls of the main castle below.

Urien's arms closed around her, but she remained quiet and aloof. He no doubt assumed this was just her lingering exhaustion, but he would give her no space to recover, silently supporting and smothering her until the sun began to sink and she prodded him gently, "Will not our host and the other lords be expecting you at banquet?"

"I care not one whit what they expect. I will not leave your side until you are well again."

"I am well enough, my lord," she murmured, sitting up. "And it weighs upon me that you have remained holed up inside these rooms, deaf to the developments of this newly forming court sitting right below our feet."

"You are right, I suppose," he exhaled, running a hand through her hair. "My fear has blinded me to proper observances. I have grown too used to having you seated at my side, surveilling all the vipers so I need not be bothered until it comes time to act and put an end to them." He kissed her, and she accepted it numbly. "Feel better, my love. I shall bring you back dinner, whatever you wish."

"I can cook for myself, thank you," she wryly joked, waving her hand and summoning instantly a steaming bowl of soup to sit on her bedside table.

Urien hissed in displeasure, cupping her face. "Do not strain yourself now."

"I am not nearly so fragile."

"Or so you believe, yet I have seen that stony facade of yours cracking far too thoroughly this trip, even before the eyes of others." He ran a finger over her lips. "They almost saw your true face. You swore that was mine alone."

"Of course it is, my lord. Who else would care to look upon it?"

"Yet I could gaze into those eyes for eons and never tire." He kissed her again, but Morgan weakly caught his wrist, pulling back her head.

"The banquet, my lord," she reminded him firmly.

"As you wish." He gave her one final kiss then pulled away, donning the rest of his robes that he had left slumped across a chair. "I shall venture forth to share discourse with our enemies. Then I shall return that we may plot their demise. That throne will still be yours, my queen."

She gave a hollow nod, and Urien departed the room, somewhat foolishly locking the door behind him. Morgan dismissed her bowl of soup without partaking of a single bite, curling back up on the bed and burying her face in the sleeve of her night shift. She was as weak and fragile as her husband so feared. She had not been able to stand up to Merlin. She had not been able to best even a fourteen year old doormat and prevent him from ascending the throne.

A knock came at the door, and she gave a sharp and violent gesture, shattering the lock and near blowing it from its hinges, as it banged open against the wall of the passage without. She did not even attempt to change her face, staring down in glaring challenge the young man who had dared make the long climb up here to leer at her.

The Tale of ~~King Arthur~~ Morgan Le Fay

Gawain straightened coolly and pretended never to have been unnerved by the violent supernatural opening of the door. "Though I am no bus boy," he grated, "I have nonetheless been charged with the delivery of your dinner." He held out the tray of soup in his hands. "As Anna is indisposed this evening and for some reason made it of urgent issue that 'the Lady Genevieve' be seen by any gossiping servant in her current, vulnerable state. And I suppose it is true that the mob would run you out of town were they to realize my uncle's wife was the same shape shifting witch that struck down my father--"

"Yet I see not thy pitch-fork," Morgan snapped, shoving herself to her feet and stalking right up to him. "Perhaps you take after your step-mother and have brought the sickly witch some very carefully seasoned stew to finally put an end to her curses." Morgan snatched the bowl of soup from his hands, sniffing at it dramatically. "Ah yes, pure suffering death with just a faint whiff of arsenic."

"You dare suggest a knight of virtue would--!"

"A crow murdering man-child would indeed seek to slaughter his enemies in any manner possible. Even if that required shooting them in the back with a poorly made bow."

"Or smiting with lightning a great king they were too cowardly to challenge in battle with a proper champion!"

"It is far more cowardly for a woman to hide behind some champion! But your 'great' father was just like you, I suppose, for he also tried to shoot me in the back. This after poisoning my mother and King Uther, his ally, in gleeful scheme alongside your step mother, so congratulations aspiring so diligently to a family resemblance!"

"If I slay thee, witch, tis going to be before the eyes of all our citizens when you have revealed your true shape as some fifty foot nightmare serpent. Then bravely, in battle, will I meet thee!"

"This is my true shape! I only wish it was something so grand as a fifty foot reptile, though your honorless peers will surely praise you just as heartily when you bring them the head of the enervated damsel. Lying is in your blood, so I am sure you shall have no trouble telling them this pale disappointment of a girl truly looked to be a dragon in the moment you struck her with your blade!"

"I have had enough of you defaming my good name--"

"As your parents defamed mine?"

"Know what?" He slurped down a massive mouthful of the soup in his hands.

"Mmm. Yes. This soup is expertly seasoned, richly made, and not at all poisoned, and thus far too good for thee!"

"Give me that!" She snatched the bowl from his hands before he polished it off, goaded by his childish taunts and the fact that this dish did indeed have quite the alluring smell. It tasted far better than conjured soup, and it warmed her considerably.

They stood awkwardly in the doorway then, and Gawain finally took note of the fact that she was in nothing but a flimsy night shift. He hastily averted his gaze, holding his tray quite purposefully before her chest. "Well... you are clearly no longer at risk of starvation, so... Give my regards to my uncle, and... do not do anything horrid to your brother. He has graciously given you rooms within these halls, and he is an honorable lad. Noble, as a king should be."

"Maybe you are not like your father after all," Morgan murmured. "He certainly would not be speaking so fondly of the rival who took his throne."

"It was never my throne," Gawain cemented, "no matter how hard Anna schemed for it. And it was never hers either."

"No, it wasn't." Morgan looked up from her empty bowl of soup, pulling the young knight's eyes back to meet her own. "What is my dear sister indisposed with this evening anyhow?"

"She is grieving her husband," Gawain muttered uncomfortably. "The 'Lord Maleagant' passed away in his sleep just the evening prior, so the other lords are of course planning his funeral while Anna is sealed up in her rooms, utterly inconsolable." Morgan rolled her eyes. "Though this particular evening I believe she will have the pleasure of yet another visit from the young king himself, who appears quite worried about her welfare and the loudly talked about fact that she has eaten nothing whatsoever these past twenty four hours."

"Yet the poor lady's callous step son feels no glimmer of concern for her?" Morgan noted, and Gawain scoffed.

"Oh yes, I am so very concerned that the grief of losing the imaginary lord she was never actually wed to may cause dear Anna to starve herself to death."

"You know Sir Lucan has been wearing the face of Maleagant these past years then?"

"Of course I know. The whole family knows. Me, the twins, and... Well, not Gareth, due to the fact that he's seven years old and an absolute blabbermouth."

The Tale of ~~King Arthur~~ Morgan Le Fay

Morgan smiled, then questioned what it was exactly she was doing just standing here barely clothed in the doorway carrying on a conversation with someone who absolutely hated her. Her smile died, and she looked down at the empty bowl in her hands. "Thank you for the soup, good bus boy," she taunted lightly, holding out the bowl. "But now the evil witch finds herself far too exhausted to endure anymore of this verbal fencing. I concede the victory to Sir Gawain, as skilled with a riposte as always. Goodnight."

He took back the bowl, and his hand lingered atop hers for a moment, eyes weighing into her with uncomfortable intensity, as a steady flush climbed over his cheeks. Finally the boy grit his teeth and averted his gaze. "Good God, you really are shameless, aren't you? Bewitching the nephew of the man you are wed to for simple delight of the torment."

"The hell are you talking about?"

"Find some other young sap to cast your spell upon if you wish to model Anna and break your vows, and leave my dreams already!" She blinked. "Standing here with such an honest face, and those dark eyes always watching me..."

He leaned in to kiss her, and she pulled back from him, shocked. She felt at her face and chest in doubtful confusion, but she had indeed changed nothing of her shape. She was just herself, with frizzing curls and narrow hips and "What the hell is wrong with you?!"

Gawain's flush only deepened, stalking right up to her and stamping his foot. "You are what is wrong with me! What awful hex is this? Where my pulse will not stop pounding and my brow beads with sweat in sight of your..." He eyed her up and down once again, and then quickly shut his eyes, shouting, "Stop pretending you didn't do this! That day in the courtyard when you fell to my arrow. You laid your hex upon me then and have invaded my dreams ever since. Now you want me to give into temptation. Showing your eyes at the tourney grounds, and smiling at my victories..." His eyes opened. "Now... your true face, all vulnerable and..."

He seized her, kissing her fiercely. She drove her fist into his stomach, breaking free of his desperate hold in a most unflattering puff of spit, as he staggered back with a surprised grunt.

"Get out!" she commanded, pointing toward the door. "Go... take a cold bath or something."

He stared at her in bemusement. "You really didn't...?"

"No! And put your hands on me again, I will... Bloody... Well..."

"Turn me into a newt?"

"Yes, a newt. So flee in terror already."

That made him smile for some reason. Then his smile turned bitter, and he swallowed, stumbling out the door. "I... Yes, ah... Goodnight, Lady Morgan. I am... glad you have recovered."

Morgan felt warm inside. She felt warm and frustrated, and certain her husband would kill this idiotic child were ever he to hear of this. It did not matter that the boy was his nephew, a vassal of Camelot's king. Urien would cut his throat and feel nothing but spiteful satisfaction. Morgan crossed her arms and turned into a shadow, hidden and untouchable. She sat as a gloomy puddle in the corner for a few minutes, then went to seek out Anna.

She found her quick enough, dabbing dramatically at her eyes, as she lingered at the side of the young king in a far too well fitted and low cut black dress that looked not at all like the attire of a heartbroken widow. "I apologize, my king. All this weeping must be dreadfully distracting, and you've an entire court waiting on your presence this eve. It is selfish of me to take up so much of your attention."

"It's alright. I don't really know what to do out there on my own anyway," Arthur murmured. "King Marcus and the others keep arguing, asking me all these questions about my father... I don't think they like me very much. I don't think they want me to be king."

"It does not matter what they think," Anna clucked, playfully brushing his lips with her finger. "Your word will be law, because the people absolutely adore you. They will accept no other ruler."

"They don't even know me..."

"Not yet, but God is on your side, Arthur. There can be no other king."

"That's what the bishop and Merlin keep telling people," Arthur muttered, "but I know little of war or peace treaties..."

"Is that humility or insecurity I hear?" Anna teased him tenderly, and Arthur flushed.

"Perhaps a bit of both. I just thought I'd be squiring for Kay this trip. That we could win a trophy or two to sell off and keep the animals fed for the winter. Sir Ector was counting on that." He paused. "But I suppose I can help out much more now, being king and all. And Merlin says the lords will all bend the knee at my coronation next month, regardless of their discontent. And he's a prophet, so... he has to know what he's talking about, right?"

"I myself have been running this court for years you know," Anna stated coyly. "I can be a far more reliable resource than that druid. And I

The Tale of ~~King Arthur~~ Morgan Le Fay

swear I shall pull myself together and join you at every future banquet. I shall sit at your side, and whisper whatever advice you need."

Arthur smiled. "Thank you, cousin."

"We are much closer than cousins. Call me Anna." She said it like a whispered secret, sitting so close beside him, holding his hand...

"What the hell are you doing?" Morgan demanded.

Anna jumped, clasping a hand to her breast and staring at the shadow become glaring sorceress before her. "Morgan. Good God. I did not see you... lurking there. You're feeling all better, I suppose?"

"Morgan?" Arthur repeated, rising hesitantly to his feet. "So you're...?"

"Morgan Pendragon, the great and terrifying. Yes," she snapped impatiently, remembering unhappily that Arthur would not in fact recall ever actually having met her.

"I wouldn't say you're terrifying. I mean... Well, it's nice to meet you." He seemed to genuinely mean that, the foolish little sot. "Are you here for my coronation?"

"No, I came here for *my* coronation. Before you went and stole my sword, humiliated my husband, and near caused me a brain aneurysm overextending myself!"

Arthur stared at her with eyes gradually widening. "Wait, *you're* Lady Genevieve?"

"Of course I am! I would think the roiling thunder clouds that accompanied my anger that day paired with the bleeding eyes and the already started rumors among the people would have clued you in to that fact!" Awkward silence descended over the room for a full minute then, and Morgan crossed her arms self consciously. "Anyway, I need to have a word with Anna, so get out."

"That's not the way you aught to speak to a king," Arthur muttered, "even if you are my sister."

"And how am I supposed to respect you when you say it like that? Have some backbone, Arthur, for God's sake."

"You should not speak to me that way!" he repeated, much more firmly this time. "I hate to say it of family but... God forgive me, you are a horrible person."

"Why thank you for stating the obvious. Now go back to the feast of powerful lords all expecting you, and let me have a word with Anna."

"I... I suppose they are expecting me." He sighed, trudging out of the room.

"Heavy is the head that wears the stolen crown," Morgan muttered to herself, firmly closing the door and turning her glare on Anna, still seated on the bed before her with an expression of pure innocence stamped across her perfectly painted features.

"Been a long while since I've caught a glimpse of that face," Anna noted, eyeing her up and down. "I thought you'd sworn off that plain little girl forever, though she does have a much more effective glare than starry-eyed Genevieve. That I will admit. Though poor Arthur never recognized you. Did you never even bother to visit your little brother?"

"He is *our* brother, in case you have forgotten, you horrid ghoul! You think I can't see what you're doing here?"

Anna gave an arrogant flip of her shining golden curls. "Why whatever do you mean? I was consoling my dear *half* brother, providing him with much needed emotional support during this important transition in his life. The boy needs a mentor, Morgan." The sorceress shook her head in disgust. "Otherwise those scheming lords will eat him alive. And if he happens to develop an all too understandable infatuation with me during our time together... What would be so bad about that? I am once again without a husband after all--"

"He's a fourteen year old boy!"

"They called us women by thirteen. So by customs, he is a man, a man in need of a wife. And the closer within the family one marries within a royal house, the purer the bloodline. It is a time honored tradition."

Morgan wanted to vomit. "It's time you showed your age."

Her words echoed in the air, and Anna's hair instantly began to gray, hands wrinkling, as her chest sagged and her flawless skin freckled with age spots. Anna stared down at her hands in horror and instantly began to hyperventilate. She looked quickly to the mirror on the wall and let out a jagged scream, closing her eyes. "Take it back! Right now! Please!"

"Why should I?" Morgan grated. "So you can swear once again to reform your ways only to revert right back to whorish villainy the second I turn my back?"

"You're the villain!" Anna shrieked, sobbing fat ugly tears, a for once genuine devastation. "You're an absolute monster, and I have had enough of your curses! Playing to your ego, living in fear that you will leave me like..." Her sobbing intensified, and Morgan's smug sense of triumph shriveled into a void within her chest. Anna crawled across the floor and clutched at the hem of her dress, staring up at her tearily. "Just take it back. You have no right to do this to people--"

The Tale of ~~King Arthur~~**Morgan Le Fay**

"You need to learn your lesson," Morgan muttered in paltry defense, vanishing from the room. She truly was the monster everyone made her out to be, haunting the dreams of all who encountered her.

xx. The Evil We Deserve

Morgan wandered the halls as a shadow for many an hour after leaving Anna's room. She gave only the briefest peek into the banquet hall where Merlin was looming and Urien scheming and Arthur sitting nervously in his much contested seat at the head of the feast. The wizard spotted her the second she stretched out from the doorway, and so she instantly retreated. She wanted to be invisible tonight. She wanted to be alone.

She was winding her way aimlessly through the stables when she came across Sir Accolon, or more accurately, the body of Sir Accolon. The knight was barely alive, his face a mangled mess and his breaths a fragile wheeze broken up by bubbles of blood that came sputtering out his broken jaw.

Morgan took the form of his queen, Lady Genevieve, without a second thought and knelt down by his head. She needn't have even bothered with the disguise. The man was unconscious, eyes blank and unseeing. He had been beaten to the brink of death, and she knew in a grim flash of insight exactly who was responsible for the assault.

"Accolon I can punish in private..."
"How often has he looked at you like that?"

Urien's grim words echoed in her mind, replaying themselves alongside the seared in image of the chilling animosity that had burned within his gaze. No doubt he would blame the death of their champion on one of their rivals, perhaps one of Arthur's own knights. He would use his personal revenge to benefit them politically and besmirch the enemy's reputation, coldly calculating as always. Still, Morgan was not about to let this man die. She had far too much suffering already on her head. Even if he woke up cursing her name, seeing her for the witch she was, she refused to let him die.

None of her potions would aid this man of course. She had to instead sculpt with magic a new face and fresh tissue, just as she did in order to heal herself when she transformed. Her experiment was successful, and the knight's shattered nose, jaw, and ribs repaired themselves with unsettling snaps.

His dark eyes fluttered open then, and he stared up at her blearily. "My lady..."

"No," she countered, realizing instantly the error of showing him the face of Lady Genevieve in this moment, only strengthening his foolish pining for the wife of his king. "I am but a stranger. You do not know me, and you never saw me here." She shoved his head from her lap and retreated back into a shadow, fleeing back to her tower and waiting grimly for Urien to arrive.

He came an hour later, exhausted clearly from his long discourse with the other kings. "Your brother does indeed have few allies." He smiled, sinking down beside her. "Still, it is a precarious..."

He trailed off, as she lifted his hand, examining the back of his knuckles. There was no bruising or blood. Clearly, he had been in no fist fights. "Of course you did not do it yourself," she whispered. "So, which of our men was so eager to beat down our champion? Sir Caradoc? He and Accolon had quite the rivalry, didn't they? I would imagine it would be him. Him, and two or three others, so gruesome was the damage, and you would not want so much as a single mark laid upon our other men to indicate their guilt."

His hand gripped hers, pushing it to the side, as he leaned in closer with smile still in place and eyes searching hers. "So, you have heard news of Accolon's passing. And as expected, you have most shrewdly pieced together every detail of the scheme which I would have of course confided in you once the attack became common knowledge. Though you would have had to have gone searching for him to have been able to find him this night, now wouldn't you? Since there were no proclamations down below yet trumpeting the discovery of the corpse—"

"He is not dead." Urien's grip tightened even further, squeezing at her hand with knuckles white, as his eyes weighed into her in rebuking suspicion. "He is *our* champion, Urien. We do not kill our own, the faithful who have in no way wronged or betrayed us--"

"Would you take him for your own then? So loyal and admirable as he is," Urien grated, seizing her jaw. "Do you take after your cousin? Of course you do. You enjoyed the attention, didn't you? You--"

Morgan vanished into shadow as his tone began to rise, slipping right through his fingers and hiding beneath the bed like a frightened little girl, invisible and untouchable.

Urien sat there frozen for a moment and stared down at his empty hand with a look of sheer agony spreading across his face. "Morgan?" he called out softly. "I... I don't know what came over me. I apologize. I did not mean to act such a bear or.... I was not threatening you, or accusing you. I would never... Morgan?"

She did not respond. She stayed hidden and quiet, curled up beneath the bed where even if he lit every lamp and scoured every corner of this room, he would never be able to find her.

"Come back. Please. I will listen as you shout at me. I will bear whatever punishment for my doubt, whatever you think is appropriate. Just come back."

She refused. She waited there silently, until finally, after a full hour of pacing, and cursing, and pleading, and panic, Urien took his leave.

He was her husband, and she had wounded him badly, terrified him twice now, day after day, with the fear that she would leave him. He had terrified her too though, and so she stayed huddled in her hiding place throughout that night and waited for the feelings to subside, waited for the numbness to sweep over her and quiet all the guilt and uncertainty that had so weakened her this day.

She retook her own shape finally, but spent that entire day huddled up in her bedroom. So did Anna. Morgan watched her sister carefully through the looking glass of her wash-basin, as the now old woman stayed veiled and covered upon her bed. She had long since shattered her mirror, speaking to no one and letting in not a single servant or visitor. Morgan kept constant eye on her sister throughout that long day, telling herself over and over that the murderous manipulator was simply acting again, trying to play upon her guilt, so the sorceress would all too quickly undo this curse Anna had well earned with her behavior. Everyone was a liar after all. No one could be trusted. They all deserved their horrible ends.

Anna stayed huddled in the corner and refused all her meals. She drank not one sip either, and she turned away even the king himself when he came to visit her. Then, in a fit of manic motion in the late hours of the night, she drew out a slew of delicate alchemical equipment from a hidden chest of ingredients and set to work grinding up leaves with mortar and pestle. Morgan remembered then that Anna did have quite the intimate knowledge of poisons.

The sorceress teleported to her room in a panic and seized her wrist, keeping her voice forcibly cold and even. "You cannot truly think I'd allow you to kill yourself."

"Why not?" Anna hissed, ripping free her veil. "You've already taken everything from me! Better to be dead!"

The Tale of ~~King Arthur~~Morgan Le Fay

Morgan raised a mirror, showing Anna shakily that she had been restored to her regular age, twenty six and stunning. Anna touched the reflection timidly and immediately started sobbing, collapsing to her knees. This truly had been traumatic for her, but Morgan had not the words to apologize. She didn't even have the presence of mind to take a closer look at the alchemical ingredients spread across the table and realize what the all too familiar recipe was that Anna had been crafting. Morgan just stared in guilty silence at the sobbing woman, laid low at her feet, until Anna finally screamed for her to get out.

She became a shadow once again, slipping off back to her lonely tower, curling up on the bed and burying her face in a pillow.

Eventually the door creaked open, and Urien poked his head in. "Morgan," he gasped in relief. "I... I shall take my distance should you wish it," he forced out coldly.

"Better for you if you did. I've been playing a cruel game too, you see. Tactics no less frightful than what you did to Accolon."

His eyes narrowed, tone darkening. "What do you mean?"

"Surely you remember my pet serpent, my dear sister? I have broken her utterly, made her nightmares a reality and made her walk in that flesh, until she was on the brink of taking her own life," Morgan whispered, turning her head finally with eyes weighing into him gravely. "She despises me now. Just as you will, in time, for my coldness."

Urien sank down at her side with arms wrapping around her. "You are not ice, Morgan. I have seen inside you. Behind that wall of stone you are fury and flame, a goddess of wrath. You have simply been burning yourself out with no one to tend you. That is why I am here." He kissed her sweetly, breathing his words against her lips. "Let the world despise you. We will burn it down together."

She curled up against him complicity, knowing deep down he was just as evil as she was, and yet still far better than a witch like her deserved.

XXI. The Beardless Boy King

The Lady Genevieve returned in all her glory for the banquet that next eve, explaining away her collapse as the delayed effect of all those hard weeks of travel through the cold and damp to attend this winter tournament that had come to such a sudden, disappointing end with the drawing of the sword from the stone. The lords all bought her excuses with fervent prayers for her good health, though she knew from her scrying that many nobles and peasants alike still whispered of her behavior and the strange events of that day, especially the women. Lady Genevieve was a witch, just like Morgan Le Fay, putting under her enchantment all the noble men at court. She should not be allowed within the king's presence, even if her husband did sign this treaty of peace between lords.

Not a single king had signed that treaty as of yet however. They had spent the past four days bickering and defaming Arthur's claim to the throne. How were they to know if he was truly Uther's son and not just a broke relation of Sir Ector lying about his heritage? How were they to know he was the rightful owner of Excalibur and God's chosen king when many of the lords had never made the attempt to pull the sword from the stone as Urien and Kay had? They spent many a long hour after those complaints out in the castle courtyard, as Arthur followed Merlin's prompt and put the 'holy' sword right back into the stone, so each and every king and earl from around the country could try their hand at freeing it.

Each and every one of them had failed of course. Then Arthur pulled it free with ease at the end of the day, though his victory was once again criticized by King Marcus as some wizard's trick, an all too accurate guess that Merlin calmly rebuffed with the false claim that he had only arrived in Camelot two days past, and thus had not even been present the day Arthur had first freed the sword from the stone.

Still, King Marcus of Tintagel and his seven like-minded peers: King Brandin, King Morkant, King Clariance, King Nentres, Duke Kador of Cornwall and the earls Cambenet and Meliodas, had stubbornly insisted there was no compelling reason for them to bend the knee to this beardless boy. These men were experienced warriors from great lines, rulers in their own right. The agreement of this tournament was supposed to be that the strongest of them be chosen to rule, not that they would be bound to accept settled borders and concede all of England's lands to the fourteen year old

The Tale of ~~King Arthur~~ Morgan Le Fay

nobody who just happened to pull a sword from a rock, regardless of his family name.

Now, those dissenters all sat together in the banquet hall of the castle, drinking up the palace stores and waiting for the arrival of the archbishop of Cantebury. That high priest was making the long journey west to put a crown on the head of God's chosen king and put a theoretical end to this endless civil war with the weight of the church's backing.

Arthur may very well be dead by the time he arrived with the way the men like King Marcus were eyeing him however. He would have been knifed in the back or poisoned already in truth were it not for the daunting presence of the dark eyed druid at his side. Merlin was God's prophet. A single word from him had been what secured his miracle-causing boy king the support of Camelot's stingy old bishop and the Catholic church at large. It was absolute hypocrisy that these priests cursed Morgan Pendragon as Satan's witch all the while revering so strongly the shape-shifting, foreign, probably fay-blooded peasant who so openly manipulated this country's kings.

"What about poison?" Urien murmured in Morgan's ear, following her glare to the imperious, posturing druid stood so cockily at the side of the throne where Arthur sat solemnly listening to the speech of one of the more neutral lords, King Leodegrance. "Something to kill him quickly, before he even realizes it. One dose for the druid, and one for the boy king."

"Never suggest poison," she whispered coldly. "It is the weapon of a coward."

"And far too obvious a treachery. You're right."

"We've no need to kill Arthur," she asserted softly. "His own expected vassals will hurl him from that throne before we need lift a single finger. He will never have the allegiance of these men. He is a beardless child who has yet to even wet a blade."

"Yet with Merlin at his side, all these cowardly kings take no action to depose him. We have wasted what is nearing an entire week beating around the bush, arguing over who should rule this country, no different than before the tournament that was to settle this. It will be no different once the archbishop arrives, so either we take action to put an end to that druid and his prop right here and now, or else we return to our troops and take this city the old fashioned way."

Her eyes became distant, still weighing hollowly into the druid across from them. "I suppose we could, but what a disappointingly short conquest that would be, a single battle with some conjured lightning on the field to remove the treacherous druid and decimate his troops…"

"We would need not your powers to win such a contest," Urien whispered fiercely. "I have the strength of arms to crush any that threaten. You need not overextend yourself."

She met his gaze and saw instantly the motive behind those words. It was not just fear of losing her caused by her recent collapse. Her king heard the whispers the same as she did, that his wife was a witch controlling and misleading him. Were his soldiers and lords to see the true Morgan Pendragon, they would all of them be terrified, and the discontent would start, leading perhaps into open revolt once the church became their enemy and…

"What troubled thoughts hang now behind your eyes?" Urien demanded, putting a hand to her cheek.

"Only a rational envisioning of our future, my king," the sorceress murmured unhappily. "For if Merlin is a prophet then I surely share that skill. There is a reason we agreed to win these lands without the use of brute force. The people here have never accepted the conquering kings such as your brother. They riot and revolt, as the church and the other lords scheme in constant opposition to those monarchs. Uther Pendragon won these lands with a legend, a lord of English birth liberating the people from Saxon invaders and savage pagan tribes. We must take charge of this alliance of kings arrayed against Arthur and use only tactics of manipulative diplomacy to win us this seat."

"Yet it would remain a seat you have no claim to, my Lady Genevieve," Urien reminded her gently, "and the church would not support us even should you proclaim your true identity and birthright, so the swift and decisive action of sending word to our troops and laying siege to this city is simply the wiser course."

Morgan's eyes darkened, and all she did was shake her head.

The doors of the banquet hall boomed open then, and a host of new knights appeared. Their armor was outdated and their hair lined with gray, but their stances remained proud and dignified, even that of Sir Ector, who needed a cane to make his way forward on foot.

"Sir Ector!" Arthur's face lit up instantly at the sight of his adopted father, and he leapt to his feet in rather unkingly fashion, only for a veiled glance from Merlin to stop the boy from rushing off down the steps to greet the retired old knight and his entourage as was clearly his impulse. "You are most welcome here, good sirs," Arthur proclaimed with attempted gravitas.

The Tale of ~~King Arthur~~ Morgan Le Fay

"Indeed, we are joyful for your company," Merlin added, "Sir Ector and Sir Baudwin and all thy fellows, renowned knights of Cambrien."

"Retired and lounging idle about your farms for the most part these past several years," King Nentres of Garlot added most savagely. "All dozen of you."

"We removed ourselves from the squabbles of greedy false kings," Sir Baudwin proclaimed, a six and a half foot juggernaut of a warrior not at all softened by his age with a slate gray beard and ominously beetling brow that seemed to swallow his eyes entirely. "There is no chivalry in pointless bloodshed. We have returned now to pay homage to the one true king, Arthur son of Uther."

He took a knee, as did all the men around him, but shattering crystal instantly stripped all decorum from the moment, as King Brandin of the Isles threw his goblet to the ground, spraying wine across the face of the kneeling old warrior. "You think a dozen old men is enough of an army to intimidate those before you, boy?" the hot-headed thirty five year old denounced. He had the second largest army of those assembled, right after Urien's own forces, and he was rumored to have the backing of the Saxons as well, who lived in peaceful treaty with his far western kingdom out on the borders of Scotland. "I am through with this farce of great warriors paying homage to some unproven child."

"You shame yourself, king," Merlin denounced.

"And you declare deadly challenge," Sir Baudwin grated, wiping angrily the red from his brow and climbing to his feet. "You have insulted my liege and my prowess alike. Draw now thy sword, and I shall cut thee in twain for the insult."

"A king gives no credit to the challenge of you country knights," Brandin spat derisively. "Lay a mark upon a great lord such as I, and you shall face the hangman's noose." Baudwin grit his teeth, for it was indeed true that he could not attack a king, not now that the lord had refused his challenge. "If the supposed king of this court thinks my uncouth words in need of silencing, let him take up arms and face me himself!"

Brandin threw off his cape, mad eyes burning into young Arthur standing weakly before his throne. Arthur did not look to Merlin in that moment, as Morgan had expected. Instead, he drew Excalibur, staring down at it doubtfully, then meeting solemnly the glare of the black bearded challenger before him. "I have no doubt, King Brandin, that you would best me in combat, for though I have trained hard throughout my years, I am perhaps not yet ready for this day."

Brandin scoffed. "You see--?"

"But," Arthur's words actually silenced the blustering monarch, though it was less the confidence in his tone than it was the subtle supernatural force Morgan could feel all too clearly coming off of Merlin that set Brandin's jaw clicking shut. "What I lack in strength of arms, I will make up for in earnest effort," Arthur swore. "I believe a good king should be fair to his subjects, so if you believe, good lords, that you have claim to be king, then this contest King Brandin proposes aught to be fair-minded and obeying of the customs of this land. Even the strongest of kings have appointed champions to fight their duels, just as Lord Brandin has said--"

"And what great warrior do you have to fight on your behalf, boy?" Earl Meliodas snarled, gesturing disparagingly throughout the room. "I see lords and knights from other houses throughout this room, but no banner of Pendragon flew at our tourney. You've no army. You simply seek to steal ours! The only vassals who have yet sworn you fealty are a band of cowardly cripples!" Baudwin flushed, fist clenching. "Old men, far past their prime."

"You name your only son to be a cripple past his prime, uncle?" Meliodas's nephew, Sir Dinadan, dramatically gasped. "Why, Tristan, my cousin, will you stand for such slander? I mean, tis true you did not win at tourney. Still, third place is nothing to scoff at--"

"Silence your prattling, boy!" Meliodas growled. "Your nonsense has zero bearing on this discussion."

"Then you were not truly listening to his words," Sir Tristan solemnly proclaimed. "You were indeed insulting my liege, father, and my own strength in turn, by saying he'd no one but cripples and old men to stand for him."

"Your *liege*?" Meliodas grated.

"King Arthur, the one true king of England," Tristan loudly declared, giving a reverent bow toward the boy king with a none too subtle glance directed toward Merlin as he did so. The druid gave an approving nod in response, and Morgan knew some underhanded deal had been struck between the pair of them.

"You betray our house!" Meliodas raved, but Merlin cut him off.

"And you betray the hospitality of the king, sitting in his hall and feasting upon his stores while seeding only spiteful discontent. If you are enemies of this kingdom, then act like men and declare yourselves so, openly, here and now." Of course, enemies of 'King Arthur' meant an enemy of Merlin and the church alike at this point, and everyone within that room knew it.

The Tale of ~~King Arthur~~ Morgan Le Fay

Still, King Brandin took no heed of the warning. "You do not frighten me, druid! I am indeed no friend of this kingdom so long as it sits beneath the soft hand of that country brat. Look for my flag on the horizon. I say this kingdom belongs to the strongest, and may all of you take heed!"

"King Brandin is correct," Urien declared, standing slowly up from his seat and ignoring for once completely the advice of his paramour seated frowning at his back. "No noble man in good conscience could leave these lands in the hands of one so weak, incapable of defending their borders. I will stand with the king of the Isles. We are peers in this discourse, and we will decide for ourselves which of us true heirs to this seat should be ruler of these lands, after we have ousted this fay-blooded charlatan," He gestured in derogatory point to Merlin. "and his all too clear puppet."

"Well said," King Marcus proclaimed, finding his backbone to face down Merlin now that two other men had stood up and yet survived his ire. "I stand with you, Urien. Now step down from that seat, boy, before we drag you from it."

"You will not lay a hand on him." The words were Gawain's, as he stepped out in front of the throne and drew his blade, chin lifted and eyes flashing. "The true heir of Orkney," Urien grit his teeth. "has sworn his life to Arthur, *God's* chosen king. Long has my family been stewards of this hallowed seat, the *Pendragon* throne, and we will all of us defend it to the death." Agravain and Gaheris and even seven year old Gareth all shouted in support, though Anna of course prevented her son from rushing with his brothers to stand with Gawain between Arthur and the glowering line of kings. "Now leave this place, all you honorless cads who declare yourselves to be enemies of our king."

"Indeed. Be gone!" Sir Lucan supported, acting only after a sharp glance from Anna that prompted him to finally abandon his drink and pay attention to the matters unfolding. "For my brother and I," He gestured to Sir Bedivere, seated at the side of the room, who raised his sword in hasty support of the claim. "have also sworn to defend this lad-- I mean, God's king. And yes, we may not have an army or any allies whatsoever besides those you see gathered here, but we will fight thee regardless!"

"Why in God's name would you tell them we don't have an army?" Bedivere muttered, putting a hand to his head. "You could have just left it at... nevermind. We swear to King Arthur! You villains shall not avail!"

"Well look at that, uncle," Dinadan declared in saucy taunt, grinning over at Meliodas. "The boy king's troops now outnumber all you 'great' kings and discontented lords packed into this room. Oh, and I swear allegiance as well. All hail King Arthur! Because he's a nice enough lad, and what is the point in inciting more pointless bloodshed and kicking off yet another civil war? I ask this earnestly to all of you--"

"You have never said an earnest word within your lifetime, you insolent whelp!" Meliodas roared. "Your very appointment as a knight is a mockery to the station! You, who will take no part in tourney and who speaks so improperly before all your betters! I disinherit you from your father's lands, and I declare you are no longer of my house! That goes for you as well, Tristan, should you not take back that impulsive vow to defend that joke of a king for which I gave you no permission!"

"I do not need your permission, father, and I do not need your inheritance," Tristan calmly rebuffed, and Morgan wondered sharply just what it is that Merlin had promised the youth to win from him such unwavering loyalty to a precariously placed and still uncoronated ruler.

"The number of impulsive young fools within this room has indeed come to outnumber we kings and our presently assembled guard," Urien cut in calmly, eyes weighing into Arthur with a look of deadly warning. "Yet our men are thousands. You will give way once they storm your gates, and your handful of knights can do nothing to defend you. This is your last chance, boy. Abandon your lies and step down from that seat. You will be the only one here to bend a knee this day, or else you will see death for your stubbornness."

"You cannot frighten me," Arthur declared, unhesitating. "I fear not your armies nor your attempts to intimidate and bluster, not any of you. Only he of righteous intent can emerge victorious in this conflict. I believe that with all my heart."

"So be gone from these halls," Gawain harshly concluded. "And look forward to the day, great kings, when we beat you into submission."

"The offer for peace will still stand," Arthur added. "But the terms will grow far less favorable should you do any damage to this city and its people, so I urge you now to reconsider your stance."

"There is nothing to reconsider," Urien retorted. "Every civilian slain and homestead burnt will be the result of your stubbornness, boy, clinging to the toxic council of that trickster." Merlin gave no response to the insult, though Arthur's eyes glimmered with doubt. Still, he kept his mouth shut and his stance firm, and the king of Orkney simply shook his head in disdain.

He held out his arm to his wife, whose mask of impassiveness was barely able to hide her seething frustration with this newly declared war.

The Tale of ~~King Arthur~~Morgan Le Fay

She could feel Merlin's eyes weighing into her, but she refused to meet his gaze, taking her lord's arm and allowing him to lead her from the room. The kings all followed after him, all but the French king, Ban, and King Leodegrance of Camlierd, who appeared far too hesitant to declare any sides in this blossoming civil war that would not directly affect their own far off homelands.

"We will meet in Caerlon to lay ground rules for this alliance and dictate what is to happen after we crush the paltry army of that so-called king," Urien told Marcus and the seven others following so close at his back.

"I do not need any allies," King Brandin scoffed in response. "I am going to storm these gates, raze this city, and put an end once and for all to you endlessly numbered little kings thinking you can declare yourselves liege lords to my kingdom!"

"So you want for us to be enemies then?" Urien pressed, and Brandin for once fell wisely silent. "You are a long way from home, Brandin, remember that, and remember how fickle the allegiance of the savage tribes that support your war efforts."

"Fine, we'll coordinate our efforts," Brandin muttered. "But I'm keeping my borders right where they are, and I am not bending the knee, not to any of you."

"An acceptable agreement." Urien held out his hand, and the black haired king shook it gruffly, stomping off and picking his own path out of the castle.

The rest of the rebelling lords of Logres seemed uncomfortable discussing anything of alliances or strategy in front of the Lady Genevieve. Women had no place in serious matters and warcraft to their minds, and so they gave nothing more than quick murmured agreements to a later meeting in Caerlon, before scurrying off with their guards to reunite with the bulk of their men and take leave of this city.

"Ready the horses," Morgan told Accolon and the rest of Urien's men, the second the kings departed.

The knights hesitated to obey, nervous about leaving their liege and his lady alone within a now hostile fortress, but Urien harshly repeated the order, and they set off immediately. Both of them knew that there was no threat within these halls that could lay so much as a single scratch upon Morgan Le Fay, no one but Merlin perhaps...

Would he dare an attack, now that her husband had so openly declared them as enemies of his precious boy king? Would he try to kill his own daughter to put a stop to her evils? Did he truly hate her, just as she hated him?

She blocked away the thoughts and turned her eyes on Urien. "There will be great cost to this conflict," she hissed. "It would have been far better to pretend to be Arthur's ally and sabotage from within his court rather than announcing yourself a threat and an invader. What is the use of taking Camelot if it is naught but rubble and dust?"

"I will not allow that savage, Brandin, to raze the city, my dear," Urien soothed. "But unless you want to use your arts and kill that brat, Arthur, quietly this very night, then we've no other practical option but to face him in battle and take this throne by force. We already control most of England. With the support of Tintagel and Lyonesse and the north, we have the enemy completely surrounded. This will not be a drawn out civil war as you fear."

"Yet the people will suffer," she whispered.

"They deserve to suffer," Urien hissed. "These ungrateful peasants who cursed you a witch and drove you from your birthright. Those that survive will make amends for that, and we will rule them justly, but the populace here has brought this suffering onto themselves by being wooed by a charlatan's tricks and calling a child a true king, able to defend them."

"The wise King Urien has a far more spurious reputation, I would say," Merlin declared, having materialized right before them in the deserted passage. "He seems just as hot-headed and hateful as King Brandin to my eyes."

Urien haughtily raised his chin, hand on his sword. "Have you come here to threaten us, druid? To bring dishonorable supernatural end to the enemies of your play-king?"

"Of course not," Merlin scoffed, eyes looking right past the posturing king and keeping locked on Morgan, glaring sullenly at his side. "But it seems you will be taking your leave of this city, so I needed to tell you first, Morgan, how glad I am to see you up and about." She flushed, knowing already the reprimand that was coming. "You really must be more careful," Merlin continued as predicted. "You pushed yourself far beyond the point of reasonable effort, and even I could barely heal the damage. I beg of you not to frighten me so again."

Urien stepped out arrogantly in front of her, eyeing the druid with open disdain. "Just because you have seen my lady during a time of weakness, does not give you the right to address her so casually. She is the wife of a king. And you are naught but a common blooded charlatan."

Merlin arched an eyebrow. "Is that so?"

"It is," Urien grated. "The pedestal of tricks that has propped you up to the position of adviser to the king worked far better when that king was a warrior of esteem. Your new little puppet is not nearly so fearsome as his father. That is why he will be so easily deposed, and you will hold no further power over this country, peasant."

"If you were an animal, Urien, it would be a goat."

The king blinked. "What?"

"Satan's companion, yet not at all fearsome. Just thick-headed and stubborn. Stubborn to the point of stupidity. You are in fact a goat."

The spell took hold before Morgan could stop it, and Urien dropped to all fours with a disoriented "bah".

Morgan grabbed him, and Urien returned instantly to his own shape, swaying dizzily from the whiplash of the sudden transformations.

His swimming eyes fixed on the druid, and he drew his sword. "How dare you--!"

Right back to a goat he went, sword clattering to the ground. Morgan changed him back just as quickly, though this time he vomited, clutching at his head. Morgan stalked up to Merlin then and shoved him. "Stop toying with my husband!"

"He is not fit to be your husband. He's an absolute ass."

Man became mule, and Morgan full on slapped the druid. "This is not a game! Haven't you done enough to ruin my life already? If you hate me so then make me your target! Just see if you can trap me in a shape and do anything worse than you already have to humiliate me!"

"I meant nothing ill, Morgan." The druid sighed. "You can change him back again in a moment. I just wanted a chance to talk--"

"We have nothing to discuss. You just want me to call off this war and support little Arthur, right? Well I hate to inform you, but my backing would be a far more thorough sabotage to his reputation, losing him instantly the favor of the church and bringing back the riots from Camelot's citizens, who clearly still irrationally hate accursed Morgan Pendragon and blame her still for everything wrong within this kingdom!"

"So you plan to hide yourself forever then?" Merlin sadly pressed. "Keep on that false face and persona and follow along complicity with that brute of a man at our feet as he--"

"I do not 'follow along'. I advise and I lead! The same as you do," she insisted, seizing Urien's hoof and turning it back into a hand, as she hauled him to his feet. He could no longer stand however, lurching into the wall, even as she tried to hold him up. She kept his arm locked firmly about her shoulders and stumbled with him down the hall before some servant or enemy could spot the great king reduced to this state.

"Will you put on pause this war and return here from Orkney to attend your brother's wedding?" Merlin called out after her, and she stopped in her tracks, glaring back at him sullenly.

"What wedding?"

"That of our newly coronated Pendragon with young Guinevere of Camlierd. Though the timeline I agreed upon with Leodegrance was two years hence, so that both may come of age. Perhaps that is too long a wait, but the engagement will still keep back the scheming vipers like Gorlois' sociopathic daughter. And I did enlighten Arthur to the fact that they are brother and sister, just as an added precaution."

Morgan pursed her lips. It seemed Merlin too had noticed the all too transparent machinations of Anna De'Gaur and had now put a deft and definitive end to them in a far kinder way than Morgan's own threats.

"And Camlierd's troops and swelling treasury will fight to defend our borders all the while before said wedding of course, so I would advise that you advise that goat-headed husband of yours to dissolve this little rebel alliance of his with all haste, before his own treasury runs dry."

"Leodegrance has lands and wealth but little military strength," Morgan countered. "Our men and our allies outnumber you in the thousands, so save your threats for when they've actual weight, you immature cad. I will see you on the battlefield."

Merlin hung his head, appearing right in front of her once more, even as she tried to storm off, with hands settled on her shoulders and eyes weighing into her earnestly. "Do not try to attack me, Morgan. I would never hurt you, but you may quite seriously hurt yourself, as happened with the sword, or else kill hundreds of innocents. Temperamental as you are, you are a kind hearted girl, and I know you do not wish that."

"You do not know me!" she retorted, batting away his hands. "You never took the time to know me. Now leave me be, before I end thee! A righteous reprisal for all your childish attacks upon my lord husband."

Urien muttered something beneath his breath, shoving himself shakily upright with quivering finger leveled toward the druid's chest. "Reprisal... Indeed... I'll kill you..." The rest of his words cut out, as he promptly began vomiting again. Morgan was not sure if that was Merlin or a lingering effect of all his rapidly inflicted transformations.

The Tale of ~~King Arthur~~ Morgan Le Fay

She hauled her shaking husband into the privacy of an unused bedroom to give him time to recover, firmly locking the door and teleporting away briefly to inform their men that the king would meet them back at their war camp but first had business to see concluded within the city.

Accolon and the others took her word without question, though Accolon did softly seize Genevieve's hand, pulling her out of sight of the others and whispering urgently, "I trust in the king's safety with whatever allies he has chosen as his guards, but you should come with us, my lady. It is not safe for you within this court. I would feel better were you to stay within my company, at least until we reunite with our troops."

"You need not be concerned," Morgan countered coldly, taking back her hand. "I will remain by the side of my king, and no man would dare threaten me there. Just as none of our men would dare to lay hand on you again, Accolon," she could not help but add. "My king will tolerate no squabbling among his troops, as he most clearly commanded this past morn."

Accolon smiled. "I sense clearly thy concern, and it warms my heart, though I fear not for myself."

He leaned in closer, fingers reaching out as if yearning to touch her, though he made not the mistake of being so bold. Still, he did dare some small impropriety, whispering firmly, "You deserve better than a man like Urien, Morgan." The woman who should only be seen as Genevieve prickled sharply at the address, eyeing him in unsettled shock. "But I will do as you command, until the end of my days. I will hang on your words and await eagerly your arrival at our camp."

Accolon vanished around the corner, and Morgan cursed under her breath the idiotic slew of men within her life able to so easily see through her disguises and yet having no aversion whatsoever to getting involved with a witch, a *married* witch.

She blocked Accolon and Gawain from mind and returned to the side of her king, pushing back his sweat damp hair.

His hand instantly seized hers, and there was nothing weak about his grip. Though his eyes had a feverish cast, they were all the more frightening for it. "He wants you." Morgan flinched, mind flashing to Accolon and wondering how Urien had known of-- "Merlin." She balked, shock turned to sickened derisive laughter. "Do not laugh at me! I can see it in the way he looks at you. How familiar he acts... He wants to make you his own. But he will never have you. Tell me he has never--"

"He's my father."

Urien blinked. "What?"

She told him the whole story then of Merlin and Igraine, and Urien relaxed considerably, running a hand through his hair. "I suppose I cannot resent a father his attacks on a son in law who has paid him insult. I did not even ask the mighty wizard permission for thy hand."

She near loudly protested the comment, before she caught sight of his smirk and realized he had been jesting.

"Still, you deceived me, wife." His smile vanished, and her heart clenched. "I will forgive you, but you must never do so again."

"I will not," she whispered. "You are the only one who knows of this truth."

"The only one you trust?" She gave a hesitant nod, and his smile returned. "As it should be." His fingers wound tightly in her hair, pulling her close. "You belong to me alone."

"So long as you belong to me," she countered, holding a finger to his lips to forestall their greedy consumption of her words.

"I am yours to command, my goddess."

"Then we will fight this war together," she insisted darkly. "I will use my powers however I see fit, and you will not attempt to stop me."

His face twisted in displeasure, but he gave a solemn nod. He had quite the appetite that night. It seemed he had recovered fully from his transformation whiplash, but he did not wish to leave that room for many an hour that followed.

"You deserve better." Those words were treason, and she tried with all vigor to exorcise them from her mind. They returned in the cold hours of the morning however, as she lay awake and restless within a possessive embrace and found new insight in the hollow feel of winter winds swirling through her chest.

The Tale of ~~King Arthur~~Morgan Le Fay

XXII. A Contest of Kings

Two years of civil war, an endless bloodshed far from the quick and wasteless victory that King Urien had promised his queen. They had lost the first battle to seize Camelot. Even with the vast host of Urien's entire army amassed outside those gates, backed by hundreds of additional cavalry from Lyonesse and Tintagel and Northumbria, they had lost the bloody battle.

Four hundred troops from Lyonesse had marched all the way up north to support them, only for Tristan to make an appearance in their camp the eve of battle. He gave an impassioned speech to the troops about needlessly endangering themselves and widowing their families for naught but the profit of savage foreign conquerors, and the men all too eagerly followed his orders and turned right around, abandoning the battle.

After all, their liege lord, Meliodas, had been stricken with a curious case of drooling madness that very afternoon, blathering nothing but gibberish, with his legs like jelly as if he had been drugged. This sudden incontinence made Tristan the rightful lord of Lyonesse in the eyes of the army, despite Meliodas's rash disinheritance of his son the month prior. He had no other heirs, and his generals wanted very badly for the talented and handsome young knight's family to continue ruling their little inlet and spare them the appointment of some foreign noble to rule in his stead.

By the time news of this coup reached Urien and his queen, they were in far too vulnerable a position to turn around and bring those troops back into line. Their army laid siege to the walls of Camelot without the aid of the southern contingent, and Morgan went irritably to check on their maddened ally, only to find him already recovered, with Merlin sitting smugly at his side in privacy of his tent.

The druid gave a patronizing speech to both the earl and the disguised sorceress of the karmatic cost of hubris and rash action. Morgan tried to set him on fire, and he vanished, but Meliodas was far too frightened to ever challenge the great wizard again. He retreated to his homeland and left the war to Urien and the other kings.

Something even worse happened the second day of Camelot's siege when Kador, nephew of Gorlois and current Duke of Cornwall, also decided to suddenly turn traitor. This man had been Urien's sworn vassal for three years now, ever since Lot's demise, when Orkney's forces had marched south and taken those lands. It seemed he had always secretly resented his king though, just as he had Uther.

He was also, as Morgan later learned, extremely religious and had been convinced by his "bishop" (a disguised shape-shifter) that he would forever rot in hell for his betrayal of his oath to Uther, unless he came to serve loyally that man's son, God's chosen king, Arthur, who had been crowned that very Pentecost by the arch daises himself. So it was Kador had with all desperate false righteousness forsaken his front of the siege at a key moment in their strategy, fighting alongside Arthur's small gathering of knights and commoners defending Camelot's gates.

Morgan the enraged sorceress had smote him with lightning in revenge for his treason, but the duke had supernaturally survived the three hundred million volts sent coursing through his body, courtesy of the druid playing guardian angel at his side. He did not attribute that miraculous healing to Merlin of course. He took it as the grace of God, defending him from the devil's servant, and his faith and that of all his men grew all the more fervent.

Morgan heard the whispers spreading throughout their war camp that day, as her temper worsened the roiling storm clouds and rumors of Kador's miracle spread throughout their ranks. She kept in the paranoid guise of Lady Genevieve and took no further sorcerous action throughout that siege, telling herself their armies did not need her supernatural shortcuts to an easy victory. Whatever she did, Merlin would just come out to counter it anyway. The might of their military would starve out the defenders and crush them the old fashioned way. It was only a matter of time.

That proved another miscalculation. On the second week of siege, the bloody French decided to join in the conflict, burning Urien's supply lines and flanking their troops. The French king, Ban, should have felt zero inclination to needlessly involve himself in this fight. The middle aged king had been nothing but a timid ghost ever since the death of his wife and sons a decade past who had been accosted by brigands on the road to Camelot. He had taken no vengeance for that tragedy. It had been an act of pure misfortune, planned by no rival lord, and the old man seemingly had no energy for hatred. He had withdrawn instead into actionless depression. He held his tiny chunk of lands in west France and he drove back invaders, but he never advanced. There was no future to his line, and with his death, his kingdom would pass to his distant third cousin. He had no apparent reason to be sailing across the sea and risking his men to save beardless boy King

The Tale of ~~King Arthur~~Morgan Le Fay

Arthur from conquest. Yet here he was, striding impassioned out onto the battlefield and guiding fiercely the charge that shattered Urien's flank, causing King Nentres and King Marcus to flee, and eventually forcing a retreat.

Morgan had tried to put an end to the rejuvenated old king and demoralize his troops, but Merlin had abruptly abducted her and solidly ruined her spell.

She had demanded at that point to know how he had secured King Ban's backing, to which his response had been, "Our good king was all too eager to aid God's chosen one. All he needed first was for his hope to be renewed. Which it was, the second he heard news that his youngest son is not dead and buried as he has long believed. He is alive and well within the realm of faerie. And I am sure I can convince Viviane to return him. I said he would return to his father's side anyway, so long as King Arthur emerged victorious in this conflict, and I have a strong feeling that prediction will indeed come to pass."

Morgan hated the wizard all the more for his lying manipulation of a father's hope to see again his long lost child. She knew that Viviane would never willingly part with her precious, pretty cup bearer, and she knew just as surely that Merlin would never attack the angelic shrew. That was two crucial chess pieces now buried within her lake that Morgan would have to somehow see to freeing, first the true Excalibur and now Lancelot, and she hardly had the time to worry about that then, with her husband's army decimated and their first move in this campaign against her brother having ended in disgrace.

The thousand troops of King Ban and another unexpected ally of Arthur's, King Bors of Brittany, chased their army far to the north, almost all the way back to the border of Orkney.

King Nentres was taken captive during one of those later skirmishes, and his little kingdom of Garlot was so bankrupted by the ransom that he became of little use in the coming years of battle.

Arthur sent another treaty out to Orkney, which Urien tore asunder and then Morgan set aflame, sending the box of ashes back to Camelot alongside the finger of the messenger who had delivered the insulting treatise.

Urien whispered in her ear that night that she should slip off back to Camelot and put an end to the young king's struggle, but Morgan retorted firmly that fratricide was an unforgivable sin. Even as infuriating and two-faced as Lot had been after all, Urien had still impressively managed to refrain from strangling him throughout their years of arguments, now hadn't he?

If Arthur needed a lesson, it would be one of ransom and humiliation, bowing and scraping at Urien's feet while declaring himself an insolent peasant. That delightful mental image satisfied Urien, and Morgan set out to see it brought to life. Merlin teleported her away the second she made it past Arthur's guards and into his bedchamber though, and so the battle returned to traditional tactics of armored cavalry clashing in the mud.

They lost nearly every battle. It was ridiculous! But Merlin's long planned machinations stripped them of ally after ally, until Arthur's horde of loyal warriors and great knights put their own increasingly paranoid and unpatriotic troops to shame. With every sorcerous tactic Morgan employed to gain them an edge in this war, the whispers among her people would grow. She was clearly a witch, and God was clearly against them. They should burn her at the stake and be free of her evil influence.

Urien had the perpetrators of such gossip dragged out in public and burned themselves, the second he heard those hateful words echoing through her scrying mirror. That cost him many a loyal general however, and angered many a knight and powerful family within his lands. Satan's temptress had a hold of Orkney and its king. The priests throughout their country continued to repeat that message.

Even if she was not a devil, the barren queen had yet to birth her king an heir even after five years of marriage, something that even the less superstitious among the nobles were rightfully concerned with.

Young Arthur started riding out to battle with his knights at only fifteen years of age, an inspiring sight that rallied his troops in a way Urien's fearful presence never could. The boy had quite the way with rhetoric. His speeches were downright moving, now that his voice had stopped cracking, and he wasn't half bad with a sword now that he had reached full height. He charged valiantly to the aid of any floundering man within his reach, be they commoner or baron, and Merlin assured that the king was never wounded during those ill advised stunts.

The enemy's weapons rebounded off the blessed king's armor without leaving so much as a scratch, and the troops never spotted the shaking mess their great king devolved into the night he first killed a man. Arthur kept his composure with stony resolve, until the moment he retreated to his tent, shaking and sobbing and murmuring fevered prayers of repentance. Merlin came almost instantly to comfort him though, and Morgan's sympathy for him turned to burning envy.

The Tale of ~~King Arthur~~ Morgan Le Fay

She wanted him humiliated, made to look a powerless child fumbling his way across the battlefield, but such disgrace never touched him, and not just because of Merlin's protection.

Arthur was skilled in his own right, a natural leader. He routed hundreds of their troops in Rockingham with a deftly planned ambush upon their camp, made all the more effective by the sudden collapse of all the tents burying their commanders and leaving them floundering to even stand, as the knights of Camelot rode through the wreckage, cutting them down. Merlin did not even need to aid him in winning on the fields of Humber, and then Trent. And in Caerlon castle, one of Urien's most important strongholds, it was the citizens and the wall guard themselves who opened the gates for Arthur's troops, swayed by their bishop's sermons of how all the recent food shortages and misfortune within their city was the fault of the witch of Orkney, a terror that could only be ended by embracing God's chosen king.

Most impressive of all was the battle of Mount Badon, where caught by surprise with none of his allies on the field, Arthur and his vastly outnumbered knights nonetheless held strong through an entire ten bloody hours of fighting with backs planted against the rockface, until back up had arrived and Urien's troops were sent fleeing into the hills.

Shining Arthur's legend was growing. His troops adored him now just as all the people did, and Morgan wished on many of those days that she had taken Urien's advice and strangled him to death.

Now, it had been two years of steady losses for the heir of Norway and his diminished allies, and there was no doubt in anyone's mind that Urien and his sorcerous queen were losing this war.

King Marcus deserted them and swore allegiance to High King Arthur, as did King Morkant and Clarience and Cambenet. The entire south was lost. Still, Genevieve and her brilliant tongue swayed King Brandin of the Isles into standing with them here in the moors of Lothian with his host of strange, blue-painted warriors. They were camped upon the rocky high-ground above the marsh where no ambush or other nefarious tactic could best them. Yet they had only two thousand men against Arthur's three thousand, and this may well prove to be their last chance, not even to conquer Camelot but just to remain an independent nation not under the heel of "God's king".

Morgan called upon a trick she had employed without success in the past and spread insidious sickness throughout Arthur's ranks, a virus that took easy hold in the chill damp of the moors and left each and every great knight without the strength to stand or even lift their arms.

Then Merlin cured her entire night's work in an hour, and Morgan shattered her scrying dish. She slumped back, exhausted, as her husband rubbed a soothing hand across her back. "I'm all but useless unless I kill him, and I can't even manage that."

"Yet you could have surely killed those knights," Urien rebuked, "unleashing sudden death instead of sickness. Then there would have been nothing for Merlin to heal."

Morgan considered uneasily that proposal, picturing in her mind the dead faces of Sir Kay and Sir Baudwin, and Gawain... "I haven't the energy for that now," she excused. "Besides, I doubt our men would accept a victory from the angel of death herself bringing mysterious end to so many."

"Rest then, my love," Urien commanded, kissing her forehead. "And think it over as you dream."

Morgan did think it over, lying awake in that command tent with Urien's arms around her, an endlessly constrictive and pressuring support. She considered it very seriously, and she slipped free of his embrace, teleporting off to the command tent of King Arthur in the moors a mile distant.

The bed there was empty, and Merlin was stood keeping weary watch from the corner of the room.

"Why do you always assume I am coming to kill him?" she muttered, grimly pushing back the hood of the menacing black robes that she had donned solely for the sake of dramatic presentation. "I came to negotiate, not to smash any skulls of lovely golden haired brats or start breaking the legs of their pretty white ponies."

Merlin put a hand to his forehead, squeezing his eyes shut as if physically pained by the thought of those acts. "I will plead yet again that you do not speak such ugly words, Morgan. Do not jest about such things, for I truly cannot tell these days what is idle threat and what is true intended cruelty."

"My threats are never idle," she stated darkly. "Though you've the awful power to erase them whenever they rear their heads. You can erase anything but death itself, and so you have left me with no choice."

"I thought you came to negotiate--"

"To negotiate your surrender," she grated. "A happy compromise for your little boy king, because fear not, father, I shall not kill my brother. Much as I hate him, I shall never lay finger on his pretty little head. I will allow him his little throne in Camelot. I will allow him to persist, and my husband's troops will never again trouble him, so long as he does as he should have that day

The Tale of ~~King Arthur~~Morgan Le Fay

in the square with *my* sword, Excalibur, surrenders it to Urien and bends the knee in deference to Orkney, to which he and all his knights will play happy little vassals, at our beck and call whenever we should need."

"Your forces have not the strength to be making that demand."

"Of course we do." She smiled, eyes wild and teeth grinding. "Because my forces are led by the right hand of the devil himself, or hadn't you heard? My forces will outnumber yours sorely should you refuse this most generous treaty, because not a single one of your knights will awake this coming morn should you spurn my kindness." Her smile vanished, eyes weighing into Merlin with all the hateful intensity of one backed into a corner with no escape from the constant humiliation and loss that had driven her to this day. "I will kill them all, druid. That is no jest or idle threat. I will kill every one of Arthur's friends and loyal servants, and I will do it with but a snap of my fingers." She raised her hand. "One burst blood vessel in the brain for each and every one of them, and they will be dead long before you can mend it."

Merlin crossed his arms, eyeing her flatly and saying not one word.

Her maddened smile returned. "Now what's with that expression? You don't think I can do it? You think of me still as nothing but a soft and temperamental girl, but you are the soft one, druid! You are too weak to kill me. You will never strike me down, as you have already declared, and thus you have no power to control me anymore! You cannot stop me. You will not. So surrender to these terms and plead upon my mercy, else your men will all..."

Her eyes suddenly began to grow heavy and her words to slow and slur. Something had appeared at the corner of her vision, though she had not noticed it until the breath of air stirred against her cheek.

She spun to obliterate the threat with a torrent of flames, turning her back to what she realized now was simply the projected image of Merlin and over to face the real druid, stood right at her side with rose in hand and the command of "Sleep." having already crossed his lips.

He caught her as she fell, murmuring his apologies and carrying her off to bed. He tucked her tight beneath the covers. Then he vanished from view of her darkening gaze, off to win yet another battle for his king. There was no one to contest him, now that his foolish daughter had been bundled off to bed, plagued by awful dreams of all that was happening in her absence to her beloved Lord Urien and his men.

XXIII. Here He Lies, in the Bloodstained Soil

The rumored right hand of the devil awoke from her slumber to find warm afternoon light already glowing through the walls of Arthur's abandoned tent. Even more unsettling was the all too familiar towheaded child planted firmly before the entrance with jaw locked and cross in hand. "Merlin said to leave you be, but I have decided to stay here and guard the slumbering dragon lest she charge out to battle and seek yet again to wound our great King Arthur and his most valiant servants, my brothers. Be assured now, with the power of Christ in hand, I shall not allow you to leave this room, witch. Now, what have you to say for yourself in defense of your years of unpenitent villainy and--?"

"Go home to your mother, Gareth," Morgan muttered, forcing herself groggily to her feet. "A nine year old page has no place on a battlefield."

Morgan teleported free of the pavilion before the boy had a chance to retort, but it was indeed already late in the day, and by the time she reached the rise where her armies had been camped, all she found were the bloody leavings of a battle long since settled. She stood upon that emptied field of churned up earth and glittering silver corpses and felt all sense of urgency bleed out from her legs. Her eyes fixed on the edge of the field, way up on the rocky ridge where the Pendragon banner flew twisting in the wind, and the emblem of Orkney lay fallen in the mud.

She walked with steps dragging slowly up to that slope, freezing instantly in place the host of soldiers that rose from their work looking over the dead and foolishly came to slow her advance on their king. The men of Orkney, all those who had survived, had already surrendered. They sat now at the side of the field with swords laid on the ground, encircled by Englishmen. There was no sign of the blue painted Picts that had supported King Brandin. They had likely retreated hours ago, alongside their liege.

The towering figure of Sir Baudwin raised his claymore in slow menace, as the black robed sorceress so grimly approached. The old knight had acted as Arthur's personal bodyguard since the day the boy was coronated, standing always at his side, just like Sir Kay, and Bedivere, and all the other familiar faced knights now gathered on that rise. "Who goes there?"

The Tale of ~~King Arthur~~ Morgan Le Fay

Gawain turned at Baudwin's shout, following his stare right over to Morgan and instantly holding up his hand. "Stand aside," he urged him. "All of you, stand aside."

Morgan's heart clenched even further, reading clearly the meaning of Gawain's guilty lowered gaze.

The circle of knights parted to admit her, and Arthur rose from his solemn prayer, knelt by the bloodstained flag of Orkney half buried in the mud. "You needn't have come," he whispered. "I wish you had not."

Morgan looked past him to the figure on the ground. She could not see his face, not through the tears that blurred her vision. She told herself it was not his body. His men were there, yes, Caradoc and Accolon, sitting alive and at the mercy of Bedivere to whom he had surrendered his blade. Her husband's men had all been killed or captured, but the king himself had surely escaped. The great king himself would never fall to some beardless boy...

She stretched out her hand, blinking the mists from her eyes and forcing herself to see. Urien's eyes were fixed and unseeing, his chest fallen still. There was nothing here that she could heal. She dropped to her knees in the mud.

"I am sorry for your loss." That's all Arthur could say. That's all anyone could say, but he was not truly sorry. He did not feel that raw regret, that suffocating agony trying to break apart his chest--

"What happened?" she murmured.

Arthur knelt down at her side and grimly closed the staring eyes of his enemy, closed them so she could not keep searching them, could not sink into them and let them swallow her. "I challenged him to a duel, to spare our men and put an end to the bloodshed. He refused, so I asked Merlin... Half your men fell instantly asleep, leaving Urien sorely outnumbered. He should have surrendered then. He did not. Still, I ordered my men not to fire, and we faced him in honorable combat. He should have surrendered."

But of course he did not, not when he thought his queen had been taken from him, imprisoned or even killed, because there was no other way she would not have been there at his side, there when he needed her, to protect their men from enchantment, to keep strong their borders and win this one essential victory....

"Every king surrenders to ransom." Merlin's voice. "All but that one, stubborn as a goat."

Morgan's grief became rage, and she climbed to her feet, eyes burning into the druid behind. "You dare denounce the character of a king? A mighty king slain by *your* trickery!" Her voice broke, and the howl of rising winds calmed to jarring stillness.

Still, the wizard felt compelled to remove her from this setting. He waved his hand and suddenly they were stood alone, far from the battlefield, isolated in the misty woods in shadow of the Welsh mountains. "I am sorry, Morgan, but there was no other way..."

"You have taken for the last time, druid," she whispered. "Now I am no more. I have no place in the world, no future, no goal, so it shall be as you wish, and I will disappear from these lands."

Merlin shook his head, charging rashly up to her, seizing her hands and trying to trample her tearful vow with assertions of his own of who she was and what she would be.

She heard nothing of his words, squeezing tightly his hands and staring deep into his eyes, as she breathed the barely audible assertion, "I will disappear, and so will you."

Her spell took hold and her hands became mist, slipping forever from his own, but she was not the one retreating this time. She was not the one trapped.

The spell was like his tower, an unbreakable infinity looping right back to the center, however you tried to force your way out, only this time it was not a dreary room of windowless cobblestone. It was a clearing in the mountains, a mirror of where they had just now stood, ringed and roofed with a mist so thick as to block out sunlight and be unnavigable. He would stay forever in that forgotten vale, that circle of magic most unbreakable, because Morgan had made no entries or exits, not even for herself. She had crafted that locked, infinite box right around the druid's head, and he would never be able to escape it. He could fly to the very tops of those peaks, but he would inevitably become turned around in the mists, until feathers froze and he plummeted back to the earth. He could walk for days through the misted woods and wind up back in the very same clearing, the lonely vale, cut off forever from the world in which he was so fond of meddling.

He would never again be there to support Arthur, to win for him battles and govern the country. He would never again bring ruin to the conquerors that threatened those lands, or steal away the wives of great lords and kings, fathering bastard children and leaving them an untrained curse upon the realm. He would stay there in her vale, eternally alone, and Morgan would not mourn him.

The Tale of ~~King Arthur~~**Morgan Le Fay**

  She had no heart to mourn him. Her heart had been ripped from her chest and laid beside the body of her husband, and she felt only emptiness in the weeks that followed, once the tears ran dry and the storming skies calmed. She had become a ghost in truth, lifeless, with nothing but a wealth of angry memories to haunt her nights, and so it was she retreated to a hall befitting of her being. She returned to Cader Idris, with the solemn vow that she would never leave those lonely halls again. These walls would become her tomb.

XXIV. The Pestered Exile

Morgan the widowed witch, the terror of all of England, retired to her ruin. She abandoned all her accursed subjects, all her husband's lords and vassals expecting vengeance for the death of their king. She left them to rot in their bankrupted kingdom and sat quiet in Cader Idris. She swore off forever the countenance of Lady Genevieve and kept her own shape for an entire year, wasting away in the darkness with all her grand schemes brought to ruin.

Sir Accolon the foolish was the first to show up on her doorstep. She had no idea how he had found her here. Anna De'Gaur was the one and only person she had ever invited to these halls, yet somehow Accolon had tracked her to this remote castle. He knew she was inside, and he would accept no common sense or obstacle of sealed portcullis and refused reception. He stood out there for days, howling for her attention, until she irritably granted him admittance to her gloomy hall. She put on no regal airs to receive him in her throne room. She just sat there all in black with a veil over her face and asked him numbly, "What do you want?"

The great knight hung back nervously at the entrance to the eerily lit hall, eyeing her uncomfortably. "Why do you hide your face from me, my queen? Will you not grace me with thy countenance--?"

"I have always hidden my face from thee," she snapped. "A veil is no different from a mask. Now what do you want?"

He strode up to her and fell to his knees at her feet. "My queen, I have searched for thee tirelessly, ever since thy vanishing so many months past. Our kingdom is in turmoil. We are in need of your guidance--"

"It is not my kingdom. The people all despise me, just as they do in Camelot. Let the other lords deal with whatever 'turmoil' it is, and go home."

"The lords are the turmoil," he hissed, hands clenching. "Warring over the seat Urien left vacant. They will not bend the knee to Arthur, nor agree on which one of them is heir to Urien's mantle in wake of his passing--"

"Gawain," she muttered. "Gawain is heir, and he is sworn to Arthur, so all of Orkney and Norway is now his property as well. Tell them that, and leave me alone."

"You wish for that druid's brat to be ruler of our country?" Accolon demanded in outrage, rising to his feet and looming over her in clear

The Tale of ~~King Arthur~~Morgan Le Fay

menace. "You will just sit back and allow him to--?"

"It is not my country!" she snapped, bounding to her feet. "It was never my country! King Urien is dead, and his barren witch of a wife left no heir to carry on his great legacy, just as the people all wail! So deal with that however you will and leave me be!"

"What shame do you hide behind this veil?" Accolon pressed, putting his hands to her face. She hurled him away from her, sending him skidding across the floor and firmly sealing the doors to make permanent his exit.

He stayed there the entire day, calling her name, her real name. "Morgan! My queen!"

He shouted until his voice grew hoarse, then still kept on calling, until irritably she teleported out into the hall, tearing off her veil and putting on the face of horrid Lady Genevieve once more.

"Not Morgan," she hissed, seizing his jaw. "Do not pretend that Morgan is the queen you came here to catch glimpse of. All you have ever wanted is the Lady Genevieve, Urien's wife. Just as all men deep down crave the talents of a changeling to give flesh to their fantasies. You care nothing for the real witch," She made her voice coarse and gravelly, her eyes becoming pitch black and her teeth feral points. "and long would she haunt your nightmares were you to dare lay eyes upon her."

Accolon seized her face, eyes wild, as madly, he smiled. "I see through your illusions. You are no devil, my lady. No clawed demon horror healed me that night in the stables. A changeling can appear however she wishes, and so yes, she is desirable. But this one is also kind, and intelligent, and wise, and so yes, long did I envy Urien."

"So you truly did not come here seeking aid for your kingdom. You simply felt cheated of your chance to bed the widow of your king, and thus went to seek her out before--"

"I did come here seeking aid," he swore, driving her back against the wall. "I need you, Morgan. But you need me as well, I can see it. You need not suffer this alone."

His lips seized hers, and she gave in for a full minute before pulling back her head, staring him down deadly with her own eyes of dull and lifeless brown.

"Leave me, Accolon," she whispered. "I can give you nothing."

She teleported him back outside and returned to her rooms, curling up on the bed. He stayed for another few hours, calling out and pacing by her gates, until wearily she called up a scried image of him to better hear what he was saying.

"I will unseat that druid's brat! And I will avenge our king! I've not your mind for brilliant plans, but I shall see it done regardless! And I will remain always at your beck and call, my lady! Yours to summon as you wish!"

The fool did not understand the sheer cruelty of that offer. She deserved to be alone, hidden away forever, just as Merlin was. Wizards brought nothing but misery to the world. They were a crime against nature, and God surely did hate them, just as fiercely as he loved little Arthur, his rightful king.

The knight mounted his horse finally and set off before nightfall settled in. The nights were quite unpleasant out in the woods that ringed this fortress, filled with predators and chill mists and wailing spirits.

None of that seemed a hindrance to the next unexpected visitor who came riding up to her gates in the dead of night only three days following Accolon's departure. The little blond haired page was far too young to be wandering the dark roads of Wales all by his lonesome. It was a miracle he had not been murdered or kidnapped already, but the boy's foolhardy bravery had left him with seemingly zero hesitation, as he charged right up to her haunted castle, squeezed right through the bars of her gates and picked his way calmly over the cracked flagstone of the courtyard overgrown with thorny vines. "Miss witch!" he shouted. "I've come to see you! If you're home, please say so!"

Morgan made no such announcement of her presence, but Gareth the half grown page pressed on with determined inertia. He was not stymied by the brambles she had allowed to grow over the main entrance of her castle. He drew a dagger from his belt and started sawing his way through the brittle limbs that made up the thicket, and the sorceress knew that even if it cost him hours of work and nick after nick of bloody thorn wounds, he would not cease until he had made his way through that entrance.

Would he be as annoyingly persistent as Accolon then and keep searching her out for days, shouting her name and allowing her no rest until she assented to his demands? And what were the demands of a ten year old anyway? And why the hell was he out here alone?

Morgan decided the balcony would be far less frightening to little Gareth than her gloomy, spider infested throne room. She teleported him up there, and the boy cast about wildly, trying hard to conceal his unease. He made a hasty show of sheathing his blade, as his eyes settled on Morgan. She

The Tale of ~~King Arthur~~Morgan Le Fay

was not bothering to wear her veil this time. This boy had already seen her true face anyway, back in Arthur's war camp.

He cleared his throat imperiously and gave a little bow. "My Lady Pendragon, witch of Orkney--"

"How did you find me, and what are you doing here?" she demanded, staring him down with arms crossed and foot tapping impatiently.

"Well, my mother had a meeting out in the woods with this deranged seeming fellow called Accolon, so I decided to listen in so I could step in to protect her should he try anything untoward. Then she mentioned a place called Cader Idris, where the sorceress Morgan Pendragon made her home, and this Accolon went charging off immediately. So I followed him of course, because I needed to speak with you. Then I fell behind and got lost in the woods for a bit, but I traded a kiss to this strange lady who came out of a tree, and she was kind enough to point me in the right direction."

"Bloody fairies," Morgan muttered. "At least you didn't run into a goblin or follow any willow-o the wisps. Now, what did you need to speak with me about?"

Gareth opened his mouth to respond, only for his stomach to let out an ugly gurgle of a growl. If the boy had ridden here from Camelot, he had clearly not packed adequate supplies for the journey. Who knows, he may not have eaten anything in days. Morgan sat down and irritably summoned a plate of biscuits and gravy to the center of the table.

Gareth plopped down across from her and reached forward instantly, only to hesitate. "Do you swear it's not--?"

"It is not poisoned! I have never poisoned anybody, I will have you know. That's more your mother's domain."

"What?"

"Nothing, nevermind. Just eat your dinner."

Gareth shrugged, digging right in and devouring the entire tray, at which point he developed quite the serious case of hiccups. Morgan summoned a pitcher of water, waiting patiently for the little convulsions to subside enough for him to speak.

That never happened however. His attempted answers to her questions emerged as nonsensical trail offs, as the hiccups refused to abate.

"Do you want for me to scare them away?" she offered, eyes narrowing in weary anticipation of what was to follow.

"Can you-- *hchp!*-- please?"

Morgan teleported right up into his face with the same black eyes and pointed teeth she had hoped to frighten Accolon with the visit prior. It worked far better on a ten year old. He fell right out of his chair, gasping loudly and clutching at his cross with heart thundering away within his chest.

Morgan had already settled calmly back into her seat, summoning a cup of tea and sipping at it coolly. A solid minute went by without a hiccup then, as Gareth climbed slowly to his feet with breaths deep and even to calm his racing pulse.

"Well, it appears to have worked," Morgan noted, "but now let me guess, you are far too terrified to speak with me."

"No. Why would I be terrified?" Gareth insisted with all prideful stubbornness, climbing back into his seat. "You said you were going to scare away my affliction, and you kept your word and did so. That is nothing to be frightened of. Though your true face is indeed unsettling, no offense. I expected it to be a dragon, not a demon, what with the whole Pen*dragon* name..."

"I'm not a real Pendragon, and I am not a demon either," she snapped. "So stop insulting me or else get out of my castle."

"Well I am sorry, my lady Pen-- Oh wait right, uh... I guess I will just call you miss witch then. Is that alright?"

"Why are you here?" Morgan irritably repeated.

"Well, miss witch, as the only nice witch I know of--"

"What makes you think I'm nice? I am the terror of all of Camelot."

"Yes, but you've never poisoned anyone, as you yourself have said, and you gave me some very nice biscuits and helped with my hiccups and you didn't try to curse me that afternoon in the war camp, so really, you're not very witch-like at all, now are you?" He smiled, though it faded in an instant, turning back to beetle browed pensiveness. "Though when I asked mother about you, she did say you were horrid," Morgan flushed, eyes lowering. "yet she also enforced that I had nothing to be frightened of because you would certainly never harm me, which I found confusingly contradictory. So then I asked Gawain about you, and he said you were tragically misunderstood. And then I was gonna ask the king about you, since you are his sister, but Lucan said that would not be proper, so I decided I needed to come here and see for myself who was right and who was wrong. And rightly nice you are." He gestured smugly to the emptied biscuit tray. "Though you wouldn't happen to have any meat, now would you?"

The Tale of ~~King Arthur~~ Morgan Le Fay

Morgan rolled her eyes and summoned a haunch of honeyed ham to the center of the table. Gareth tore into the offering with the typical enthusiasm of a preteen boy. He really hadn't eaten anything of substance for some time now it seemed.

"Aren't you going to eat any?" he mumbled, and Morgan's stomach chose that moment to let loose an ugly rumble of its own. Gareth held out a plate and obligingly she took it. It was true that she had not been eating regularly these days, as she had not the motivation for it.

"So to get this straight, you came all the way out here just to determine for yourself how evil I am?" she pressed.

"No, I came to ask you to stop the plague, because no one can find Merlin and everyone thinks you sent it, but if you did do that, then it would be easy enough for you to cure it, now wouldn't it?"

"I don't know anything about a plague," Morgan muttered. "And no, I did not send it."

"Well good, but... Can you still cure it? Because it's spread throughout the city and the castle now, and I'm real worried for Lucan and the king who were showing the first signs of that really gross sounding cough the day Sir Accolon came barging into town."

"Why not do what everyone else in Camelot does and just pray for God to cure it?"

"Well, I have been, and so has everyone, but he must be terribly busy somewhere else, because even the bishop has come down with it now, which has everyone on edge."

Morgan's eyes turned to the star filled sky, thinking of Merlin's long ago words about Avalon, Excalibur's sheath. The true holy sword was said to protect its wielder and all those around him from wound and disease. Arthur never would have fallen ill if he were carrying the true Excalibur at his side instead of Merlin's replica sword in the stone.

"It is time you went home."

Gareth gave a vehement shake of his head. "Sorry, miss witch, but I'm not going anywhere unless you're going with me--"

She waved her hand and summoned up a portal, tossing the boy right through it with a surge of telekinesis to land safe upon his bed back in the manor outside Camelot where Anna's family resided. The portal instantly started to close, and Gareth bounded angrily to his feet, passionately proclaiming, "If I've not persuaded you to aid us yet, then I shall simply ride back to your gates and try again! However many times it takes, and however far away you send me--!"

The portal snapped shut, and Gareth deflated, looking instantly toward the door of his bedroom. "Off I go again, I suppose. Though it was rather a long ride, and now I've lost my horse..."

"Your horse is back in the stables, and you are not going anywhere," Morgan enforced, causing him yet another serious scare, near jumping out of his skin, as he clued into her presence stood right at his back. "You are going now to find your mother and tell her you've come home, and you are not going to do anything nearly so reckless as charging off alone into the Welsh mountains or the woods until you are over six feet and can hold a full claymore, are we clear?"

"You think I'll be over six feet?" He smiled. "That would make me taller than Gawain *and* Lucan, and mother would be ever so proud... I really should say hello to her now. You're right about that. I never gave a proper farewell when I set off last month."

It was right at that moment that the door burst open, and Anna came sweeping into the room, Gawain at her back. "I heard it. It was his voice. I know it..." She trailed off, and her eyes flooded with tears, as they locked with those of her son stood so casually in the center of the room.

"Mother." He gave a little wave, and Anna instantly crushed the breath from his body, holding him tight to her chest and kissing his cheeks and forehead.

"You cruel... idiotic... thoughtless boy! Where in heavens have you been? And why the hell are you here?!" she shouted at Morgan, glaring up at her fiercely with arms clasped protectively around little Gareth's back.

"I brought her here to help us," Gareth asserted, the words completely muffled by his mother's shoulder, shoved up against his face. "She's going to cure Lucan and the king."

"I made no such promises," the sorceress muttered, melting instantly into shadow to escape the wary, glowering stare of her sister.

"Morgan, wait..." Gawain reached for her hand, but it slipped right through his fingers. He sighed, staring right at the spot she had vacated and seeming to know that her shadow still lingered somewhere within the room. "If you did set this plague upon us in vengeance for Urien, then punish only he who struck the final blow. Your brother offered him mercy, yet I slew your husband, my uncle. I am the only one who need be punished!"

"Liar." Her whisper echoed through the room.

She had scried that moment of her husband's death a hundred times in painful replay, and she knew it was Arthur himself that had killed her lord. He and his men had encircled the king and demanded he surrender. Urien had spurned the offer and lunged to end the boy. Sir Baudwin wrested the blade from his hands, and Arthur speared his fellow monarch through the heart. An uneven contest, and an image that would hang in her mind forever, just like her husband's lifeless eyes.

Quests for vengeance had never brought her anything but failure and further loss however, and so she felt no need to waste her energies on thinking up further torments for her brother and his aged bodyguard. But of course Gawain did not see that. Of course he thought she had punished an entire city with deadly illness in reprisal for a single man's act. Tragically misunderstood he'd told Gareth. Morgan the widowed sorceress was tragically misunderstood, yet he believed her capable still of terrible things, and he was right to fear her.

She was not a noble healer rushing off to Arthur's rooms to nurse him back to health. She was a villain with nothing left to lose, and no reason or need to do anything she did not wish.

XXV. Avalon

The great King Arthur lay sweating in his sheets, skin flushed with fever and armpits swollen with blackened blight, the mark of the terrible sickness that had swept over his city. The budding warrior king, savior of all of Britain, dead at only the age of seventeen. It would be such a temptingly poetic loss, a fateful squelching of grand potential, dashing all the million hopes of all his fanatical acolytes who had wanted so desperately a just and fair king at the end of these decades of civil war and strife that had torn apart their country. This boy was supposed to grow into a man, to reign long and unify the country with holy Excalibur in hand…

But he had been duped just as soundly as his people, and therein lie his doom. The sword laid out at his bedside was naught but an imposter, a blasphemy to the true relic that still lay buried at the bottom of a lake. The dark eyes of his sister, the accursed witch and changeling, weighed into the unconscious king, and she decided coolly that it was long past time he learned of his folly. This teenage dunce was in sore need of revelation of all the many lies of Merlin and his daughter who had manufactured miracles for the wizard's little chess piece who was in reality naught but an average boy. Arthur would have to awaken of course, in order to process those much humbling truths. He would need to be freed of his fever and his delirium, else Morgan's words would be but pointless sounds, echoing off the walls and into the deafened ears of one dying.

Morgan knelt at the weakened king's bedside and laid a hand upon his chest. She understood the science of the little creatures who had invaded her brother's body, destroying him with a steadily growing host of attackers, just as his own armies had laid waste to her lord husband's troops. These invisible creatures needed to be cleansed. Arthur's own microscopic soldiers were fighting to slaughter them even now and drive them from his tissue. Any potion she fed him to bring down his fever, or bleed the poison from those sores, or clear the phlegm from his lungs would be an all but meaningless treatment of symptoms. It would not ensure he won this internal war. Luckily though, she was not only an enlightened alchemist and doctor. She was a wizard no less learned than Merlin, and the power of sorcery, enhanced by knowledge, could burn away in an instant any enemy that arose, no matter their size.

The Tale of ~~King Arthur~~Morgan Le Fay

She focused on Arthur's weakly pounding pulse, and brought swift and brutal end to every invisible invader she detected, clearing away the remains and the waste in a stream of sickly yellow liquid that came streaming out his mouth and nose, as he came lurching awake, spewing into the bowl she held calmly up toward his face. He spent a solid five minutes after that coughing, no doubt still feeling dreadful, but his temperature was already coming down.

"Sister?" He seemed surprised at her presence, and who could blame him? The chillingly dark eyes, fixed frown, and sallow freckled face were not a sight any man would wish to be greeted with upon waking.

"Your life is in my hands, as always, little brother," Morgan stated hollowly, sinking back in the chair at his bedside. "What a poor king you have proven without Merlin to guide your every step. Laying there powerless as your city is consumed by plague..."

Arthur flushed but bit back the prideful retort clearly brimming on his lips, eyes sad and distant, as he answered instead, "Tell me truthfully you did not send this curse."

Morgan ground her teeth. She had saved his life, and just like Merlin, he had given no thanks for it. Instead, he simply assumed like everyone else that she had been the one to conjure up this sickness. She aught to return him to his sickbed, set him to burning with fever and vomiting his guts out and--

Arthur seized her hand, eyes weighing into her gravely. "If you did send this horror... It surely sprang from grief, and so I feel I've no right to my wrath. I would feel no anger in truth had I not walked through our streets and seen the bodies of mother and child alike laid out in the gutters. For all your attacks on the battlefield, your curses then ate only into soldiers and knights, those strong enough to weather death. I respected that line, and if I have pushed you past it..." His hand tightened over hers. "Forgive me. I grieve for your loss. I do. But do not punish the people. Do not heal me only so that I may continue to watch them suffer--"

"And have them rioting at your gates, defaming you rightfully a pretender and fool?" She ripped her hand free of his grip. "God's chosen king indeed, the one God loved so much he would have spared him the evils of this world by putting a painful drawn out end to his story at the ripe old age of seventeen! But I guess the devil is not done with you, Arthur, for behold, I have cometh! Satan's most wicked curse upon the world has stolen into your castle and healed you this day, only that you may suffer!"

"Even if that is so," he declared, speaking so passionately and somehow missing completely the absolute sarcasm in her tone. "I beg of you to heal this city. Take only righteous vengeance and inflict whatever suffering upon me that you wish, but spare the people."

"Do you know how many house visits it would take, how much time and energy and effort it would require for me personally to cure even a handful of your citizens?" she snapped. "Even if I was so willing to exhaust myself, I'll show up at their bedsides, and their family members shall instantly scream and attack me, and I won't get to heal a single soul before the mob drives me from the city."

He shook his head. "I... I suppose, but I don't understand why you would have to go into their houses. You sent this curse with but a wave of your hand, or so I thought. Surely, you can dispel it just as easily--"

"I did not send this plague! It is no trick of sorcery, you blinded, bigoted, idiot!"

He stared into her raw and wounded gaze, and his own eyes widened in pained realization. "You didn't...? Then I have wronged you sorely. I--"

"Do not bother with your worthless apologies! Because even if I had sent a plague, you know what would have protected you? Avalon. Excalibur's sheath."

He looked to the blade at his feet, seated in a plain leather casing, since neither Merlin nor Morgan had crafted a sheath for their replicas sunken in the anvil. "Then... where did you hide the sheath when you cast the sword into rock?"

"I never hid the sheath, because *this* sword has no sheath. *This* sword is not Excalibur. It was never Excalibur. I never had the real Excalibur, because that sword is the closely guarded possession of the closest thing I have met to a real devil who sits at the bottom of a lake out in the faerie woods."

His eyes narrowed, shaking his head. "What is the purpose of these lies? Do you wish for me to abandon the true holy relic and set off on meaningless quest for...?"

She held her hand out to the side and summoned instantly another replica Excalibur, tossing it at the floundering king and letting him feel the heft and run his hands over the inscription in the all too real steel. "By God..." He looked again to the blade at his feet. "So the sword in the stone... It truly was all just a performance, a trick?"

The Tale of ~~King Arthur~~ Morgan Le Fay

"A trick and you were simply the pawn, hauled up from the audience and used to sell the magician's lie," she gloated. "God did not choose you that day, Arthur, Merlin did, despite my best efforts to combat him. You stole my throne and ruined my legend, and you have nothing to show for it but a fake replica of a holy relic that does nothing to protect your country from famine and plague."

Arthur sank back on the bed, hands clenched and eyes lowered. "Merlin never said anything about any of this."

"That's because Merlin was a lying coward. He did not care if you had the true Excalibur and its protection, so long as the people believed you wielded the true holy relic. And he did not care to tell you the truth, because he was a selfish and short-sighted cad."

"Where is Merlin? I have not seen him since that day in Lothian..." Morgan instantly turned her back. She turned her back to hide the pain and guilt twisting over her expression. "You struck him down?"

She did not answer the somber and quiet question. She raised her cowl and kept her voice cold and even. "If you want to save your city, brother, brave the path to distant Dozemary lake and lay claim to the true Excalibur. Your people will be healed at but a touch of its sheath. Though best make haste. With the trade routes still open, this sickness is already manifesting in Caerlon and London. Your little kingdom is crumbling."

Fear shone poignantly in his gaze, and she melted into shadow, commanding herself to savor his dismay rather than feel pained by it.

XXVI. Healings and Grudges

The all too tender hearted witch of Camelot headed out from Arthur's rooms, but was stopped dead in her tracks by the sound of sobbing echoing down the corridor. She followed the crying to its source only a few rooms down from the royal chambers and stared somberly at the painful vignette of little Gareth, crying at the bedside of Sir Lucan, with hand clutched tight within a limp and unresponsive grip and forehead pressed against the blankets, the *infected* blankets.

Morgan dropped back into a solid shape and stalked angrily over to the boy, grabbing his wrist and pulling him back from the plague-ridden knight. "Do you understand nothing of the principle of quarantine? Who the hell let you in here...?"

She trailed off, as she saw Gareth wince and noticed the darkened indents of deep bruising around his wrist. Gareth ripped his hand free of her grip, wiping at his eyes and pridefully pretending he had never been crying. "No one let me in. The maids are all sick or retreated to the countryside though, so they can't very well keep me out." He raised his chin, forcing a smile and staring up at her hopefully. "I was worried you already left, but you came to heal him, right? To help?"

Morgan crossed her arms, tapping her finger on her arm. Lucan was vapid, shallow, and not particularly bright. He was also a serial adulterer whose only talents outside the bedroom seemed to be running people through on horseback. Besides, she was already tired...

She looked again to Gareth's swelling wrist. "What happened there?"

He tucked his hands behind his back, solidly avoiding her gaze. "It does not matter. I am not the one in need of healing."

"Give me the truth, and I will heal him," she promised, and Gareth brightened. "Who did that to you?" Her brow lowered, tone darkening. "Did your mother...?"

Gareth blinked, shocked by the accusation. "*Mother*? All mother did was kiss my cheeks and hug me til I near suffocated and tell me not to leave my room for the next week." He paused. "I did leave though, right after she did. I wanted to check how Lucan was doing, but I ran into Agravain out in our stables." He rubbed at his wrist. "He gets angry. I cause him a lot of trouble when I make mother worry like that. He usually just shoves me, or trips me, but when I make mother this mad at them..."

She laid a hand on his shoulder and sensed instantly the bruised ribs and stomach hiding beneath his shirt. She pulled him into an instinctive hug and instantly healed all the damage. "Tell me where Agravain is now," she whispered.

He stiffened, pulling back from her. "Why?"

"I'm a witch," she grated. "I punish the wicked, so tell me where he--"

"I will not forgive you should you do anything evil to him on my behalf!" She stared at him wordlessly, stunned. "I am to be a knight. I do not allow others to fight for me my battles."

"You do not have a battle, Gareth. You're ten years old. Someone needs to be protecting you."

"I hate when they're protecting me! All mother does is coddle and fuss and that just makes him angrier. Then Gawain finds out or sees something and beats him so bad that..." He swallowed. "He broke his arm the last time, and Agravain couldn't hold a sword for months. They used to be close, before I came along..."

Lucan let out a dangerously wet sounding cough, and Gareth rushed back to his bedside, grabbing hold of his hand. "The only one I can talk to is Lucan. He doesn't treat me any different from anyone else. He just nods along, and he can't give any advice, but that's better in some ways. Then he lets me feed the horses, helps me practice my sword forms." He smiled, a bittersweet grin. "I don't think he knows what's going on with Agravain and Gawain. He sees even less than mother, but that's alright." His teary eyes turned up to fix on her. "Don't let him die. Please?"

Morgan gave a heavy sigh and once again pulled him back from the bed, planting him firmly in the corner. "Do not touch the deathly ill, you tender hearted fool. That is how you get sick. Just stand back here and keep quiet."

She put her hands on Lucan's chest and cured him the same way she had Arthur.

Lucan's eyes opened to fix on her, and he instantly cursed, lurching up from his bed and reaching for his sword. "Witch!"

"You shameless ass, how many favors have I done for you now?"

He settled back into a sitting position on the floor, blade still held out before him. "Well, I don't know. What's happening? Oh, Gareth. Wait, your mother does not want you speaking with this woman. Do you understand?"

Morgan's hands clenched, and she exploded past him in a burst of violent wind, streaking up to her abandoned childhood bedroom in its isolated tower. Sir Kay and Sir Baudwin and a host of others within the castle were already in the late stages of this illness. They might not live out the night without her intervention.

She did not care. Let them all die. She was done exhausting herself for ungrateful fools. If Arthur wanted to save such cretins, then he had best retrieve Avalon already and get it done himself. "Because I've nothing but hatred for you, all of you," she murmured. Well, everyone except little Gareth perhaps, but he wasn't even allowed to speak with her anymore.

She curled up into a ball and prayed for her exhaustion to drag her under. When she awoke, it was already late in the morning, yet she had absolutely zero motivation to get up from beneath her covers. There was something dreadfully comforting about her childhood rooms. They stayed always the way she had left them, no matter the years that passed between her visits, and her little window gave view to sunny skies that almost never graced her fortress in Cader Idris. In here, she could just curl up beneath her covers with no ghosts or arachnids to pester her, safe within her quilted cocoon where Merlin had always come to sit at her side and tell her stories...

She left the bed and dressed immediately, keeping her mind consumed by business before the tears could come to choke her. She pulled up an image of Arthur in her washbasin and found he was already deep within the western woods, well on his way to lake country, with only a single pair of bodyguards, Sir Elliot and Sir Daniel, riding at his side.

He had set out with all impulsiveness the evening prior, almost the second Morgan left his side and paid her visit to Sir Lucan. He had taken the time beforehand only to outfit himself in armor and make a brief appearance before his court, hale and healthy with 'Excalibur' held aloft and the bold words that he was setting out because he had learned of a cure for this plague and need only go out himself to seize it. His nobles gave weakened cheers, and the coughing and enervated populace echoed those supports as best they could, as he rode down the street and out through the gates with the loudly repeated words that a cure was on its way.

Morgan had not expected him to leave in the middle of the night, and she really had expected him to send word to Gawain and at least a dozen other of his still healthy knights staying in the countryside safely away from the disease ridden castle. Instead, the impetuous youth went riding out into the hostile wilds in that gaudy golden armor of his with only two of the closest men on hand as his escort. Perhaps he was too used to

The Tale of ~~King Arthur~~ Morgan Le Fay

having Merlin at his side, making him invulnerable and putting swift and decisive end to any enemy that threatened. Arthur and his men had already been accosted by brigands, almost as soon as they set foot outside the city limits. The three young knights had fought fiercely the host of untrained criminals and narrowly survived the ambush, but now Sir Elliot especially appeared worn down and battered, barely keeping his place in the saddle. Sir Daniel was not looking much better, and just a mile up the trail, Morgan could see the dust trails of another group of armored men riding them down. These men were much better outfitted and more capable seeming that the ragged band of bandits from before.

The black armored figure of Sir Turquine rode at the head of that force, and so Morgan wearily guessed that this was the opportunity the old brute had been waiting for to slay the young king and finally put an end to Uther's line. She teleported out to that trail and changed the enemies' horses into cats and their armor into sand, all but that of Sir Turquine, whose midnight outfittings curiously resisted her sorcery.

The knights fell naked to the ground atop their furry, hissing mounts, and descended into a confusion of yelping and flailing limbs, as the disoriented felines clawed at the bodies of those crushing down upon them. Morgan almost smiled, remembering with wistful fondness how delightful her little pranks could be when they descended upon the cruel and unsuspecting.

"W-witch!" the clawed-up knights shrieked, leveling a finger at her chest. "It's the witch of Orkney, come to curse us!"

"I am not from bloody Orkney," she spat. "Now flee for your lives and all that."

"We wish you no offense, my lady," Sir Turquine pronounced, giving a low bow with eyes glittering ferally through the narrow slit of his visor. "We are allies of your fallen lord husband, set to watch the movements of our enemy, King Arthur, on behalf of King Brandin and all we unjustly unseated barons of these lands stolen from us through a wizard's underhanded tactics." The rest of the men gave shaky nods, still naked on the trail with their transformed steeds long since run off into the brush. "This day has given rise to a grand opportunity, and we ride forth now to take vengeance on that lying wizard's prop. If you would kindly stand aside and return our weapons--"

"You have zero right to call yourself a knight, *Sir* Turquine," Morgan mocked. "It seems you challenge one on one only babes and old nursemaids, and now that the boy is but barely full grown thou art left quivering in thy boots, needing an entire host of men to dare confront him."

Turquine flushed. "I fear not some beardless boy!"

"Then fight him like a man, and kill him on your own. You still possess that dreadful armor of yours and the strength of arm to strangle some beardless teenager surely, unless tales of thy savage prowess have been naught but lying embellishments... Perhaps beneath that armor there is naught left but an aged, withering, soon to be corpse."

His savage eyes narrowed into a glare. "Stand aside, saucy wench. Witness for yourself the strength of the great black knight, and do not dare attempt to lend any sorcerous aid to your brother this day. I long ago made myself immune to such tricks."

"Remove then thy helmet, good sir, and let me gaze upon that crooked nose from that glorious face-plant you apparently feigned the last time I cast my spell upon thee."

"Be grateful my king does not wish you dead yet!" Sir Turquine hissed. "There are powers other than you that roam these lands, woman. Powers to rival even that of Merlin himself."

"Then clearly you've nothing to fear this day. Go on, Turquine, carry on now." She waved him on down the trail. "Though you'll be going on foot of course, and no man from this armsless little army shall follow."

Her eyes flashed to the naked host of men still quivering behind the black knight, and sure enough, they took off at a run back up the trail, all but two of them. One, a peach-fuzzed boy even younger than Arthur who must surely be a squire of some sort. That shaking teen said nothing, but looked to Turquine in fearful indecision.

The second was a much more muscled warrior in his late twenties who gave the solemn vow, "I shall not abandon thee, father. Though if my lady would be so kind as to restore my brother and I our trousers, so that we may fight with some measure of dignity--"

"There is no dignity in outnumbered ambush, good sir," Morgan countered. "You may fight as you are, or you may turn tail and run."

"I give you leave to depart from here, Pellinore," Sir Turquine announced. "You as well, Lamorak. You need not debase yourselves, and I require not thy aid. I will beat that boy's skull in with naught but my bare hands and return to thee anon."

"Anon then!" Lamorak stuttered, turning hastily to depart, only for his elder to catch his arm.

The Tale of ~~King Arthur~~ Morgan Le Fay

"We would both surely benefit from witnessing this great victory, father," Pellinore proclaimed, "though I will not cheapen your challenge by revealing myself before a king in this state. I shall watch deep in cover, as will my brother."

"Very well."

The black armored brute and his buck naked sons continued on down the winding trail, though Pellinore and Lamorak did manage to forage some basic armor and coverings from the bodies of the bandits that Arthur had earlier slain. Morgan allowed them that one small mercy, but disintegrated every knife and club the pair laid their hands upon, until Turquine once again lost his temper. "You call it a fair contest?" he railed at the sky. "Stripping men of arms and sending them against a mounted entourage of fully outfitted knights?"

"You said you needed naught but your bare hands to beat down that boy," Morgan reminded him coyly, a breath of wind tickling past his ear. Turquine cringed away from her presence and tossed aside angrily the stub of a sword hilt, muttering curses beneath his breath and slogging on along the trail.

A sharp whinny echoed from up the road suddenly, and Morgan's brow lowered in concern. She took the form of a crow and flitted on ahead, swooping down just in time to glimpse Arthur rolling his way free from the body of his war horse, as a sharp and savage bit of nothing stabbed down into the neck of the already collapsed stallion, silencing its panicked cries and then whipping out toward Arthur like a blade of razor-edged wind.

Morgan erected a barrier around the fallen king, and the unseen blade rebounded. Whether is was fairy or ghost, she was not quite sure, but the ugly slashes of its attacks along the legs and neck of Arthur's horse had the look of a sword and not claw marks. Morgan could feel eyes weighing into her, but she could see nothing of their owner, and thus had no target to attack. The invisible assailant seemed fearful of her regardless and retreated off into the brush in a rush of snapping branches.

Arthur noticed nothing of his true enemy's passage however, sitting up dazedly with helmet askew and head ringing. His eyes fixed wearily on the crow settling down to roost in the branches right above him.

He looked sadly back to the corpse of his fallen steed. "That was a cruel trick, sister, bringing unjust end to a faithful friend."

"My king?" Sir Daniel pressed, pulling him to his feet. "You know what it is that attacked you just now?"

"I know all too well." Arthur sighed, and Morgan's feathers ruffled up in rage. She really aught to let Turquine beat his face in.

She let loose an angry caw, spreading her wing and gesturing dramatically back down the trail from whence she had come.

Arthur's eyes narrowed, and he followed her point, keying in finally on the stomping steps of the black knight and his sons drawing slowly up the trail. "Good day to you, sirs!" Arthur called out in greeting. "What brings you to this neck of the woods?"

"We've come to kill a king," Turquine declared with impressive boldness, fist whipping out to take out the wounded Sir Elliot as he struggled to draw his blade. A single punch and the man was down for good, as savage Turquine plucked the blade from his fingers and swung for Arthur's head.

Daniel moved to intervene, but Pellinore and his brother tackled aside the young knight, and the three fell to grappling in the mud.

Arthur had drawn the false Excalibur and raised it in expert block of Turquine's strike. The blade shattered. Turquine's stolen sword cut right through the steel, carrying on in a broad swipe across Arthur's chest.

His breastplate deflected the worst of the damage, even when Turquine's next blow to the side began to cave in the metal, so the black knight aimed the next stab at the weaker chainmail covering his armpit.

The sword puffed to mist, the second the point made contact, and Turquine cursed, glaring back at Morgan standing calmly in the shadows behind them. "With my bare hands. That was the victory that was promised. I understand, witch," he derisively spat.

"Bare hands. Alright then," Arthur shakily assented, tossing aside his broken stub of sword and swinging out with his fist toward Turquine's head. Gauntlet struck visor, once, twice, and Turquine never even flinched. Instead, he seized hold of Arthur and threw him bodily to the dirt.

"Sire!" Daniel cried out in panic. He gave a savage strike to Lamorak that knocked the boy sprawling, only to get caught up in constrictive grapple by Pellinore whose superior size and weight gave him quite the advantage in this fight without blades, just like his father.

Turquine's hands were around Arthur's neck, squeezing mercilessly with weight settled on his chest. Arthur's panicked blows grew weaker and weaker, face red and eyes bulging…

"Damn it," Morgan muttered. She really was a tender hearted fool. She held out her hand, with the firm order of, "Sleep!"

The Tale of ~~King Arthur~~ Morgan Le Fay

The spell did nothing, and Turquine's visor swung over to face her, eyes glittering with triumph. She knew then his earlier words about being invulnerable to her spells had not been lying blusters. With his visor in place, he was seemingly immune to all magical influence. Still, she was not willing to give up just yet without at least trying to disintegrate him. The flames could not touch him, neither could the frost or the sickness. No enchantment could reach this brute, so long as that armor lay about him.

"How about a knife to the face?" she muttered, summoning a dagger, not into her own hand, but into Arthur's, who plunged it dutifully right into the eye of his opponent. The black armored goliath collapsed dead on top of him, and the boy was most thoroughly pinned, coughing into the dirt.

She refused to go over there and roll aside that ponderous corpse. Still, Arthur appeared in no state to manage it himself, and now Pellinore was stalking over there, having broken the neck of Sir Daniel and taken his sword for his own.

Morgan stepped calmly in between the shoddily armored wrestler and his floundering prey, staring him down in grim warning.

The knight settled into fighting stance with sword menacingly raised. "Stand aside, my lady." At least he wasn't calling her 'witch' or 'wench' like his father had, and that tone of reverent respect did have a somewhat soothing effect on her temper. "I must avenge my father and put an end to that usurper--"

"Your father is the usurper, ambushing his lawful king," Morgan retorted sharply. "And you this day have killed a loyal guard," She gestured to the body of Sir Daniel. "and bereaved his own family, so enough with the noble pretense. Just carry on your way with that broken-nosed brother of yours, and be grateful I don't incinerate you."

Pellinore pursed his lips, chin raising in haughty consideration. He looked once more to the dripping visor of Sir Turquine. "His body must be laid to rest with proper ceremony."

"Take Sir Daniel's horse then, and be gone from here," Arthur croaked, finally fighting his way out from under the fallen giant. "Enough men have died already this day, and I've no desire to fight thee."

Pellinore considered those words and shot another unhappy glance toward Morgan before seizing the reins of Sir Daniel's skittishly dancing mount, heaving his father's body onto its back, and setting off back up the road with his limping younger brother in tow.

Arthur kept a look of stoic resolve upon his face until the men had long since vanished from sight. Then he dropped to his knees at Elliot's side with hand to his forehead and eyes tearing. "Ah, the death will never end, now will it?" he exhaled, looking in dismay to dead Sir Daniel, staring up at the stars. "The cycles of endless vengeance for good men fallen to senseless violence..."

"Sir Dinadan doesn't really strike me as the vengeful type," Morgan shrugged off, thinking of Daniel's elder brother, a quite cavalier sort not at all interested in traditions or bloodshed.

"*You* are the endless vengeance!" Arthur snapped, whirling to confront her. "Your torments know no sense of limits or fairness. From my childhood onward you have taken from me and left me without peace. And I tried hard to understand, to show mercy and compassion, only to find that you punish every enemy that spares you, just as you struck down Merlin..."

She started laughing, an unhinged cackle, high and shrill and littered with sobs, as she took in the sheer irony of the completely warped viewpoint of the spoiled king before her.

His words trailed off, and he stared at her in tense unease, so she closed her eyes, clasping her hands to her breast and envisioning this scenario as it aught to have played out. "'Thank you, sister. Thank you so very much for saving my life this day.' Why you are so very welcome, Arthur!"

"Why would I thank you?! You killed my horse, and broke my sword, and egged on enemies to--"

"I did not break your sword. The sword broke because it was not a real sword, it was Merlin's conjuration, given life and solidity only by concrete belief in its existence, so now with Merlin gone..." Her voice caught.

"And that as well! How can you expect me to forgive you for that?" Arthur shouted. "Merlin was your teacher. Time and again he defended you to me, and time and again did he spare you his wrath! He was nothing but kind, and you--"

"Kind? *Kind?* Oh yes, he was just as kind and as thankful as you are!"

"For what do I owe you thanks?!"

"Oh gee, well let's think real hard, shall we? Not only did I *yet again* save your life, even though you did not at all deserve my intervention, you idiot, riding out alone, a king, in a king's shining armor, announcing your departure to all your enemies first then isolating yourself out alone in the woods so an entire armored contingent can ride you down and kill you! A contingent I disposed of by the way, all twenty men save for the magically resistant Turquine and his sons. Though you've left them their evil magic

The Tale of ~~King Arthur~~ Morgan Le Fay

armor and just sent them on their way, so they may attack you again in the future! Just like whatever that invisible creature was that killed your horse that you did not even have the perception to notice!" He blinked, clearly taken aback. "So yes, I am sorry you got your men killed. But oh wait, no I'm not, because it is enitrely your fault and I hate you!"

She burst into the shape of a crow again and vanished off into the woods. She expected Arthur to turn around then, to give up his foolish quest and slog off back to his dying city. Instead, he just sat there on the ground, appearing to be deep in thought and staying that way for nearly an hour, before he finally rose to his feet. He composed his men solemnly and laid them at the side of the trail, saying a prayer over their bodies, then setting off alone, ever deeper into the woods with darkness already descending.

His steps were somewhat staggering. Morgan thought at first that was simply exhaustion. The longer she studied his movements though, the more she began to suspect that Turquine's mighty blows against his breastplate had cracked a rib, if not several. Sure enough, his face grew paler as the hours wore on, and his breathing more labored, but Morgan saw no need to tend to his wounds. In fact, it was perfect pathetic bait for the selfish warden of these woods who would surely take covetous pity on the wounded young king now wandering so close to her domain.

A light appeared in Arthur's path as the sun vanished below the horizon. A single hovering orb of blue, then another, and another: a clear line off the road and into the deeper wilds. Everyone knew it was folly to follow the trail of a will-o the wisp, yet Arthur paid no heed to that wisdom. He went walking right after the lights, but luckily for him, this wisp had a master beyond its own mischievous intent.

Arthur arrived at the shores of the lake and collapsed to his knees, staring down at his ragged reflection in the waters below. Blood dribbled out his split lip and speckled the mirror-like surface with gory ripples of excitement.

Then a pale glowing hand reached up from the depths and cupped Arthur's chin, forcing him to meet the glorious green eyes of the angelic creature knelt now before him on the surface of the lake. "What grave misfortune has befallen you, my king?"

"If you are God's envoy, I am not yet ready to go," he gasped. "I cannot abandon my people. They need me."

"Do they now?" Viviane cooed, pushing back his hair. "Well perhaps I will return you to them then, but what favor would you give me in return?"

"Whatever you ask."

Viviane smiled, a glowing and absolutely chilling look to Morgan's eyes. "Rise then, my king. I've the power to cure all that ails thee."

She pulled him to his feet and out onto the surface of the lake, guiding him to the mirrored image of the moon in its center. "See there." She raised his hand toward the rippling image of the true Excalibur, shimmering just beneath the surface of the lake. "Stretch out thy hand."

His fingers reached beneath the water and clasped tight around Excalibur's hilt, drawing it free of the depths. The sword glowed with dazzling golden warmth the second he gripped it, and Viviane's lips parted in covetous awe, hands tightening around the wounded vassal that her stolen sword was clearly announcing as its destined master.

Arthur held the glowing blade in both hands and raised it up before him in wonder, straightening without pain now, with the color quickly returning to his cheeks.

"There is your favor." Viviane beamed, fingers stroking his head, as she whispered insistent command into his ear. "And now my request. You must bring me Merlin."

Arthur's face grew pained, and he wearily lowered the blade, looking back at her sadly. "That is something I cannot do, my lady, for even armed with so glorious a weapon, I cannot reach beyond the realm of death."

Viviane laughed in dangerous disbelief. "What fiend could slay Merlin?"

"Morgan Le Fay."

Viviane's smile died, eyes searching briefly past Arthur and scanning the darkened woods for some sign of her invisible quarry. "Merlin's carnivorous little bud did not fully devour the great druid, I sense. She has simply hidden him away... But until he is returned to me, I am surely due a replacement." Her eyes went back to Arthur, but Morgan did not wait for the suddenly swirling waters at his feet to suck him down into Viviane's kingdom along with the prized relic in his hands.

A burst of fire exploded right against the possessive fairy's chest, as the invisible hand of magic seized Arthur from behind, yanking him through the air and back to shore. He hit the ground with Excalibur in hand, and Morgan teleported him back to Camelot, the second his feet touched soil not under the fairy's water-based enchantments.

Arthur sat up in his bed and looked blearily around the room. He then looked down at the sword in his hands and announced in solemn vow, "I shall put you to good use, my friend, in honor of Sir Daniel, and Sir Elliot, and Merlin."

The Tale of ~~King Arthur~~**Morgan Le Fay**

Sure enough, the earnest young king set to such good works immediately. He took not one moment of sleep that night, but instead visited every sickened soul within his castle, healing them of their illness with but a tap upon the shoulder. He then rode without rest onto Caerlon and then London, calling the people to mass with the help of the town bishops and healing them all of their afflictions. Excalibur truly was a holy relic, bringing miracle after miracle in the hands of its true wielder. The people rejoiced, and the crops flourished that spring, while Morgan retreated sullenly back to her distant castle with the small comfort that at least horrid Lady Viviane felt just as angry and slighted as she did now, as they had both of them been cheated of their prize.

XXVII. Sir Lancelot Du Lac

Morgan the aspiring shut-in was allowed only a single month of solitude within her haunted home, before the bizarre spectacle of a donkey-pulled cart carrying within it the bulky figures of a pair of richly armored and all too familiar knights caused her to yet again open her gates. She had done almost zero scrying recently, telling herself firmly that she never wanted to see Arthur, or Anna, or any one of her cruel, accusing family members again. And so it was that she had zero idea just what it was that had prompted Sir Gawain to come riding up to her gates on a donkey of all things, pulling with him in his cart an absurdly beautiful man with loosely curling dark hair and eyes a warm and heart melting chocolate.

The damn lounging lout made Morgan's heart flutter the second she so much as glanced at him in her mirror, and she cursed herself a girlish fool, knowing that could only be Lancelot, full grown now and gorgeous. Though how the hell had he escaped from Viviane's greedy clutches? There were literally a million questions caused by this odd couple's appearance, and she could answer none of them while keeping them locked outside her gates.

She waved her hand and teleported them inside her throne room, sitting haughtily back in her seat in a flattering dress of deepest purple. She arched an eyebrow in clear and cocky question, then tried to snuff out the flood of warmth that filled her chest, as Gawain responded with a relieved yet curiously close-lipped smile. "Morgan. Thank you for seeing us. We are in dire need of your aid."

"Because you lost all dignity in some back-country town when you traded your horse for a donkey and cart?"

Lancelot flushed, trying unsuccessfully to shove himself upright from the spot of floor where she'd dumped him. There was an arrow straight through his knee however, and another sitting perilously close to the artery in his thigh, so he stood no chance of standing. "You mock an earnest fellow, a man who is still technically a knight, even now that he has set aside his meager pride to secure a means of transport for his wounded comrade."

"My *meager* pride?" Gawain repeated, tone darkening. "And what exactly do you mean I am still *technically* a knight?"

"Well, you failed comically to defend your king, then lent zero aid whatsoever in my storming of the enemy stronghold, so really it is audacious you dare call yourself a warrior at all."

The Tale of ~~King Arthur~~Morgan Le Fay

"Says the man who went charging straight at the arrows, after stealing my horse!"

"I did not steal your horse. I was in need, and I borrowed it."

"And now he's dead! Just as you aught to be! You, a boy, not even *technically* a knight who--"

"I am the knight and uncontested champion of the Lady of the Lake."

"A fairy cannot just declare you a knight. The king has to knight you."

"I need not that thief's validation!"

"Your every posturing act is a desperate cry for validation."

"How dare you--!"

Morgan started laughing. She couldn't help it. This scenario was enrapturingly confusing and absurd, and after so much time alone, she was very much in need of a good story. "Bravo!" She clapped. "You have me utterly hooked, just brimming with interest, so what the hell are you talking about? And how did you two even meet?" She gestured to Lancelot, trying to keep the derision from her tone. "Last I saw you, you were six years old and being sent off to bed in permanent imprisonment for breaking your psychotic lady's rules and going out without permission."

Lancelot's fists clenched, cheeks reddening with a pretty flush of anger. "I warned you before, witch, and I will warn you again, do not insult my lady."

"Mmm, so she is still your lady," Morgan dryly mused, unable to hide her disappointment. "Alright then, back to the first question; how did you two lovebirds meet?"

Both men flushed in anger that time, and Gawain put a hand to his forehead, eyeing her darkly. "You've really an unfortunate talent for getting under people's skin."

"How can I help it? You quarrel like an old married couple. Now go on, tell the tale. Entertain me, jesters!"

The candelabras burst to life with atmospheric lighting, but Lancelot gave no heed to her command, raising his finger in warning point. "Were I at full strength, witch, I would strike you down for such mockery, righteous vengeance for your attacks against my lady--"

"Well it cannot be righteous vengeance, because you've just announced that striking me down would be for the sake of your pride, a response to my mockery, not an act of loyalty."

"Don't try and argue with her. It will only leave you more frustrated and her all the more amused." Gawain sighed, and she arched an eyebrow, unable to help but wickedly smile.

He turned away the instant they locked eyes, doing everything and anything he could to avoid her 'bewitching' gaze. "Anyhow, we are fortunate that she allowed us into her halls," he continued unsteadily, "and we are in need of her aid."

"So you claim," Lancelot murmured.

"Please, you so called lake knight. You cannot even stand right now, and even if those arrow wounds do not fester and kill you, you will never use that knee again without the skill of the sorceress before you."

"So you dragged him here simply for me to heal him?" Morgan prompted boredly. "I feel not so inclined, given how frequently that brat has insulted me, both now and in the past. Though I will suffer your presence to hear of how he became so prickled with missiles. But do start at the beginning, because all this jumping about is making your tale hard to follow."

Gawain gave a low bow, eyes finding hers once again. "As you wish. It all began when this dunce came riding up to Camelot's gates."

"Dunce?" Lancelot snapped. "You know what, this is my story, so you, defeated fool, may sit quiet and I shall tell the tale." He looked stonily to Morgan. "This all began when--"

"Actually, you were not even there for the beginning, *young* sir," Gawain interrupted. "Since this all began with King Leodegrance and the delayed wedding of our king, so really I must tell the tale."

"That's it." Morgan sighed. "Both of you sit quiet. We can all watch together."

She rose to her feet and motioned them over to a massive pool of water at the end of her grand reception hall. Gawain was in the process of helping Lancelot to his feet so that he may limp his way over there, a process that required a great deal of grunting and dripping wounds and pained expressions, until irritably Morgan teleported over there, mercilessly yanking out the arrow in his knee.

He fell back to the ground with a howl, and she yanked out the second arrow in his thigh, sealing the wound and fully healing the damage before he could bleed out on her floor.

Lancelot sat there for a minute, pale and shaking, staring down at his now mended legs. "Thank you, madam," he forced out. "Though you've all the grace and gentleness of a blacksmith who breaks the iron."

"Know what, only Gawain gets to speak from here on out. How about that?" She twitched a finger, and Lancelot's tongue caught. He could not force out so much as a single word now, and his face flushed with anger.

The Tale of ~~King Arthur~~Morgan Le Fay

Gawain stifled a laugh. "Wish I'd the power to do that. Would have made all these weeks of travel much easier."

"Yes indeed. Tis what all men crave after all, a pretty face at their side with not a word able to cross their lips and pester the ears of their lord."

Lancelot tried to snap out a response. It emerged as nothing but a wheeze of wind, though Gawain's solemn words spoiled her enjoyment of the moment. "Have you truly that low an opinion of me? Saying I like my women silent."

She met his eyes and defensively crossed her arms. "Your sense of humor is dull as a pebble, if you think I was being serious," she muttered.

"And your sense of humor is rather unexpected," he countered, studying her intently. "I have never seen you smile so much as I have these past few minutes."

"What can I say?" she nervously dismissed. "I've been driven mad in isolation, and your presence is an unexpected delight. Now... come along already."

They sank down by the side of the pool, and she summoned up an image of the day Gawain indicated, the day Sir Lancelot Du Lac had come riding up to Camelot.

Arthur sat in his throne, completely ignorant at fist as to the approach of the richly armored knight riding up out of the woods, engrossed as he was in listening to the report of Sir Bedivere stood before him.

"We thought at first that the lack of word was yet another tactic of King Leodegrance to delay yet again the wedding, and we fully expected this meeting to entail yet another challenge for you, my lord, or an increased demand of dowry, just like what he had presented us with these past several correspondences as recompense for the expenses incurred during your campaign to drive out the rebel kings. Yet I have spoken with Leodegrance, face to face this time, and he assured me he had earnestly intended for you and his daughter, Guinevere, to be united in matrimony this very spring. But the princess has, to his panic, simply vanished from Camlierd castle, and from the grief in his eyes, my king, I believe this to be no subterfuge. He pleads earnestly our aid now in retrieving her from whatever felon it was that hath stolen her away."

"Has he any other information to provide about this fiend who kidnapped my betrothed?"

"Only that the attacker somehow slipped unseen through every gate of the castle, and that the guards around Lady Guinevere's room were cut down with blades undrawn. The lady's drinking glass lay broken as well, with bits of torn

clothing at the scene. It churned her father's guts with fearful rage to even recount the sight. He believes it firmly to be the work of the witch of Orkney, Morgan Le Fay, for no other enemy could have slipped so easily through his defenses."

"This is not the work of my sister," Arthur instantly protested, and Morgan blinked in surprise. "If she took it into her mind to kidnap my fiance, she would have done so without leaving any dead men, nor any trace of her passage. This invisible kidnapper sounds far more like whatever creature it was that attacked me in my bed just this past month."

"I remember all too well the day, my king," Sir Lucan supplied. "It was through miracle alone that you survived your wounds, but I thought you slew the creature, even as he made his perilous stab."

"Nay, Sir Lucan. Even the blessed edge of mighty Excalibur could not cut fully through what felt like solid steel. My attacker received but the shallowest scratch I suspect, before fleeing out the window, never to return."

Morgan pulled back from the mirror, turning her eyes to Gawain. "And did you ever catch this invisible assassin you did not think to mention to me?" she demanded, thinking back to that day in the woods and the bladed demon that had killed Arthur's horse.

"No, but we know now its villainous scheme, thus we shall see it slain, just as we will rescue Lady Guinevere soon enough, with your aid. Just watch and you will see. This pool of yours truly is a marvelous trick. You can see every detail of the day." Those last words emerged rather tentative, and she could tell the great knight was self-consciously dreading the images to come. That only further stoked her excitement of course, and she turned her attention back to the mirror.

"....intruder at the gates! He demands an audience with the king." A brightly clad messenger had interrupted the knights' solemn meeting.

"What is the name of this man?" Arthur prodded.

"He announced himself as Sir Lancelot Du Lac..."

"I have never heard of such a man," Lucan muttered in his liege's ear.

"Nor have I," added Gawain and Baudwin.

"I will receive him regardless," Arthur resolved. "For his bearing is clearly noble and his manner sounds that of a man on urgent mission. I have time at the hour of noon. Tell him to wait in the guardhouse until then. I will meet him there, since he is but a stranger and thus unproven in his intent."

"He is already inside the castle, sire!" the messenger blurted out in a panic, clearly wanting to have relaid this important news earlier but not daring to interrupt the king and his nobles. "He beat down the guards at the gates, and

The Tale of ~~King Arthur~~ Morgan Le Fay

the ones at our inner portcullis as well. Now he is on his way..."

The doors of the room burst open once again, and the dazzling figure of Sir Lancelot emerged, sword aloft in derogatory point toward the king, with the groaning figures of a dozen knights laid out in the hall behind him. "King Arthur, cretin and thief! I have come to reclaim the sword of my Lady Viviane which you so insolently pilfered from our kingdom."

Gawain abruptly waved his hands through the waters, scattering her image and distorting the voice that rose to contest Lancelot's demand. "You can skip this part. It really isn't important. Just fast forward to the moment when the black knight comes in."

Lancelot smiled and let out some unheard taunt, and Morgan pulled Gawain smugly back into his seat. "No, I think I would like to watch all of this in order as it unfolds, thank you very much."

"It's just Lancelot peacocking. There is really nothing of worth to..." He trailed off, as the images resumed, and the voice of his past self rose boldly to drown out his present pleas.

"I will beat down this intruder who dares slander your reputation, my king," Sir Gawain proclaimed, drawing his sword and advancing grimly down the steps to face the silver armored knight in the center of the floor. "You face now Sir Gawain, boy. King of Orkney and hero on the fields of true and mock battle alike. From the tourneys of London and Camelot, to the fields of Mount Badon and Lothian, no man has ever defeated me, least of all a beardless boy of unknown house and origin. Your rude assault upon this castle and its loyal guards shall not be pardoned. Flee now, or see death for your--"

Lancelot disarmed Gawain in a single strike and sent him to the floor, walking carelessly past the groaning tangle of limbs and continuing his advance upon the king.

Morgan started giggling.

"It is not something to mock. I was defending my king!"

"Oh, but you gave such a glorious lead up to such a short and comical defeat!" She cackled.

"You've the cackle of a true witch, do you know that?" She cackled all the harder, slumping against him and losing her breath.

"Oh, alright. Oh. Where were we? Oh yes." She wiped at her eyes, restoring clarity to the rippling image before them.

Sir Lancelot fought with impossible speed and fluidity, gliding among the dozen knights who came to surround him and stripping each of them of arms, just as he had Gawain, all without dealing a single deadly blow.

He brushed aside Sir Baudwin last, sending him tumbling down the steps to land in a heap atop a moaning Kay. He then raised his sword toward Arthur, on his feet now with Excalibur held calmly out at his side. "Return now our relic, or truly, I shall end you."

"You are a warrior of great skill, Sir Lancelot," came Arthur's cool response, eyes flitting out over the groaning bodies of his men. "And great mercy as well, for you have killed not a single one of my loyal friends and vassals, for which I am most thankful." His eyes locked with Lancelot, steely blue cutting shrewdly into soft brown. "You've never killed a man, have you?"

Lancelot stiffened in shamed anger at the perceived insult, cutting Excalibur from Arthur's hand and driving him back against the wall of his throne with blade at his neck. "This is the bidding of my lady. She does not wish you dead, for surely she is merciful and kind, the most beautiful creature on this earth, and you have stolen from her! Betraying her trust by denying her favor, then refusing to return the gift that was loaned you!"

"I apologize if I have offended the great Lady of the Lake," Arthur offered earnestly, "but I know too well the story of this sword. It was never hers to keep. Keeping Excalibur locked within the depths of her kingdom has caused my people great suffering, suffering I cannot allow to renew."

"Thank you, young stranger, for clearing the path to my vengeance!" a second intruder most boldly proclaimed in sudden jarring baritone. It was Sir Pellinore, savage son of Sir Turquine, and clad now in his same shimmering black armor with visor lowered and feral eyes glittering. "I came to these halls on simple instructions to relay a message from King Brandin of the Isles. The King of Northumbria has stolen away your pretty queen, Arthur, and demands now that you turn over Excalibur and give way for him to assume your throne. Striding unopposed into these halls however, and finding you in such a state, I think I shall instead lift Excalibur from your corpse and carry it back to my king."

Gawain lurched to his feet at the words, seizing up his sword and lunging to put an end to the black-armored menace-- Pellinore's boot slammed into the young knight's face before his hand even fully closed around the weapon, sending him back to the stones in a spray of blood and skittering teeth.

"Ooo." Morgan winced, shooting Gawain a look of grinning sympathy and pulling up his lip to reveal the missing teeth she had not previously spotted.

He batted away her hands. "He is a big bloody brute, and I was already dazed."

"Of course you were," Morgan soothed. "But you had such a decent face before that boot, and what potential wife will take you seriously now, all gap-toothed and crooked nosed?"

The Tale of ~~King Arthur~~Morgan Le Fay

He was not truly crooked nosed. It was just a little scar from the time she herself had kicked him in the face and bloodied it. She still healed it now regardless, along with both teeth, a peculiarly sentimental gesture, with her hand even lingering on his cheek after the fact. Perhaps she was simply drunk on company. Perhaps she wished sorely that it was Gawain who had come to her castle instead of Accolon that day with craving in his eyes and the heartfelt offer to be always at her disposal whenever she should need…

Lancelot cleared his throat, gesturing impatiently back to the now dissolved scrying images.

"Yes, of course. Black knight, looming threat. Though I'm assuming this is the part where you beat back Pellinore and defend Arthur, because if you did kill my brother I'd of course turn your insides outside," she casually warned the pretty boy, and his eyes narrowed in wary uncertainty.

"That is very kind of you, Morgan." Gawain smiled, a full toothed, actual smile that fluttered her heart even more than fair Lancelot's face. "And it is very good to hear, I must say."

"Curb your enthusiasm. I did not say I would help Arthur. I just said I'd kill anyone who kills him. It is a very different thing," she insisted. "I care nothing for his wife to be, and I have zero inclination so far to waste my energies running off to rescue her.

"I am enjoying this diverting tale of action and menace however, so let's watch it to its conclusion. Then you can tell me where the donkey and the arrows fit in."

Sir Pellinore strode past the dizzily lurching bodies of Arthur's knights tangled up with one another on the floor and toward the king and his young attacker.

Lancelot lifted his blade from Arthur's neck and swung to face the black knight with a look of cocky outrage. "You intrude upon my business, you uncultured lout. You have won no contest to earn you passage into these halls as have I, so be gone from this place."

"The trial I have weathered is the loss of my father to sorcerous tricks," Pellinore grated. "And before that the loss of my home and the disgrace of my family. Vengeance gives me entitlement to stand within these halls and lay challenge upon that boy. A false king, a thief and a cretin, just as you, young sir, have named him!"

"You have no right to revenge for an attacker slain in battle." Arthur sighed.

"Pick one of your slovenly knights to act as your champion, king, if you are too craven to face me yourself. In the meantime, I will leave you to the blade of that youth."

"Sir Lancelot's blade can no more kill me than your mighty claymore," Arthur boldly proclaimed, holding up his wrist to reveal that the cut Lancelot had earlier dealt him to disarm him of his weapon had already fully closed. Pellinore warily slowed his advance, and Arthur picked up Excalibur from the place it had fallen. "Ask any of my men, and they will tell you it is so. I am God's chosen king, and I cannot fall to any wound, so long as I remain within His favor."

Excalibur began to pulse with shimmering golden light, and Pellinore halted, sword hesitantly lowering. "What wizard's trick is this?"

"It is no sorcery or magic. It is God's own protection. This is why I did not fear the blade at my neck but a moment past and why I neither fear your challenge. Now, do you wish to fight me and fall to God's wrath, or will you face my champion?"

"I... I can best any man in this room," Pellinore pridefully growled. "None of the pathetic damsels spread out before me here shall ever defeat me."

"Yet when you are defeated, you will profess your loyalty to this throne and abandon your war-mongering ways."

"If I am defeated."

"I hold this as a binding oath then, made before the eyes of God and king alike," Arthur proclaimed, raising Excalibur, whose brilliance instantly lightened tenfold, forcing Pellinore and even Lancelot to shy away from its harsh glare. "Sir Pellinore, you will fight my champion, and should you lose, you will swear solemn allegiance to atone for thy brutish deeds."

"Fine, I assent!" Pellinore growled. "But when I win, you will hand over that sword."

"If you win," Arthur replied, "I will do so. I name now my champion."

Gawain forced himself back to his feet in weary expectation, but Tristan waved for him to stay down, as did Sir Baudwin, just now coming awake after yet another insistent shove from Kay pinned beneath him.

"Sir Lancelot Du Lac."

The boy looked at him askance, and Pellinore blinked. "You cannot name your attacker your champion!"

"Surely I can, for he is no ally to your cause," Arthur retorted, eyes shifting to Lancelot. "And if your lady wishes her sword back, then it can hardly be allowed to pass into the hands of King Brandin, now can it?"

Lancelot scoffed. "You've a clever mind, little king, and as the uncultured brute behind us has declared, if you will not fight your own battles, then I fear not thy challenge."

The Tale of ~~King Arthur~~ Morgan Le Fay

"Come forth then, fairy knight!" Sir Pellinore taunted. "I can cleave apart that pretty skull of yours with a single swipe of my--"

Two rapid fire parries and a single swipe, just as it was with Gawain, and Pellinore was on the ground with body twitching. That last blow to the back of his neck had soundly dented his gorget, causing no doubt painful trauma to his spine.

"There. I have won your contest," Sir Lancelot proclaimed. "Now give me back my sword."

"Your sword?" Arthur coolly noted. "I thought it was your lady's sword."

"My lady has bestowed that holy weapon unto me as a symbol of my station as her champion. Now hand it over."

Arthur eyed his golden glowing blade with calm appraisal, eyes somber with a solemn and earnest sense of responsibility and resolve. "It is God's will I have Excalibur. It began shining with His warmth the moment I laid hands upon it, and He has allowed His miracles to pass through my hands and into its length. My people need its presence here in this court as assuredly as they need a just king to rule them. Even so," His eyes locked with those of the young knight before him. "I shall abandon this seat for a time and go with you willingly to speak with the Lady Viviane and persuade her to allow me continued stewardship of this blade. I will go willingly, so long as you first lend me the strength of your arm to save my beloved fiance, a pure and sinless damsel, from the hands of the evil men who have stolen her away."

"If they have abducted a damsel, they surely deserve the wrath of my blade," Lancelot haughtily agreed, sheathing his sword. "For I am as any knight of virtue. Only better. Obviously." The room gave a collective groan, and this time it was not the pain of their injuries, and everyone but Lancelot knew it. "And following my triumphant return, boy king, you swear you shall accompany me with Excalibur in hand back to the domain of my lady?"

"I vow I shall go to that lake or wherever it is you wish upon your successful return with the Lady Guinevere."

Lancelot smiled, and even though there were no ladies within the court, all the men within his eyeline other than Arthur did instantly swoon, though surely they would later claim it to be their injuries and not the enchanting glory of that expression.

Morgan herself was feeling unnaturally woozy from that look, and she quickly dashed apart the image, rolling gracefully back onto her heels. She brushed the dust from her skirt and walked calmly away from the mirror.

"Your lady gave you a bit of fairy magic, didn't she?" Morgan demanded, keeping her tone as cold and detached as possible, as she restored Lancelot's ability to respond to the question. "It's not enough that you're naturally gorgeous and talented, she had to soak you in enchantment as well, just to ensure no harm would befall her pretty cup bearer."

"I am the *champion* of my lady, a knight, not a cup bearer."

"For the moment." Lancelot flushed, fists curling in rage. "Though her little bewitching spell does not appear to extend to arrows, now does it?"

"There is no spell! My lady is not a witch. I battled through that castle and won each crossing of blades with earnest skill and effort. Well, barely any effort, but you get the point."

She studied him in cold consideration for a moment, but found herself staring far too long and hard at his lips with her knees buckling once again and so coldly jerked away her gaze, insisting to herself that there was most certainly a very strong and layered enchantment around him, though it could be resisted with enough willpower. All one had to do was focus on the narcissistic words coming out of that pretty mouth, and all attraction instantly vanished. Yes, best to leave him speaking for now.

"Well, the skill of Sir Lancelot is clearly no joke," Morgan remarked, "so tell me what clever enemy it was that so wounded him and sent you pleading to my doorstep."

The Tale of ~~King Arthur~~ Morgan Le Fay

XXVIII. The Cart Knight and his Quarry

Morgan curled up happily on her throne and listened with eager attention, as Gawain (with no small amount of interruption from Lancelot) recounted to her the lengthy tale of how they'd wound up in that cart.

Sir Gawain and an entire host of knights had gone with Lancelot to the gates of Glastonbury where Pellinore had divulged King Brandin to be waiting for them. The fortress was right on the edge of Arthur's territories, and his men had ridden up there to deliver deadly challenge, demanding that Lady Guinevere be released to their company at once, else Britain's entire army would come charging to these gates. There had been no response, and so the knights had stormed the gates of the seemingly unmanned parapets, only to find the citizens inside those walls were all cowering in terror.

King Brandin had been slain, his body discovered strung up outside the castle with ominous message scrawled across his chest that 'the true lord of these lands hath returned'.

Those peasants knew nothing of the Lady Guinevere or her whereabouts. The knights searched every inch of the deserted fortress and found no trace of the princess, so the group sent Sir Dagonet and Lamorak riding back to Arthur with the news.

"And we were all of us glad to be rid of Lamorak," Gawain asserted, "since as the brother of Pellinore his presence at our backs was by nature suspicious."

"Nay. I think you needlessly sent away an additional warrior of skill," Lancelot countered. "Eager to prove himself our ally, though you gave him no chance to do so."

"Regardless," Gawain took over again. "We sent word back to Arthur, and the rest of us stayed within that city for another few nights to continue investigating the crime scene, as well as give comfort to our terrified citizens."

"And exactly what sort of comfort did you strapping lads provide the young women of Glastonbury?" Morgan demanded wickedly, and Gawain rolled his eyes.

"Do not so defame us. We are all men of chivalry. And I for one would never lie with then leave a maiden, no matter how sweet their praising words and pleas," he added somewhat smugly. "At most I grace them with a kiss, or a few hours of kisses, before sending them on their way. Though during this particular stay, half the village just followed around Lancelot, staring at him yet not even daring to approach, as if they were seeing the second coming."

"Because I am an uncommonly impressive sight," Lancelot stated coolly, "but you have wandered dreadfully off topic. We must speak of the attack."

It came suddenly during the third night of their stay, and an invisible creature near gutted Gawain's brother, Gaheris, before he and Lancelot had driven off the beast. They had then gone to wake the rest of the men, only to find the halls were suddenly flooded with armored enemies. Gawain carried his bleeding brother upon his back, as he and Lancelot fought their way free of the trap--

"Well, I fought our way free of that horde of hundreds as Sir Gawain gave piggyback to his brother, a needed pack-mule certainly, but you still cannot say that *we* fought our way free of there--"

"Can you silence him again?" Gawain pressed. "Before I silence him." He raised his fist, and Lancelot scoffed.

"Hush, children. Let's get back to the story, now shall we?"

The Saxons had flooded the halls, and they had narrowly escaped out the castle gates with the help of the gatekeeper's wife. "Who, let me guess," Morgan interjected, "asked nothing in return. Just that she be allowed to gaze upon Sir Lancelot but a few moments more, as his glorious backside went trotting off away from her."

"That's not too far off actually," Gawain admitted. "Anyway, we made it out into the city."

There they also found Sir Lionel and Sir Balan, whom they'd nicknamed the red, on account of the solid sheet of red that had covered him after he had fought his way free of that same trap in the halls above. The stable boy and a slew of other all too willing civilian accomplices had then smuggled the five knights and two of their surviving horses out the city gates and into the safety of the woods beyond.

"We had planned of course to regroup in Camelot and return with greater numbers," said Gawain, "since Gaheris was so badly wounded and Sir Lionel in a sorry state as well. But some of the thicker headed among us five," He pointed to Lancelot. "did proclaim that to be cowardice--"

"As surely it was," Lancelot retorted, "for you have glossed over that disgraceful dawn where the foul villains who had ambushed us in the night and driven us from the city did send out in ignominious parade before the

The Tale of ~~King Arthur~~ Morgan Le Fay

gates the trussed figures of our comrades, Sir Bors and Bedivere, and even Sir Agravain, thy own brother, whom timid Gawain cared not to attempt to rescue from shameful ransom--"

"Because it was obviously a trap. And we all agreed it was a trap, so we kept our cover, preparing to set off and get the wounded to safety, only for me to discover that my horse, one of our only two mounts, was suddenly missing, and so was young idiot Lancelot, who with a great and foolhardy howl announcing his presence, went riding alone in head-on charge--"

"To rescue our fellows."

"To *attempt* foolish rescue," Gawain saucily corrected, "and make it just clear of the treeline before the archers on the battlements raised sights and of course shot him down."

"My horse may indeed have fallen to their arrows--"

"You mean *my* horse."

"...and come crashing down on top of me. But lo, did I surrender? Nay! I waited for the approach of the fiends who believed me fallen to their missiles. I waited until they rolled aside the body of my steed. Then with shaky stance and shattered ribs, I nonetheless laid waste to their ranks--"

"You took one man by surprise. Then I came running on foot to lend aid and carried you off that field and into cover."

"And thus ensued a harrowing flight," Lancelot took back up his narrative, seeming not at all abashed by that correction. "Whereupon I took another mount--"

"Whereupon Sir Lionel, with his broken arm, gave up his seat upon what was now our only horse, you mean, so you could ride with Gaheris--"

"While Sirs Gawain and Balan and Lionel slogged along on foot beside us, yes, just narrowly outpacing the army on our heels. It was indeed a trying day."

"The Saxon patrol gave up about a mile into the woods," Gawain dryly corrected. "It wasn't really all that harrowing a chase. We pressed on to the nearby village of Wyght, and the monks there assured us that my brother would soon recover from his wounds. The slashes were fairly shallow. He had simply suffered a bump on the head that left him concussed. The case of our arrow-prickled Sir Lancelot however--"

"Was much more grave. My only hope, Gawain professed, was to head north with him to the doorstep of the witch before us, Morgan Pendragon," Lancelot grated, "the sworn enemy of my lady."

"She's declared me her sworn enemy?" Morgan laughed. "How delightful. Tell her thanks, I hold her in equal disdain. Though I don't think of her as near important enough to be my sworn rival."

"And I of course scoffed aside his absurd proposition that we come pleading to thee!" Lancelot angrily continued, pretending not to have heard her. "I did not in fact require the aid of a witch of such dubious character. My lady could have healed me just as easily as you did--"

"Then perhaps I shall undo such unwarranted mercy," Morgan cut in coolly, "send you back to her a bloody, groaning mess, so you can go weep in your watery cage of a bedroom."

"Be not so quick to spiteful action. I was not yet finished my recounting," Lancelot forestalled. "For I soon realized, with great wisdom, that it is indeed a necessary evil that we enlist your aid, Madam Pendragon, for the threat to our king's betrothed has in no way resolved. She is in the hands of the enemy still, and we've no way to track her. So, to honor both my vow as a knight and my mission from my lady, I shall put aside my pride and ask you to employ your talents in scrying to track down this captured damsel, so that we may return her to her waiting groom."

"Let me think about that... No. Goodbye now." She waved her hand, and Lancelot vanished, dumped to wait with the donkey back outside her gates.

She then turned on Gawain with hands menacingly raised, but he turned up his palms in meek surrender, dropping to one knee as he proclaimed, "Ah, but Morgan, you have not yet heard about the cart and donkey."

Her fingers curled back beneath her chin, with grin returning. "Ah yes. Indeed I have not. Very well, natter on, conclude your tale." She settled back into her throne.

"Thank you. Though, honestly, there's not that much to tell. Lionel and Balan returned to Camelot with Gaheris and our one horse, and the village of Wyght had no other mounts, save a little farm of asses."

"The perfect mount for young Lancelot."

"Come now, do not slander the faithful donkeys. They are not nearly so arrogant as to suit that posturing ponce." She smiled. "Anyhow, the good farmer lent me a cart as well, to haul our wounded lake-knight, and that is how we wound up here, pleading at thy doorstep."

"I do find myself appreciating the pleading," Morgan nervously admitted, with Gawain still on his knees before her and her lonely heart already thinking of pleasing ways to spend the night...

The Tale of ~~King Arthur~~ Morgan Le Fay

He was Urien's nephew though, she reminded herself, rising coldly to her feet. Urien, whose loss had not been forgotten. No matter the time that passed, it would never be healed, and she had no right to bed this boy. Though he was twenty years old, not much younger than she was, and hardly a boy any longer…

"Anyhow," Morgan forced her tone to remain insulting and callous, bereft of all warmth and desire. "I'd say you at least, good jester, have earned your dinner." Gawain rolled his eyes, but also could not help but start, as he looked behind him and spotted a table already spread with succulent fare. "Feast away." She took the seat at the head of the table, picking away at a dinner roll in awkward pantomime.

Gawain took the seat right beside her, the bold little fiend, though he did instantly ruin the mood by requesting, "Lancelot may not have the grace to admit it, but he is likely also near starving from our long voyage here. Our rations ran out days ago, so abrasive as his tongue may be, any proper host would invite him to dinner nonetheless."

"Yet I am not a proper host. I am a cackling witch who makes a habit of chasing company from her halls, as you aught to have noticed."

"Not the way Gareth tells it," Gawain coyly countered. "First Accolon. Now me…"

"I aught to throw you outside, you entitled… cur."

Gawain smiled, cocking his head. "Now that insult seemed considerably lacking of creativity and venom alike. In fact, you seem to be getting flustered."

"Well why are you leaned right up in my face irritating me? Graciously I have provided thee with dinner. Dinner and nothing else. Because nothing happened with Accolon, and this is not some private audience, so stop being so smug. Look." She summoned Lancelot back into the seat across from Gawain. "Your pretty partner's back. Stare at him for a while, why don't you? He's got a nicer face than I have anyhow."

"Venison. Excellent." Lancelot eagerly rubbed his hands, digging right into his graciously provided meal without a single word of thanks.

He spent the entire meal talking about how "The venison at my lady's table is far more succulent of course" and "the wine is far sweeter" and "the candles far warmer than this gloomy ruin, though truly none of her exquisite décor nor any other dazzling sight can compare with those eyes. Ah, if only she were here right now to grace me again with her kiss…"

"I'd feel irritated, if I weren't so sorry for you, really," Morgan muttered, disgusted once again by Viviane's behavior, having groomed this kidnapped child then acting so inappropriately toward him the second he was grown. Maybe she really aught to make Viviane her sworn enemy. She certainly deserved some type of punishment for all her centuries of selfish kidnappings.

"Sorry for me?" Lancelot was laughing. "Of what do you speak? I am the most fortunate of men. Ah, you speak of my suffering. The pain of my wounds so worsened by your cruel yanking of those arrows. Well, I forgive you, madam. You healed me in the end, so you are pardoned your brutality."

"And there dies all sympathy. And we're right back to irritation."

"I'm impressed you have the sense to be irritated at all," Gawain praised. "Every other maiden we've encountered just kept hanging upon his words, staring at him dreamily. Though maybe that was simply that enchantment you spoke of."

"I'm sure he'd be getting along well enough without it."

"Yes, but would the *monks* have gotten so flustered at a mere glimpse of his countenance if not for that spell? Now of that, I am truly curious."

"I'm sure a few would have still been tempted," she whispered wickedly. "Yet you yourself feel no allure bewitching all thy senses?"

"There is only one alluring presence here, and she is seated right beside me, consuming all attention."

Morgan blushed and broke quickly free of his gaze, magically changing her skin tone to hide the reaction.

"Tis impolite to ignore the compliments of the guest before you and sit there with heads pressed together in sinful gossip," Lancelot cut in dourly.

"Compliments?" Morgan pressed, having indeed tuned out the last five solid minutes of his rambling in dangerous distraction with Gawain. "And what compliment have you paid me? I heard only tiring praise of your lady."

"Because my lady is deserving of endless praise, and you aught to see that about her. But I said to you, this past remark, that this butter is rather good." He gestured to the smeared topping on the roll before him. "My lady has no butter within her kingdom, for whatever reason. Nor any cheese. Though I've heard that gives dreadful dreams…"

Lancelot rambled on about his perfect lady the entire meal, as Gawain gave clever comments, and Morgan spent her willpower keeping her hand carefully away from his, laid so open and inviting on the surface of the table right before her.

The Tale of ~~King Arthur~~ Morgan Le Fay

She remembered how Urien always used to play with her fingers, whispering comments into her ear, not so different from what Gawain was doing... Though Urien's muttered words had often been cruel and chilling, threats to those around them that had made her blood run cold. Whereas even as Gawain mocked young Lancelot, he did so with earnest mirth and not the slightest trace of envy or spite. His eyes were so much softer, his smile so much more genuine...

Morgan shoved back her seat, announcing coldly, "Well, I have certainly had my fill of all this. I suppose it is too late to send you merry lovers back out into the wilds, so you may stay the night if you wish. You've plenty of rooms to choose from." And would Gawain be so bold as to seek out her bedroom? She hoped sorely that he did not, for she would not have the strength to turn him away.

"If the rooms are all as dusty as this, I shall have a hard time sleeping," Lancelot noted. She shot him a glare, in response to which he cleared his throat, actually appearing abashed. "Ah, my mouth did comment there before my mind had time to think better of it. That was not a fitting remark to make to one's host. I should thank you and not criticize. Dust is an all too tolerable sufferance, since the hospitality of a witch must by nature be somewhat uncomfortable and insect ridden," he made his earnest yet horrible apology. "I assume the spiders are simply drawn to you like--"

"Like naive young women to pretty faced posers calling themselves knights," Gawain cut him off dryly, and Morgan once again could not help but grin, though the look died out, as they once again locked eyes. "Still, Morgan, my mind would be greatly eased were you to call up an image of the Lady Guinevere before we all retire for the evening, just so we may rest knowing no harm is befalling her--"

"I will do nothing of the sort, because as I said before, I've no interest in helping Arthur or rescuing his bride," she stated, tone cold and flat. "You may rest here tonight, but you must leave these halls come morning and see to such futile searches yourself."

She walked off without another word, but Gawain followed doggedly after her, seizing her hand. "That girl is in grave danger," he pleaded. "You've no idea what awful things might be happening to her in hands of whatever demon it was slew Brandin."

"And why should I feel guilt for that? I've no desire to know what's happened to her," she snapped, and Gawain blinked, shaking his head and clearly not at all understanding.

If she never scried this Guinevere, then she would never have to see her suffering, and thus there would be nothing to feel foolish pity for. Maybe she had run off on her own the night Brandin died, or more likely she was already horribly ruined by the men who had taken her or else dead, and Arthur would have to find some other wealthy airhead to wed. That was fine with Morgan, because she knew nothing of this girl. All anyone talked about was her beauty after all, so she was probably just some pretty, spoiled brat, just like Lancelot, but without even the grace of a tragic backstory to earn her sympathy.

"I care nothing for this princess," Morgan repeated. "She is a stranger, so even if she is not already dead, I will not waste my time and energies chasing after her."

She turned again to leave, but Gawain held her captive, eyes glowing with earnest fervor. "Wrongfully in the past I have assumed you to be so callous, but each and every time I made such denouncements of your character, I was swiftly proven wrong. You care about this kingdom, and you care about your brother--"

"No, I absolutely despise my brother," she corrected shortly. "And he will never thank me, no matter how many times I lend him aid. Now let go of me, and go to bed!"

She tried to pull free her hand, but he only tightened his grip, pulling her to face him with all urgent insistence. "We need you, Morgan. We do not even know where to look for this devil now. Even if he is still within that fortress at Glastonbury, we've no way to retake it with just the pair of us, and by the time the king's armies storm those walls, young Guinevere may already be--"

"Sleep!"

He slumped to the floor in a poof of dust, snoring away into the cobwebs.

She stalked angrily away from him and sealed herself up inside her rooms, pacing from side to side in angry consideration for a few tense minutes before hurling herself upon the bed and forcing shut her eyes.

She could not sleep. Not at all. Even keeping her eyes squeezed shut and holding herself rigidly immobile to keep from tossing and turning, she was no closer to rest as the minutes ticked past.

She gave up her futile efforts in an hour and set to scrying. She replayed first that night in Camlierd when Guinevere had been taken from her rooms, needing to know the exact likeness of the girl to be able to search her out in an unknown location.

The Tale of ~~King Arthur~~Morgan Le Fay

The girl was indeed a beauty beyond compare. Sixteen years old, she was tall and willowy yet with the curves and ample endowments that gave Anna such power over every man within her reach. The face of Guinevere put Anna's to shame however. Her shining golden locks were just dark enough to keep beautifully defined her eyebrows and long brown lashes, lashes that framed perfectly her sparkling eyes of clearest blue. This girl possessed more than a superficial beauty. She seemed to almost glow with life. She would have made stunning Lady Viviane seem a cruel-eyed pretender and exquisitely crafted Genevieve appear a dull and blank-eyed doll were either to dare stand in company with her freshly bloomed grace, as she squealed with delight and gave a pretty blush at whatever line of poetry she had read in the romance spread open on the bed before her.

A thud sounded in the hall without, and Guinevere hastily flipped shut the book, shoving it into hiding beneath her pillow.

The door creaked open, and Guinevere scrambled to extinguish the light of the candles on her nightstand. "Father, I was going to bed, truly. I needed a sip of water, that is all. I was not reading. No," She whirled about with an innocent smile. "Prudence took that filthy book home with her, just as you..." Her brow furrowed in confusion, as her eyes settled on the empty doorway before her. Then her gaze drifted downward to the armored hand falling listless to the ground, the only yet visible sign of one of a dozen deadman spread throughout the hall beyond.

Invisible hands clamped down on Guinevere's arms, as some unseen terror leaned right up in her face, foul breath stirring against her cheek, as he rasped, "Your new king wishes to see you."

She swooned.

Morgan rolled her eyes. "Of course she fainted. What is with noblewomen? Are they all just trained to collapse at the merest glimpse of trouble?"

Though admittedly, the gore stained hallway filled with dead knights was probably a sight the sheltered girl was better off blind to, as the invisible terror scooped her up and carried her off, down toward a boat moored by the lower levels of the keep where he had first made his incursion.

Morgan dismissed the image and shifted her focus to Glastonbury and the night King Brandin had been slain.

The savage king of the Isles had Guinevere locked in the highest turret of the fortress, a gloomy room of no windows where she sat sullenly huddled on the bed, still in her ragged night shift with knees pulled to her chest. Her enchanting warmth was severely dampened now by an all too clear fear pulling her perfect pink lips down into a worried frown, with eyes darkly circled for want of sleep.

The bolt on the door screeched open, and Guinevere lifted her chin, squashing down her terror and assuming an admirably regal pose with ankles crossed and hands neatly folded.

King Brandin eyed her up and down with a chilling smile, rubbing at his beard. "It's been weeks, girl, and still no response from that father of yours."

"It is a vast distance between Camlierd and Glastonbury. You must give it more time--"

"I must do nothing." He sank down upon the bed, and Guinevere prickled, hands clenching. "I am not a patient man, and the woman I had last night... She was nothing compared to the ripe little dish I had waiting for me up in this tower." His hands locked around her wrists, forcing apart her hands.

"My father will not forgive you and neither will Arthur should you defile my honor, lord king!" Guinevere snapped. "Entire armies will come in retaliation. It is far better to wait. I have sent the letter, pleading that my father call off officially my engagement to Arthur and give his blessing for us to wed. Then after that day you may... you may have me, but not before!"

"Yes, yes. I indulged your scheme these past weeks, my future queen, but thinking it over, there is in fact no reason to wait. I will simply take you tonight. Then your father will have no choice but to see us wed, else you will die a filthy harlot."

He shoved her down onto the bed, and Morgan wished this was happening in the present so that she could portal over there and put a stop to the filthy brute.

Another supernatural presence stepped in right at that moment however, and seized hold of the king, instantly paralyzing his limbs, as the cold currents of a rising wind hurled him away from young Guinevere and onto the floor.

"You dare lay hand upon my prize?" the voice boomed through the air. It seemed oddly familiar, though Morgan could not quite place it.

"Ah, dark lord," Brandin stuttered. "You were absent for so many days. I was not sure you would return--"

"And yet in my absence you have schemed to steal from me my bride," the disembodied voice continued, shaking through the walls and causing Guinevere and Brandin both to cringe in fear. "taking her for your own."

"Our marriage would be a trio!" Brandin desperately defended. "You wanted her for your bride, and I serve still as your faithful and much needed vessel, do I not? So now that you've returned, you can take hold of me once

The Tale of ~~King Arthur~~Morgan Le Fay

again," he begrudgingly offered. "And we'll both have the pleasure of deflowering our little queen over there--"

"You are no longer a fitting vessel," the voice chillingly denounced. "I have caught wind of another, far stronger and fairer than thee. I shall take him as my puppet and proclaim my true name, as I use him to lead our armies for decades to come, rather than the brief candle of time your wrinkling, booze-soaked corpse could provide."

Brandin flushed with rage. "You treacherous--!"

The force seized hold of Brandin once again, and he was powerless to defend himself, as his neck gave way with an awful snap and his limbs broke and twisted. Guinevere screamed and squeezed shut her eyes, as the invisible force ripped open Brandin's shirt and began to carve words into his chest: **The True Lord of these Lands Hath Returned!**

It hauled Brandin out the door. Then the dreadful force returned to seize Guinevere, tilting up her chin and appearing as some image in the air before her that made her tearing eyes widen in terror. "The time will come soon, my bride. From this moment on, you are mine."

The image went dark.

Morgan frowned, trying to call back the vision of the room and see what had happened to the girl and where she had been taken. The waters remained black and clouded. She could no longer even replay the scene prior with Brandin's death. The entire city of Glastonbury was now shrouded in shadow, and her eyes grew hooded with anger. This was sorcery, a studied wielder of the dark arts blocking her scrying the moment he noticed her spying upon him.

That voice _had_ been familiar, but it was not distinct enough for her to remember and put a name to it. What was even more troubling was that the first invisible fiend to seize Guinevere and then the second force that had killed Brandin were not only different speakers, but different creatures. The first acted like an ordinary man with an invisibility spell, walking down hallways and opening doors, while the second enemy seemed a mere ghost, passing right through objects and wielding powers like paralysis and telekinesis.

Gawain and Lancelot would stand no chance against these enemies. They might, with a bit of luck, manage perhaps to wound or slay the first felon, but a ghost would render them dead in an instant, especially a sorcerous ghost that even a prideful warlord like Brandin referred to as "dark lord".

"Though clearly we're dealing with an egomaniac here," Morgan mused. "He has a 'true name' and he's surely just some dead king, yet he calls himself the dark lord in reference to Satan." All that posturing and lack of physical form did not make him immune to hellfire however, and Morgan was sure that should she herself encounter this fiend, he would be sent on to his torturous afterlife in an instant, just like every other ancient poltergeist and banshee that dared challenge her.

She spent the next five hours searching the land for the now clouded face of Princess Guinevere. Despite the sudden scrying block around the city, she was almost entirely sure that this invisible terror was not still in Glastonbury. Gawain and his peers had searched that castle quite thoroughly after all, and the army of Saxons settled there and the lure of the captured knights made that city seem far more likely to be a tactical diversion for Arthur and his army. The real fortress of this fiend would be a place thrumming with ghostly energy, yet still a hall befitting a king as this "dark lord" would surely demand.

There were no such castles throughout the lands of King Brandin and the Picts. There were no such places, until she looked back east within Arthur's own domain and came across the halls of Dolorous Guard. That entire spiry keep sought to vanish itself from her sight the second she called upon its image. She could not peer inside its windows nor search through its rooms, and she knew this was the place where this fiend, the 'true lord' of Glastonbury, had hidden away Guinevere.

Dolorous guard was the home of one of Arthur's vassals, Lord Dolor, whom, unbeknownst to the king, had been secretly slain, his seat usurped by the sorcerous terror that had abducted Guinevere. Morgan peered through time and saw clearly the sight of old Count Dolor's body being chucked out into his moat three months prior. She spent hours eavesdropping on the gossip of the village folk within his domain who had fished his body out of the river downstream. Those peasants had been silenced by a visored knight wearing the colors of King Brandin who came riding through their villages, burning and intimidating as he went, so that word of this pagan incursion into his lands never made its way back to King Arthur.

If Merlin were here, he would have immediately put a stop to this evil. That thought filled her with instant grief and regret, and she stubbornly blocked the druid from her mind, telling herself firmly that the people did not need his protection, because she would nobly act in his stead to put an end to this terror. And not because she had to. It was just because... she felt like it.

"I feel no obligation to my brother, no guilting from Gawain, and no pity for Guinevere. None at all," she insisted aloud, trying futilely to give the words more power than her doubt-filled thoughts. "I am simply setting out to save that girl and all of those peasants under this dreadful tyranny, because... because no man nor ghost has any right to block my scrying. It is an insult to even attempt it, and I will retaliate now with deadly force."

She nodded firmly, staggering away from her wash basin with limbs heavy with exhaustion and the sun already rising, as she set off to find Gawain and haughtily inform he and Lancelot that she would carry out the king's charge in their stead.

XXIX. Dolorous Guard

"Morgan." Gawain tried hard to mask his worried study of her features, as he took in her red, circled eyes and disheveled hair. "Good morning. Did you, ah, sleep well?"

"No, and you know I didn't, because I look awful. Now go running back to Camelot and tell Arthur he'll have his bride back in a day or two," she grumbled, sinking down at the breakfast table and conjuring up a cup of extra strong tea. "I'll portal you over there, right after my tea."

"You've found her then?" Gawain pressed, sinking down beside her. "I am heartened by the news, but of course we will not be returning to Camelot. We must set off immediately to rescue our--"

"You will set off nowhere, except home." Her eyes narrowed. "Though come to think of it, shouldn't you be in Orkney right now? Ruling your country, instead of running around on pointless errands for Arthur?"

"They are not pointless errands. They are perilous and vital quests. And with the help of my liege I ended the civil war in Orkney months ago, as you have probably seen, but I have a steward there to hold the throne. I do not need to waste my time sitting in that remote chair seeing to pointless--"

"Essential matters of state?" She shook her head. "What a poor king thou art. You make my brother look like a downright master of state craft, so little effort do you put in for your people."

"I am a knight. A warrior, not a politician," he stubbornly defended. "That is where my talents lie, and this is all of it far from relevant right now, because I need to rescue Lady Guinevere, and I will not be headed off to either Orkney or Camelot until that duty is accomplished."

"You cannot rescue Guinevere. She has been kidnapped by the powerful ghost of some dead sorcerer who has hidden her away within the now cursed fortress of Dolorous Guard," Morgan harshly illuminated. "And since you and foolish Lancelot and every other thick-headed knight all have zero weapons that will work against a ghost, the burden falls to me to break into this fortress and save the helpless maiden from being made the unwilling bride of this dead warlock, as seems to be his plan."

"That is indeed grave news," Gawain breathed, "and surely we will be grateful for your aid, but we must of course accompany you, to defend you from--"

"Defend me?" She gave a weary laugh.

The Tale of ~~King Arthur~~ Morgan Le Fay

"What part of 'sorcerous ghost' did not make it through that thickened skull of yours? And since when have I ever needed defending? I am Morgan Le Fay. Warriors and ghosts alike all quiver in terror at my presence."

"I have seen you exhaust yourself before," Gawain cut through her bravado. "If my sword can spare you even some small measure of effort, surely that is worthwhile. We must accompany you, both Lancelot and myself. It is our duty."

She rolled her eyes, groaning, "Fine. Your pretty faces can follow along posturing at my side. Come on now." She gulped down the rest of her tea, slamming down her empty cup and shoving herself to her feet.

Gawain caught her arm, still eyeing her in concern. "Perhaps you should grab a few hours of sleep before we depart."

"Five weeks that girl has been within that monster's clutches," she reminded him. "Do you know what's been happening to her all that time? What's happening to her right now?"

His hand dropped from her arm. "No. No I don't. Has he…?"

"Maybe not, but I've no idea," Morgan snapped. "This thing has blocked my scrying, and I've no idea what is going on within that fortress, so let's break inside already and save the damsel so I don't have to sit here any longer thinking about it, alright?"

He smiled, seemingly thrilled at her all too rightfully predicted compassion. "Alright. Give me but a moment to don again my armor and…"

Morgan waved her hand, and Gawain was instantly outfitted back in full metal, sword belted at his side.

"Should you really be wasting your energies on such needless tricks?"

"Oh I'm sorry. Do you want me to take it all off again, so the little man can dress himself?"

"I'm sure you would love to remove all my clothing," he smugly countered, "but as you've said, we've no time to waste, so let's just grab Lancelot and be on with our rescue."

"Where is the young lake night?" she yawned.

"Outside. This way."

Gawain led her off down the hall, and they soon came across Sir Lancelot, bare chested out on her terrace in light of the misty morn, his skin glistening with sweat as he practiced his sword forms.

That sight was far too swoon-inducing, and Morgan woozily turned her back, stating testily, "You could have warned me there was a shirtless Adonis peacocking out on my patio."

"This is not him peacocking actually. He does it every dawn. Works just as hard, even with no one watching. Surprising as it is, he is in fact a warrior of discipline."

Morgan turned her gaze back to Gawain and noticed his eyes were glued to Lancelot's muscled back, and though he did not seem in danger of fainting, it was nonetheless quite the attentive study.

"Enjoying the view?" she whispered in his ear, and he jumped, cheeks turning bright red as he quickly averted his gaze.

"It is a bloody strong enchantment, alright?" he gruffly excused. "Lancelot, hey! We're leaving to save Guinevere, so stop strutting around half naked and get your armor on!"

Lancelot lowered his sword and turned coolly to face them, wiping at his brow. "An uncouth greeting, yet I understand haste is required, so abide thee but a minute, Gawain, and I shall be ready to depart."

"You're not going to magic on *his* clothes?" Gawain pressed her dryly, as her eyes unconsciously drifted right back to Lancelot, just now reaching for his shirt.

"No. I don't think I shall."

"Can you just transport us out to this haunted castle already? I'd much rather be fighting ghosts than having to endure anymore of this…"

"Soul-crushing envy?" she taunted, eyes locking with his. "Indeed, the bright flower of Sir Gawain must be wilting after so many weeks of neglect with no single maiden able to pay him notice, for fair Lancelot doth drink up all worship and praise."

"Yet here before me I have a maiden whose eyes keep glued to mine far more often than not, and she has paid fair Sir Lancelot not a single earnest compliment."

He was standing far too close to her again, and Morgan angrily turned her back. "And we're leaving now," she ordered, waving her hand and summoning up a portal.

Her sorcery could not touch the space within the walls of Dolorous Guard, no matter how clear the picture in her mind called up from detailed schematics, and no matter how stubborn her efforts.

The closest she could transport them was the burnt ruins of a village a full mile outside the castle walls.

"Now *that* is a strong enchantment," she noted, pointing to the castle ahead plunged into permanent shade by an unnatural halo of storm clouds. "I suppose you two are here for a purpose. It may turn out however, that we

The Tale of ~~King Arthur~~ Morgan Le Fay

need an army to storm those walls, since I've no idea just how many troops await us within those gates."

"However many they have gathered, we shall batter through their ranks and find good Lady Guinevere," Lancelot vowed, lowering his visor. "For any villain that dares abduct one of virtue and noble blood, helpless to resist them... Such a villain is due no mercy from my blade."

"You have just described exactly your lady," Morgan noted, and Lancelot blinked, head swinging to face her with an irate glare.

"What nonsense do you speak? My lady is--"

"A kidnapper, who stole away the helpless three year old son of King Ban and enslaved that poor little boy forever with her enchantments. And yes, your father is King Ban of France by the way, and he near died of grief thinking you dead for years."

Lancelot stood frozen in stunned shock.

She had nothing else to say, so she walked uncaringly past him, starting toward the gloom soaked castle ahead.

"Kind of a blunt way to break that to him," Gawain muttered, falling into step at her side. "I think you may have broken him."

"She lies. Yes?" Lancelot called out desperately, head finally lifting. "That was but a cruel falsehood designed to make me doubt my--"

"No, she wasn't lying," Gawain told him earnestly. "I know your father well. He is a good man. The king's prophet, Merlin, told him you lived and that he might one day see you again. He talks about that all the time, says that hope alone is what has given him the strength to carry on and keep fighting, what with your brothers and all the rest of his line dead."

Lancelot fell back to silence and moved not one step, until irritably Morgan slowed, staring him down expectantly. "Now see, *you've* broken him," she chided Gawain, stalking back to the paralyzed knight and seizing his arm. "Innocent maiden in great distress and terror," she reminded him sharply, and Lancelot blinked, quickening his pace and striding off ahead of her, though he said not one word, not for that entire hour, as they slogged on toward the blackened castle.

They were walking exposed over open ground, and Morgan considered briefly outfitting them with disguises or a cloak of invisibility, but she decided in the end that she could instead simply deflect any arrows, and hopefully that would get their enemy to open his gates for a more direct attack and provide them with a path inside.

No arrows were fired, even as they drew within a dozen feet of the walls, yet the gates did swing open at their approach, and an armored contingent rode out to encircle them, each of the dozen outfitted in menacing black steel. "What fools approach the dark lord's fortre--?"

Lancelot knocked the speaker from his horse and drove his sword through his neck, fighting with far less grace and mercy than the last time Morgan had seen him in combat.

"You definitely broke him," Gawain remarked, lifting his own blade and preparing to join the fray. "But at least he can still…"

"Brutally end all challengers," Morgan finished the thought, as five horses and twelve men all fell broken to the dirt before she or Gawain could even get in a blow.

The surviving riderless steeds went galloping off into the dawn, and Lancelot cleaned the blood from his blade, whirling to face her with tone strident and eyes wild. "My lady would never lie to me. You are the liar! My family is dead. She saved me from savage beasts and said I should not even ask about such things as who my father…" He shook his head. "No. No. Such is trivial. It matters not. She is all I need, and all I shall ever need, and I shall bring back her sword, and she shall be happy once again!"

"It is not her sword, and you are not her slave," Morgan replied.

"Stop calling me a slave!" He leveled his sword at her chest. "You know nothing of what you speak! You…"

Gawain stepped solemnly in between them. "Stand down, Sir Lancelot. She speaks only truth."

"Truth? No. Or maybe? But even so, for what manipulative purpose? She is a witch! An evil… And she hates all the fay. She said it herself, so this is just her petty vengeance, making me doubt she who is most…"

A chorus of cries drowned out his words, as more men came charging to aid those who had fallen outside their gates. Lancelot turned without a second thought, beating them back.

"I think he's going to have to work through some things here," Morgan noted.

"Well the violence seems to be helping," Gawain supplied. "Either that or worsening his temper. Stand back." Gawain stepped foolishly out in front of her, as one of the black armored knights lunged to challenge them, but Lancelot cut him down from behind before Gawain could lay a mark upon him, stealing the kill as he had all the others. "And now I am feeling rather pointless," Gawain noted ruefully.

The last of the men dropped dead, and Lancelot whirled to face them once again, not even bothering to clean his blade this time and flinging spatters through the air as he gestured. "Behold! What man can

The Tale of ~~King Arthur~~ Morgan Le Fay

even hope to challenge me? No one! And do you know why that is? It is because of my lady. She gave me the *best* of instruction from her fairy knights, and the *finest* of armor and blades, and it is my love for her that makes me strong and able to work so tirelessly so that I may be worthy of being her champion! So do not dare defame her sweet and glorious--"

The open portcullis began to drop down with a grating screech. Morgan quickly raised her hands, holding it up with telekinesis to keep it from closing between them and locking she and Gawain out. "Through. Now," she grunted, but good God that thing was heavy. She could hardly move herself while holding it in place.

Gawain seized hold of her wrist, as he noticed her frozen there, and pulled her forward through the barely five foot hole before the gate could collapse on top of her.

"There was probably a smarter method to hold that," she panted, but the space within this castle would not allow her to teleport, and even that small bit of telekinesis had seemed harder than it should be. There was a foul dark energy sunk into the soil and stones here, almost as if a barrier had been erected to stymie her arts.

More armored knights were charging out the castle doors now, and Morgan decided it was time she test just how effective her magic was in here. Their flesh caught fire with a flick of her wrist, and all two dozen fell screaming to the ground. "Well, they are not outfitted like the true black knight with magic resistance, so that's a relief. Onward we go."

"You have not seen how she cares for me," Lancelot was rambling on.

"I do not want to see how she 'cares' for you," Morgan retorted, picking her way past the smoking corpses and through the castle doors. "She is hundreds of years old, and you are seventeen, so this entire 'love', inappropriate and twisted."

"Her face is fresh as a new spring day!"

"And her mind as lewd as an aged pedophile." His fist clenched, and Gawain once again put a hand upon his chest, holding him back from her. "Just please," Morgan continued, "I entreat you, go speak with your father. Stay free for a few more weeks and find someone your own age. Then you will see all too clearly that what you and your lady have is far from love. You are her possession, dearly and disturbingly regarded, yes, but still just a little trophy beneath her palm."

"I will hear no more of your insidious words," Lancelot denied, stalking off ahead.

"Maybe you should drop it. Leave him his denials," Gawain suggested.

Morgan simply shook her head, eyes sad and distant. "Happy lies serve no one. They simply make it so the wound is never treated," she whispered, an embellishment of a quote that Merlin had long ago comforted her with.

She drew up short then with eyes scanning the empty grand foyer around them. "I've just had a quick thought now though, and does this whole three man invasion of an enemy fortress not seem just a bit too easy to you?"

"You burned twenty men with a thought, Morgan," Gawain reminded her numbly. "Yes, you make it look easy."

"Yes, but look at this," she insisted, gesturing around them. "An empty hall. We've seen only a few dozen soldiers. No arrows. No reasonable tactics to keep shut the doors and gates. Just that pittance of resistance with zero sorcerous support from their 'dark lord'. He's not even hurling any objects at our heads. And look up, right there." She pointed to the iron ring of darkened candles directly above them. "Now wait for it... Nothing. See? No falling chandeliers. And poltergeists *love* to set falling some chandeliers."

"So you think we're walking into a trap right now?" Gawain predicted, and she gave a grim nod.

"Highly likely this is a trap. Yes."

"Lancelot, slow down! It's a trap!"

"If you have not the resolve to carry onward, then turn back, ye craven dog!" the boy shouted, already a good ways up the sweeping staircase before them. "I will not leave a fragile maiden to torment and imprisonment. She will be free, just as I am. Free. I. For I am not, nor have I ever been a prisoner!"

"You definitely should have broached this topic of his lady *after* we were done with the rescue," Gawain noted, jogging forward up the stairs.

Morgan followed along after him, but her brisk walk rapidly slowed to a panting trudge, as they continued from the initial branching staircase onto a long set of spiral steps winding up to a tower.

She had already walked over a full mile this day. She had not walked that far in ages. She flew or she teleported, but these passages were too narrow to make it worthwhile fluttering about as a crow potentially smacking into a sudden turn or doorway and breaking her wing. Maybe she aught to shape-shift into a mimic of Gawain or some other fighter with the bare minimum of lung capacity and cardio requirements for this lengthy trek.

She was considering it seriously when Gawain came tromping back down the stairs to look for her. "I was waiting for you on the landing, but it had been so many minutes that I was worried some enemy had fallen upon you in ambush."

The Tale of ~~King Arthur~~Morgan Le Fay

"No... enemy... just... tired. Go." She waved him on ahead, but instead he hooked an arm around her legs.

"What are you doing?" she protested but gave no serious resistance, as he scooped her up into his arms. She had always been rather curious what this felt like.

"You are but a fragile, exhausted maiden," he taunted, "so now, I am going to carry you. Lancelot's stealing all the kills anyway, so I need some sort of exercise. Though you are alarmingly light for a full grown woman."

"Because I'm five foot two with all the voluptuous curves of a twelve year old boy."

"Oh how you exaggerate. I have made keen note of your subtle curves, Lady Morgan, and they are not at all boyish."

"You lustful fiend! If I feel these hands of yours wandering, I will..."

"...turn you into a newt." He spoke the threat with her with a sort of irreverent fondness, adding wryly, "It may not be so bad, being a newt for a time. They're rather fetching little lizards, don't you think?"

She stifled her laughter, clearing her throat and reminding him dryly, "Serious mission, Gawain. Perilous castle, evil ghost, helpless damsel."

"Yes I know, but my dear friend, Sir Dinadan, says laughter gives fresh energy, even on the brink of battle, and I find I much agree with him. Your saucy tongue doth give me courage to brave the terrors, my lady."

"Blowhard."

He smirked, striding on up the stairs, as she clung to his neck and gave far too much enjoyment to this little reprieve for her already blistering feet.

Gawain set her down at her insistence once they reached the top of the staircase, at which point her feet were already swollen, so she quickly healed them of blisters before setting off down yet another irritatingly long hallway, hopefully in the same direction Lancelot had wandered. "Dark lord pretender!" she shouted. "Reveal thyself! The great Sir Gawain doth challenge thee!"

"I challenge he?" he whispered, and she shrugged.

"Well, he's not going to rise to my challenge. He might be hiding from me already should he know my true identity, cowering in fearful anticipation of my flames that can all too easily burn apart his essence and send him on to hell."

"Is that the plan here?"

"The rough outline, yes."

A sudden gasp drew them onward down the hall, and they rounded a corner just in time to see Sir Lancelot scrambling out the door of a bedroom right at the end of a passage, struggling to redo the buckle on his weapon's belt, as Guinevere followed him coyly out into the hallway with lips turned up into a wicked grin.

"My lady, control yourself. You are indeed fair. The fairest I have ever..." He shook his head, snapping out of the entranced study of her face. "But this is not at all the proper conduct--"

"Just hold still, will you?" Guinevere commanded, driving him up against the wall and kissing him soundly.

"Another maiden fallen to fairy magic." Gawain exhaled. "Going to have a hard time explaining this one to the king."

"Hold on. Something's not right," Morgan doubted, but too late, as something passed into Lancelot and his body tensed in pain.

His hovering hands seized hold of Guinevere in a sudden lewd caress, and she collapsed limp within his arms. Lancelot pulled away from the unconscious maiden, and the eyes skipping over her face now were cruel and hungry. Guinevere was staring up at him blankly, and he gave an irritable sigh. "Perhaps my departure has left you dazed. What a pity."

He scooped her up into his arms, carrying her back into the bedroom.

"Ho!" Gawain shouted. "What do you think you're doing, lad?"

Lancelot stopped in his tracks, looking over at them cruelly. "Ah yes, the other intruders. It's time you die."

The ceiling came crashing down on them. Morgan dissolved the stones into mist. Though she could not attack this ghost at the moment, not without burning young Lancelot to death.

"So the witch herself has come to pay me visit," the possessed knight noted, lowering Guinevere to the floor and beckoning her haughtily closer. "You've the talents to serve me, if you debase yourself first in a satisfying enough manner, so kneel now at my feet or else suffer my vengeance."

Morgan laughed in derision. "*Kneel*? To *you*? Who the hell even are you? Some long dead charlatan no doubt, who learned a few little spells and thus thought himself a sorcerer. And maybe you were born to some distant noble line, and thus gave yourself the title of lord. Or wait, I'm sorry, it's 'your dark majesty', as you prefer to be addressed, correct?" she jeered.

"I am the great King Maleagant!" Lancelot roared, drawing free his blade. "Given new flesh and form, and I shall reign forever over these lands!"

"You're the ghost of Maleagant?" Morgan shook her head, remembering the lustful old warlord she had cursed. "The pig who parked his disgusting backside in my brother's castle for a month and thus thought himself to be King of Camelot? No. I don't see how that could be. Maleagant was an

The Tale of ~~King Arthur~~Morgan Le Fay

ordinary idiot, so where did you learn all the scrying blocks and sorcerous enchantments?"

"I see what you are doing, witch." Lancelot gave a wicked smile, and even with that disgusting soul behind his eyes it still weakened her knees thanks to Viviane's cursed enchantment, forcing Gawain to reach out and steady her. "You are but stalling for time while you think up some desperate plan to escape my wrath. You have not the hardened heart to set your flames upon this handsome young host of mine, now do you? You have always been a weak and gutless sort, more bluster than bite, and that is how I survived thee! Now I will carve apart your flesh, again and again, as you beg for death at my feet!"

Lancelot stalked toward them with blade bared, and Gawain stepped out in front of her with sword raised. "Get out of the way!" she ordered, but he ignored her, warning Lancelot:

"I've no desire to do thee harm, but if evil has seized hold of thee, then I will put an end to thy suffering. I shall not allow you to lay hand on this--"

Gawain got in an entire third parry that time, so fierce was his conviction, before Lancelot's bladework sent him bleeding to the ground. The sword puffed to mist, as it descended for the final blow over her self-determined champion's throat. Lancelot looked to his empty hand, then shot Morgan another chilling smile. "You think I need a blade to end him?"

An invisible force seized hold of Gawain, and his arm gave way with an awful snap. Morgan hurled his possessed attacker from his feet, breaking his focus before the spell could complete.

Gawain's screams had already shifted into prideful cursing, as Morgan dropped down in front of him and quickly healed his wounds.

"Hellfire," he grated. "Hellfire the hell out of that bastard."

"Not yet," she whispered, distractedly deflecting the vase sent hurtling toward her head and rising calmly to face anew her pathetic challenger just now struggling his way to his feet.

"Flee now, you simpering witch! You cannot kill me! But should you bruise this perfect packaging of mine, I will ensure your torments are endless! You will beg for death--"

"Yes, you've said that already," Morgan cut him off. "And I grow tired of your empty threats, so how about instead you tell me how you've manifested here as such a powerful ghost, you pig."

"Yes, you would be curious, now wouldn't you, witch? You thought it was a death sentence surely, sending me off to that farm in the insulting flesh of a tuskless beast, but I am a warrior of unparalleled strength, and you clearly know nothing of my legend! I clawed my way up from the mud once, and I did it with ease a second time!

"You placed me in that pen amidst a host of fearful little pigs waiting docilely for their deaths, but I whipped those cowards into frenzied shape and led them in an assault against our captors, that foolish old farmer and his family. We gored them all beneath our hooves, and with the remaining bones and entrails I did paint my plea to Satan and his demons to lend to me their strength!

"Sadly, they gave no answer. It appears that even with the proper sigils, a mere animal can attain no sorcerous power, so I rid myself willingly of that cumbersome flesh! I set out from that massacred farm onto a nearby ignorant locale and laid myself beneath the butcher's knife there, swearing with my dying breath that I would cling to life and gain my dominance over the spineless witch who had consigned me to this fate!

"My spirit ripped free of that swine, and I flew to the lands of the old north and paid visit to the young witch, Ceridwenn, in the land of the Picts. She trembled in face of my glorious anger when I seized hold of her flesh in séance, and reverently did she obey my demands, teaching me the spells of possession of even those guarded and all the extent of her craft. I strangled the life from that heathen then, seized for myself the body of a healthy young warrior, and went on to ally with superstitious King Brandin who thought himself a great enough man to serve as my permanent host.

"But no! I would not fall back into the trap of age and weakness. No more was I some aging lord, and no need had I to take by force the adoration of women which I was always due. My puppets now will be only the strongest yet fairest of men, my wife, the most beautiful woman in the land who will eagerly feed my lust and bear me countless sons to serve as my vessels the second they are grown. I will reign eternal! Feared and envied and--"

"Good God, is there no end to this monologue?" Morgan sighed, twitching her finger and silencing the man. "You are an absolute windbag, but I guess I have my answers. You are in fact Maleagant, the pig."

"You cannot silence me... Snrt!" He had broken apart her silencing spell, yet even as he spoke a much stronger enchantment had already taken hold of the body he was inhabiting, transforming fair Lancelot into a pig. Now granted, it was a much prettier pig than Maleagant's own aged iteration from years past. Even snouted, Lancelot had perfectly smooth skin and twinkling eyes.

The great lord was still stricken with panic regardless, barreling toward them with an ear splitting wail. He ripped free of his beastified vessel the

The Tale of ~~King Arthur~~ Morgan Le Fay

instant he reached them, flooding right into Gawain at her side before she could act to stop him.

The possessed king of Orkney raised his sword, swinging for her with an angry shout. "You think you can imprison me? You--"

"Swine? No wait, that's you."

The sword puffed to mist, and Gawain also shrunk into a pig, scampering back from her in oinking dismay, as Morgan leaned right down to glare at him. "You will always be a pig, you dead fool. Whatever host you take, I will see them turned to a shape befitting the one puppeting their limbs. No harm shall come to them of course. They shall have happy little lives scuttling about some farm until you decide to leave them. You learned a few chants to demons that stir some wind and toss some furniture, but that does not make you a changeling, now does it? You are incapable of changing the flesh of your container, thus you will be trapped forever as a filthy pig until the day you leave these lands. Go on now. Run away."

The ghost ripped free of pig-Gawain's flesh with a howl of rage and went reaching straight for Morgan. "Then I will have you, witch!" Maleagant's true voice echoed through the air. "A changeling puppet to dance to my desires--"

"There's that ugly old face, such a nice clear target." Morgan seized the specter by the throat as it flooded up against her and revealed to her its image. Hellfire burst beneath her fingertips the second her grip closed around the hairy jowls of the dead warlord. Maleagant clenched his teeth and ignored the flames beginning to eat away his essence, pressing up against her in a disturbing flood of cold.

"I will fill you and break you--"

"Please. I am Morgan Le Fay," she grated. "Wizard of unparalleled power, daughter of Merlin, greater than all you pretenders! Now GO TO HELL!"

The flames turned white, a searing, blinding brilliance, and those awful spectral hands ripped free of her chest. The awful cold burnt away, erasing Maleagant's filthy essence with a mournful howl, as his palely glowing form lost definition and dwindled down into the floor, a little spot of ash, brushed away with the wind.

Morgan slumped back against the wall, shivering and cursing that the ghost had flooded so deep inside her before she'd managed to exorcise him. It would be even worse for Gawain and Lancelot of course, who would be left both transformation dizzied *and* defiled. Not to mention how Guinevere must be feeling, ensnared for weeks by the filthy old pervert.

"Back to men," she mumbled, waving weakly over the heads of Gawain and Lancelot to restore them to their proper shapes.

The men lurched dizzily to their feet, and Gawain gave a heavy sigh. "That was brilliant, Morgan." His tone was weary with strain. Still, the compliment seemed genuine. "I was worried I'd have to slay him." He gestured toward Lancelot. "Or haul him all the way to a church, but you hardly even hesitated. You outsmarted that ghoul most thoroughly."

Shouts sounded in the halls beneath them then, and Gawain reached for his sword, only to find his sheath empty.

"I disintegrated it," Morgan reminded him. "But I can call it back. Here."

She ignored her drooping eyelids and summoned the blade back into her open hand. A horrible mistake. The act sent her pitching sharply forward.

Gawain reached out to steady her, taking back his sword and stating earnestly, "Thank you, but you should have saved your energy. You look exhausted."

"Nonsense," Morgan mumbled, walking away from him. "Twas a... simple conjuration. I am... not at all..." She swooned.

He swept her up and carried her off at a run, shouting for dazed Lancelot to bring a just now awakening Guinevere and follow, as the bulky shapes of black armored knights still loyal to their dark lord flooded the corridor.

Morgan tried with earnest effort to keep open her eyes, so she could open up a portal within this now exorcised castle and teleport all four of them to safety. They would never make it free of this fortress otherwise, but her hand dropped listless to her side before she could even attempt it. Great and mighty wizard indeed. Merlin would not have passed out from one single exorcism.

A tear leaked out the corner of her eye, and she ducked her head into Gawain's chest, murmuring beneath her breath in delirious plea for the wizard to return from his prison, here in this moment, so that he may for once in his life give aid to his poor, weak daughter. Nothing happened of course, and her senses gave out, the tears still running down her cheeks, as they fled for their lives from the enemy closing in on them.

The Tale of ~~King Arthur~~ Morgan Le Fay

xxx. 𝕳𝖆𝖗𝖘𝖍 𝕾𝖕𝖔𝖐𝖊𝖓 𝕻𝖎𝖓𝖎𝖓𝖌

Morgan the fainted and carried off damsel felt zero desire to open her eyes. At first it was shame that she had collapsed just like some prissy, anemic noblewoman. Then it was the begrudging admission that she was in fact far too exhausted to stand even should she choose to open her eyes and look about. Finally, it was a peculiar enjoyment of the feel of those arms cradled around her back and thighs. It was far from comfortable, bouncing up and down with cheek chafing against Gawain's breastplate, yet she was enjoying it regardless. Why was that? Was it because he was clinging to her with such fierce determination, hoisting her up, again and again, despite the weakening of his arms and the dragging stumble of his steps.

"Here they come." Lancelot's voice, yet so oddly grim and subdued. "Run ahead, fair lady, with Sir Gawain and his fainted witch."

"You cannot face them alone!" Guinevere protested in panic.

"I can, and I must."

"Bloody hell, just set me down and help him," Morgan muttered, forcing open her eyelids. "What are we fighting?"

"Lie still, Morgan. You cannot yet be ready to stand," Gawain stubbornly protested, but she shifted her weight, and he had no choice but to drop her, at which point she shot him a defiant glare, struggling stubbornly up from hands and knees.

"I am ready when I say so," she grated, turning her weary gaze to the open plains behind them where dozens of armored enemy knights were riding out from the gates of Dolorous Guard only a hundred meters distant. Lancelot stood with sword raised, fully prepared to face on foot the armored contingent.

"We fought our way out from the halls through a secret passage the Lady Guinevere led us to," Gawain filled her in. "But now it appears they've sent their cavalry to chase us down, and without any cover, we've no choice but to stand and face them."

"I know you're too bloody tired to keep carrying me, so do not even attempt it this time, alright?" Morgan mumbled, and Gawain looked to her with a forced smile.

"I cannot be tired. You are light as a feather. Now what are you..?"

She pointed her finger at the forty mounted knights now only fifty meters from their quarry and envisioned them as what they were.

"Insignificant pests." The men puffed into fruit flies, and their horses confusedly slowed their gallop, stomping about in confusion.

Morgan swooned once again, and Gawain completely ignored her command, cradling her close to his chest, even as his own exhausted legs gave out. *The lovely fool.* It was her last thought for... she was not sure how long, but when she opened her eyes, she found herself laid out beside a campfire in a cozy little cave.

Gawain, seated on watch at the entrance to the little hole, turned attentively to face her, as she forced herself up onto her elbows and asked the obvious question, "How long has it been?"

"Two days," he breathed, kneeling at her side with eyes so rife with worry, the same expression Urien had worn that morning in Camelot... "How are you feeling?"

"Don't look at me like that." He blinked, taken aback by the sharp hostility in her tone. "I am perfectly fine. One exerts themselves, they get tired, and they sleep. It is a natural occurrence. I am not some fragile damsel in need of thy coddling care."

He sank back on his heels, scoffing in clear offense. "Alright then. I apologize. Clearly I should feel nothing but callous indifference toward those I must carry off the battlefield. I should feel no concern whatsoever for even grave wounds I cannot understand, those that leave them unconscious for days, moaning in discomfort--"

"Moaning?" she demanded. "Did I truly spend the entire two days writhing about and moaning without even realizing it?"

"You were not writhing about. It was just the occasional... little sound, of pain or sadness, but whatever it was I was worried, alright? And that is nothing to mock. You saved us all, twice in one perilous day, and clearly you were not and are not 'fine'. I would have shown the same care to my brothers or any other knight I saw before me in this state. You are not weak just for needing occasionally to be taken care of."

"So if I had you stripped of armor, laid out on the ground, and I leaned down fussing all over you the second you awoke, you would not then feel weak?"

He flushed, clearing his throat and looking quickly away from her. "Do not mock me with salacious taunts. I was being earnest."

She arched an eyebrow. "Salacious? What part of that was--?"

"Oh please. A wounded knight awakens in his sick bed with your beautiful dark eyes shining over him, offering him care..." He swallowed.

The Tale of ~~King Arthur~~ Morgan Le Fay

"Damn it, stop making me want to kiss you, because I know you're only going to mock me or strike me the second I try it."

"I suppose it is salacious," she murmured to herself, envisioning now the bare and bandaged chest of Sir Gawain lying helpless upon her bed, indebted to her for healing him... "But I am not some wounded patient in thy care," she asserted, kneeling primly across from him. "I am perfectly rested and recovered, so long as I do not attempt any elaborate spells or long distance portals for a few days." Her eyes scanned the little cave around them. "What happened to our actual rescued damsel?"

"Princess Guinevere has gone riding out with Lancelot in search of a standing village in order to secure us rations. Most of the towns around here have been burned by that monster, Maleagant's, hordes. Lancelot wanted to ride out alone of course, but Guinevere requested she go with him. She said she could not sleep on the cold stone and needed the brief reprieve of a night in town on a soft down pillow."

"So she is a spoiled brat."

"A sheltered girl who has been through a terrible ordeal," Gawain gently corrected. "And she seemed at great unease huddled out here in the dark, so perhaps she simply wanted solid walls and... well, Lancelot to guard her I guess. She does not think too much of my fighting abilities due to the fact that I was carrying you and thus unable to engage in most of the combat during our harrowing struggle free of those Dolorous halls."

"And then you had the added displeasure of hanging back to guard my drooling, unconscious body, as all the lovely adornments of our company left to go spend the night in comfort. Clearly, you have made a poor judgment call, Sir Gawain. It is surely a betrayal of your king, abandoning guard of his freshly rescued betrothed just to give care to cursed Morgan Le Fay, the longstanding enemy of his country."

"You are no enemy, Morgan," Gawain insisted. "You saved our lives and defeated a great evil. The people aught to be praising your name--"

"But they won't, so do not mention my involvement, not to my brother and not to any within Camelot."

He shook his head. "What do you mean? Of course I am going to tell tale of--"

"The great Sir Lancelot and the mighty Sir Gawain," she insisted, "two *lone* knights who stormed the halls of evil enchanted Dolorous Guard and fought through hordes of enemies to liberate young Guinevere from the ghost of Maleagant that slew King Brandin and had been holding her captive."

"You think me some lying peacock?" Gawain snapped. "As if I would take credit for your--"

"I do not want a legend! I do not want a horde of people questioning and slandering me and all those in my company whom I lay my 'evil bewitchments' upon. I just want to be left alone. So go back to Camelot, tell your damn story the way I have ordered it, and leave me alone!"

She started to her feet, reaching to summon a portal right back to Cader Idris. She was still not nearly recovered enough for that however. Her vision instantly began to blur and her stance to sway, until Gawain seized worried hold of her shoulders, firmly scattering her concentration. "Morgan, please."

She slumped back against him, hand dropping listless to her side. "I see, so I am your prisoner this day."

"Don't be absurd. You are not a prisoner. You just need to rest."

"I am not tired," she insisted with childish petulance, batting away his hands. "And I will show you truly, I am capable still of a million simple spells, for they require little energy." She gave a wicked smile. "Like this."

His armor vanished along with all his clothes. He tensed, and she expected him to instantly cover himself, accusing her of shameful taunts or toying with him. Instead his hands dropped to his sides and he straightened, staring her down in haughty challenge. "And the salacious games continue, but if I'm to be standing here naked..." He eyed her up and down, and she crossed her arms defensively.

"Truly you have no shame, nor any sense of modesty."

"Nor do you."

She was indeed staring at him, staring at a sight she had seen many times before that she knew all too well how to handle. "I assume you've had a hundred women just throwing themselves at that thing?" she taunted, hoping the answer might quiet the near suffocating craving so quickening her pulse.

"I have indeed. Tiresome airheads, admittedly quite pretty, some of them sincere, talking endlessly about my greatness and the strength of my arm and their eagerness to bear me sons, and it is all of it a little bit sickening to be honest." He advanced toward her. "Not that this should drive me to admire and endlessly fantasize about a sharp tongued woman who spends every conversation we have just scathingly insulting me, yet curiously, it does, because she is not only witty and brave and self-sacrificially kind and criminally underappreciated, but she also wants me just as fiercely as I want--"

Her lips seized his, subduing his words with her wickedly skilled tongue. Finally, she pulled back, gasping, "Sorry. I cut you off before you could finish your confession. I want you, yes, just as fiercely as you want Lancelot, correct?"

"You insufferable...!" Her own clothes vanished, at which point he was far too distracted to finish his retort.

She lay exhausted anew in the aftermath of the drawn out satisfaction of both their cravings. His fingers stroked her gently, and she kept her head upon his chest and for once felt nothing but warmth as she drifted off into dreams.

XXX. Sinful Folly

Morgan the cheating harlot awoke to the setting sun, feeling no longer warm or full or any other of the pleasant feelings that had filled her but a few hours prior. Urien would cut Gawain's throat for this... Urien was dead. But he had never deserved her anyway...

"*He is not fit to be your husband. He's an absolute ass.*" Merlin's smiling face, then that bleak look of realization flooding his eyes, as her final spell took hold and he was sealed away forever in horrid isolation, an act that was only righteous because she would remain alone forever as well. She was a ghost. She was dead, gone, exiled. Like Merlin. Like Urien. If she was not, then...

"Morgan?" Gawain brushed back her hair, searching out her gaze. He could tell that something was wrong, but she did not want his burdensome concern, his prying questions. He had gotten what he wanted from her already. He did not have to pretend to be kind. She was cruel and treacherous, and a serpent stretching out against you in search of warmth was not a creature to be pitied.

She let loose a lazy moan, sliding her fingers between his legs. "You don't have to call me Morgan, you know." He arched an eyebrow but bit off his response with a gasp of pleasure, as her hand continued its wicked work. She pressed up against him, tongue tickling his ear. "Whatever shape or exploit those *endless* fantasies were picturing, you can call me her name. I'm in a hungry mood, so no need to pretend. I'll be anything you want."

He seized hold of her wrist, fighting past his natural reactions and forcing her eyes to meet his. "Morgan," he repeated. "what is this?"

"Come on, don't be shy. I know the bony witch may have some skills, but that weak nonsense from last night..." She laughed. "I could hardly tell you were there, so let's go a little harder, shall we? Hurt me."

"Hurt you?"

"Choke me, hit me, make me bleed, whatever you feel like," she breathed. "Just make sure it hurts."

He held her back. "I am not going to hurt you. Is this what my uncle...?" He shook his head. "I would never hurt you."

"What a bore." She shoved away from him, snapping on a low cut black dress. "Come on then, let's find what's befallen young Guinevere and Lancelot. They weren't meant to be gone for two entire days surely."

The Tale of ~~King Arthur~~Morgan Le Fay

She conjured up a brass bowl and poured their waterskin into the newly made scrying dish.

Gawain sat up and pulled his knees to his chest in self-conscious cover, looking down in embarrassment, as he waited for the instinct she had awakened to fall flaccid. "I don't suppose you plan to give me any clothes."

"Hmm? No yes, of course. I'm done with you anyway."

She snapped her fingers, and he was back in his same bulky armor from the day prior, though his defensive posture of crossed arms and pulled in knees had not at all abated. "You're certainly in a mood."

"No, I *was* in the mood, but then you went and ruined it, so let's focus on the quest at hand ferrying pretty Guinevere to Camelot, and we can revisit our other business when you've grown up a little and can give me what I want."

The look in his eyes then drove a knife into her chest, a far more bitter ache than the punishing pain she had been looking for. He started to his feet and stalked right out of the cave.

Morgan turned her eyes back to the scrying dish, waving her hand over the surface of the shallow rippling water and calling up an image of Guinevere.

She was seated in the saddle right in front of Lancelot, as they rode at a gentle canter toward the distant lights of Glyngarth, with the rain drizzling down upon their uncovered brows.

Guinevere's shoulders shook, and Lancelot looked down at her in concern. "Are you cold?"

"A bit."

"It rends my heart that I have no cloak to lend thee."

"And that rain-speckled steel doth lend no warmth the way differently clothed arms might, circled tight around me," Guinevere nervously noted.

"I did not even think of that. I shall remove my armor and consign it to the saddle bags," Lancelot stated with all seriousness, reining in their horse and hopping down from the saddle for a moment while he stripped off his breastplate and gauntlets. Guinevere watched him closely out of the corner of her eye, waiting anxiously for him to return to his seat.

He climbed up behind her once again, grabbing hold of the reins. "Is that better?"

She leaned contentedly back into his chest. "Mmhm." Her voice had the nervous high pitch of a young girl enjoying a scandal. She was grinning yet blushing quite furiously, though Lancelot did not catch sight of the expression, eyes fixed on the lighted city ahead.

"We shall be inside soon," he promised, nudging their steed back into a trot. "In rooms befitting your station."

"I shall feel content in any room, so long as you remain to guard me," Guinevere whispered. "You did promise you would not leave my side."

"I will allow no harm to befall thee."

"I know you won't." She burrowed even closer against him, closing her eyes.

Lancelot cleared his throat, shifting positions nervously. "I am surprised you feel no aversion."

Guinevere's eyes snapped open. "Aversion?" She laughed. "Toward what? Toward thee? Why ever would I feel aversion toward the brave knight who rescued me?"

She craned her neck, but Lancelot desperately avoided her gaze, cheeks burning with shame. "I... do not wish to awaken unpleasant memories for you, but... I allowed myself to be taken over by evil, and I took advantage of you in your weakened state."

"It was but a kiss," she murmured. "A kiss I do not well remember. It was all of it, as if some dream, distant and cloudy... I do not remember most of it. I know only that I was not myself. There was something awful, all inside... Then your kiss..." She put a hand to her lips. "It freed me. The nightmare ended. I came awake and saw an angel standing over me." She gazed upon his face. "He pulled me to my feet. He enabled me to stand once again, and he held so tight to my hand," She twined her fingers through his own, and Lancelot gave no resistance, staring down at those long slender fingers with an almost tangible desire. "never dropping it, as he fought a path free of that fortress, that cage. He kept hold of my hand, and he drove back so many enemies, and even with his great skill, a few cut him, and he bled, and I realized then that he was but a man. A man who was my savior. Who would not leave my side..." She swallowed. "I do not wish to leave your side."

"This is why you wanted to come with me?"

She nodded. "I need not fancy furnishings, nor warmth. You are warming enough, so long as you are here." She settled back against him, folding his hand against her.

"I'm afraid I need... The reins, my lady."

She quickly dropped her hold, blush returning. "And I have taken captive your ability to steer. Yes. Of course. I apologize."

She covered her face in cringing shame, but Lancelot kept looking down to gaze at her regardless. Each time his stare came to linger on her though, he would nervously force away his eyes, time and again, to focus on the streets of the city closing in around them.

The Tale of ~~King Arthur~~Morgan Le Fay

They stopped outside a brightly painted inn. Lancelot dismounted and held out his hand to Guinevere who took great delight in guiding that hand to her waist and allowing him to lift her down from her seat.

They were both gazing at each other now, faces only inches apart, and Morgan thought what a miracle it was that Guinevere had not already fainted. Then she noticed the little golden charm of the stylized cross hung about the girl's neck, a talisman to repel enchantments.

Morgan gave a little grin. It was a wise and customed gift to many a girl from a royal house, provided usually by the old country priests to protect them from being switched out by changelings at birth or lured off by fairies. Morgan had burned her own necklace at the age of seven, infuriated that it had never done anything to combat the constant hurtful whispers that she was nothing but a changeling imposter who had devoured Uther's heir. Still, she remembered well the design of that sigil. Guinevere had not had it around her neck back in Dolorous guard, so Maleagant must have taken it off in order to possess her. It appeared she had found it again afterward though, and what it meant right now is that Guinevere was completely immune to Lancelot's enchantment. Every dreamy eyed look and clinging touch was motivated only by natural attraction, paired with potent, teenage hormones.

"Horses get quartered around back," a harsh voice cut apart the tension between the two rain soaked teens, and Lancelot ripped his eyes free of Guinevere's stare, holding out the reins of their mount to the innkeeper in the doorway.

"Take our horse and see it stabled then."

The old man flushed. "Now look here, I am no stable boy. We do not have a stable boy. What we have is a post, so you can head around back and tie it up yourself..."

Guinevere opened the purse at her side and held up a solid gold coin. The old man snatched it greedily from her hands, shouting over his shoulder, "Tom! Leave the bar and come tie up this horse!"

"What?!"

"Just do as I say, boy!" The innkeeper held the door open for his now realized to be wealthy patrons, smiling invitingly. "Come on inside, my lady, my lord."

"Two rooms, side by side," Lancelot ordered, and Guinevere grabbed at his hand, whispering brokenly,

"No please. You promised. I cannot sleep, alone in the dark."

Lancelot cleared his throat uncomfortably. "I understand, but it would not be proper..."

"Come on, lad, no need to pretend," *the old man advised him, steering them forward up the stairs.* "Whoever's daughter she is and however loud the sounds, we've a strict policy of confidentiality in this--"

Lancelot's hand went right to his sword hilt, and he turned on the old lech with eyes deadly. "Two separate rooms, for a maiden of unrivaled virtue and her guard."

"Yes sir. Of course." *The man held out a pair of keys, and Lancelot snatched them from his grasp. The innkeep tottered off down the stairwell, and Lancelot unlocked the door beside them, holding it open for Guinevere to gracefully enter.*

She turned back to him then with shining eyes of worried plea, and the boy hesitated only a moment before tucking away the extra key, stepping in behind her and softly closing the door.

"Well that's going to be trouble," *Morgan murmured to herself, but she had neither the energy nor the inclination to go teleporting over there and put a stop to the young couple's rapidly escalating flirtation.* "But maybe they will just go to sleep. They've been through an exhausting and harrowing ordeal these past few days. Just because they're teenagers, alone in an inn room..."

She called back the images just to assure herself that Lancelot was lying respectably on the floor right now and not...

"...Your aim in preserving my honor is valiant, good sir," *Guinevere laughed,* "but a noble knight cannot sleep on the filth stained floor. There is more than enough room beside me on the bed."

Lancelot looked doubtfully to the double wide mattress in a room made for nobility. He was not staring at the mattress though. He was staring at Guinevere, stretched out in her night shift with delicate fingers patting the space right beside her... "I fear, good lady, that I have not the willpower to lie there." *His voice cracked.*

"Then I shall sleep upon the floor."

"I could never permit that."

"But you have suffered so much already for my sake." *She strode right up to him, hands clasped to her breast.* "I have read many a tale and..." *This time her voice was the one to slant suddenly high pitched and break, as she fiddled with her hair and turned quickly away from him to hide her growing blush.* "You are due some sort of reward for all your heroic deeds, Sir

The Tale of ~~King Arthur~~ Morgan Le Fay

Lancelot," she asserted with forced confidence. "Whatever you ask of my father, I am sure he will give it."

It was obvious what she wanted him to ask for, but Lancelot answered simply, "I require no reward. If I have done you service and freed you of suffering, then that is reward enough."

She turned back to face him with eyes glowing with admiration. "You are a knight of true virtue. I have never met a man such as thee."

"Many have said as much," Lancelot nervously deflected, and Guinevere's face fell.

"But of course." She laughed, back to avoiding his gaze. "Every maiden must feel a similar fluttering of the heart within thy presence. Surely you've a hundred proposals from beauties much fairer than I."

"No one on earth is as fair as thee." The fierce declaration stopped Guinevere dead in her tracks. "I thought once that I had seen perfect beauty, that heaven itself could sculpt nothing more glorious. Then I looked upon thy countenance and I saw a warmth, and a need, and a love..." His voice caught. "It made each sight before feel shallow and faked." He put a hand to her cheek, and Guinevere leaned right into him, eyes shining with hope. "There is no one in creation more beautiful than Guinevere."

He kissed her, and she melted right into it. He broke away after a minute, forehead pressed to hers and breath still mingling up against her lips. "I should not have done that."

"I wanted you to," she breathed, kissing him once again.

He lowered her into a dip, then lifted her back upon the bed... and Morgan hastily dissolved the image, turning her eyes to the ceiling. "And as predicted, Arthur has quite definitively lost his bride."

She dusted off her skirt and rose primly to her feet, stalking outside to inform Sir Gawain what had become of the pretty princess he had been honor bound to escort to the altar.

Her smile died the second she spotted him, stood brooding beside his already saddled horse, kicking at the dirt with a clear impatience to be off. She remembered the cruel, confidence crushing words that she had spoken to him, and she knew she must apologize.

He spoke even as she opened her mouth however, and the words died upon her lips. "You found them I trust?" His voice was cold and bitter, the closest thing to loathing that she had ever heard within his tone.

"In Glyngarth, in an inn called The Mermaid. It's a full day's ride from here."

"I'd best get going then. I can reach them by sunrise." He mounted his steed. He still had not looked at her, not once.

"Would you prefer for me to ride in front of or behind you?" She said it with a tone of teasing coyness, and his fist clenched around the reins.

"I would prefer for you to retire to your castle. You're clearly fit enough to travel on your own, and we require not your aid any longer." He looked down. "You've already had your fun. No need to see to the boring bit of escorting a stranger safely to her king."

Morgan crossed her arms. "A stranger she may be, but to leave mid quest seems a bit--"

"It is not your quest," Gawain snapped. "I do not need your aid. We ride for Camelot now, and I've strength enough to keep us from being ripped apart by bandits on the way, so there will be nothing to amuse you. You are done with me. No need to pretend anymore that you care anything about the welfare of that girl." He scoffed, shaking his head and staring up at the sky. "I should have believed you the first time you said it. You care nothing for her, or your brother. You care nothing for anyone."

He kicked his horse into a gallop, and Morgan shrunk down into an insect without even realizing it. She told herself sternly after a few moments of near tears to stop being foolish and forced herself into a mentality of flight.

She burst into the shape of a falcon and easily overtook Gawain and his horse. She considered landing right in front of him and stopping him, forcing him to halt and hear her out. It was at that exact moment that he looked up at her however. She saw in his eyes then the look of an enemy, a son whose father she had slain. She had bewitched him for a time, but now he had taken what he wanted and he saw through her games. He remembered all the reasons he had to hate her.

She zipped up into the clouds, safe from his sight, and soared on to Glyngarth. Even if he did despise her now, that did not mean he got to command her when and where to go. She would finish this quest and see Guinevere safely to Camelot, because that is what she felt like doing.

She quickened her pace to a blistering dive, climbing and gliding like a streak of quicksilver across the night. She reached Glyngarth in mere hours and fluttered down to the windowsill of the rooms where she knew Guinevere and Lancelot were quartered.

Their clothes were laid out in crumpled piles upon the floor. It was late in the night, yet Lancelot was sitting up in alarm, as Guinevere

The Tale of ~~King Arthur~~Morgan Le Fay

uncomfortably shifted positions, and he made a closer study of her tear-filled eyes.

"Have I hurt you?" he pressed, voice thick with concern, as he followed her stare to the blood on the sheets.

"No," she breathed. "Tis as it should be between a lady and her first. I am not truly in pain. It is just..." She pulled him gently back onto the bed. "I will not be sad at all," she asserted. "I have no reason for sadness. My father will understand. His heart will lighten with joy when I introduce him to the handsome and fearless man who rescued me, a knight of unrivaled skill and kindness." She smiled, closing her eyes and snuggling up against him. "He will understand I cannot marry Arthur, and we will put peaceful end to that promise, for my heart belongs, from this day forward, only to thee, Sir Lancelot, my knight."

Lancelot stiffened, pulling away from her.

Her eyes snapped open. "Was that not... was that not eloquently phrased enough for a confession?" she half-joked, fear shining in her eyes.

"I am not your knight. I cannot be your... I do not deserve such words, good lady, and you should not have spoken them."

She swallowed, hands wrapping to her chest. "What... Whatever do you mean? Do you not love me? Was this but...?" Her voice broke.

"This was but sinful folly," Lancelot answered mercilessly. "We have both of us broken faith to those who have been promised our devotion."

"By mere betrothal?" Guinevere desperately laughed off. "Then you are also betrothed? But you can call it off, surely..."

"I have already lain with my lady." Guinevere flinched. "My heart is hers, for all of time. She is..."

The tears returned, and Guinevere turned from him. Lancelot's eyes flooded with pain, reaching to comfort her. "I beg you not to weep--"

"Don't touch me!"

Lancelot flinched away, sinking back in his seat and staring on powerless, as she sobbed into the sheets.

Morgan's heart was breaking, for the second time within one day, and she stormed into the room without a second thought. Guinevere screamed at the sight of her, pulling the sheets tight around her, as Lancelot leapt away from the bed and snatched his trousers from the floor, hissing, "You make a rude and inappropriate entrance this day, witch!"

"Rude and inappropriate is a rather redundant phrasing," she sniffed. "And I did not mean to intrude. Only..." She did not have the right words, looking awkwardly from Guinevere to Lancelot then just blurting out, "Sir Gawain is on his way, so you had better both of you get dressed already."

Guinevere clenched her hands within her hair, shaking her head. "How am I to hide? It will do no good. I am no longer fit to wed a king."

"Then don't marry him. Seriously, girl, you are clearly no good for Arthur, so he can find some other..." Guinevere wailed, collapsing face first into the pillow. "I did not mean..."

"Is there no limit to your cruelty?" Lancelot snapped. "You have always the exact words, don't you? To wound as no other can."

Morgan's eyes drained of life, and she vanished into mist, falling weakly out the window and drifting away in the vague direction of distant Cader Idris.

The Tale of ~~King Arthur~~Morgan Le Fay

XXXII. A Slowly Unraveling Curse

Morgan the thoughtless curse could never undo the damage she caused, yet she marched off to a hidden vale deep within the misting Welsh mountains with the determination to at least try to undo her cruelest mistake. "Even infinite spells can be rearranged and twisted," she reminded herself coolly, taking her position within the center of the glade and grimly raising her hands.

She remembered that day in vivid detail. Merlin teleporting her away from the battlefield and out to this clearing, his hands on her shoulders, and that look in his eyes, as he took in her words and finally realized what she had...

"Focus!" she commanded the shaking weakling within, wiping at her eyes.

She reached out into the ether. She reached for the touch of that parallel plane and the druid who should be standing right before her. She would call him back, and he would be standing there, **right there**, the second she opened her eyes.

She opened her eyes.

She was alone.

She cursed, stamping her foot and repositioning herself imperiously.

She tried for hours. And then days. A million different approaches, and warpings of space, and portals. She could not even feel the corners of her box. She could not even sense its walls. Her spell had been perfect. There was no trace of it. No entrances, and no exits. No weaknesses to exploit.

She ripped her fingers through the air and tore through the fabric of reality but found nothing and no one behind it. Her ripping claws of energy broadened their search, cutting deeper and more chaotically, until a black hole nearly swallowed the mountain range, and she had to spend the next three days reining it in and eliminating it before it destroyed the earth.

By the end of the third week, she was not rationally trying to undo her spell at all. She was sending forks of lightning just ripping through the air, disintegrating trees and causing avalanches, until her energy gave out and she curled up into a ball on the charred and ruined grass, weeping into the dirt. "I'm sorry. I'm so sorry..."

Her spell had been seamless, folding away forever a distant and unbreakable prison. Her cruelty could never be undone.

She trudged on foot all the dreary miles back to Cader Idris.

She did not heal the blisters, even when they broke and she was limping and bleeding into her boots. She soldiered on through the rain and mud, because she deserved the suffering. She deserved far worse suffering. She ruined forever everyone she loved. Everyone except Arthur maybe, because he was too perfect and good for anyone to ruin him. "Except perhaps Guinevere. Though she's run off with Lancelot surely, no longer to be married, so I guess that ruins nothing," she talked to herself deliriously.

A pack of goblins tried to eat her on the winding path back to her fortress. They did not seem to realize who she was, so miserable and filthy did she look, and though she was a glutton for punishment at the moment, that did not give her a tolerance for being nipped at and gnawed on by dreadful creatures such as that. She ripped them all to bloody pieces, and the entire forest quickly realized just who it was taking a stroll through it this night.

No other fairy or spirit dared accost her on her journey, and she made it all the way back to her castle, only to draw up short, as she saw the rusted gates hanging wide open with a whinnying white stallion tied to a post deep within her courtyard.

"What suicidal idiot invited themselves into **my** castle?!" she thundered, her fury shaking the walls.

No coward came screaming out the doors in response, and she surged forward as a shadow. The formless wraith ripped through the halls in angry search of the intruder, dropping back into her body, as she burst through the doors of her throne room and finally spotted the fiend lounging sideways across her throne.

"Of all the insolent... What are you doing here?" she demanded, and the wine glass in Lancelot's hand shattered into fine dust. There was no wine left within it, just as there was none left in the dusty bottle sitting uncorked at the foot of the chair.

The lake knight turned his bleary eyes upon her and rose swaying to his feet. He had not shaved in what looked like weeks. Unfortunately, the rugged beard and tangled locks still somehow suited him, and even with bloodshot, glossy eyes and slovenly dress, he remained annoyingly attractive.

"Madam, you have returned. I was sitting on your throne. I know. And I've no place on a throne, no place at all..." A look of utter dismay twisted up his features, and he collapsed back into the chair. "Aye. Aye me. Oh. You really must think of leaving around some extra chairs for company, madam.

The Tale of ~~King Arthur~~ Morgan Le Fay

This dusty block of stone is not at all comfortable. My entire rear has been solidly numb for hours."

"What are you doing in my castle?!" Morgan repeated, and he raised his head, eyes locking with hers.

"Oh. I'm here so you might kill me. Worry not. I will fight. Wait, here." He fumbled around the back of the throne until he found his sword. "There we are." He raised it before him, taking his stance. "Attack me now, witch! Burn me to a cinder. I am the champion of thine mortal enemy! The treacherous champion..."

The tears flowed over, and he collapsed upon the steps, sword falling useless at his side. "Ah. Your wine is terrible by the way," he informed her, kicking away the empty bottle. "Near vinegar, but strong. So very strong."

"Have you lost all sense of pride?" she snapped, stalking up and yanking him angrily to his feet. "What kind of knight comes staggering drunk into a witch's den?"

"I am not a knight. I was never a knight. I am an honorless cad!" he shouted, seizing her shoulders. "A pretender! A fool! Who broke the heart of a pure and gentle damsel..." His head dropped against her chest, despite the utter amount of stooping that required almost folding him in half. "I cannot return to my lady. I betrayed her trust, and every moment within my heart I continue to betray her! I belong in hell!" He straightened, maddened eyes burning into her. "Yes, hell. You must send me to hell. So summon forth your hellfire. Come now."

Lancelot had stepped into far too close proximity with her face however, breathing his booze soaked demands right up against her lips. She could already feel her consciousness fading. "Bloody... enchantment..." She swooned.

She awoke, and she was lying out on her balcony staring up at the stars. Lancelot was seated right beside her, and she made a point of not looking at him directly, shuffling irritably away from his swoon inducing body heat. *He is a child.* She reminded herself. *A narcissistic, insufferable child, who at the moment reeks of wine.* Which was all the more reason to be away from him.

"Awake, madam? I though the fresh air might do you good. No ordinary maiden could long survive in the cough-inducing interior of your dust filled nightmare of a castle."

"I did not pass out from breathing dust, you thick headed..." She trailed off, as her glare settled on him and she noticed finally the bottle in his hands. It seemed that he had taken the time to secure more vinegared libations from out of her ancient wine cellar, no longer even bothering with a glass, as he forced down more of the mundane numbing potion.

    He followed her stare to the wine and drew it away from his lips, holding it out to her. "I have no glass to offer you. Still, if you wish to partake--"

    "Of course I do not wish to partake!" She instantly disintegrated the dangerous inebriant. "And you will not take in another drop, you drunken fool!"

    "Aye. I am a fool." He raised a hand to his forehead, nodding along deliriously. "A cursed fool. For you were right. What you said before of evil magics hanging about me. I am indeed cursed. I have seen it too many times now, magic of the cruelest kind, but I all too well deserve it. Don't you see?" His voice broke. "She knew I would not be faithful. She knew I would betray her, thus provided me this charm to blacken the senses of the poor, vulnerable women I might lay my filthy hands upon... My curse was even stronger than her blessing though, and most wickedly have I ensorcelled young Guinevere. Aye Guinevere..."

    He started sobbing again, and Morgan shuffled even further away from him in case he opted to try and lean into her again. "That spell of your lady's is no blessing," she grated. "It is a perverse and possessive charm to provide you with protection and favor, yet instantly knock out any who dare lay hands on you with any trace of desire within their mind." She exhaled, taking his hand and feeling nothing but motherly pity for the child. "And I am definitely going to unravel it for you, alright? Because I find it not only disturbing, but also extremely irritating."

    He scoffed. "And what of my other curse?"

    "You don't have another curse. That's just your face. Guinevere liked your face, and that whole air of knightly nobility. You did not ensorcell her. She has a charm of magic protection, just as Arthur does, so she cannot be ensorcelled. And what kind of idiot are you anyway, raving about your lady right in front of her? Why did not the pair of you just run away together, and where the hell is she now? Do not tell me you just left her disgraced and alone in that inn."

    "Of course I took my leave! My presence was a torment! But she is not alone. She is protected in the care of noble Sir Gawain, a true knight, free of the thoughtless lust that is the ruin of lesser men such as I."

    She bit back her protest of that comment, thinking sadly that Gawain's thoughtless lust toward his enemy had indeed brought him to ruin. He was broken now just as Lancelot was. Only Lancelot was acting far more stupidly

The Tale of ~~King Arthur~~Morgan Le Fay

of course, for he had been the one to drive off Guinevere by clinging to the ownership of his lady.

"Sir Gawain is escorting her safely to Camelot," Lancelot sighed. "where she will wed that thieving cretin, Arthur..." His voice broke. "Oh, but I am the cretin..."

"Enough with the pitiful self-loathing! If you're so broken up about this wedding, then why not put a stop to it?"

"And leave her without a husband? She needs a husband, to restore her virtue, the virtue I have stolen..." He broke off sobbing once again. "Aye, but I did love her. I loved her in that moment truly. Deeper and truer than anything my lady and I had..." The words were a fearful whisper, then his eyes turned to hers, shining with panicked horror. "To hell. I must immediately to hell. Strike me down."

"I am not sending you to hell. This is not your fault, alright? Well, not most of it anyway. You are simply young and stupid, and you need to go home to your father."

"Father?" His bloodshot eyes became distant and bleary. "Yes, I have a father. Did you know I have a father?"

"Yes. Obviously I..."

He vomited, and she scrambled quickly backward, just narrowly avoiding the foul stream. He blacked out then, and she lifted him quickly away with her magic to keep him from falling into the puddle. This boy was badly broken.

"God damn you, Viviane. You win. We're mortal enemies now. Look here, your mortal enemy, cleaning up your mess."

She hauled Lancelot off to bed and strained to her limits her skills of blind telekinesis, as she stripped the booze-soaked knight of his soiled armor and clothes without the need to look at or touch him.

She spent the entire night after that in study, running over again all the legends and messy details of undoing fairy enchantments and love spells. Her swimming eyes fluttered closed on their own accord around four in the morning. She peeled her cheek off the pages hours later with the morning sun streaming through the windows and decided firmly that her eyes still needed further break before they would be ready to resume her research.

She checked in on Lancelot and found him still soundly unconscious, murmuring deliriously, "My lady... but I have betrayed you. I cannot return..."

Her eyes narrowed in suspicion, and she peeked into his dreams and found unnatural visions of Lady Vivianne speaking into his thoughts.

The Lady of the Lake prickled in rage the second she sensed Morgan, but it did not matter. She was all but powerless beyond the borders of her woods, and the sorceress absolutely refused to suffer her intrusions into the beleaguered mind of Morgan's guest.

"You will visit him no more," she declared, and just like that, Viviane was forever blocked from Lancelot's dreams.

The boy started awake and instantly winced, clamping a hand to his skull. This was not a result of her spell. It was a self-inflicted ailment that far too many men in court did saddle themselves with on an almost weekly basis. "My skull is splitting open."

"You wanted hell," she reminded him dryly, summoning one of the brews from her potions cupboard and holding it out to him insistently. "But if you've had your fill of suffering, drink this. Then water. Lots and lots of water."

He took the mug from her hands, and she quickly took her leave of the room before the brush of those fingers could set her to swooning again. "That jealous curse is breaking right this day," she muttered to herself.

She finished her readings and realized finally the method of undoing this spell, at which point she gave an angry curse and took to pacing once again, seriously doubting she had the strength to pull off such a gargantuan challenge of willpower. "A lustful enchantment of possessive taint can be cured only by a pure-hearted gesture." She sighed. "Alright damn it, let's try it. You have to at least try."

She stalked back into Lancelot's rooms, and he was sitting on his bed all bearded and shirtless, and she angrily turned her back. "Put on some bloody clothes!"

"What point is there at pretended decorum and dress?" he muttered. "Unless..." He straightened, exhaling in relief. "Ah, you have come to end me, and as a man of noble blood I must die with sword in hand, to leave this world with dignity. Yes, I understand--"

"I am not going to kill you! I am going to end the foul enchantment of your lady that is keeping you from happiness, so put on a bloody shirt already!"

"To end the enchantment..." His eyes were troubled and distant. "What right have I to erase her protection? She is my lady. I must return to her... No, no. To hell. A traitor belongs in hell--"

"Good God, you poor boy," she murmured. "Wait, that's it! You are in fact a kidnapped child, a little boy."

The Tale of ~~King Arthur~~Morgan Le Fay

Her spell took hold, and Lancelot turned back into a six year old, the same soft hearted child who'd found her crying on the shoreline and offered her a flower.

She walked right up to him and kissed him on the forehead, a gesture of pure, motherly compassion. "I love thee truly," she declared, and Viviane's enchantment forever dissolved.

"Haha!" she laughed in triumph, turning Lancelot back to his ordinary age, bare chested on the bed with her arms around his back. Even in so scandalous a position though, she felt absolutely zero attraction to the unshaven mess. Really, all she could focus on was the fact that he smelled of sweat and vomit. "God, you reek. Go take a bath," she ordered. "And if I ever catch you in my wine cellar again, I will turn you into a mouse."

She steered him toward the door, and he looked down at her blearily. "You love me? That is a highly inappropriate confession. My heart belongs to my--"

"Love need not be erotic and disturbing the way you were raised to believe," she snapped. "I love you like a sad little puppy I found abandoned in the street, and it is that pure and virtuous regard which has freed you of your curse. You may go now to any town or tavern you wish and... Well, most of the women will still throw themselves at you to be honest, but they will *not* fall instantly unconscious the second you shoot them a smile, so... progress."

She drew Lancelot a bath, then sat down alone by her scrying pool, calling up an image of Guinevere to ensure the girl really had made it home safe to Camelot.

XXXIII. Of all the Loves Unrequited

The Lady Guinevere had arrived safely in Camelot in company with Sir Gawain a full week prior. She had kept cloaked and hooded throughout the journey, as Gawain led them shrewdly through back roads and remote hamlets without ever announcing her name or his to avoid another attempt at kidnapping or ransom. That hood stayed raised even as they passed through Camelot's gates and Gawain announced their identities to the soldiers on the walls. She stayed cowering within those folds of fabric until they were well within the throne room, stood before the king himself.

"The Princess Guinevere, your majesty," Gawain presented her, and Guinevere dutifully lowered her hood, giving an elegant curtsy.

"It is an honor to meet you, my lord. Tales of your greatness are known throughout my kingdom."

"As tales of your beauty have echoed throughout mine," Arthur gently replied, staring entranced at the face of his bride. "Though such a simple word as beautiful could never describe…" He cleared his throat, remembering suddenly that he was before all his court. Besides, this woman had been through a great ordeal. She needed not his empty flattery in this moment. "I am pleased to make your acquaintance, my lady, though much has befallen you, so surely you wish to rest and recover, not be forced to stand here and endure the fumbling compliments of a stranger."

"The compliments of a great king are no trial to endure. They are to be cherished," Guinevere responded soullessly. "I am to be your bride, so I am at your service, whatever you require."

Arthur studied her in wordless concern for an instant. Then his eyes moved past her to Gawain. "I am grateful to see you returned to our company, Sir Gawain, escorting my betrothed safely into these halls, but where is Sir Lancelot?" Guinevere's face further drained of color at the name, but Arthur's eyes were on Gawain, so he made no note of the reaction. "Did he fall?"

"No, the young lad did not fall in battle," Gawain responded dully. "Most bravely did he fight, storming the gates of Dolorous Guard and almost single-handedly driving back the hosts of our quarry. I did precious little but follow useless in his footsteps to be honest. It was he who rescued the Lady Guinevere from her prisonous rooms, and he who guided her free of those hostile halls. Then he took his horse and rode off without a word once we reached the safety of Glyngarth."

The Tale of ~~King Arthur~~ Morgan Le Fay

"For what reason?"

Gawain spread his hands. "I truly do not know. He was guarding Lady Guinevere's door. I arrived there, and he left."

"He said nothing of his mission from his lady?" Arthur pressed, and Guinevere answered in Gawain's stead, a polite toned yet definitive assertion:

"Sir Lancelot did cry to me that he had been absent too long from his lady's side. He aided a damsel out of knightly duty alone and wished no reward for his great deeds in rescuing this princess. He will never again return to these lands. He made that clear."

Arthur smiled. "Then he and his lady have realized Excalibur belongs to England? That it is needed here?"

Guinevere shook her head, eyes veiled and distant, and Arthur's smile died. "I do not know, your majesty. He never mentioned the sword."

Arthur broke free of his study of Guinevere's somber countenance and turned back toward Gawain. "Perhaps we should speak in private. I would like to hear in much greater detail the tale of your quest to defeat this sorcerous foe and rescue my lady."

"So you wish me gone from your sight," Guinevere numbly noted. "I understand. I shall withdraw." She turned to leave, and Arthur scrambled panickedly to his feet, holding out his hand.

"My lady, I meant no such offense. Just know... you have been through a great ordeal," he repeated. "But you can rest now in peace. No harm shall befall you within these walls."

"That I know, my king," Guinevere acknowledged, giving another curtsy.

"And I would very much like to join you," Arthur rambled on, "at dinner. Should you wish it."

"Then I shall await thee in the banquet hall, your majesty," Guinevere submitted, forcing an empty smile.

She glided out from the throne room, and Morgan skipped forward to watch the awkward dinner with Arthur that night. Guinevere picked politely away at whatever dish the servants placed in front of her without seeming to taste a single bite of the fare, agreeing hollowly with whatever praise Arthur gave of the seasonings or the wine. In the end, Arthur wound up talking more to the servants than he did to distant Guinevere, and those old maids all blushed and beamed at his compliments, singing his praises to his beautiful bride-to-be seated coldly at the other end of the long table.

"I have never served a better master," the eldest of the maids told Guinevere in earnest prodding, as she cleared away her dishes at the end of the meal. "You could wish for no better a husband, my lady. And you make such a lovely match, the two of you, cute as a pair of buttons. I'm sure your children will be just as radiant."

"Indeed." Guinevere smiled, and the maid smiled right back without seeming to sense any of the utter deadness of the expression.

"I can escort you to your chambers," Arthur offered, holding out his arm, only to lower it just as quickly. "Or I can have Cara do that. That is probably a better idea."

Guinevere shook her head, closing the distance between them and calmly taking his arm. He guided her rigidly down the empty hall toward the temporary rooms she would be staying in until the wedding ceremony that was to be held at the end of the week once the procession from Camlierd arrived with Guinevere's father. "You wish for me to feel more comfortable within thy presence," she noted softly, "yet you stand rigid now, as if repulsed by my touch."

"Repulsed? No, I... I simply worry for your comfort, as you noted, and to hold you is... Well, I know tis not impropriety. But I... I am not a... worldly man."

"No, you are a worthy man." She sighed, voice shrinking down into near silence. "A man of virtue I cannot hope to match."

"You, uh... You think so highly of me?" Guinevere gave no direct answer, and Arthur looked away nervously. "Most of those tales that you have heard of me, they are... Look, the legends sound impressive, I know, but..." His rhetorical skills had seemingly deserted him, as he floundered to connect with his distant fiance.

He dropped her arm and took a deep breath in to steady himself, cementing in his mind what it is he wanted to say. Guinevere was just staring down at her empty hand, then she too gave a nervous swallow, crossing her arms. Arthur opened his eyes and took in that expression, and he turned his eyes away from her, before declaring, "I know it is..."

He took another deep breath, tone steadying. "Tis a strange thing indeed, to meet the person you are to spend the rest of your life with only days before the ceremony. I wish there had been chance for a proper courting before this day, that I might have seen your home and that you may have come to know me. Alas, I have not had the luxury of idle travel and pleasant pursuits.

"Since the day I took this throne, there has been death, and war, and turmoil. The people say I bring an end to such things, that I quiet the disaster that has plagued this country for decades, but in truth, I am just barely keeping my head above the waves." He took up a grim pace, up and down the

The Tale of ~~King Arthur~~ Morgan Le Fay

corridor, wringing his hands and avoiding her gaze. "Most shrewdly has your father made note of this turmoil and the continued misfortunes, first the fracturing of Orkney and then the plague... and though it has lain quiet for a time, I am sure he is but looking for an excuse to have back his beloved daughter and find for her a husband less contested than this perilously positioned young king."

"You are the only king of worth, good Arthur, and I would never so slander your works," Guinevere whispered. "My father wants very badly this union, to see his grandchild on this throne. And it is my duty to bring about that future and unite forever our houses. It is just..."

"You need not marry me for duty." Arthur took her hands, eyes earnest and tone firm. "I would not wish for your unhappiness. Seeing you for the first time..." He swallowed. "I could dream of no lovelier a bride, but I could see in an instant that you did not feel the same." She shook her head, about to deny it, but his hold and gentle words pressed her into silence. "You need not lie to me. Our countries will remain as friends, until the end of my days. This I vow. I will explain things to your father, so that there is no slight to you returning home. You need not subject yourself to a match you do not wish."

"Aye, but you are kind," she breathed, putting a hand to his cheek.

It was at that exact moment that Sir Lancelot walked into Morgan's throne room, his eyes glued to the image of Guinevere, as he sunk grimly down beside the pool.

Morgan looked over at him worriedly. "As you can see, the princess did indeed arrive safely in Camelot. There is no need to keep watching any further--"

"Be quiet, please," Lancelot pleaded, hanging upon the words of the lady before them.

"You are sincerely kind," Guinevere continued to praise Arthur. "And handsome." She kissed him, searching desperately to capture a desire and banish all past diversions from her mind.

It was an awkward gesture in the end however. Arthur was clearly caught off guard, and he had not Lancelot's experience or skill. Guinevere broke away quickly and turned her back to him, hand flying to her mouth. "I apologize. You must think me frightfully lustful now as well as unjustly melancholy."

"There is nothing to apologize for." His strong voice was quavering, eyes glowing with clear desire, as he laid his hand upon her arm and gently turned her back to face him. That kiss had clearly stirred his heart, even if it had not hers. "What is to be criticized about a man and a woman who are to be wed sharing but a simple kiss?"

He kissed her, and tears started running down her cheeks, and he pulled back in confusion. "Ah...? Now I have turned the lustful cad it seems." It was a half-hearted joke at best, but he knew nothing of Guinevere's troubles and so of course could not understand her behavior.

"Oh, my lord, you are as good as they say, and I do not deserve you." The tears ran more quickly, her voice breaking with sobs. "I am not fit to marry a king. I am no longer pure."

Lancelot flinched at the words, face twisting with pain, and Morgan exhaled. "Alright. I think that's enough of--"

"Wait!" so fierce was the order that Morgan sunk back grimly and allowed the scene to play out to its conclusion.

Guinevere collapsed against Arthur's chest in desperate search of comfort, and unhesitatingly he embraced her, eyes shining with compassion. "You aught to be disgusted with me. I am not fit for someone such as thee."

"No, my lady, I will not hear you condemn yourself," Arthur commanded, lifting her chin and wiping the tears from her cheeks. "Whatever evil has befallen you, it does not diminish your worth. No one need know of it."

Her lips parted in wonder. "So even hearing of my sin... You would have me for your wife regardless?"

"Gladly would I have thee. If you feel love for me as well, then I will stand proudly and patiently by your side and silence any that ever dare defame you. You will heal from the wounds of these past weeks, those terrible days, however long it takes. And even after the bishop has pronounced us man and wife, I will do nothing you do not wish. I will never force myself upon thee."

"You are a true gentleman." She sighed, the tension bleeding from her shoulders, as her lips spread into their first genuine smile.

"Aye, that smile..." Arthur clasped a hand to his chest, staring at Guinevere with all the fixed infatuation of a boy and his first love. "I love thee truly."

"You do?"

"To the end of my days."

She held him close, and her smile remained joyful and serene.

And Morgan dissolved the image before Lancelot could slump any further forward into the pool. "I guess they're still to be wed then, and Arthur sure is taken with her. Though that was not entirely an honest connection, since he clearly thinks her abused by her captors when she is in fact still pining for you--"

"Do not speak such manipulative lies," Lancelot gasped, wiping at his eyes. "She is happy. I can see it. She is forgiven, at peace, and her husband-to-be is not a thieving cretin. He was never a cretin. He is worthy of her, a noble king, and she will be his queen. His most beautiful queen..."

"Bloody hell, just ride over there already and stop the wedding," Morgan ordered him. "You said yourself you love this girl."

"No, Arthur loves her. You can see how he loves her."

"I can see that she does not love him," Morgan countered coldly. "And Arthur knows absolutely nothing about her. He is in love with nothing more than her pretty face--"

"Do not speak such slander of our good king's character!" Lancelot snapped, having pulled a complete 180 on his opinion of the man and now defending it fervently. "He loves her truly, and she will be happy. She must be happy, so she can move on and forget my sinful ensorcellments."

"For the last time, when she slept with you, that was not an ensorcellment. That was entirely voluntary--"

"She will be happy!" He nodded to himself, stumbling back from the mirror. "She'll be happy. I can die now in peace." He held out his arms in the pose of a martyr. "Go on, witch. Strike me down."

"For the last bloody time, I am not going to kill you!"

His face fell, and he clenched a hand to his forehead, sighing. "Aye, because you too have been ensorcelled into believing you love me. Right."

"I am not ensorcelled! And you are no longer cursed. I broke said curse with my selfless act humiliating myself before a dense and thankless cad!"

"If I have slighted you, then kill me."

"No!"

"Very well." He stalked over to her throne, snatching up his sword and weapon's belt. "Then I shall go forth and find a monster of merit to see to the deed."

"You'll be betraying your knightly duty if you allow any such monsters to slay you," she coldly illuminated, "because that would mean you are permitting such evil to go on harming the innocent."

"Then I shall fight with earnest ferocity, and we shall both myself and the monsters die within the same fateful breath!"

He spent that entire day and then well into the night trekking hungover through her woods until he found a den of goblins and cut them all to pieces. Morgan watched on wearily and kept back the specters and the more deadly enemies. Lancelot cut in twain the final fleeing creature and wheeled about with sword aloft, shouting into the darkened woods, "Is there no one else? Are there no stronger challengers who dare face me?!"

A pack of wolves gave a mournful howl in response to his screams, and Lancelot went stalking toward the sound, only for Morgan to teleport him irritably back to her castle. "No killing the wolves! They're out there minding their own business, and I don't want you charging in there and hurting the poor dogs."

"So I am to be your prisoner then?" Lancelot panted, tossing down his sword. "You think I will betray again my lady? Try whatever seductions you wish, you tiny witch. With earnest willpower I shall easily resist your wiles."

"My wiles?" she repeated in outrage, but he kept rambling on, completely ignoring her.

"Even should you change your shape, as I have heard tale of, I will stand aloof and avert my eyes. Even should you take the form of Guinevere...." His eyes filled with sudden wistful lust. "Could you do that? Would you appear as Guinevere? Then I would not be hurting she, it would only be--"

She slapped him. "You have a serious problem, and I would feel nothing but pity for you did you not infuriate me so, you absolute ass! I am not some lewd seductress, and why the hell does everyone label me that?! I have only ever slept with two men, I will have you know. The first of them, my **husband**, and the second--" Her voice cracked. "A dreadful mistake, no different from you and Guinevere, because even if I could permit myself to love him... I killed his father, and I do nothing but tear him to pieces."

"You slept with a man after killing his father?" Lancelot demanded in disgust, and Morgan's hands clenched.

"It was not right after! That was years ago and... Get out of my castle, you ungrateful lout! I hate you!"

"No, by your own confession you 'love me truly'," he repeated deliriously. "Just as my lady and poor Guinevere did."

"No, far different from how Guinevere feels, and so many miles removed from that twisted possessiveness that your lady has toward you that I am seriously offended you would accuse me of such feelings. Earnestly did I pity you, which has saved you of your curse, and now I am sending you home to your father, before your spiral of disturbing destructive behavior gets any more serious."

The Tale of ~~King Arthur~~ Morgan Le Fay

She called up a portal to Brittany where King Ban was staying at the moment in company with his friend, King Bors, but Lancelot quickly shook his head, near fleeing from its presence. "No. I will ruin no one else!"

"Whatever are you talking about?" she sighed.

"You heard Gawain, my father is a good man, a noble king! He would feel nothing but shame were he to truly come to know his son, a lying drunkard and pretended knight who steals the virtue of pure young maidens through wicked enchantments..."

"You had one night of drinking. That does not make you a drunkard. It makes you a grief stricken teenager. And Guinevere fell for your charms, not some enchantment. Your father wants to see you--"

"No! If you will not send me on to hell then..." He looked about the gloomy throne room with its eerie green candles and skittering spiders. "Wait, yes. I see. This castle is already hell, a hell on earth, and these dusty halls shall be my prison. Yes, I am indeed your prisoner."

"Bloody hell, I cannot stand you. Now get your things and *get out of my home!*"

She vanished in a dramatic flash of fire and returned to her studies, but Lancelot refused to leave on his own accord. He sat in his rooms and treated it like a prison, never opening the door, or coming out in search of food, until angrily the next day she stormed in there, asserting, "Your horse is going to die, if you do not go down there and feed him."

"Stephen is a proud and noble horse," Lancelot sniffled. "Worthy of a far better master. Send him home to Camelot. He belongs there, with the true knights."

"Oh no. You brought him here, you care for him. Feed him, and brush him, and take him out riding, and get all those massive piles of crap out of my courtyard already!"

Lancelot did as she demanded, only because he truly did not want the noble beast to fall ill. The animal clearly loved him, and he fed it and cared for it dutifully, though he ate not so much as a single bite himself, and so angrily she began just delivering his meals, picking dishes with purposefully tantalizing smells and just summoning them onto his nightstand. Inevitably he gave in to the rumblings of his stomach, then she cleared away the empty dishes and repeated the irritating room service at every meal.

Yet other than those few hours of visiting his stallion, he never left his bloody rooms.

"You really do need to be getting some sort of exercise," she told him irritably on the morning of the seventh day.

"So you have come to try and tempt me into lustful--"

"No! I am telling you to pick up your sword and practice like you used to, and if you will not shave, then you at least need to wash your hair more frequently, alright?"

Lancelot sniffed in carefully concealed embarrassment, scratching at his face. "Very well. I shall do as you request and resume my regular routines, but in return, you must do for me a favor."

"What favor?"

He wanted to look upon Guinevere, to watch her with pointless pining on her wedding day, as she walked into the church in her dress of pristine white, and Arthur stood proudly at the altar, waiting enraptured for her to walk up there and join him.

"There's still time for me to teleport you over there so you can confess your feelings. It's your last chance, child, I mean it."

"See how radiant she looks," was Lancelot's only response, voice cracking.

Guinevere was indeed near glowing with happiness, as Arthur lifted up her veil and stared into her eyes. They spoke their vows with earnest conviction, then she kissed him passionately, and the assembly cheered, and Lancelot exhaled in jagged suffering.

"And that's the end. They're married." Morgan dismissed the image. "Arthur really does seem happy, I suppose, and so does she. It seems you made the mature decision, Lancelot. Congratulations."

"I would look upon her but a moment more. I beg you."

Morgan arched an eyebrow. "Fine, but afterward you are... to clean the entire throne room. Deal? Dusting and de-webbing."

"I am not thy servant! But fine. Show her to me. Quickly."

Lancelot kept his eyes glued to Guinevere's face, as they sat there for hours watching the newly united lovers leave the church and head to the evening feast.

King Leodegrance congratulated Arthur and presented his new son in law with an expensive and oversized gift, a massive circular table with 150 artistically carved seats, all made of the finest oak, to sit in castle Camelot's long abandoned war-room. "Your father, Uther, was the one to give me that table during our own peace accord two decades past," Leodegrance illuminated. "It seems only fitting I return it, now that our kingdoms will once

The Tale of ~~King Arthur~~ Morgan Le Fay

again be unified. Though this time, it is an alliance that shall span the generations, never to be broken."

"Indeed." Arthur smiled. "I am a man of my word, your majesty, and I shall endeavor to fairly mediate and keep peace and justice throughout my reign."

"And may you reign long and bless me with many grandsons."

Lancelot's hand clenched, but Morgan paid him no mind. She was rather enjoying sitting in on this day. It was almost as if she had been invited to attend her brother's wedding and could share with all those many esteemed guests this important milestone in his life.

"Even before she is pregnant, you mustn't allow her to exert herself," Leodegrance continued to embarrassingly advise his new son in law. "My daughter is a delicate flower in need of constant attention and care."

"Father!" Guinevere blushed.

"Oh, and you may call me father as well," Leodegrance carried on merrily. "There is no further need for all this 'your majesty' nonsense. You are my son now, and I shall punish you as casually as any father would, the second you upset me." He gave a wicked laugh, and Arthur laughed along nervously, until Guinevere mercifully excused the both of them from the discussion, telling her father that they were neglecting sorely their other guests.

Arthur spent a good deal of time after that introducing Guinevere to Sir Ector, clearly feeling far more at ease in company of his adoptive father than he did in formal address with the higher ranking nobles and clergymen around them.

Guinevere stayed beaming throughout that feast. She clung unwaveringly to Arthur's arm and welcomed happily all the courtiers and well wishers giving praise to their new queen. She smiled even through the cringe-inducing ceremony where the heralds announced that the bride and groom would retire now to the royal bed chambers to consummate their marriage. Arthur appeared ready to sink into the ground, muttering for the men to just return to their feasting already, as he led his wife briskly off down the hall with the raucous and envious shouts of his knights chasing after him.

"You are truly not a worldly man," Guinevere giggled. "Just be grateful we are not in France where they sit in and observe the royal bedding."

"They what?!"

"Come now, my king, you needn't sound so wild," Guinevere whispered, pulling him inside the bedroom and firmly shutting the door. "This shall be a night unlike any other." She nodded to herself, unlacing his shirt--

"Quite definitively the end," Morgan declared, dissolving the image. "They're married. They're happy. And now my back hurts from all these hours stuck leaning over this thing scrying, not to mention the massive crick in my neck."

She arched backward to try and alleviate the pain, and Lancelot reached over uninvited with hands working over her back and shoulders.

"Ho, no touching!"

"I am but repaying you your kindness," he whispered numbly, thumbs digging into her back muscles. "I can rest easy now. She has forgotten all about me."

"Stop sounding so bitter, you... Ah. Oh..." He really was quite the talented masseuse, and she sat there compliantly, as she felt the knots in her neck and lower back rapidly easing. "You are almost too good at this."

"My lady taught me."

He leaned in closer, and she stiffened, squirming free of his hold. "And now my skin is once again crawling. Keep your hands to yourself, you confused ball of damage, and go to bed."

He did not show up to the banquet hall for breakfast the next morning, so she flitted off to his rooms and found him just lying there on the floor, staring blankly up at the ceiling. "You would not allow me to return to my lady, even should I wish it, yes?" he croaked. "I am your prisoner."

"You are *not* my prisoner. You let yourself into my home, and I don't know why you're clinging to the bizarre idea that I wish to keep you here. I will let you go wherever you want. Though I will *request*," she enforced, "that you not return to your lady, because having eaten the food of the fay, you would be instantly imprisoned back within that kingdom the second you set foot in those woods."

"I know," he murmured. "And I know just as fiercely that I must go back, so that my lady might punish me for my unfaithfulness. I had a dream of her, the first night I came here. She called me home, said all was forgiven and she needed me... But you silenced her." He stared at her with brow lowered, whispering raggedly, "Now I find I do not wish to go back at all. I would rather be a prisoner in this hellish haunt of spiders and spirits than back at the side of my lady, a position any man would be fortunate to..." He shook his head, putting a hand to his forehead. "Your bewitchments are indeed the most potent in the land."

"Are you actually attracted to me?" she demanded flatly, and he frowned, eyeing her up and down in weary indifference.

The Tale of ~~King Arthur~~ Morgan Le Fay

"Well, no. You are nothing special to look at, yet you have made me doubt my lady, and I feel now a steady comfort and relief within your presence, and your council of endless lies starts to echo in my ears as if it were true wisdom, so surely you have made me your slave just as--" He bit back his words.

"Just as she did?" Morgan filled in the confession, and Lancelot gave a vehement shake of his head.

"Every day within this hell, so far removed from her presence, I come closer to believing such lies. But it is guilt alone that keeps me from returning to her side. Yes." He nodded. "I have betrayed her most thoroughly, thus I do not deserve to be back within that paradise."

"Do you know what your lady's request was to Arthur in return for Excalibur?" she prodded.

"No. I know only that he betrayed their bargain, stealing the relic and running off--"

"She requested he bring Merlin back to her kingdom."

Lancelot shrugged. "Well... the druid is an enemy, I suppose, and a threat to her subjects, just as thou art--"

"The druid was her lover," she corrected scathingly. "A bedfellow she kept imprisoned in an infinite tower so that he could never choose to leave her and no other could lay hands on him, yet she could visit whenever she pleased. She wanted him back to resume that twisted status quo, and when Arthur said he had no way of delivering the druid, she stated aloud that she would take him as a temporary replacement, because just like you he is young and pretty and his naive little heart makes him no doubt desirable to her corruptive clutches."

Lancelot stared at her, heart-broken, shell shocked.

"Fairies are inhuman and unfeeling creatures," she illuminated harshly. "They feed off the souls of mortals, and they love nothing more than to be the ones to devour their firsts, first kisses, first loves. They will drink up every emotion inside you, until you reach that place of 'immortality' that your lady no doubt offered you, but once you reach that place? Where you've grown up and will never again feel age or new experience? All that was once you just withers and dies. You feel nothing anymore. You are just a blank puppet, a slave to the master's whims. And after a few decades such mortals are no longer very filling or much fun, so they find someone fresh to replace you, and around and around it goes."

Lancelot denied harshly her words at first, even after she showed him in her scrying mirror the stories of the few abducted mortals to ever escape a fairy's clutches, how they spoke about that time, and how hollowed out it had left them once they returned to the real world and lost all interest in life.

Lancelot spoke no more of his lady in the days that followed. He began showing up to mealtimes, and practicing the sword, and going out riding with Stephen, or "patrolling" as he called it. He pestered her every evening however, begging her time and again to show him some image of Guinevere.

She gave in at first, showing him Guinevere sitting attentively beside Arthur at some meeting of state, then eating her dinner alone, then brushing her hair, then luring Arthur away from his late night work slaving over missives to his allies by candlelight, tempting the exhausted king into bed--

"Alright, this isn't healthy," she told Lancelot bluntly, as he sat there near ripping at his hair.

"You are right. We should all of us immediately retire for the evening."

"And what will you be dreaming?" she sighed, but he refused to answer, and she rolled her eyes.

In the third month of his stay, the boy did finally put in the effort to cut his hair and shave. Though suspiciously that was the very same evening that they looked in on Guinevere and caught her criticizing Arthur about his freshly grown in beard.

"But I liked you better without a beard," she wheedled, pressing up against him and putting a hand to his face. "I don't like all these whiskers scratching against my lips."

"Yes, but I have a summit with King Nentres and King Marcus in Caerlon this week. They are reluctant vassals at best, and now, well... I need them not to be able to term me the beardless boy king anymore."

"You can be a dashing, beardless man," she pleaded. "The great, clean shaven king."

"I'm sorry, Guinevere, but this is a matter of state, and it must come before personal preference."

Despite those words, Arthur seemed far too proud of his beard, and Morgan highly suspected it was with no small amount of selfishness that he kept growing it out, even after that summit was concluded.

"Aye, but that is a glorious beard," Lancelot noted after another week. "But a lady's preference must always come before selfish vanity, and you aught to know that, lord king."

The Tale of ~~King Arthur~~ Morgan Le Fay

"He cannot hear you, you know," Morgan chided, yet Lancelot continued to stare at and talk to the images of Arthur of Guinevere he so insisted on spying upon. He never wanted to leave that scrying pool, not for hours at a time, and Morgan slowly began to realize just how pathetic the both of them were, hiding away from the world yet watching on so fixedly the actions of their loved ones, as if they were still a part of their lives.

"This gravy is so watery as to be tasteless," the spoiled brat noted that night at dinner. "I'm rather suspicious as to where you got it from. Also, this meat is horridly tough."

Morgan threw down her fork, rising slowly to her feet with face a darkening storm. "Actually, I think it is in fact under-cooked." She set his plate aflame, burning the slab of venison to ash.

Lancelot exhaled. Then he smiled, palming at his forehead. "Ah yes, I requested that this prison be hellish, so the texture of this meal was clearly designed to feed into that atmosphere. I apologize, good woman."

"I am never cooking for you again! You can bloody well starve to death! See if I care!" She stormed out of the room.

He set out hunting the next morn and returned to her gates in the evening with a self-made bow and an entire stag slung across the back of his horse. "Bloody show off," she muttered.

Lancelot butchered the stag and seasoned it expertly, serving her up a steak.

"Who taught you to cook?" she asked him suspiciously.

"A little green skinned fellow named Leidshaft. It was a precise and hallowed art, the capturing of meat for the feast table and the butchering of its carcass. Just as it was of particular procedure the airing of the lady's wine…" He fell silent.

"It tastes delicious," she praised him gently.

"Yes, of course it does."

She threw down her fork.

He caught her arm, as she shoved back her chair at the end of the meal and turned to leave. "Will you summon your mirror, so I may look upon the Lady Guinevere?"

"No, because it's creepy that you just sit there and stare at her so often, and you need to let go. Honestly. She is a married woman."

"Yes, yes you're right." His hand dropped from her arm, and he slogged off to bed.

He was right back to pestering her the next morning however, though on an entirely new topic. "Can you fetch for me paints?"

"Paints?"

"Yes, brightly colored pigments of gold and red and blue."

"Why on earth do you need paints?"

"So that I might begin work on a portrait."

Her eyes narrowed in suspicion. "A portrait of who?"

Lancelot flushed, storming out of the room. "If you will not lend me aid, then I will make the pigments for myself!"

He spent days foraging in the forest, until he'd found berries and roots that boiled down into heavy dyes the colors he was looking for. He then began work with sweeping lines all across the walls of his room. Morgan peeked in on him curiously near the end of the days long project and saw that sure enough there was now a massive portrait of Guinevere plastered right above his bed.

She threw up her hands. "You have a problem," she repeated, and he jumped, hand jerking and ruining the highlight on the golden spiral of hair he had been so meticulously shading.

"Jealous witch! You've ruined it. I must now repaint the entire lock."

"Either that or simply let her go, you obsessive fool. Though that truly is a beautiful portrait." She studied appreciatively the stylized lines of Guinevere's glowing face. "You really are good at everything."

"Yes, I know," he muttered, scrubbing away the jerky line with a wetted sponge, then setting back to work repainting the entire section.

He knelt there for hours at a time once the portrait was finished, just gazing at Guinevere's face. Then he started singing to it, and that was the final straw, because he had an infuriatingly lovely singing voice, like low and whispery velvet. It tingled her spine just to hear those soft refrains when passing by his rooms, and that was not at all fair!

"How long are you going to stay here?" Morgan angrily cut into his song.

"Until the day I die. I told you that. I belong in this prison, to keep safe the maidens of the world from my evil, lustful--"

"I don't want you lounging about my castle for all eternity, singing your laments and redecorating my walls! I did not invite you here. So pack your things, and go visit your father already."

Lancelot swallowed, ripping his eyes free of Guinevere's smiling countenance and telling her quietly, "I... I will visit my father. One day. Once I have become a true knight, a man worthy of being his son."

"Your father is a king," she countered flatly, "just go to him, tell the tale of Dolorous Guard, and he will knight you."

The Tale of ~~King Arthur~~Morgan Le Fay

"Dolorous Guard?" Lancelot whirled on her angrily. "Where I gave myself over to evil and defiled the innocent damsel I was honor bound to--"

"Forget it. You're hopeless."

She stalked out of the room and mulled over the prospect of just teleporting him out to King Ban's court, but in the end she found herself strangely procrastinating that decision. Lancelot was horrible company. Even when he trained hard and took care of his horse and made his own dinners, he still spent every night just pining endlessly over Guinevere and every morning complaining about the hellish gloom of this "prison" to which he had consigned himself. Still, she felt better these days than she had the entire past year, wasting away in lonely grief, for with Lancelot here, the needy teenage son she had never asked for nor wanted, she did not have to think about Merlin or Urien or anything of consequence. She could spend all her energies berating him, trying to motivate him to get over himself and return to the world so that he may set right his perceived sins instead of sitting sealed up here brooding about them.

It was an entire four months into this joking "imprisonment" scenario that another uninvited guest came crashing through her gates. She raised her head irritably up from her book, as she heard the deranged yet gleeful shout echoing up her stairwell. "Morgan! My queen! It is indeed a joyous day!"

She shut her book and coolly gestured open the doors of her throne room, as the all too familiar voice of Sir Accolon drew steadily nearer her position. The wild-eyed knight came striding through the open doors, and his face fell visibly, as he spotted her seated there with just her ordinary freckled face and not the sculpted cheekbones and full lips of his Lady Genevieve.

He forced a smile regardless, sinking down on one knee with forehead bowed. "You wear no veil, and you have cleared the brambles from your entrance, keeping open your doors and lit all these candles to welcome my return to thee, yes?" His smile broadened. "You have been waiting for my arrival, waiting to congratulate me on this most joyous of occasions." He rose to his feet and strode right up to her, reaching out his hand. "I had hoped you would be watching me. If you would only grace me with your true countenance. Surely I have earned at least that boon."

She caught his wrist, rising coolly to her feet. "What is this occasion you speak of? I have not been watching you, sir, so I know not these reasons I have to be so joyous."

"Surely you do. Yet you remain as coy and poised as always. If you wish for me to brag of the details, then I will indulge you, my queen." He seized her hands. "I have retaken our homeland. I ousted that neglectful pretender, Gawain, from King Urien's throne."

Morgan's brow furrowed. "How?"

"The ransom of his brother, Agravain, which I took quick and careful charge of following the death of King Brandin."

"So, you bankrupted him?" Morgan pressed, her worry ebbing, for it was surely no tragedy that the man who had never wanted to be king had lost his seat along with his family fortune. It was no tragedy at all, so long as he remained unharmed...

"No, my lady!" Accolon laughed, winding his fingers in her hair. "I demanded such an outrageous, unfullfillable sum of gold that the false king Gawain and his allies could not hope to pay it. Then I said we would immediately execute Agravain unless his brother returned alone to Glastonbury to meet our demands. He came and attempted a rescue of course, and I challenged him to single combat and..." His breath caught. "Oh, tell me you watched the duel. You always watched so closely my duels. I know you saw this one."

"What happened to Gawain?" she snapped, the panic returning.

"A fierce clashing of blades, yet I got around his guard and delivered the fateful blow from the tip of a poignard that pierced through the chainmail. Now he dies, a slow and painful death, and his tyrannical liege, King Arthur, will be next."

Morgan hurled him away from her, sending him skidding on his back across the floor, with her hands shaking and eyes flooding with tears. "Dies? What do you mean he dies? Then he is not dead yet?" she reassured herself. "How long ago was this duel? How...?"

"I came that we may watch his end together," Accolon grunted, sitting up. "Our men wait for us not far from here with that trussed and weakened cad, and we will haul him back to Orkney where a coup is already underway to dispose of that boy's foolish old steward. Then, with he and his brother executed before them, the rest of his supporters will fall silent, and you will have back your throne."

"It is not my throne!" she snapped. "And what do you mean his supporters will fall silent? He has two other brothers! Not to mention that Arthur, the liege lord of that entire territory, will not permit an overthrowing of the current steward, you fool! Now tell me **now** where *exactly* is Gawain?"

The Tale of ~~King Arthur~~Morgan Le Fay

Accolon's eyes darkened in angry confusion, and she did not wait for him to give answer, stalking over to her scrying pool and searching out Gawain. There was a hood over his head, and he was hanging limply off the side of a horse amidst a mounted patrol of armored northmen. There was no twitching of his fingers, no struggle against his ropes. He might already be dead for all she could tell. She pulled quickly back into a much wider view to determine what exact road it was where they were waiting so that she might instantly portal there.

Accolon caught her wrist, pulling her back from her mirror.

"Do not dare lay hands on me!" she hissed, then her anger died, for there was such genuine hurt and confusion in the cruel idiot's eyes.

"For what cause are these tears?" Accolon gently pressed, wiping at her cheeks.

"I did not ask you to do this!" Morgan tried to explain. "I told you to leave me be!"

"No, you told me to retake Orkney by my own power, and I am doing so now. I am proving myself to thee. I am thy loyal servant, and I have waited so long for your summons…"

"A loyal servant would not cause such an expression on the face of his lady," Sir Lancelot denounced. Accolon's eyes widened at the sound of that voice, another man's voice. He looked to Lancelot and let out a shaky breath. "Get your hands off of her, you uncouth villain. The lady of this castle most clearly did not invite you here."

Accolon looked madly back to Morgan. "So you have found a fairer champion and given him the boons of which you would never indulge me." He gave another jagged exhalation, tenderly brushing back her hair. "It matters not. I will share. I am your servant, as I said. I was always willing to share you, so long as a little piece of that lady, my queen, might be given to me as well."

He leaned in to kiss her, and Morgan broke free of her paralysis and dissolved right into shadow, slipping out from under him and setting him stumbling forward.

"Who is this madman?" Lancelot demanded, as she rematerialized beside him.

"Sir Accolon of Orkney," she murmured. "Just leave him be. Gawain is in danger, and I must get going."

"I shall accompany you," Lancelot declared. "Sir Gawain is a noble knight and a cherished friend. I would see no ill befall him."

"Come along then." She opened up a portal to the borders of her woods where Accolon's allies and their prisoner were awaiting her arrival.

"What have I ever done to so earn your disdain?!" Accolon screamed after her.

"You're doing it right now," she muttered, seizing Lancelot's wrist and quickly fleeing through her portal.

The Tale of ~~King Arthur~~ Morgan Le Fay

XXXIV. 𝔒𝔩𝔡 𝔓𝔞𝔱𝔱𝔢𝔯𝔫𝔰

𝔉ifty knights were set to guard the defeated king of Orkney, a paltry obstacle to the threat that was coming to obliterate them. The sky boiled with sudden blood red clouds, and the boredly lounging warriors scrambled quickly to their feet. Deep within the shadows of the trees, the air itself seemed to tear apart and out stepped the witch of Orkney and her fully armored tag along. She wore the face of hated Lady Genevieve, for the sake of instant recognition, but the angelic queen was clothed this time in no pretty dresses or sparkling crowns. She wore instead the black cowled robes of a sorcerer, and her blue eyes flashed with rage as deadly as the lightning now crashing down in front of her.

"This scene is as unsettling as it is overdramatic," Lancelot sighed but fell silent the second he met her gaze.

Her rage in this moment was no mere performance.

The men dropped to their knees the instant they spotted her. "Your majesty," their leader greeted her reverently, then looked confusedly toward Lancelot. "Where is Sir Accolon--?"

"Your queen did not give you permission to speak." The thunder shook the stones, and the men bowed their heads, cringing. "You will utter only answers to the questions I ask. Now, which of you fools truly believed you were doing my will?"

"It is your husband's will we follow and his legacy we preserve," their captain harshly replied. "We have knocked down the pretenders who seized his seat. Though if you had but returned to us before... If you had but born him an heir--"

The lightning touched down right upon the captain's forehead, and he fell smoking to the ground, as the rest of the men scrambled back from him in panic.

"You are traitors to your king," Morgan denounced. "Gawain is your king, son of Lot and nephew of Urien, an heir of royal blood whom you have tricked and defeated through dishonest contest. Those who are truly loyal to me, cut him free immediately, place him gently on the ground, then flee."

The crimson clouds crackled with static, and the men mounted their horses and attempted to set off with the limp form of their prisoner still tied to the saddle of treacherous Sir Caradoc.

"You have failed your chance at mercy," she hissed. "Now you are but dust and bone."

The words echoed in the air, and the flesh of all fifty knights shriveled into ash and leaked through their armor like sand through a sieve, leaving behind only lurching skeletons incapable of steering their mounts.

Lancelot drew his blade and whirled to face her with a look of clear unease upon his face. "You are indeed a witch. There is no honor in--"

"Silence." She strode uncaringly past the silenced lake knight and raised her hand in a quick and urgent claw, ripping free the ties around the motionless figure she knew to be Gawain and pulling him into her arms.

Genevieve melted away, as she lowered the still unresponsive captive most gently to the ground, lifting free his hood. The roiling red clouds churned all the more tumultuously, as she laid hands on that face, so disfigured with bruising. The less swollen eye was open at least, alert and aware yet glossing with fever.

"Morgan," he breathed. "If I am seeing you here, in the moment of my death, then I've truly no idea if I am headed off to heaven or..." He trailed off, as his gaze wandered past her and caught sight of a set of armor filled only with fleshless bones tumbling from its saddle and clattering to the ground right before him. "Hell. Definitely hell."

"No demon will lay hands on you. I have come to end your suffering." His eyes glimmered with fear at the words, and it was like a knife to her heart, for how could he ever assume she had meant--?

It did not matter. She pressed her forehead to his own, searching beyond the bruises and battered ribs in search of more serious threat. She found finally a slow-acting venom eating its way through his veins. The toxin would take weeks of regular doses to fully kill him, but it attacked the nerves and instantly weakened the muscles, which is surely why Accolon had bested him so easily. The second he'd cut him with that poisoned blade, Gawain had stood no chance of fighting back. Still, she knew now the antidote to his suffering.

She healed his bruises and summoned the antivenom from the potions room of her castle, holding it up to his lips. "Drink."

He pulled back his head. "What is it?"

Curse that hateful suspicion within his gaze, ripping at her heart, so that her hand became a claw knotted in back of his hair and she forced the tonic down his choking gullet with all compassion and grace abandoned. "There! You're healed!" she snapped, shoving his head from her lap and starting angrily to her feet. "You need not suffer my presence any longer.

The Tale of ~~King Arthur~~ Morgan Le Fay

"You, stay here and nurse him back to health," she ordered Lancelot scathingly. "He is in no state to defend himself should any other conspirators ride up here to attack him, and I'm sure he'll be grateful to see those lovely dark eyes of yours shining over his sickbed."

"Morgan, wait..." She ignored the weakened grunt from the dazed knight sitting up so slowly and reaching out after her. She ignored his words, because she knew that even should it be a begrudging thanks crossing his lips in this moment, it did not change anything between them. She was a villain who had used and then abandoned him, and he had every right to hate her. No healing could make up for what she'd taken from him, and she could not stand to see that look in his eyes, not for another second.

She teleported back to Cader Idris and curled up on her throne. Sadly, Accolon was still seated there pathetically on her floor, and his face brightened with such hope at her appearance, and he fell to his knees before her with that thankful exhalation, "You've come back."

"And that makes you happy? To see the wicked witch returned here to torment you?"

"Torment me all you like, if I have earned such a punishment," he replied with earnest conviction, kissing her hand. "My heart thrills with hope for but the chance to be within thy presence."

She knew what he wanted. How little it would take to make him happy, to see that love and adoration in his eyes... She sunk back into the shape of Lady Genevieve, straightening from her previous defensive huddle. "Do you truly love me?" she pressed. "No matter what I do to you, you will continue to love me?"

"Yes. I love you with all my soul, my queen. I will always love you. No other can compare."

She allowed him to kiss her, then she took him to her bedroom, and she tried to steal back from him some of the pleasure and joy he was taking from her body. It worked to a point, but she was even lonelier at the end of it than when she'd had spoiled Lancelot wandering her halls, giving her nothing but criticisms.

"Leave me now," she commanded.

And his answer was, as always, "As you wish." He gave Genevieve one final, passionate kiss and then withdrew from her chambers.

The villainous pretender had reverted to filthy old patterns, and she lay alone on that bed and she wept, knowing that all Gawain's pretty words to her that one perfect night had been utter lies, because she deserved no better.

XXXV. An Enemy of No Conscience

"I would wish to never leave this paradise," Accolon whispered in her ear, pressed up against his Lady Genevieve, with hands endlessly exploring and words endlessly praising.

He had been here an entire month now, a pleasing distraction during the night and a constant bother during the day, speaking only of affairs in Orkney as well as his many feats of arms that she had missed seeing this past year. She watched those tournaments and contests through her scrying mirror just to indulge him. Then she watched his fight against Gawain and insulted him scathingly. "If you needed to poison him to win, then you are no knight of merit."

"Yes, I understand," he murmured, hands wrapping around her waist. "You disdain the use of poisons, because of your mother's death. I should have remembered. That is why you set our enemy free, correct? Because I had not earned that victory?" She gave no response, but he did not really need her to, so assured in his own rightness. "The next time I face that usurper, it shall be an honest challenge, I swear it, and I will run him through with you at my side..."

She faded into shadow and hid from him for an entire day after that remark, but he was so utterly clueless that he did not understand her behavior. Still, he was no danger to Gawain or anyone else, so long as she kept him here in exile. Every dangerous and awful thing he had done this past year had all been for the sake of impressing her, proving himself to his queen.

Keeping him here meant constantly pretending though, and she knew she was steadily losing the small corner of self she had managed to rediscover these past months. She never appeared in anything other than the shape of Genevieve now, because that was the woman he was in love with, and she wanted him to be happy. He could be happy, and she could suffer as she deserved to. And it wasn't entirely suffering. He could be generous and comforting, and she had felt something for him, on many of their nights together.

But not tonight, as he finished his work and stared solemnly into her eyes. "This is indeed paradise, yet we have hidden here too long, my lady, ignoring the world outside."

The Tale of ~~King Arthur~~ Morgan Le Fay

She did not want to hear those words. She broke free of his gaze and coldly turned her back.

He settled down beside her and kissed her neck, continuing on with his unwanted words. "I can see it in your eyes, my queen, that distance and malcontent. You are not yet happy."

"You can do no more to please me, Accolon," she whispered. "You have performed with expertise, but your queen is a woman who will never be satisfied, no matter the momentary pleasure."

"That is because this room is not your proper position," Accolon insisted. "You should never have run into hiding. Your thrones sit waiting in every warmly lit hall from Camelot to Orkney. Even the most prideful lord will kneel in awe the second you return in all your glory to seize that birthright, Morgan Pendragon, our one true queen."

He insisted on calling her Morgan, even as he insisted that Genevieve was her 'true countenance'. He wanted to be the vassal of Morgan Pendragon, sister of Arthur and unrivaled tyrant who had once so easily seized Camelot's throne by smiting the pretender who had been seated there.

"Seizing a chair does not make you a queen," she whispered, thinking once more of Merlin and his endless, patronizing advice that she had hated so fiercely at the time but now heard constantly replaying through her head.

Merlin probably hated her by now, sealed away forever in isolation as he was. He hated her, or he was completely insane already, but she knew that even so, if he could see her in this moment, he would feel no disgust. He would feel only sadness, and disappointment.

She let all the lovely curves of Genevieve melt away and felt Accolon stiffen in alarm. "I tire of this game, and I am not your play thing," she murmured, standing up from the bed and dressing herself in a set of plain and unflattering robes.

"Play thing? Of course not. I love you, my queen. Whatever shape you pretend, I see your loving heart behind those breasts, or lack thereof..."

"How poorly you pretend," she exhaled, striding out of the room.

"I have upset you again. I apologize." He rushed right after her, seizing her wrist. "I will make it up to you, I swear it, whatever you wish."

"I wish to be left alone." She ripped her hand free of his grasp and could feel his eyes following her down the hall. Should she look back and meet that stare though, she knew she would find no comfort in it, no desire to turn around and fall back into his arms.

Accolon would use her just as happily as Urien had, to lay waste to their enemies then warm him in the night, trapped forever in a pretended persona that he labeled as paradise. His paradise was her hell, and every day within this self-established prison she was slipping further down the slope. She did not want to sink any further this night. Her thick-headed champion could lie alone and dream of Lady Genevieve, the discontented sin of which she had once accused Gawain. Gawain... The only man who had ever loved Morgan the girl, never tempted to exploit her gifts, as every other man desired.

She knelt down by her scrying pool and called up an image of Orkney's true king. He was safe and alive, and that undid a worried knot within her stomach that she had not realized had been plaguing her all these weeks. Of course, with Lancelot camped there beside him as his bodyguard, she supposed it would have taken an entire army to pose threat to the knights.

It was already late in the night, yet she stayed up past sunrise and watched with wistful interest every encounter and struggle the two of them had faced these past four weeks.

They had indeed put a stop to the coup in Orkney, rescuing Agravain from his prison and restoring their capital city and the surrounding lands to a state of quiet stability. Though more accurately, it was Arthur who restored that status quo. He had ridden north with a section of his army at the same time Gawain had ridden off alone to Glastonbury to fall prey to Accolon's trap. Arthur's rhetoric and shows of military strength had brought into line the scheming lords of the north, even as his presence there worked to reassure the people.

Gawain then made use of his own mundane talents to the best of his abilities by offering his conspirators a chance to be spared the headsman's axe by fighting him in single combat and proving their claims that he was too weak to inherit his father's mantle and rule their kingdom. He fought the champions of the three most powerful lords and beat them all back, giving them the option after they yielded to either swear him allegiance or lose their heads in place of their masters. Each man took that bargain, and the old nobles were executed.

"A most brutal failure," Accolon noted, sinking down beside her just in time to see the conspirators' heads set to rolling. "My plan was indeed flawed, but as I said before, I've not your mind for brilliant strategy. Advise me now, and we shall surely vanquish all that--"

She clamped her hand to his mouth, staring him down determinedly with her own glowering eyes and thin lipped mouth, and asserting icily, "I am not the queen of Orkney, and I am certainly not the witch of Orkney. I am not a Pendragon, and I am not your Genevieve. I am Morgan Le Fay, a

The Tale of ~~King Arthur~~ Morgan Le Fay

wizardess who is indeed done with hiding, but who wants no part in your desperate schemes to reignite a war already ended. You are not my champion, Accolon, and our time together is ended now, because I am done pretending. Now get out of my castle. Right now. I mean it."

She removed her hand from his lips to allow him to respond, but he just stared at her with pained confusion. "I am not your champion?" It was such a broken plea, and her will instantly wavered.

She clamped a hand to her forehead, squeezing shut her eyes. "Fine. You are still my champion, so act as a proper knight. Obey my will, and *go away*. Now."

"I will act as a proper knight, your knight." He pulled her in, attempting once again to kiss her.

She did not run from him this time. She teleported him outside, getting the distinct sense that he would continue to ignore and grope her until she took back even this tiny show of resolve and caved to him once more. "I hate all men," she muttered to herself. "You're all overbearing, and selfish."

And she was very badly missing at least one of them regardless of all those facts, so she called back the images of the rebellion in Orkney and continued to drink in every detail of those pivotal days she had been absent from the world.

An assassination attempt had been made upon both Gawain and King Arthur in Orkney's castle the very night the treasonous cabal's executions were carried out. That flood of forty men who came sneaking through the corridors at midnight was repelled by Sir Lancelot, who cut down most of the horde himself before the commotion of the fighting awoke Gawain and the other knights. Morgan found it curious that Lancelot had not simply shouted that there was an attack taking place, in order to wake them sooner. Though he did make a point of never removing his visor in company with Arthur, so perhaps he was simply too ashamed of his sinful forays with Guinevere and thus wished to keep hidden his identity.

Arthur asked Gawain of course that next morning who this brave knight was who had defended so valiantly his kings.

Lancelot elbowed Gawain in the stomach, even as he went to answer, then stone-walled Arthur's request that he remove his visor, so Arthur simply arched an eyebrow and remarked, "Well, when good Sir Lancelot does feel so inclined to present himself before us, I shall be eager to reward him for his many brave deeds. I shall await you in Camelot, good sir."

Lancelot refused staunchly to meet Arthur's gaze, and Gawain demanded tersely what was wrong with him.

Lancelot gave no answer, so Gawain stalked off to bid farewell to his liege.

King Gawain did not stay long in his kingdom however. A damsel, Lady Gwenellen, came riding up to his court in pitiful plea only a week after the near civil war there was averted. King Arthur had already returned to Camelot, but Gwenellen had been wanting desperately to speak with him. She needed a worthy knight to avenge her fallen lord husband who had been slain by a sorcerous, invisible terror that had broken into their manor in the night and attempted to carry her off.

Gawain and Lancelot both volunteered immediately for the quest, as did Sir Balin, a knight from the nearby duchy of Reince and the close cousin of Gwenellen's fallen husband. The trio set off in company with the damsel, leaving in place yet another steward to watch the throne in Gawain's absence.

"That fool will never learn," Morgan muttered to herself with a grin. "He's more interested in chasing down quests than he is in ruling. Why doesn't he just step down already, trust the seat to Gaheris? Gaheris at least puts in the effort to run your family estate. Maybe I should visit and tell him that..." She shook her head and forced her exhausted eyes to focus back on the vision unfolding in front of her.

The Lady Gwenellen was slain by a spear the very first night of their hunt. The weapon was thrown from seemingly empty air and struck right between her shoulder blades, killing her in an instant. She fell dead in Gawain's arms, and despite how Lancelot strove to ride down the fiend who slew her, it was not easy to follow a trail when there was nothing but the drowned out sound of hooves to clue him in to the enemy's location.

This seemed the same invisible enemy that had first abducted Guinevere and before that attacked Arthur and killed his horse that day in the woods. The fiend was still rampaging unchecked through the countryside, and Morgan could not help but doubt that Gawain and Lancelot would be able to track their magically cloaked quarry, despite the fervor of Gawain's swear to avenge this young maiden.

Balin returned back to Orkney with the body of Lady Gwenellen to see her properly interred in her husband's crypt, promising to rejoin his fellow knights in Carbonek at the end of the week to continue the hunt. Gawain thanked him for his dedication.

Lancelot said nothing, giving a little wave.

Now Gawain and Lancelot were camped out in the woods in solemn silence by the flickering light of their campfire as the sun sunk steadily below the horizon.

The Tale of ~~King Arthur~~ Morgan Le Fay

Morgan herself was exhausted, stretched out by her pool for nearly sixteen hours straight just watching the adventures of those she could not be in company with.

"But why not?" she asked herself, lying on her back staring up at her cobwebbed chandelier. "They are facing a great danger. Surely they would be grateful for my presence. He'd be grateful for my…"

She set off on impulse before the doubt could finish ripping apart that assertion. She did not portal straight to their campsite, not wanting to trigger a reaction of startled knights leaping to their feet in alarm with blades warily raised. She decided instead that it had been far too long since she'd done any flying. And oh how she'd missed that feeling, gliding through the air with the soft feathers of an owl, ruler of the night skies, with the wind ripping past her and the moon shining so brightly above.

She reached her targets just as dawn was breaking over the horizon and fluttered down onto a tree limb right over the sleeping king of Orkney's head. *"And what a poor king thou art,"* she wanted to taunt him. *"Running away from your subjects and putting yourself in danger out here on the road, so open and vulnerable."*

Though he was not truly at risk. He had his pretty bodyguard, already up and practicing his sword forms. Lancelot halted his swing the second she landed, sheathing the weapon and stalking right up to her.

Her feathers ruffled in irritation that the lake knight had already unmasked her perfect disguise. Her irritation turned to instant amusement however, as Lancelot began to emphatically move his lips, only for no sound to emerge. She realized then that his taciturn behavior these past weeks had not been some shamed vow of silence. Morgan had simply forgotten to lift the silencing spell she had cast over him when rescuing Gawain an entire month past.

Her owl let out a little chortle, and she fluttered to the ground and took her own shape, as was needed for any spell casting. "I just wanted to impart you with some discipline," she joked. "I have removed the distraction of words, so you may focus on only your bladework. I'm sure the power of your pretty face will still secure you any boon you wish regardless."

Lancelot stomped his foot and mouthed what appeared to be a very flustered threat. It was downright comical, and she could not help but cackle.

Then Gawain awoke to that sound and turned to face her. Her smile died, and she waved her hand numbly over Lancelot. "Speak, be free. You are free of my curse. I'm sorry."

"I am not sure so simple an apology doth cover so many weeks of...!" The lake knight trailed off, as she melted into shadow, becoming one with the dappled patterns of the leaves on the forest floor and pretending she'd deserted them.

"How long has she been following us?" Gawain pressed, staring deadly at the empty space that she had occupied.

"I believe she just arrived," Lancelot replied. "She was an owl, an owl who did not even seem to realize that she had stricken me with permanent muteness, the thoughtless witch."

"I'm sure it was just her idea of fun," Gawain doubted. "She's had her way with you. Now she continues to toy with your mind, until the mood strikes her again. If it ever strikes her again..." he muttered, eyes distant.

"To what do you refer when you say she has 'had her way with me'?" Lancelot demanded, and Gawain cocked an eyebrow.

"Please, I'm not dense. The two of you both disappear from Glyngarth on the very same evening, after I've upset her. Then you appear together out in her woods months later, so clearly you spent at least some of that time in the bedroom as her--"

"Bite your tongue! Even if I had a desire to pursue such sinful indulgence with that plain and bony witch, she would no more take me than she would some dog she found in the street, for that is how she loves me."

Gawain stared at him, completely baffled by the poorly worded denial. "What?"

"That was her analogy, but regardless, by her own confession she loves me truly."

Gawain exhaled. "Sure she does, as deep as she is capable of it." Morgan flinched, curling ever deeper into the darkness. "Every bloody woman loves you, thanks to that enchantment."

"The Lady Morgan lifted that enchantment," Lancelot retorted. "She freed me of my curse, and she acted most selflessly in the months that followed, so it remains that even though her love of me is unrequited, I will nonetheless defend her. She kept me as her prisoner, and she treated me in a manner in which I have never been treated."

"Yes," Gawain grated, putting a hand to his forehead, as if physically pained by the images now assailing him. "She is very skilled in such... Know what, we've no need to talk about this. Not ever. I did indeed suffer less when you were silent."

He gathered up his things, angrily strapping on his armor, but Lancelot rambled on. "She treated me as a child." Gawain froze. "Which was

The Tale of ~~King Arthur~~ Morgan Le Fay

strange, yet oddly comforting. She berated me most sternly into acting again with discipline and restraint, and we never shared so much as a single kiss the entire time I was imprisoned there."

You were not imprisoned! Morgan felt like leaping up and yelling, but she held in her temper, as a strange expression flooded Gawain's eyes and he sunk back in his seat.

"So when she said she loved you truly...?"

"She meant purely. Like a brother perhaps?" He paused. "She is a good woman, and at the same time, she is as evil as my lady decried." All the warm feelings within Morgan withered. "And I speak not of her petty games cursing me with silence, though that was not at all appreciated," he enforced, staring directly at the spot of bush where she now cowered. "No, I speak of her horrors wrought when rescuing you that day, acts I have not been permitted to speak of until now, and perhaps that was purposeful... She turned true knights, her very own servants, into shriveled husks with but a word. There is endless wrongness and villainy in such acts."

"I know. I've seen her do such things before," Gawain whispered, "for years on the battlefield. Lightning and plagues, though never anything that... disturbing."

Because I love you! She wanted to cry. *Because I did not want you taken away and hurt! You were already so hurt...* She shrunk down even further, wanting to disappear entirely.

"My uncle was an evil man," Gawain continued fiercely. "He pushed her to do such things. I wanted to believe he pushed her to do those things, that they were not her idea, yet I have seen now her creative cruelty and..." He trailed off, eyes fixing on the spot of brush Lancelot had given away as her hiding place. "If she would but come out here and explain, I think maybe... Well, I'm not sure it could be explained, but... Well, this is just ridiculous. Morgan, if you're there, come out. I hate the idea of you watching me all the time without me knowing it. Or to deludedly think you are watching me, when you are in fact otherwise diverted and could not care less how I..."

Morgan the twenty four year old sorceress sat huddled like a little girl now in plain and baggy robes with knees curled up to her chest and back planted firmly against a tree, staying stubbornly deep in shadow, just visible enough to not be an utter coward as she whispered, "I watch when I care to, but even when I am not watching, that does not mean I do not care."

"You care enough to see us not dead," he muttered. "I suppose I understand. That's why you show up now when we're caught in dangerous circular chase with this invisible beast, correct?"

"I thought you would be glad for my aid, but if you wish me gone, just say the word and I will leave you to your..." She sighed. "No. That's a lie. I will not leave you in peril. Much as you may despise me, you are..." Her courage shriveled. "I could never despise you," she corrected somewhat sheepishly.

Gawain rolled to his feet and stalked right into the underbrush, seizing her hand and pulling her to her feet. "Why then do you flinch?" he observed, for she had indeed jumped the second he touched her and even now made a point of avoiding his far too piercing stare.

"You thought I had come to kill you," she grated. "When I came to save your life, you thought I would... as if I would ever..." Her eyes were tearing, throat closing up and making it far too difficult to speak. "When have I ever threatened you?"

"Besides afflicting me with horrible illness, and bringing sudden death to people right beside me on the battlefield, and killing my father, and--"

She melted instantly into shadow, slipping from his grasp.

"Wait, stop!" He fumbled desperately to catch her, to no avail. "That was the wrong thing to say. I know. I'm sorry. It's just... It is difficult to care for you, alright? Your champion, Sir Accolon, was the one to challenge me at Glastonbury. He poisoned me in the name of his queen, Morgan Pendragon. He said he worked to give her back her throne, and I could not help but think then of the meaning of that night we..." He turned his eyes up to the sky, struggling to keep his composure. "It seemed you wished simply to wed again a king and have back your seat. Then you changed your mind, after having your fun with him and determining he was not near as skilled as your previous--" His jaw locked, voice breaking.

She appeared instantly before him once again, with arms wrapped tightly around him and head buried in his chest. "Do not..." He pried free her hands, holding her coldly at arms length. "I am not in the mood for this, alright? We are on a serious quest, to avenge an innocent damsel and her noble lord slain by some invisible fiend... And sure, you can help with that. I suppose we need your help, but if you came here simply to gloat about that then--"

"I love you," she confessed, and that admission terrified her, especially as his own expression remained so withdrawn and suspicious. Still, she had decided to be brave. She could not hide from him any longer. "I love you," she repeated, stronger, with conviction. "You did not disappoint me that night, in that cave, and it was not some evil scheme." Her voice cracked. "I do not care about having a throne. I hate being in court, and I did not ask Accolon to go beat and abduct you! I was terrified that day! Thinking you dead. Because you mean everything to me. Our night was perfect, loving in a way that I had never known before, and you enraged me that morning because you would not ruin it and treat me as I deserved. You are a man of too much character for that, and I will never ask it of you again."

She seized his hands. He did not pull away, and her fingers twined all the tighter. "I will never ask anything of you again. And you do not need to hold me or love me in return. Just do not hate me, please. I cannot stand to see that in your eyes, even though I know you've every right to feel that way, to despise me for all I've--"

Her words cut out with a soundless gasp, as a spike of what felt like pure heat punched jarringly through her spine. She folded like a rag doll, and Gawain's arms snapped up to enclose her in panicked embrace. "Morgan! Oh God…"

She melted into shadow, then rematerialized in an instant with her body whole and mended and the bloody spear that had struck her in the back clattering useless to the ground. She could still feeling the imminent chill of death descending down upon her, but the feeling would pass in a minute. She was far more irritated than frightened. "Bloody spear ruined my speech," she grated.

Gawain left off staring at his empty, blood-soaked hands and turned toward her voice. He closed the distance between them in an instant, dropping to her side, with hands clamped tight around her head and back. She noted with dry amusement that he was shaking far worse than she was. A bubble of laughter escaped her chest. "Why the hell are you laughing?" he snapped.

"Well why the hell are you trembling?" she countered. "You well aught to remember that sharp object through the back is a completely ineffective method of murdering me, no matter how expert the aim. So if you could hold me please without the needless, suffocating concern…" she prompted, peeling away his hand and turning her face up toward his own. "Honestly, what kind of knight sets to shaking like a leaf when--?"

"Do not mock me. Not now. Don't you dare." His harsh retort quickly silenced her taunts, and she glanced down blearily at the solid sheet of red covering the front of Gawain's breastplate, splattered right up to his cheek.

"I suppose that is a good deal of blood, now isn't it? But the thing with solid metal outfits is that the stains will wash out with ease, I assure you. My robes on the other hand will simply have to be burned and replaced. A terrible waste." Gawain's exasperated exhalation had the ghost of a grin buried beneath it, and Morgan leaned in closer, her lips hovering hungrily right under his own. She heard his breath hitch. "Perhaps I should remove them now, ruined as they are..."

"And you wonder why everyone speaks of you as a lustful seductress," Lancelot noted, stomping back through the trees in a clamor of metal. "Yet even in the midst of danger, having suffered grievous wounds, there remains only one thing on your mind."

Morgan prickled, shooting him a glare. "Your tongue is the far more offensive to my ears, Sir Lancelot. Need I silence you again?"

"You are a woman of neither conscience nor caution!"

"He is right." Gawain swallowed, starting to his feet with fierce eyes sweeping the maze of foliage around them. "We cannot relax our guard. Which way did he flee?" he asked Lancelot, who had taken off after their quarry at a dead run the second that spear had come arcing out of the bushes.

"To the south. He left a clear enough trail, but even his horse remains invisible to the eye, and I stood no chance of catching him on foot."

"We'll continue on as before then and follow his tracks," Gawain resolved, taking hold of Morgan's hand and leading her over to his stallion, as if it were the natural course.

"I'm to ride with you then?" she noted smugly.

He hesitated, looking back at her with a forced grin. "Your presence would be much appreciated, yes. So long as you abstain from getting speared through the heart as we fight."

"That really did frighten you, didn't it?"

He wiped the smear of blood from his cheek. "It would have frightened anyone," he excused. "I just got you back. Then to suddenly lose you like that..."

"You will never lose me," she informed him wryly, clearing away all gory evidence of the incident with a twitch of her finger. "I am basically immortal. I will never be slain, certainly not by something so weak as this cowering cretin. He has run fleeing from my presence every time we have crossed paths, and he has surely realized after today that he cannot harm me in the slightest, yet I will burn him to a cinder the second I lay eyes on him."

"Take care all the same," he beseeched her quietly. "For I cannot bear to see you hurt like that, not again."

Of course he could not. He'd had to watch Gwenellen die like that, only a few days past. That thought caused a lump in her throat for some reason, but she forced aside all doubt and sadness, teasing him coyly, "Then guard me as close as you like, my good sir." She held out her hand, and he accepted it tenderly, guiding her up to his horse.

    He settled in at her back, and Morgan leaned contentedly into his chest, feeling more at ease than she had for months, as they set off down the road in deadly pursuit of an invisible enemy who might even now be watching them.

XXXVI. Sir Balin The Savage

Gawain did indeed keep a most protective hold about his sleeping passenger that day, as she leaned into his chest and drifted off to sleep.

"She dares indulge in slumber, at a time like this?" she heard Lancelot loudly demand, in response to which Gawain harshly shushed him, but the boy rambled on without paying heed to the rebuke. "I will permit that only if she is simply playing dead in order to lure in our quarry. And aye, that is a sound strategy, I suppose. Alright, well done, witch, snore away--"

"You are indeed no knight, you uncourteous windbag," Morgan muttered, cracking open an eye. "Berating an exhausted damsel simply for resting her eyes. I have been awake for days, so I am going back to sleep now, and should we get attacked, only then do I permit you to use your freshly regained voice to warn me awake. Until then, be silent."

She closed her eyes, and they carried on at a gentle walk, until gauntleted fingers digging into her side awakened her once more. She let loose an irritable groan and glared up at Gawain, demanding an explanation for his sudden prodding. "You were falling out of the saddle."

"Hold me tighter then," she murmured, "and take off your gauntlets. That scratching metal is far too cold and abrasive."

He rolled his eyes, but did as she requested. She smiled, laying her hand atop his own folded firmly against her stomach.

He did not pull away, gazing down at her solemnly. Her smile widened, and she settled back into a happy doze.

"Castle Carbonek." Gawain's whisper tickled her ear, and she opened her eyes once again to find the sun already setting, painting a blood red glow over the blocky turrets of the fortress before them. "I would not have woken you, but I figured you'd want the chance to wipe the drool from your face before we announced ourselves to the gatekeeper."

"A lady does not drool," she muttered, wiping at her lips. "And when a sorceress does allow some minor leak of bodily fluid to escape her lips, that is deadly ammunition that aught to set you to quivering with terror."

"You can cast spells with spit?"

"But of course." She smirked, holding up her moistened finger. "This right here, water of life, a potent weapon that can break through enchantments and wreak deadly damage."

"So your drooling was intentional."

The Tale of ~~King Arthur~~ Morgan Le Fay

"Of course not. A lady does not drool. Of what nonsense do you speak?"

He scoffed, smiling in spite of himself. "You're the one speaking nonsense, you infuriating witch."

"Witch is a discriminatory term," she rebuked. "From now on, you may call me only 'madam wizardess' or 'miss great and powerful sorceress'. Or Morgan. That I will also accept."

"Morgan it is then," he replied, and she was not quite sure the meaning of that, whether it felt affectionate or cordial and distant.

She was careful to hide such insecurity of course, seamlessly shifting the topic and demanding, "Why are we headed into Carbonek anyhow?"

"Because our invisible terror, as you yourself have noted, is no beast or mythic creature," Gawain calmly replied. "He fights with mundane weapons of sword and thrown javelin, and we have seen the hoof and boot-prints, and found even left behind blood trails from the night he attacked our king within his bedchambers. He is clearly but a man with one simple skill, to turn himself invisible."

"And to fight with deadly prowess, and keep keen surveillance on his enemies, ambushing them most expertly," Lancelot dryly interjected.

"And with all that tactical expertise, he has the great Sir Lancelot quivering in his boots. Duly noted," Morgan countered, and the boy flushed in rage, vehemently denying such defamation.

"I fear nothing. I simply urge a reasonable caution from those possessing of far lesser skill and instinct than I."

"So I am the one you fear for?" Gawain clarified, with brow darkening.

"I would say you are both of you equally fragile little mortals," Morgan teased. "Now let's get back on topic, shall we? I agree this is indeed an ordinary knight with a spell of invisibility about him, but what makes you think he hails from Carbonek?"

"This invisible terror first surfaced acting at the behest of that ghost king, Maleagant, and I think it logical to conclude that villain is from whence he learned this evil glamour."

"Admittedly so," she agreed. "Yet Maleagant could have gifted any killer with an invisibility spell, so I see not the link to--"

"Dolorous Guard is a strange choice for a sorcerous refuge," Gawain responded. "It sits right in the middle of King Arthur's lands. It was dangerous to seize that location, and killing Lord Dolor benefited only one family, King Pelles of Carbonek and his line."

"King Pelles..." Morgan reflected, trying to dredge up memory of politics she had been completely removed from for almost two years. "Ah yes, relatively penniless cousin of Lord Dolor and heir to Dolorous Guard and all its vast and profitable lands, now that Lord Dolor has been so unceremoniously slain without an heir."

"Precisely. Not to mention that all of this terror's recent attacks, most suspiciously the murder of Lady Gwenellen and her husband," His voice darkened with anger at the memory. "all took place within a few mile radius of this castle. Pelles is known throughout the land as a holy man, most loyal vassal of God's chosen one, King Arthur, yet he never lent a hand in the civil war or went to pay our good king homage in Camelot. Despite this, every man and woman in this county that I have spoken to seems almost afraid to criticize the man."

"So his reputation seems spurious and his motives for serving Maleagant an apparent gain," Morgan concluded. "Still, this explains not why he would carry on with his attacks now that his dark lord is destroyed and Dolorous Guard and all its lands already entrusted to his family."

"He acts now for selfish interest," Gawain countered. "The Lady Gwenellen spoke of it to me our first day of travel. Landless King Pelles wished a union of their houses, for Lady Gwenellen's father carried much wealth and influence. Our conniving king entreated that Gwenellen be betrothed to his brother, Garlon, a skilled competitor at tourney and the lady's close childhood friend. Gwenellen's father called off that engagement however, when Garlon somehow slighted him, and Gwenellen married instead the aged duke of Reince, a noble man whom she says she truly loved. Then Gwenellen's father fell dead of mysterious illness, almost immediately after that wedding, and Garlon came pleading to her doorstep in the night that she run away with him, almost as if he feared for her well being. She refused, and a week later, she was attacked in her bed."

"So Pelles was slighted by the rejection of his family and decided to kill all those responsible," Morgan filled in, and Gawain nodded somberly.

"She died in my arms. Collapsed dead, right in front of me, even as she was telling me that story."

Morgan's heart clenched, and all the words caught in her throat. She had seen that moment of Gwenellen's death replayed in her mirror. Gawain had been holding her in embrace the moment before she was slain. Perhaps he had finally been moving on from his infatuation with the cruel witch and falling in love with a much more gentle lady. She did not resent him for that. She had no right to. Instead, she grieved with him. After all, if she had only looked sooner, she could have saved the girl and spared him the loss.

The Tale of ~~King Arthur~~ Morgan Le Fay

"We will avenge her though," Gawain continued on, oblivious to her pain. "And we will save countless others by slaying this fiend. He will die by my hand, the second I lay eyes on him."

"You must prove first that King Pelles is the villain you suspect," Lancelot councilled. "For this theory of yours is, as of yet, but unfounded speculation. The people said he was a just and proper liege and that their land prospers under his rule."

"And that their daughters and sons being mysteriously slain or carried off is nothing but hearsay, for which they all have strangely no comment," Gawain countered.

"Regardless," Morgan weighed in, "you cannot just charge right up and stab a powerful lord within his own hall."

"Surely not," Gawain retorted. "I shall first denounce his character before his entire family and court, then he shall surely challenge me to duel, and then I shall run him through."

"Even if it does play out like that, that in no way confirms his guilt," Morgan criticized.

"So you're taking Lancelot's side?"

"It is not a matter of taking sides. I am simply cautioning you to--"

"Cautioning me?" He scoffed. "You are the most rash and overconfident individual that I have ever met. Since when do you approach situations with caution? You go charging right in, be it Dolorous Guard or hell itself, and you think nothing of conserving your energy or--"

"And acting rashly like that has caused me more suffering than you will ever know!" she silenced him, thinking of Merlin and that dreadful impulsive mistake she could never undo.

"The faithful guards of this city shall surely be alarmed should they hear you two quarreling and speaking such open defamation of their lord," Lancelot noted dryly.

"We will speak no more of it," came Gawain's muttered response, and Morgan felt a swell of bitterness, knowing he resented her lack of support for his theory and his mission of revenge, but resenting him in turn for being so easily wounded by her words, even when it was nothing but sensible council.

Was she supposed to speak nothing but jokes and empty praise? Would that earn back his favor? Would stroking his ego earn her the forgiveness she so desperately craved? Her honest confession of love and even her honest apology had clearly not worked to soothe over the rift that divided them, but she should have realized it wouldn't. Being plain, crass Morgan was never enough.

As it turned out, the guards would not have heard them, even had they continued quarreling. They had their hands full already with a tank of a man outfitted in full platemail with a massive shield slung across his back that carried an emblem Morgan found most ironic, that of a hairy, tusked boar on a field of white and blue crosses. It was the emblem of Sir Balin, The Savage, as he was known throughout the land, and the man was certainly acting a boar.

The brute had ordered the guards for the final time to open the gates "...so I may avenge dear Lady Gwenellen and beat your foul lord, Pelles, into bloody pulp!"

The guards of course refused to open the gates to that demand. In response to which the boorish knight smashed his sword hilt into the face of the captain on the other side of the bars, and the men on the parapets all raised their bows in outrage.

"Oh my lords, I beseech you! Lay down your arms!" Morgan wailed, though she was no longer in the shape of Morgan. She was the Lady Gwenellen, with her flaxen braids and dewy green eyes. Gawain stiffened at the sight of her, jaw clenching with hurt, but she ignored him completely, rushing right into the fray and throwing herself at the body of the invading knight who had turned instantly at the sound of her voice.

Now his wild eyes appeared ready to fall out of his head, as she hurled herself upon him, and those massive, meaty hands quickly caught hold of her shoulders, holding her up. "Gwenellen? No, it cannot be..."

"Oh, good captain, my friend, Sir Balan, is not well."

"*Balan?*" he grated, eyes becoming instantly suspicious. "I am not Balan. I am Sir Balin--" Morgan twitched a finger, silencing him, and the man's grip grew all the more rigid, seizing her by the throat.

What are you? Was the question he mouthed, but no one heard it. They saw only a maniac, seizing by the neck the damsel who had run to shield him.

"Has the madness progressed so rapidly?" she wept. "That you do not even recognize now the wife of your cousin?" Balin's grip wavered upon seeing those tears, and he staggered back from her, shaking his head.

"Oh, my good sirs, I beg of you, lower your weapons and open your gates!" Gwenellen pled to the men before them. "Sir Balan—er, Bal*in*, is a noble knight whom I ran to for aid when my lord husband, Duke Vanceor, was most brutally slain. Alas, the sight of the horrid demon responsible did

The Tale of ~~King Arthur~~ Morgan Le Fay

afflict brave Balin with madness and he did becry strange falsehood that he witnessed me most brutally slain and now I was but a specter, my words a meaningless haunt.

"I knew I must seek the aid of pious Lord Pelles and his bishop to cure our brave knight of this demonic torment of the mind, for there is no more hallowed chapel in all of England than the sacred hall of Chapel Perilous, as knoweth all good Christians.

"Mighty Sir Gawain and his squire--"

"Squire?" Lancelot scoffed, but Gawain shot him a sharp look that prodded him into silence without need for a spell.

"...did accompany me from Orkney to escort our dear friend here to Carbonek. Alas! Sir Balin ran off ahead of us in the night. Yet surely his soul doth cry deep down for the Lord's salvation, as he has found his way here of his own accord. Listen not to his crude ravings, I entreat you. Instead, open your gates and most kindly restrain him, so that we may carry on to the chapel and see him cured."

"You are not Gwenellen!" Balin's angry cry echoed through the air, as Morgan lifted from him her silencing spell so the guards would not clue in to her sorcery through his continued shouted silence.

"You believe me still to be some specter, good sir?" Morgan wept. "Oh, I cannot bear to see you in this state, sick with incontinence of mind and body alike."

His legs turned to jelly at her words, and he lurched into the wall, foaming at the mouth and struggling to hold himself upright.

"Good God, men! Open the gates already!" Gawain commanded, finally playing along with her lie. "We've little time to waste!"

"Indeed, open the gates!" the captain repeated the order. "That is indeed the Lady Gwenellen, wife of Duke Vanceor whose death I am greatly aggrieved to hear of."

"What sorcery is this...?" Balin's words were barely audible, with the foam still pouring out his lips.

Gawain quickly dismounted his horse, passing his reins off to Lancelot, much to the boy's irritation, and rushing over to stand at Morgan's side. He took Balin's arm, advising him quietly, "Tis I, your fellow, and I have not forgotten my vow, nor our quest here this day. Come along quietly, and we shall have vengeance for your cousin and his lady."

Balin looked from Gawain to 'Gwenellen', and then just shook his head. "I see her right there before me, Gawain... Have I truly gone mad?"

"Yes. Now keep quiet, else your mouth will start foaming again," Morgan ordered, and Gawain's eyes darkened. He could not openly rebuke her of course, not now, with the gate grinding open. Pelles' guards seized hold of Sir Balin, hauling him off and escorting them successfully through the gates.

XXXVII. The Keeper of the Hallow and his Kin

The noble captain of Carbonek's guard accompanied the false Lady Gwenellen and her drooling friend, Sir Balin, all the way to the entrance of the Chapel Perilous where awaited a reception of nobles containing not only the town bishop, but a richly dressed and well groomed man in his forties, who presented himself as strong of arm and dignified of stance, yet his eyes were strangely tender.

Morgan used her sorcery in that moment to send Balin to the ground in a sudden fit of twitching limbs, creating an opportunity for her to fall crying into Gawain's shoulder, as if unable to bear the sight.

"What are you--?"

"I believe that to be Lord Pelles," she hissed into Gawain's ear, "but I will have no rash denouncements or challenges from you until I've a chance to tease out his guilt, for I do not believe him to be the true villain here."

"You can tell that at but a glance--?"

"He is utterly unsurprised to see the Lady Gwenellen here before him," she retorted, "as are all these men, because word has not had chance to travel from Orkney and Reince yet, so the only one within this city who should be shocked to see Gwenellen alive and well before them is the one who struck her dead."

"That guard ran ahead to announce our arrival," Gawain argued, "so clearly Pelles had time to compose himself and prepare to face you."

"Then he should be eyeing me with scrutiny or a carefully guarded gaze, not beetle browed concern," she noted, shooting the man another glance out the corner of her eye, as she wiped dramatically at her eyes and pushed herself away from Gawain. "Oh, I apologize, your majesty, for my frightful behavior, but the sight of the great Sir Balin reduced to such a state..." Her voice broke.

"You need not apologize, my lady," the man she assumed to be Pelles pardoned her gently. "We should all of us shed tears of compassion for this man, so savagely attacked by demons. Bring him to the cells of the chapel, good bishop, so that we may see this evil driven out with all haste."

Morgan twitched a finger to free Balin of his fit, though the poor knight did then collapse exhausted within the hands of his new captors, giving no resistance, as they hauled him away toward the cellar door of the rather ominous looking church set up before them. The Chapel Perilous was certainly not a normal name for a place of worship and healing, yet it had been called that for as long as anyone could remember, and not even the locals could say why.

Gawain was still glaring at her on Balin's behalf, which was not at all appreciated, since King Gawain had no reason to be glowering at the Lady Gwenellen and really aught to remember his manners and play along better with her genius plot to unmask their invisible foe.

"Your majesty appears of a sour disposition this day," Pelles noted, and Gawain finally lifted his eyes from Morgan, turning his glare upon the mild-mannered lord.

"I see a fellow knight suffering for no reason while a lady most inappropriately embraces me," Morgan's fist clenched covertly behind her back. "and some stranger stands coldly judging before me, having no grace to introduce himself."

"Ah, I apologize, lord king." Pelles gave a shallow bow. "I am King Pelles, ruler of Carbonek, and we have made previous acquaintance, Sir Gawain, during your tourney in London."

Gawain's brow furrowed. "Forgive me then. I cannot say I made note of you there. Perhaps you were watching me unseen." Morgan resisted the impulse to roll her eyes at the utter hamfisted bluntness of that prodding.

"Indeed, good sir, you were otherwise involved that day and perhaps did not make note of my speech to your liege lord, Arthur, and the other kings about the poor example set by frivolous violence feeding our war mongering culture."

Gawain arched an eyebrow. "You dare call good King Arthur a war monger?"

"I gave no such slander," Pelles denied, "yet he doth continue amassing troops and seizing lands he does not need..."

"For the sake of unity! That just laws may be enforced throughout our country and an end put to squabbles of territory and the division of our people!"

"Forgive me, your majesty." Pelles gave another bow. "I meant no slight. I am glad you survived the recent bloody coup that threatened your own reign, though it is a tragedy so many had to die to seat you back upon that throne, a throne I must say I never have in fact seen you upon, so often are you away in travels and tourneys."

Gawain reached for his sword, and 'Gwenellen' stepped frantically in between them, teary eyes weighing into King Pelles. "For what reason do

The Tale of ~~King Arthur~~ Morgan Le Fay

you pick at the noble knight who escorted me safely to your city, sire? Sir Gawain is indeed a king, thy equal and thy superior in terms of lands and influence, yet he is also a noble warrior, who left his seat at my request, so that he might help with the curing of Sir Balin and the avenging of my husband, our duke."

"Of course. And as I said, I meant him no slight, my lady."

"Yet slights are all you have spoken, so spare me the patronizing lie that you meant them not," Gawain snapped. "You have insulted my character and competence, and that is to declare deadly challenge. In fact, I am tempted to most justly denounce thee in turn…"

Morgan looked back at him, and surely Pelles presumed it was a gentle-eyed plea and not the stare of flaming eyes and clear rebuke that set Gawain to remembering her cautions. "Yet I am in fact a far more chivalrous man than thee," Gawain begrudgingly concluded. "And since you, Lord Pelles, have forgotten yourself, I will remind you that the poor Lady Gwenellen here has had a long and tiring journey of great emotional strain."

"Yes, of course. I am sure our pious damsel wishes nothing more than to sooth her worried soul with prayer," Pelles supplied.

"Right. Yes." Morgan found it a struggle to feign enthusiasm, heading reluctantly toward the chapel doors.

"We shall join you inside, my lady, though the men before me must first surrender their arms, as no weapon may cross onto these hallowed grounds."

Gawain surrendered his sword and shield without hesitance or complaint. His lance had been left along with his horse and 'squire', Lancelot, at the town stables.

What followed was an entire two hours of prayer, during which Morgan found herself entirely disappointed that no invisible enemy charged in to attack them. She would have welcomed the conflict. This mass was so dreadfully dry that she was on the brink of breaking character.

She made repeated study of Gawain, knelt right at her shoulder, but he refused to so much as glance in her direction. From his clenched jaw and brooding expression, she could tell his attention was most certainly not on the sermon. He seemed wounded by her appearance taking on the shape of dearly departed Gwenellen, but she could not very well just abandon the ruse, not before the eyes of Pelles and his men. She supposed simply taking on a woman's face was no substitute for having that person back in your life and perhaps only aggravated the pain of their loss.

She lifted her gaze from Gawain and forced a half-hearted study of the eerie and interesting décor of this gloomy little church. A roman-style spear stood upright beside the altar, a strange choice of relic, given that Pelles had said no weapon could dare be brought within these hallowed halls.

The lengthy minutes of kneeling silence finally ended, and they headed for the doors, as the bishop told Lady Gwenellen he would be working tirelessly along with his fellow priests throughout that night to exorcise the demons from brave Sir Balin. They could all still hear him even now, tantruming down below, though this time it was not a sorcerously triggered fit.

"You need to end this awful ruse," Gawain whispered in her ear in response to those indignant cries.

"Sir Balin will be fine," Morgan assured him coolly. "I will free him once we find our villain and take our leave of this dreadful place."

"That is not nearly soon enough. He should not be forced to suffer this, and you should not be wearing that face."

She flushed, eyes becoming glued to her shoes. "Really? But she's such a pretty little damsel. I would think you would be glad to be in presence with such a glowing countenance once again."

He looked over at her with brow furrowed. "Whatever are you...?" His eyes widened. "You think I fancied her?"

"I saw the way you were looking at her, that final embrace..." She blushed all the harder. "And that is... none of my business. I'm sorry. I just came up with a plan on the spot at the gates, and this seemed the best... I'm sorry," she repeated, striding off toward the doors.

Gawain caught her arm, steering her back to face him. "I felt pity for Gwenellen, because her husband had been brutally murdered right in front of her. I was giving her comfort. That is all. She had zero interest in anything else, and neither did I. It isn't right for you to wear that face, because it is horribly unsettling. It's staring at a dead woman, even harder for Balin than it is for me. We both feel anger at her loss, but that is not because I fancy her. I barely knew her."

"I suppose I understand. I'll remove it as soon as I am able," she murmured, eyes weighing into him tentatively. "Though... how on earth is it you felt nothing but pity? She's gorgeous, all delicate and dewy eyed..."

He gave a subtle grin. "This sounds to me as if you are the one who caught a glimpse of Gwenellen and became instantly infatuated."

"Well damn. How right you are."

The Tale of ~~King Arthur~~ Morgan Le Fay

His smile broadened, and she wanted most desperately to lean into those lips... Then she clued into Lord Pelles and his men, staring back at them expectantly, and she scurried out the door with Gawain right on her heels.

They headed out into the crisp evening air and found Lancelot waiting for them with arms crossed. "Sir Gawain, my lady. Our horses are quartered in a strangely well surveilled stable, and your weapons all confiscated. They even tried to take my sword."

Morgan looked coolly to the bleeding wrists and battered armor of the guards standing warily around them. "Tried and did not succeed, I see."

"A squire must defend loyally the possessions of his lord. I understand, boy," King Pelles condescendingly pardoned. "But should you wish to be granted rooms for the night within my castle, as your master and the Lady Gwenellen shall have, then you must first surrender that weapon. It shall be returned to you when you depart this city, but I have sworn an oath before God that the halls of my home, attached as it is to this chapel, shall remain always as a place free of violence and blooded weapons."

"I am not a squire, and he," Lancelot pointed rudely to Gawain. "is not my master. I am his fellow and comrade. Still, I respect your vow and your rules of hospitality, good king, so I will offer up my sword for temporary safe-keeping, trusting that it shall indeed soon be returned."

He held out his sword to Pelles himself, who accepted it graciously before passing it off to his bleeding captain. "And your name, good sir?"

"Lancelot d... Just Lancelot."

"Well, my young Sir Lancelot, were this a tourney, I am sure you would have most decisively defeated all these challengers and won for yourself great acclaim. Yet you have this night abused loyal guardsmen but doing their duty, so you have earned instead my most heartfelt rebuke." Pelles smiled as he said it, and Morgan thought that this was indeed an unsettling man.

Pelles guided the trio into his hall and insisted they all join him for dinner. "I have provided of course a change of dress for all of you, as no noble man can come outfitted to my table as if charging off to battle."

"So first he strips us of weapons, and then our armor..." Gawain muttered in her ear. "I would not lay myself so willingly down like a lamb for the slaughter were my lady not here to resummon such adornments the second we should need them."

"Your lady is aware of your anxiety, and she is watching you most carefully, dear sheep," Morgan soothed, giving a covert squeeze of his hand before following the prompt of the servants guiding her to Lady Gwenellen's provided rooms.

The dress Pelles' servants had laid out for her was an appalling creation of sunny yellow cloth covered with flower patterns and frilly lace right up to her chin. It made Morgan want to vomit, but Gwenellen of course simply smiled and remarked how lovely it was, and then tried not to punch her maid in the throat when she scraped back her hair into a painfully tight crown of braids that gave her unpleasant flashbacks to her childhood in Uther's court.

Gwenellen walked out into the feasting hall and worked hard to subdue her wicked smile and put a stop to her roving gaze, as she spotted Gawain in a dashing tunic of deepest green whose too-tight trousers did wonderful things for his backside and calves. The Lady Gwenellen would not leer at him so openly of course, so she jerked her eyes to a rosy cheeked girl of perhaps fourteen years of age whom Pelles was introducing to his fellow monarch as "...and my daughter, the Lady Elaine."

"Pleased to make your acquaintance, sire," the girl meekly noted, giving a low curtsy. She then turned her eyes to Gwenellen, and her smile became all the broader and more genuine. She rushed right up to her and seized her hands.

"Lady Gwenellen! I had so worried you were--" She bit off the words and cast a veiled glance back at her parents. "I am happy to see you," she corrected. "You visit so rarely."

Morgan embraced her with a smile, as if they were long-parted sisters, and whispered covertly, "You need fear no evil, Elaine. The sorcerous terror that has been stalking these lands, these brave knights will put an end to him this night. Does that not gladden you?"

She studied closely the girl's expression as she spoke. There was indeed genuine relief, but also fear, rife within her gaze. She tightened her hold around Gwenellen and muttered most urgently, "Your confidence is misplaced. You must flee. Now. However strong your champions, they cannot hope to..."

"You act as if two siblings long parted." The laughing words instantly caused Elaine to jerk away from her, fixing her desperate smile on the dapperly dressed lord now looming at Morgan's back. "I had no idea the two of you were so close, Elaine."

"She was almost family," Elaine excused, voice cracking. "Oh how I wished the two of you had wed. You make such a lovely pair."

The Tale of ~~King Arthur~~ Morgan Le Fay

"Elaine," Pelles chided, eyes darkening. "I'm sure your uncle does not like to be reminded of such things."

"Oh, brother, there is no wound to recall," the man insisted, lifting Gwenellen's hand to his lips. "I am simply glad to see you once again, my lady," He lowered her hand and pulled her in, daring a kiss on the cheek as he whispered, "so beautiful and full of life. Yellow was always your color."

Morgan knew these eyes. They were Urien's eyes. The eyes of a man who hated and coveted yet concealed it all behind perfect walls of cool indifference, who played every reaction and could never be unsettled by even something as shocking as the living and breathing reemergence of the lover he had murdered walking in on his dinner.

"Garlon," Pelles rebuked, and his brother quickly dropped his hand from Gwenellen's cheek.

"Yes brother?"

"I know you and the Lady Gwenellen share much... history between you, but her husband has been gone not even a month."

"Yes, a dreadful tragedy," Garlon breathed, painting compassion across his face and holding firmly still to Gwenellen's hand. "And I will comfort her as any old friend would. Is that not your wish?" he asked her, and she smiled with manic rage.

"Oh, my lord, I do but wish I could find comfort within thy presence, yet surely you understand that due to the nature of my suffering, I cannot at this moment *stand* to be so close to you."

She could just incinerate him, right this very moment, so sure was she now that Garlon was the sorcerous enemy that had killed Gwenellen and her husband. An invisibility cloak could be used by multiple perpetrators however, to kill rivals and attempt to assassinate kings, meaning the rest of his family's guilt was still yet to be determined, so she held off on such rash impulse.

Gawain interposed himself between the pair of them, taking back her hand. "You heard the lady. Now keep your distance."

"Has the Lady Gwenellen already found herself a new suitor then?" Garlon chillingly joked.

"He is my champion. He shall avenge my husband, for that is his vow. And it shall be just as I told you, Elaine," she reassured the girl still hovering nervously beside them.

The child said nothing in response, looking nervously to her uncle and retreating back toward the feast table. She made it only a single step before she stopped dead in her tracks, but it was not terror this time that forestalled her. The last person invited to this private feast was just now making his entrance. He was dressed all in white like an angel from a painting, and being tall and muscled and gorgeous as always, his simple act of pausing in the doorway and looking around to assess his surroundings drew instant rapt attention from every servant and noble within the room. Elaine herself had lost her breath, gazing at him as if some mystical enchantment were still in place, causing her pulse to quicken and her legs to give way.

She swooned, and Morgan caught her, only for Lancelot to shoot her a sharp and suspicious look, stepping toward the pair of them and whispering, "Yet you claim your kiss unraveled the enchantment."

"Bite your tongue. It did," Morgan hissed through the close-teethed concealment of a smile. "Our Lady Elaine has just had a sudden rush of blood to the head, forgetting to breathe. That is all. And she is still awake."

Elaine was indeed still awake, blushing furiously with open eyes fixed on Lancelot leaned so close right over her. "I-I apologize, sir...?"

"Lancelot," Morgan supplied. "Lancelot, Elaine, a girl who wants very badly to stand up now, yes?"

"M-my legs do not yet appear to be working." Elaine nervously laughed.

Lancelot slipped an arm behind the girl's back and titled her gently upright, demanding, "Yet you truly just felt faint? There was no mysterious sudden darkening of your senses?"

"N-no, good sir. I am truly baffled at this talk of enchantment. Though thy countenance is perhaps somewhat enchanting, and... Oh my. That is... solid." Her hand had found its way onto his bicep, which her fingers were most eagerly exploring.

"Ah... my lady?" Lancelot pressed, and she stepped quickly back from him, folding her hands behind her back.

Lord Pelles and his wife, Nanette, were watching most unhappily this exchange, and Elaine loudly declared, "I am sorry, lord father. I am, uh, utterly starved! Feeling faint. And our guests were kind enough to steady me. I shall... take my seat."

She sunk down in her assigned seat to the left of the table's head, and Pelles looked narrowly to Lancelot, announcing darkly, "Yes, we should all take our seats and say grace, that the Lord might bless this meal and purify our thoughts."

"But of course, brother," Garlon announced with a smile, sinking down in the seat right across from Lady Gwenellen. "for we gathered here are all so very thankful for everything the Lord has provided us this evening."

The Tale of ~~King Arthur~~ Morgan Le Fay

A priest came in and gave the king a flowery Latin blessing over the meal. Then the prayer finally ended, and they were permitted to begin eating.

Elaine scrambled to her feet, as the servants emerged out of the kitchens with a jug of wine. "I plead that I might have the privilege of serving our noble guests their libations!"

Pelles arched an eyebrow, and Queen Nanette frowned in disapproval. The king waved his hand in permission regardless. "If it pleases you, daughter. A good host must indeed be first and foremost a servant to their guests, just as a good king is a servant to the people."

"And just as a good lady is the servant of her husband," Garlon added, still staring right at Morgan.

She was in no danger. She had to keep reminding herself of that. This disgusting fiend could not lay so much as a single scratch upon her...

Though he already had with that spear through the back. She had healed in an instant, but she still felt it cutting into her. He had done the same to Gwenellen, poor, powerless Gwenellen, who had run from him before he could have his way with her, prompting him to end her in a fit of jealous rage once he saw her with Gawain. Now before him he had a perfect replacement though, and there was so much more he was wanting to do to her. She could see it in his eyes, and it was making her skin crawl.

She visibly flinched, as a hand seized hers beneath the table. Then she realized it was Gawain, seated right at her side and squeezing tightly her hand. She met his eyes, and her terror calmed. He knew something was wrong, so she cast a very deliberate look to Garlon, and Gawain understood instantly that this was the villain they were looking for.

"Sword." The near silent word was not a question but a demand, yet she instantly shot it down.

"Not yet."

"How inappropriately familiar the two of you act," Garlon noted, tapping his cup impatiently, as Elaine drifted past with her pitcher. Elaine picked it up and meekly filled it to the brim, moving around the table and doing the same for all the other goblets, one after another.

Garlon kept talking at Gwenellen, but she was ignoring him completely now, eyes shifting from Elaine to her parents and then back again. The king and his wife were watching the girl with uncomfortable intensity, especially as she moved to fill Sir Lancelot's cup, keeping her back turned to them and whispering fiercely, "Drink not."

"What was that, dear niece?" Garlon prodded loudly.

"Yes, what was that you whispered to our guest?" Pelles more bluntly pried. "For such conduct is surely an impropriety."

Morgan stole the girl's voice and spoke from her lips, "He had a leaf in his teeth, and I did not wish to embarrass him."

Elaine clapped a hand to her mouth in unsettled shock at the mysterious puppetting, but that had the desired effect of selling the lie of a girl who had just blurted out something embarrassing. She set down the pitcher and slunk back to her seat, as Pelles guiltily cleared his throat. "Well then, ah... I am sorry for chiding you, daughter. That rebuke was unearned."

"My *Gwenellen*, you are a woman of so many talents," Garlon toasted her, drinking down his cup and staring at her in clear challenge. Maybe the wine wasn't poisoned. Or maybe the fiend really was a sorcerer, who had more than a simple spell of invisibility but the talent for crafting and dissolving poisons as well.

Morgan met his gaze boldly and drained her own goblet after a quick whispered word that replaced it all with nothing but clear, clean water.

Lancelot looked to her uncertainly, and she motioned for him to take a sip and avoid suspicion. It was perfectly safe for him now. There was nothing in there but water, just as she had done for Gawain at her side. The boy left his chalice just sitting there though, and took not one sip. "I find I have no appetite this evening," Lancelot rather rudely declared. "If I might be excused, I would retire."

Pelles was considerably disgruntled by that request, but Lancelot pressed the issue, until reluctantly he assented.

"My armor is still within my chambers, I trust?" the young knight demanded, and Pelles' glare deepened.

"I am offended at what you imply, young sir. Have you no courtly training?"

"Perhaps not, just as you've no directness, for thou hast not answered my question."

"Oh, good sir, it rends my heart to hear you so insult our host," Lady Gwenellen rebuked. "Can we not all dine as friends? We are all of noble spirit, and this most holy king would certainly never seek to do you harm."

"Yet perhaps Sir Lancelot cannot help but be terse, so tired and strained as we have made him," Elaine piped up nervously. "So if he cannot be good company and wishes instead to retire and set to perhaps polishing his armor to work out his... frustrations, that is certainly a wise decision."

"Elaine," her mother hissed.

The Tale of ~~King Arthur~~ Morgan Le Fay

"I am sorry, mother. It is just... I find his face far too distracting, and it surely is in fact my leering stare that has put him so on edge!"

"Elaine!"

She turned bright red, as did her father, muttering quickly, "Perhaps it is best that Sir Lancelot withdraw."

"Thank you, lord king." Lancelot gave a shallow bow and strode briskly out from the feast hall. Elaine's eyes trailed wistfully after him, until her father's stare of outrage set her to ducking her head in shame.

"If that boy were your squire, I would request you punish him for his discourtesy," Pelles prodded Gawain.

"Yet a squire he is not," Gawain countered coolly. "He is in fact a champion of the fairy court of ancient waters in lake country, so the tutelage of his conduct was perhaps somewhat... unorthodox."

"You jest," the queen demanded, and Gawain stared her down with blunt composure.

"No, I do not. He is a warrior of great skill, yet as I said, he had a peculiar upbringing, thus he knows not when to check his tongue. I must thank you in his place though, Lord Pelles, for providing us with such delicious fare this fine evening." He took a long draw from his goblet, and he and Morgan played along in quiet strain throughout all three courses, as dish after dish was placed in front of their assigned seats and Morgan plied her crafts to disintegrate and purify each bite before it could be swallowed.

She had no time to replace the food with fresh fare without the unwavering gaze of Garlon and their host making note, so it was she was forced to simply vanish it all the second it crossed behind closed lips.

"I'm famished," Gawain whispered to her on their way out the doors hours later. "Horribly famished. I do in fact feel a bit light headed."

"I'll bring you something in your chambers once the servants have left me," she soothed, "and I'll be sure to first put on a more frightfully familiar face of endless freckles and dull brown eyes."

"I love your eyes." Such a blunt and earnest statement. It flooded her with warmth, and she smiled over at him coyly. "And that expression..." He grinned in return. "I can already see your true face in every glance, every word you say..." He cleared his throat nervously, turning his eyes to the corridor ahead. "But that is hardly important at the moment. We need to deal with Garlon."

"I shall cage him myself this night, and you can bring him before Arthur and make him account for all he's done. How does that sound?"

He blinked. "That sounds shockingly merciful."

"I can be merciful!"

"I'm not saying you can't. It is just... surprising," he muttered, clearly unhappy with the decision.

"You can fight him in some duel avenging Gwenellen and her lord, if you so wish, but I want that fight happening far from this castle and away from Elaine. And I want to see how it is he's turning invisible and just what other powers he has, so imprisonment and questioning is clearly the wisest route."

"My lady, my lord?" the eldest maid called. She and her coworkers had drawn a good dozen meters ahead of their crawl of a walk and had finally looked back and noticed how far back their guests had fallen. "Your rooms are in different wings, so this is where our groups would naturally part ways."

"And you are of course unsettled by the impropriety of us, hanging back here with heads bowed together," Gawain noted. "Yes, I apologize. Lead the way, good madam."

Gawain headed off to the right, as Lady Gwenellen drifted docilely down the turn opposite. Morgan too was feeling a mild queasiness of the stomach now. Perhaps that was simply because she had taken in nothing but water for days, or perhaps it was how suddenly uncomfortable she felt sealed up in the skin of Lady Gwenellen. Maybe it was Gawain's unease or Lord Garlon's sickening gaze, but she felt the sudden desire to start scratching off the skin of this dead woman, peeling it off in bloody chunks until she could rip her way free of its prison.

That thought was absurdly extreme, and she forced herself to keep calm and patient until she reached her room and suffered her maids their expected duties of unbraiding her hair and unlacing her bodice so she could slip into a simple night shift and usher them out of her rooms. She gave a sigh of relief then and sunk back into her own shape.

At least, she tried to. Her body would not change. Her skin just tingled with awful numbness. No matter what shape she envisioned, be it sorceress or crow, nothing shifted. Her breathing quickened, and she tried to calm, telling herself she was simply too light headed to focus.

All she needed was to sit down for a second and eat something. She summoned a bowl of soup to her nightstand, and that worked just fine, so she sighed in relief, wolfed it down, then tried once again to change back into Morgan.

Nothing. Bloody. Happened. "What the hell is this?!"

The door creaked open, and a wicked low laugh echoed through her chambers. "Were you trying to change?"

The Tale of ~~King Arthur~~ Morgan Le Fay

She whirled frantically toward the sound and unleashed a burst of fire, but there was no one bloody standing there. Then something struck her in back of the head, and her vision flashed red. She pitched forward, only for uninvited hands to close around her chest.

"I like you in this shape, little changeling." The disgusting words tickled right against her ear. "You must stay like this but a few hours more."

She resummoned her flames, and the hands jerked back from her, but her stance was swaying and she had no visible target, no way to effectively resist, as her invisible attacker shoved her back upon the bed with hand clamped tight over her mouth.

"Now, dear, I thought we agreed we had to dispose of the others first," a woman's voice noted, and Morgan turned her swimming eyes to the raven-haired beauty, Queen Nanette, stood imperiously in the doorway. "You can't do much of what you're wanting now in that full set of plate with just your hands uncovered." The hands locked around Gwenellen pulled back with a growl of irritation, and the cold weight of steel pressing down on top of her lifted. "Run along now, love. She'll still be here when you get back, just as you like her."

Footsteps thudded out the doorway, but Morgan clung stubbornly to consciousness and raised her finger toward Nanette. "I'll burn you to a cinder--"

"You are as powerless as the bones that bind you." Nanette raised a little straw doll in the yellow dress of Gwenellen with ropes of strange vine wrapped tight around its body, and Morgan's flames died out to smoke. "Lie still now." She set the doll down on the night-stand, and Morgan felt herself pinned in place, laid rigidly flat upon the bed with arms at her sides.

Nanette sunk down right beside her, clucking in disapproval. "You young witches, always so overconfident. Though I have never in all my hundreds of years met anyone as loud and haughty as you, Miss Morgan Le Fay." She brushed playfully at her nose, and Morgan glared. "Changelings are indeed a rare and most troublesome enemy. You cannot even wound them, so long as they can keep shifting like quicksilver, reknitting their flesh, and to find one so schooled in true sorcery as well... You truly are a special little girl." She pinched her cheek, and Morgan tried to punch her, but she could not move. That damn voodoo doll was infuriatingly effective spellwork.

"The poison was in the lining of your cups, by the way," Nanette smugly illuminated, "not the wine itself. I assigned you seats and specific compounds based on your individual strengths. For the King of Orkney and his squire, a simple poison to kill them in the night, but for you, my pretty pet. For you I was forced to put in much more labored preparation. You drank down this eve the powdered blood and cursed spirit of Gwenellen, to hold you fixed to one shape, until my lover Garlon has had his way with you."

"Who are you?" Morgan grated.

"I am the Lady of the Marshes. Known these days as the wife of King Pelles, Keeper of the Hallow, that tainted spear stained with Christ's blood that gives such wonderful power to witchcraft, if you know the proper corruptive rituals. I tell you what though," She took her hand. "I will save you from Garlon's most brutal delights should you swear a simple blood oath and act as my apprentice. I could teach you so much, and as I said, you are a very special girl. I could wish for no more brilliant a student."

"I serve no one, you evil hag." Morgan spat, and the spittle hit Nanette's eye with an angry hiss.

Nanette wiped away the oozing wound with nothing more than a mild irritation. "Acid. How crude. Do you want to see what a real witch can do?"

She licked a finger and held it to Morgan's forehead. It burned straight through her skull, as Morgan's screams shook the ceiling.

Nanette kissed the wound and healed it in an instant, a second before her death. "And even if I had let you die, I could still bring you back as a blank, breathing puppet that Garlon would no doubt still be satisfied with. Now how does that sound, little witch?"

"I am **not** a witch. I am a wizardess, more powerful than all you Satan-worshiping lunatics!"

"A witch you are not then, and never shall be it appears." Nanette sighed, dropping her hand. "That ignorance makes you powerless in hands of a true master." She trailed a finger along her thigh. "I shall watch most happily your torments this night, for I am also the grandmother of Sir Turquine, and I did not at all appreciate your humiliations, allowing your brother to kill him. Still, I am beyond such petty emotions as vengeance, so cry to me for mercy at any time tonight and I shall take you on still as my loyal disciple and slave--"

She had leaned right down in Morgan's face to deliver her threats, and so it was she had not noticed the young lady creeping carefully over to the doll on the dresser and untying its sorcerous bindings.

Morgan hurled Nanette away from her the second she was free, killing her in an instant with the shouted curse, "Burn!"

Nanette burst into wicked green flame with a shriek of pain, and Elaine clamped her hands to her mouth in horror. "Mother! Oh God. I'm sorry, I'm

The Tale of ~~King Arthur~~ Morgan Le Fay

so sorry... I just wanted to help him." She fell sobbing to the ground, and Morgan felt an instant swell of shame that she had given the girl's mother such a brutal death right in front of her.

She found herself wishing that she could mimic her mother and put on the air of a gentle princess to comfort the weeping child. Though the other part of her insisted sharply that she had nothing to apologize for here. Murdering this monster had been basically self-defense after all, and killing Garlon would be just as justified.

"Thank you for freeing me," Morgan muttered. "I am... sorry about your mother, though assuredly she deserved her fate."

Elaine did not respond, still screaming into her hands, as The Lady of the Marshes' burnt skeleton crumbled into dust.

Morgan jerked her to her feet with no further time to be compassionate or gentle. "Your mother's potions room, where is it? I need to know."

Elaine just shook her head, refusing to meet her gaze.

Morgan shook her. "Damn it, girl! You said yourself you wanted to help. Sir Gawain is dying as we speak--"

"I don't care about Gawain! I needed you to help Lancelot! He did not drink the poison, but he does not have his sword, and now Garlon is going to kill him. He's already killing him." Her sobbing increased, and Morgan took off down the hall, yanking on her hand and forcing her to keep pace.

"Fine. We'll slay the invisible savage first. There will still be time to cure the poison afterward," she told herself. "All he felt so far was a bit light-headed. That is nothing grave, right? It is a slow acting harm. Plenty of time for antidotes."

The angry clash of metal drew them on ahead. Surely every servant within this entire wing could hear that, yet no one was coming out of their rooms to ask questions, and no guards were charging in to investigate. It was as if the entire castle had been cleared of those who might interfere this night.

They skidded around a corner, and Sir Lancelot jerked toward the sound of their emergence with sword point lowered, eyes closed and back planted against the wall, as he seemingly listened for the approach of his attacker. Something slammed across his shoulders the second he turned toward them, accidentally putting his back to his true quarry lurking right beside him. The blow sent him to the ground, adding yet another dent to his already much abused breastplate, but the agile knight rolled to the side the second he hit, swinging blindly upward with the blade still clutched tight within his hands and hitting his enemy with a solid clunk that sent the invisible juggernaut crashing into the wall with a curse.

Morgan keyed in on that impact and swallowed the area in a burst of white-hot flame. The man screamed and went lurching away from the site, but there was no smoke trail or outline of flames to keep following his movements as Morgan would have hoped. Steel did not make for very good tinder.

Lancelot opened his eyes at the sound of those screams and just narrowly restrained his instinctive jab lashing out at Elaine who had dropped down weeping at his back with arms closed about him. "Gah. I ah... I cannot see who this is," the tinny voice sounded from within his visor, bent solidly in over the left side of his face. "But you are clearly a maiden, and with those screams and the smell of smoke... Morgan?"

"You think I would drop to my knees weeping over you?" the sorceress scoffed. "I'm off to your left here, but Garlon is not dead. He is no doubt still right in front of us, so get up already!"

"Easier said than done," Lancelot grunted, fighting against his soreness and the weight of his armor, as well as the oozing slash wound in back of his knee.

Elaine eagerly slipped her hands beneath his arms, helping to lift him to his feet. "You wrested away his sword and took it for your own. Oh, you are a warrior of such skill. But you must beware his axe and dagger. I will not allow him to kill you. I could not allow him to kill you," she deliriously rambled, clinging to his back, still firmly within his blind spot.

"Ah. My lady Elaine," Lancelot filled in finally. "I told you to flee--"

"Your lady?" She near melted at the idea, staring at him so dreamily, even in this moment when all she had to look at was scratched and dented steel.

"Ah... We really must stop speaking. I cannot hear him when there's--"

Something slammed into his helmet with enough force to split the metal, and Morgan decided she needed to respond with a blunt impact of her own. She disintegrated the stones right beneath the invisible attacker's feet, sending him crashing to the ground two stories below.

The sword had already dropped from Lancelot's limp fingers, and Elaine pulled him frantically back from the hole before he could topple in after Garlon, collapsing beneath the weight of the bleeding knight. She held him close and scrambled for purchase beneath the lip of his visor, lifting it free of his head, though both the metal and the leather cap beneath seemed far too inclined to stick to the bloody locks ratted up within the tear.

"Oh!" Her hands were shaking at the sight of what lay beneath that helm, split scalp oozing red all down the bruised left side of his face. She pressed her face right against his own and began to sob, as if that would help anything.

"Stand back. He is not dead yet, but he will be if you keep getting in my way!" Morgan shooed her, kneeling beside them and laying her hands on Lancelot's forehead and chest, envisioning him to be whole and mended.

His eyes snapped open and he gasped, grunting at the unsettling feel of his broken rib snapping back into place. "Good God," he groaned. "Your healings are a trial in and of themselves. It feels as if I've some invasive evil scratching at my insides."

"Oh, my lord!" Elaine threw herself on top of him, kissing his cheeks.

"Ah... I am glad you are glad I am well, but this is not the proper behavior, my lady. Do remember, we have only just met."

Elaine pulled back from him with cheeks of burning crimson, wringing her hands. "I-I apologize, good sir, but I was so v-very worried my uncle had..." She swallowed. "And I of course would not have dared a true kiss. Unless," Her eyes drifted longingly to his lips. "you wanted to.... kiss me?"

She swooned at even the thought of it, and Lancelot reached out quickly to steady her, at which point she let out a nervous giggle. "F-far too much excitement tonight. I apologize. Such behavior... Whatever would my father and mother--?" Her voice cracked, and her eyes flooded with tears, chin dropping against her chest.

"Oh, good lady, do not cry." Lancelot fumbled to escape this deeply awkward encounter. "I am perfectly well. There is no reason to weep."

"She's not crying for you. I killed her mother," Morgan coldly illuminated, staring warily down the hole she had opened to the hallways below. The fall wasn't nearly far enough to kill an armored knight, but she was too vulnerable right now to risk floating down there alone to finish off their enemy. "Nanette was a witch working with Garlon. She may have even orchestrated everything for him and Maleagant both, but we've little time to sit here consoling each other." She seized Elaine's hand, pulling her to her feet. "Where is your mother's laboratory? I need antidotes. Now."

"So you fools drank the poison?" Lancelot demanded. "Even after good Elaine warned us to 'drink not'?"

"I was shrewdly outmaneuvered," Morgan grated. "Now I'm stuck in the skin of this anemic little damsel with a concussion I cannot heal, and we need to find and cure Gawain, who is likely suffering far more seriously right now!"

She stalked off down the hall, dragging Elaine along with her, as down below she heard a grating drag of steel and felt a sharp chill within her chest. Their enemy was still alive, and he was coming for them.

XXXVIII. The Dolorous Stroke

Gawain was not within his rooms. He was keeled over in the corridor not far from Lady Gwenellen's chambers, vomiting bile and shaking, and making Morgan wish most fervently that Elaine had not delayed her so in running to his side. The girl had been useful at least in that she knew the exact poison her mother had used against Gawain, sparing Morgan the need to see him first and diagnosis him before running back and forth from that laboratory of black magic to fetch the antidote.

She dropped down by his side, and Gawain flinched at the sight of her, shaking his head. "Still seeing you as... Doesn't matter. If you're really here, you need to know... poison..."

"I know." She hastily uncapped her bottle, pushing back his sweat damp hair and tipping back his head.

"A damn... strong..." He clutched at his stomach, vomiting again before she could get the antidote in his mouth. The bile that time was mostly blood.

"I am so very glad I incinerated that sadist," Morgan hissed, tipping hopefully fast acting salvation down his throat. He convulsed, as if something were forcing him to reject it, but Morgan kept her hand clamped tight over his mouth, and her fingers softly stroking, until he calmed.

"Definitely... worst dinner," he panted. "Ash in the mouth, then ten times as bad on the way... out."

"The queen lined the cups with poison, so it did not matter that I swapped out the contents," Morgan murmured in apology.

"Pretty sure I'm still hallucinating," Gawain murmured in response, eyes uneasily searching her face.

"I still look like Gwenellen. I know." She sighed. "That was my own personal prescription of poison. I cannot shape-shift, or heal myself, but at least my regular spells all still seem to be working, so it is nothing to worry about," she insisted.

"So that scream...?" His hand tightened around her own. "I knew it was you. I came running. Then the ground started to tilt, and I couldn't run... They hurt you?" His hand went to the bloody stain in back of her tangled locks, and his eyes instantly hardened. "I'll kill them. I'd like to say that. Sadly... Damn it, I'm pretty much useless here, aren't I?"

"It's alright," she soothed, holding him close. "We've only one enemy left to worry about, and he is surely in a somewhat sorry state since Lancelot got a few blows in then I dropped him down two floors."

"Sounds promising," he grunted, forcing himself into a sitting position. "I think I'm good to stand up now."

That proved a gross overconfidence on his part. The poison had badly damaged his body, leaving him enervated and feverish, and those side effects were such a complex chain of cause and effect that Morgan was left powerless to heal them. It was not like burning a virus or setting a broken bone where there was only one concrete action to envision. It's why she used alchemy in the first place. For certain afflictions, it was far easier and more effective than sorcery.

"You won't be ready to stand for at least a couple of days," she agonized. "Let alone fight."

"I bloody hate poison," he breathed, slumping back to the floor.

Her eyes searched the corridor around them in paranoid watch for Garlon's inevitable ambush. "I will come to you as soon as this is over," she swore.

"What are you..? No. I can stand... just fine, and I am coming with you--"

"Sleep."

He fell limp, and she summoned up a portal to send him safely on to Camelot. At least, she tried to. Nothing happened. "Damn it! Why?!" she shouted.

"Keep your voice down," Lancelot hissed, stood on guard at the head of the passage with Elaine still clinging to his back.

Morgan ignored them both, closing her eyes and reaching out into the ether in search of what was blocking her efforts. This entire castle was covered in the same barrier that had been laid into the stones of Dolorous Guard. She could not have portalled into this place, and she could not now escape. She could not even shape shift into something stronger able to carry Gawain to safety.

She slammed her fist into the floor. "Lancelot. Get over here. You need to carry him."

"We will have no one then to defend us--"

"I will bloody defend us. That fiend is going to die painfully and instantly the second I hear a footstep. But for now we're running for the exit."

"How then will you hear his footsteps--?"

"Enough arguing! It's either this or I go with my plan B and collapse the whole bloody castle in an attempt to bury the bastard!"

The Tale of ~~King Arthur~~ Morgan Le Fay

Lancelot and Elaine were both quite averse to that casualty heavy back-up plan, so he picked up Gawain and they set to fleeing.

"We need to take the passage from my father's rooms," Elaine advised. "It leads down into the cells of Chapel Perilous."

"And why ever would we go there?" Morgan criticized.

"To free you of the vestiges of Gwenellen's corrupted spirit that bind you now to her shape. You must pray at the altar, and then you will be purified and able to heal yourself."

"Alright, but I am not actually a Christian, since the church had me excommunicated as an abomination and all that," Morgan dryly illuminated. "So this strategy of pray and be miraculous cured, I seriously doubt that is going to work."

"It is the only way," Elaine insisted. "Unless you know the counter spell to mother's--" Her voice cracked at even mention of the woman, and she reached for Lancelot, clearly needing to assure herself that saving him had been worth the cost. "I can keep this close to you, yes?" she pled, clinging to his elbow.

"Ah, yes. Stay behind me, and I shall endeavor to protect you."

Her face calmed, and she leaned her forehead against his shoulder.

"Fine. I agree it's worth a try to go visit your church, but we are going to need you to guide us there," Morgan prodded her dryly.

"I can give directions from back here," Elaine murmured, keeping up her awkward shuffle glued to Lancelot's side. That only further hampered his exhausted movements of course, as he balanced the substantial weight of Gawain slung across one shoulder yet kept his stolen sword in hand.

They reached Lord Pelles' chambers and found him sound asleep, stretched out on the bed with face serene, oblivious to the conflicts happening throughout the halls around him.

"Sleep enchantment," Morgan noted, and Elaine gave a sad little nod.

"Mother does it on many nights when she needs to see to her work."

"So he is a good king," Lancelot asserted. "One who knows nothing of the villainy of his brother and wife."

"He is a pious man," Elaine agreed. "He tries so hard to be righteous, and I wanted so badly to tell him the truth, but I was so frightened…"

She wrapped her hands around Lancelot's waist, and he looked down at her nervously. "All is well," he offered hollowly. "It will all… be well."

They opened the private passage and followed its dank, winding corridor down through the levels, emerging out into the cells of Chapel Perilous.

"If he is a holy man then why does his private passage lead to the church dungeons instead of the atrium?" Morgan pressed.

"So he may visit those in direst need of his time and comfort," Elaine answered fondly. "We keep down here those assailed by demons, and my father believes through speaking to the soul within, he gives them strength to keep fighting. The Lord rewards acts of labor and charity far more than empty words and--" Her speech cut out with a scream, as the cell door right in front of them ripped free of its hinges beneath the weight of a mighty kick, crashing to the floor.

Sir Balin stalked free of his prison and turned instantly toward the cry. His eyes flooded with rage the second he spotted 'Gwenellen', and he charged. "Unholy revenant! You die this night!"

The much encumbered Lancelot stood no chance of stopping the maddened knight, but Morgan calmly raised her hand, gluing his feet to the ground with blocks of solid ice. "Do not delay us. I am not a revenant. I do not even wish to appear as this dead duchess, but I have been cursed by the witch of these lands, the now dead Queen Nanette, and I need to get up to that chapel to restore my true shape."

"More lies!" Balin snarled, shockingly shattering her ice, so great was his strength, and lurching on toward her. "Your words are but endless lies--!"

"I do not wish to kill you," Morgan snapped, "but we have no time to waste! That invisible terror is surely right on our--"

A hand clamped over her mouth and white hot pain slid into her side, purposefully far to the right of her spine and vital organs. "You burned me badly, whore," Garlon snarled. "You are going to heal that flesh, and then you are going to feel it, right up against you, as you bleed out on the ground."

He shoved her into the open cell beside them. Her head hit the stone, and it was such an effort to keep the blackness from dragging her under. The rage could keep her going though. It always did. "Should have killed me, you idiot," she grated beneath her breath, forcing herself back up onto her elbows, even as the cell door slammed shut. "You think a door is going to stop me?"

Lancelot had admirably instantly tossed Balin his sword. The knight took it without hesitance, swinging blindly for where their quarry's head should be. He hit nothing but air, and Garlon cut the unarmored savage a near fatal wound across the chest.

Balin lurched just in time to avoid it, turning it into but a shallow graze and hitting clearly something with his retaliatory strike.

The Tale of ~~King Arthur~~ Morgan Le Fay

Lancelot set down Gawain, closing him and a protesting Elaine up safely within an empty cell, with his eyes never leaving the desperate fight between Garlon and a blindly flailing Sir Balin.

Balin's insane fighting style was somewhat effective for now. Garlon did not seem able to get in a blow with his shorter weapons Elaine had warned of, the axe, and the dagger that Morgan had just felt. But Balin was bound to exhaust himself rather quickly just slashing that longsword rapidly through the air at every level around him.

Morgan for her part had already disintegrated the bolt on her cell door, crawling along the floor toward the nearby set of stairs leading up to the Chapel Perilous. She was just barely conscious by this point, losing blood rapidly, so she decided in an instant that there was no point just blindly attacking the air with her flames in the hopes of wounding Garlon again. Lancelot and Balin could keep him occupied while she slunk off to pray for the Lord's salvation, so she could become herself again before she bled to death. She almost laughed at the thought. This was shaping up to be the most bizarre and terrible evening she had ever experienced.

She made it on hands and knees all the way to the top of the stairs and straightened shakily, reaching for the doorknob. Then came the thudding steps, and a fist knotted tight in her hair, jerking back her head. "My instructions for you were clear. I do not like having to repeat mys--"

She set her hair on fire, and Garlon's hand released with a shout. Morgan herself did not care about the pain. She extinguished the blaze as soon as it reached her scalp and tumbled with only minor burns, smoking and laughing, through the open doorway, kicking it shut behind her.

"Come on! Look how pious I am!" she shouted deliriously at the ceiling. "I have forsaken my vanity, and I come before thee, Lord, with shaved head and modest night shift and so much… bleeding wounds…" Her exhausted cackles increased, and she lurched her way onward the remaining few feet to the altar, even as the door behind her thudded back open.

Balin smote that invisible fool, stuck in that narrow passage with nowhere to dodge. The mighty blow slammed into his breastplate with a thunderous cracking of metal, sending the villain crashing to the ground, though Balin's next swing hit nothing but flagstone.

Morgan kept her back to the pair of them and folded her hands, elbows propped up on the altar just barely keeping her upright. She did not pray for selfish miracle as had been her initial plan, but requested sincerely instead, "Please liberate the spirit of poor Lady Gwenellen, good Lord, and free her of this heinous binding. She deserves to rest in peace."

Something tore free of her chest with an echoing sob of relief, and Morgan gasped, collapsing to the ground. Her skin began to tingle, and she saw the back of her hand freckle with a trio of little spots that had been there on her true skin for as long as she could remember. Her long black hair tumbled back into existence and the wound in her side closed over, her vision clearing of black.

"Thank you," she breathed, looking up at the cross. "Though this does mean that whole excommunication nonsense your servants have been bandying about is absolutely meaningless, now isn't it?"

Balin came crashing down right beside her then, ripping the cloth from the altar. The walls of the chapel shook with a feeling of indignant rage.

"Maybe we should try and move this outside..." Morgan cautioned, but too late.

Lancelot was fighting off Garlon in the center of the aisle with the sword Balin had dropped, eyes closed and brow knotted with focus, as he felt out and parried every one of the invisible knight's attacks in the narrow confines of the space between pews. He got a solid stab in finally that sent Garlon stumbling backward, blood dripping from what appeared to be his arm, as his axe became suddenly visible and dropped to the ground with a clatter.

With that drip of blood, Balin saw clearly his target, and his hand closed around the ancient spear right beside him without a second thought.

"No! Not the--" Morgan's warning was ignored, and Balin drove the spear point straight through Garlon's back.

A massive thunderclap split the air as that tip pierced flesh, near bursting their eardrums, and Garlon dropped dead to the ground, with all the concealing spells laid into his shattered armor burnt away in an instant.

The walls were shaking much more seriously now, as Morgan leapt to her feet, and Elaine stood quivering at the head of the undercroft steps, and Lancelot shouted for her to run--

And the roof came crashing down.

Morgan tried to turn the stones to mist. Her spell had no effect on the hallowed grounds, and she just narrowly avoided being crushed to death herself by turning into shadow right as the first chunk of stone made contact with her shoulder.

She saw Balin drop to the ground, still holding tight to the corrupted Hallow, and miraculously the piece of ceiling that should have smashed him flat fell braced against the altar, forming a little stone tent that held strong under the cascade of other rocks, saving the dazed knight from deadly injury. Though it would take several hours of labor from some very strong volunteers to get him out from under that mound of hundred pound stones.

Morgan looked then for Lancelot and found a much graver scene. He was lying atop Elaine to shield her from the rubble, and even the brief sounds of his initial pained grunts had fallen silent, as those last two pieces of rock bounced off his breastplate and helmet, and he collapsed into the swirling dust.

The ragged breathing of Elaine was littered now with whimpers, as she lay pinned beneath the knight and stared fixedly at the blood dripping through his visor. "Help him. Help him. Somebody help!" She did not seem to notice her own bloodied foot, crushed beneath the rubble, and Morgan suspected she was slipping into shock.

"But I've a feeling you need first healing," the sorceress murmured to Lancelot, rematerializing at his side and making a quick examination of his injuries.

His insides were beaten to a pulp, spine bruised, ribs cracked, leg broken, and brain hemorrhaging, and he was oh so very lucky he had the world's most talented healer at his side in an instant to save him. "Alright. Let's start with the vital areas."

It was a rather intensive labor, seeing first to his head and waking him up so he could use his now healed back to hold up the rubble enough to allow Elaine to squirm out from beneath him.

Then Morgan shifted into a copy of Sir Balin and used that set of much more impressive muscles to lift the stone off of his shattered leg then hold up the other massive slab of rock pinning his left side as he crawled out from under it. That slab unleashed another little avalanche of debris the second she dropped it, and the trio just narrowly made their way safely to an exit and escaped being buried once again.

Once they were safe out under the open sky, Morgan finished healing Lancelot's leg, then saw to Elaine before the internal bleeding from her crushed foot could send her into unconsciousness. That final healing devoured all the last of her energy, and she herself collapsed, cursing in her mind absolutely everything to do with Garlon and Nanette and the Chapel Perilous, as she decided that there was no place on earth she hated more than Carbonek.

XXXIX. A Perilous Position

She sensed Gawain's presence at her side long before she opened her eyes, but her glowing smile turned to glaring irritation, as she realized that weight pressing up against her stomach was not his hand, or his back. He was not lying romantically stretched out beside her, waiting for her to awake. He had his feet up on the mattress.

She shoved them from the bed and disturbed his graceless slumber, reclined in the chair at her bedside with jaw hanging open and drool leaking out the corner of his lips. He started awake with a grunt, and bleary eyes flooded instantly with warmth as they locked upon her own.

He opened his mouth to say something, then just as quickly bit back the comment, noting ruefully, "I'd ask how you were feeling, but I've the sense I'd only get snapped at in response. After all, you are hardly a fragile maiden in need of my 'coddling care'."

"I think I preferred being coddled to being your footrest," she noted archly, forcing herself into a sitting position. "What kind of gentleman puts his feet up upon his injured lady?! You aught to have been holding my hand, sitting up in attentive vigil until I awoke."

He rolled his eyes. "Even the most stalwart knight cannot keep a waking vigil for three days straight. I simply needed to rest my eyes."

"You should have lay down beside me then," Morgan sniffed.

"The sheer impropriety of such a position would have surely offended our host." Gawain cast a glance toward the doorway behind him, and Morgan made note finally of the little viewing slit through which a glowering pair of eyes was most steadfastly surveilling them. "Pelles did not even want to allow me in the room, but I said I was honor-bound to not leave my lady's side until she made a full recovery. We are being most vigilantly chaperoned however, and even now that you're awake, I don't suspect they will unlock the door until their king gives the order."

Her eyes narrowed. "Did you not explain to him what happened? All of Garlon and Nanette and their abominable schemes?"

"I explained with impressive conviction, yes, when the royal guard came and found me locked in that cell in the undercroft of their now collapsed church with no idea how I had ended up there or what had happened to you or Balin or anyone else. I nonetheless did manage to persuade their king that I was neither possessed by demons nor a terrorist bringing purposeful ruin to his city. I enforced that it was his brother Garlon who was the cause of all this violence, as the man was a villainous cad and his queen a wicked witch.

"Sadly, such arguments did not go over all that well, even with the Lady Elaine there to support the testimony. You see, the lady's father seemed more focused on the fact that his daughter would not give up her hold hanging off the arm of a far too blunt and of little aid Sir Lancelot. Pelles declared before the entire court that his daughter had been bewitched and had Lancelot hauled off in irons and Elaine locked in her rooms. Though at the very least the stubborn fool did not have the discourtesy to chain up the unconscious damsel he had never seen before that day lying helpless out in his courtyard."

Morgan exhaled, sinking back against her pillows. "Well then. There goes yet another of my altruistic efforts repainted as horrible terrorism. At least Pelles does not know his strange unconscious guest is Morgan--"

"Pendragon? Yes. Yes, he does know that actually. I told him." Gawain shrugged, and her eyes flared wide, a mix of anger and dismay.

"And whatever made you think that was a good idea?" she grated, fist clenching.

"You are the sister of King Arthur. That means he cannot execute you--"

"That means he'll want me burned at the stake! Just like all the rest of..." Her voice broke, and she looked away from him, but Gawain gently took her hand.

"That seems a little dramatic, does it not? Stuffy and naive as King Pelles may be, he still aims to be a holy man, a just ruler. He is not going to have you, or I, his fellow nobility, executed. Though perhaps if you were to shift into Gwenellen briefly, show Pelles that we did not in fact murder the good duchess as he presumes along with his wife and brother..."

Morgan instantly shook her head. "I can never again take that form. Not only because it would feel wrong and I'd be disturbing Gwenellen's ghost, but because I am intuitively positive that doing so would instantly invite divine punishment from the God who freed me of that shape."

"Well then," Gawain sighed. "with proving our innocence off the table, I've rather run out of ideas of how to resolve this diplomatically and get us all free of this place. Lancelot's still locked up in the dungeons, last I heard, despite the fact that winning the affections of a king's daughter really isn't legal grounds for such imprisonment."

"If they're throwing around accusations of bewitching and witchcraft a 'holy man' can justify any punishment," Morgan muttered. "Though the only one of us who committed any sort of sin here is Sir Balin, defiling a holy relic of Christ by using it to stab a man in the back and all that."

"I fear Sir Balin was already quite brutally punished for that error," Gawain noted somberly. "They say the entire chapel came down right on his head. There is no way I can think for him to have survived that. They've been digging through the rubble for days from what I've heard, and they have yet to hear a sound, or find a body..."

"He's alive," Morgan disagreed. "I can sense it. I can also sense how very deeply cursed he is. Perhaps I've inherited my father's prophetic gifting and I can now just start spouting out solemn predictions of who be-ith cursed and who shall prosper..."

Gawain's brow furrowed in confusion. "In what way was King Uther a prophet?"

"In no way," Morgan scoffed. "But Uther was not my father. Merlin was."

His brow raised. "You failed to mention that."

"It is hardly that shocking. And I am fairly certain I blurted it out right in front of you all the way back in Dolorous Guard. Though you were a pig at the time, so perhaps you were not listening. Anyway, Merlin never told anyone other than Arthur and I..." She swallowed. "But I am tired of being a shameful secret. I think I shall announce my true esteemed heritage to most everyone from now on. Then perhaps people will stop calling me a witch, and I can start walking around with my own face again.

"Though more likely it will not change anything, because it's not like he's here to vouch for me. Not like he would speak out for me, even if he were here. And not like he now can..." She had tried so many times to undo that spell and free him, and she was far too weak at the moment to make it even worth attempting it now. Perhaps Merlin's return was the miracle she should have prayed for at the chapel, instead of her own selfish salvation. She hardly deserved to be saved, after what she had done.

Gawain put a hand to her cheek, wiping the tears from her eyes, and she just then realized she was crying.

"No looks of pitying sympathy!" she rebuked, wiping embarrassed at her dripping nose. "I imprisoned my father in a permanent unreachable prison, and I am just going to have to live with that. He was never around before that anyway, so it's not like I changed much in truth."

"Even if he was a poor father, that does not mean you do not miss him. My own father was a flawed man as well." She shrunk down at even the mention of Lot, staring up at Gawain in cringing guilt. "I was but the son of

The Tale of ~~King Arthur~~Morgan Le Fay

his least liked wife, and he paid me no praise or attention, yet when he was gone for good, it was a far more painful absence."

"You do not still hate me for that, do you?" she whispered.

"I love you far too much to hate you," he murmured.

Her eyes widened in wonder, shimmering with tears. "You love me?"

He arched an eyebrow. "Don't act as if you did not know it."

"How would I have known it? You never bothered to say the words! I gave you an entire heartfelt confession articulating most clearly my feelings, yet you keep silent for each day afterward, then let that most precious of phrases just slip out offhand because you figured I knew?!"

"How could you *not* know? It's been clear as day in my every reaction to you. You tease me to madness, you wound me most seriously, yet I meant every word I said to you that night, after Dolorous Guard. I mean it all still. There is no one like you, Morgan. From the day we met, there has been no one else able to make me feel the things you do, so of course I am in love with you. I will always be in love with you. I simply was not ready before this to say it plain and let you start gloating about it yet." He paused, growing solemn. "As for my father... I forgave you for that years ago. He poisoned your mother, betrayed his ally, then framed a little girl for both their deaths. That I blamed you at all after hearing your side of it was my own childishness, failing to see you as anything other than the rumored, inhuman witch the people were always whispering of."

"And... what do you see now?" she prodded nervously, sitting in her own skin with frizzing bedhead and chapped lips, neither intimidating nor alluring whatsoever.

His eyes locked with hers, and he smiled. "I see you."

She exhaled in heady joy, leaning in suggestively and waiting breathlessly for him to close that final finger of distance and--

The crossbar screeched, and Gawain turned away from her and over to the opening door of their prisonous guest rooms. She wanted to set the guardsmen on fire, so rude and unwelcome was their timing.

"The King of Orkney and his witch will stand in formal trial before King Pelles and the clergy to determine accountability in the death of Lord Garlon and the disappearances of Queen Nanette and the Lady Gwenellen. Your companions, the pagan knight and the savage, shall share whatever sentence you earn."

"Meaning the savage Sir Balin has been excavated from his almost tomb and is fit enough to stand trial. See, what did I tell you?" Morgan gloated to Gawain, slipping out of bed and taking his arm. "Though the fact they're openly denouncing me a witch means this trial is assuredly already decided, so what do you say we take our leave of this place before they've got my pyre completed?"

"I will allow no harm to come to you," Gawain swore, "but let's at least attempt to settle things civilly first. I am confident I can get Pelles to see reason. Failing that, we can resort to brute force and fight our way free of this city as you suggest. Either way, we'll be safely home in Camelot soon enough." He said that with a smile, already headed out the door.

Morgan did not share in his grin, allowing her arm to slip from his grasp. Whoever said anything about returning to Camelot? What was the point of fleeing this cursed fortress just to foolishly seek refuge in a city no less hostile?

Gawain had already slowed, looking back at her with brow furrowed. "Morgan?"

Her eyes locked with his, and the sense of dread twisting its way through her insides did calm, at least somewhat.

Camelot was not her home. Going back there would mean putting on some false face and persona and convincing Gawain and Lancelot to maintain that cover, else it would incite riots in the streets from an entire city and court who feared and disdained her.

She explained nothing of that to Gawain at the moment however. Instead, she threw her arms around his neck and pulled his face toward her own, savoring the feel of his warmth, and making that kiss last as long as she could bear with the guardsman all staring on in judgment and the doubt already swelling over.

Good things never lasted, and Morgan Le Fay would never be a hero to be praised.

Here ends Book One of the Twisted Tales of Camelot.
The Story Continues in Book Two, The Greatest Knight in the World.

www.ingramcontent.com/pod-product-compliance
Ingram Content Group UK Ltd.
Pitfield, Milton Keynes, MK11 3LW, UK
UKHW041537090126
10018UKWH00035B/266